SHATTERED LIGHT

SHATTERED LIGHT

LEGEND OF THE SPEAR SAINT
BOOK TWO

A. T. Valentine

Podium

To my family

Cover design by Narendra B Adi

ISBN: 979-8-89539-396-3

Published in 2026 by Podium Publishing
www.podiumentertainment.com

Podium

SHATTERED LIGHT

CHAPTER ONE

Heroic Calling

Rowan,

I really hope this letter finds you in good health and spirits. ~~It has come to my attention that~~ *Sorry, been writing too many of these lately. You don't want to know how stuffy nobles and royalty insist on acting.* ~~I really just want to~~

Didn't send this letter to complain! Listen, things aren't great in the kingdom right now. Even with our summoning, there's a lot of tension and doubt that we can defend against the demon lord's invasion this time.

A ton of stuff is happening in the background, and I've been sent on so many missions to track down demon sympathizers, cultists, and more. Who even really believes that "demons are just escaping a hostile world and we need to help them"? For real?

Anyway, the person who brought you the royal missive should have explained the Big Problem already. I know he can be a bit abrasive, but you can trust him—please believe that!

Just in case, though, here's some details.

The invasion is happening much faster than it should. Months ahead of schedule, even. The mages have started detecting heightened demonic activity that precedes the arrival of a demon king, and the sudden rush of demons also broke through the defense line, threatening the civilians of a border barony.

You should know that already, though. I think you're in that territory, right? Baron Kayden?

Well, in response, the king can't wait as long as he'd like for us to get ready. We need to do something about the problem now. That means that we're all three of us getting deployed as quickly as possible. I have some loose ends I need to wrap up over here, but then I'll be joining you and Kayla on the frontier.

Now, I know you didn't get the best of Heart Cards. Don't worry! I'm not going to let anything happen to either you or Kayla. I know they expect us to push deep into the demon territory and clear the path to their king so we can end him and his invasion.

So, that's what I'm going to do.

I know the nobility will support me, so I'll try to wrap this up as quickly as I possibly can. It's going to be simple! My class is pretty much made for killing demons. Again, that means you don't need to worry. Just hang in there, and I'll make sure you guys can go home safely.

Sincerely,
Your best friend, you butt
Blake

Rowan laughed, loud and sincere. Relief surged through him. Maybe everything was complicated with Kayla, but at least it seemed like Blake was the same kind, slightly goofy person he'd always been.

"Is this all some big joke to you, Hero Rowan?" Kayden growled.

"Sorry, I'm . . ." Rowan held up his letter. After the messenger left, Kayden had unrolled the scroll and discovered a smaller letter accompanied the royal missive. Seeing Blake's name front and center on the letter, Kayden had handed it to Rowan. While the baron read and reread the scroll, Rowan had busied himself with the letter.

"Just because the Radiant Hero sent you a letter doesn't mean that the royal order is nullified," Kayden said as he paced around the room.

"Uh, what's the problem?" Rowan asked. "Wasn't I supposed to go to the frontier anyways?"

Kayden whirled around, and Rowan saw a kaleidoscope of emotions running through the man's eyes. Anger seemed to be the primary ingredient, but there was also fear and anxiety.

"You think this is about you?" Kayden said through gritted teeth. He leaned forward into Rowan's face.

Before Rowan could respond, he was saved by the door. In came both Olivia and her mother. Both paused when they saw the scene, but Camilla thawed first.

"Oh, what do we have here?" she asked.

"Royal decree," Kayden sighed as he tossed the scroll to her. "Our hero is being sent to the frontier."

"All of the heroes," Rowan added softly. "Blake and Kayla are also going."

"Oh." A dark look flashed across Camilla's face.

"Are things that bad?" Rowan asked.

"'Hero Rowan and his party are expected at Rest's Remorse within three weeks of reading this decree,'" Camilla pulled open the scroll and read. "'Hero Rowan will officially assume the role of leading the town upon his arrival. Additional information on your assignment and expectations will be available there.'"

Rowan blinked. "That's it?"

"That's it," the baroness confirmed.

"So what does that mean?"

"It means that something has gone very, very wrong. Rhys might not be a large kingdom, but we are a civilized one," Kayden replied, bringing his emotions under control. "The kingdom is duty-bound to give the hero proper training, to be presented before the envoys of different kingdoms when that's done and then sent with the best of the kingdom to the frontier."

"And something changed," Camilla said. "The kingdom can't deploy the heroes to the frontier early unless a serious change has happened."

"Maybe it was the recent wave?" Olivia offered. "We fought an Epic-tier demon at Felton's Mill. It shouldn't have gotten this deep when the invasion hasn't even begun."

"Blake mentioned it," Rowan said, and felt a slight panic when all the eyes in the room turned to him. "Apparently, demons are moving way ahead of schedule. They're months ahead of where the kingdom thought they'd be at this point."

Kayden stepped closer to Rowan. "Read me exactly what Hero Blake wrote. Word for word."

Rowan began reading the letter. Only when he got to the fact that the mages had detected heightened activity that precedes the arrival of a demon king did Kayden stop him.

"That's bad," the baron admitted with a sigh, dragging a chair close and collapsing into it.

"What are we going to do to improve our daughter's chances of survival?" Camilla said, as serious as Rowan had ever seen her. Olivia coughed forcefully, drawing her mother's attention. "And the survival of our sponsored hero, of course."

"We're strong now," Olivia said proudly. "I'm a [Combat Alchemist], a Rare class. And Rowan's close to getting to Rare as well. We both have decks that synergize well."

"But not Epic." Kayden traded a glance with his wife before turning to Rowan. "Before anything else, Rowan, I need to apologize. I didn't think that there would be any true danger in Felton's Mill. This was meant to be a break for you. Instead, you've been dealing with two demons that would have leveled this village. Thank you, and I'm sorry."

"No, it's okay." Rowan awkwardly put his hands out in front of him. "I'm glad I was able to help in the little ways that I could."

"And the second part of my apology is about your tier. I was told that Hero Kayla played a role in defeating the demon. I'm sure that you've noticed that she's already at the Epic tier. It's my fault that you're not keeping pace with her. I insisted on ensuring that you had a foundation instead of relying on dungeons to level. You could have been at the peak of the Rare tier by now."

"It's not on you," Rowan said, also serious now. "You were there in the capital. No one else was willing to sponsor me. If it weren't for you, I'd probably be in an alley somewhere. Or I'd be dead to a minor monster I picked a fight with, without even knowing how to fight. I owe the Sutton house a serious debt, one that I promise to repay."

Kayden's gaze on Rowan softened slightly, only to harden again when Olivia moved across the room to grab Rowan's left hand, dragging it closer and giving it a soft squeeze. "You've done plenty, Rowan.

There is a bit of good news. The kingdom still needs to follow the rules put in place by the allied council. That means that every hero gets a town and at least some funding. We might need to pry it out of the hands of whatever official is there, but it's a start."

Rowan tried to follow along. He really did. But Olivia's hand was making it really hard to focus. All he could think about was the cuddling, and the late-night talks, and the hand-holding . . .

Are we an actual couple?

Olivia chose that moment to furrow her eyebrows, and Rowan couldn't help but notice the creases that formed. She was dealing with enough on her own that he didn't need to add the extra struggle of managing a relationship on top of that.

Yeah, I'm not going to be a dense idiot. She likes me. But even if we cemented our status, what would we even do? Go demon hunting for our first date?

"Rowan? Hero Rowan," the baron called out.

"Yeah, sorry. I got lost in my thoughts for a second," Rowan said. His hand itched for his spear to clear his head of all the distracting thoughts.

"As I was saying," Kayden continued. "This might actually turn out to be a good thing. The frontier is a place known for growth. If you can survive the initial period of deployment, your tier and level won't be an issue."

"But the issue is surviving that initial period," Camilla added. "Rest's Remorse. You're being sent to the one town that was hit by the demons the hardest."

Olivia, for once, was completely flabbergasted. "You mean the one frontier town that was almost left in ruins? The town you told us lost its leader to the horde that eventually made its way here? That town?"

It was almost funny how similar the resigned looks on Kayden's and Camilla's faces were.

"Yes. However, remember that I said this might actually be a good thing," Kayden said. "When a hero takes over a town, they do so mostly in name. Their control over the town's resources is tentative at most, with actual power in the hands of the mayor. But with no one to contest your control at Rest's Remorse, that won't be the case."

"Sure, but what's there to control to begin with? Ruined buildings and corpses?" If bitterness were weaponizable, Rowan was pretty sure that Olivia could kill the demon king on the spot.

"The mayor is dead, yes, and the city heavily damaged," Kayden said sternly. "However, there's no talk about it being removed from the list of frontier towns. That means it's still relatively if not fully functional."

"So, we can expect to find more than just rubble upon arrival?" Rowan asked.

"Yes, Rowan, you can expect to find more than just rubble." Camilla sounded amused, her hands falling to massage her husband's tense shoulders as she spoke. "Make no mistake, it *will* take money and time to fix the town. However, once you've done that, you'll *own* it, because the town has no mayor. That's a very rare opportunity. Other heroes usually are granted a frontier town after the invasion has been repelled. You're getting one right now. That's an opportunity. One that most nobles would be willing to risk life and limb for. You'd become a duke."

Rowan wasn't sure how excited he was by the prospect. To begin with, he was a contractor. This wasn't his world, nor was this meant to be his life. If he could actually make it through everything, the death of the demon lord would mean an opportunity to head back home.

Even with all the awesome powers he'd gained in this new world, he wasn't sure he could resist the urge to go back.

It wasn't so much that he desperately missed his friends and family. Frankly, he didn't have much of either. He did have his cat, though, and he did have safety. Security. The assurance that people on Earth were unlikely to try and kill him.

In his new world, even if he chose to stay, he wasn't sure what the king's reaction would be. After all, the man had forced him and his friends into a death match upon their arrival, all based on some vague supposed prophecy.

A prophecy Rowan wasn't even sure was *real*.

"Rowan?" Olivia's voice tiptoed its way into his head.

Rowan flinched a little, realizing that he'd wandered off again and missed at least part of the conversation. He found Olivia looking at him, worried.

"I'm fine. Sorry. Just thinking. A lot's happening, and I just needed a second," Rowan assured her once again when her eyes narrowed, but, thankfully for him, she didn't push. "Really, I'm fine."

"Is that all you wanted to talk to us about?" Olivia asked instead, turning her attention back to her parents. "You can see that he's tired. The rest of us need a break after all this, too."

"Ah yes, I'm sure you'd love to go off and *rest* together." Her mother put emphasis on that particular word in a way that made the two of them blush scarlet and her father scowl. But it broke the serious mood that had been hanging over the room. "But we need to discuss your party arrangement."

"Party arrangement?" Rowan asked. "What about it?" For some reason, Rowan felt very defensive. The twins were great, and they'd already fought alongside each other enough times for him to trust them almost implicitly.

"Before we got caught up in everything, I was assembling a party for you," Kayden said, twisting the scroll in his hand as if that was the source of his troubles. "The Sutton barony may be small, but there are dozens if not hundreds of talented men and women that would be good pairings in your four-member party. The timing might be a bit rushed with his decree, but we can still—"

"It's fine," Rowan cut in. He traded glances with Olivia in almost the same way that the baron and baroness had done earlier. "Marcus and Milena are both good additions to the party. Marcus is an [Aura Guardian], a defensive class that pairs well with my [Reckless Spear] class. And Milena is a [Elder Shaman] and covers the gaps of [Combat Alchemist]."

"Those are surface qualities. There are dozens of other candidates that can accomplish the same thing." Kayden paused. "The real question is whether you believe that you can trust them. Do you believe that Marcus and Milena will stand next to you as a wave of demons bears down upon you? Will their resolve waver? Or will they prove to be worthy of your trust?"

"I trust them," Olivia said. "They were among the few people who went outside the walls and fought with us in the first wave against a scouting demon. And when all was lost against the

Epic-tier demon, they didn't run. They fought until exhaustion and then some."

"That's well and all, but I was asking our hero. Rowan?"

Rowan nodded. "I trust them. I want them in my party."

For a second, Rowan thought that Kayden looked relieved. Then the baron stood up from the chair and looked in Olivia's direction. "Well, I guess that solves it. Can you go get them? Might as well formalize everything now while we're all here."

A few moments later, Olivia returned with the twins in tow. Kayden gestured for them to take seats.

Marcus sat with his tail clasped firmly in his hands like he could use it as a barrier between himself and what was about to happen. His wolf ears also twitched erratically.

Before Marcus could get more uncomfortable, Rowan spoke up. "Marcus, Milena. Would you like to join my party on a permanent basis?"

For a moment, the two looked more shocked than anything, then amusement sneaked onto Milena's face.

"Oh, I don't know. It sounds like a lot of work," she said with a wink.

Marcus nodded immediately. "Yeah, and a guaranteed place to stay, steady meals, and official recognition of the local authorities doesn't sound very fun."

"Okay, then, we won't impose on you further," Olivia immediately shot back.

"Sorry, too far?" Milena asked. "Of course, we'd be happy to. Who wouldn't want to join the party?" Judging by the way Milena had leaned forward, letting her tail happily wag behind her, she seemed pretty happy.

"Typically, people who don't already have Epic-tier Heart Cards of their own." Camilla's cold voice cut through the air. "I'd like to know why two distinguished members of a major tribe would be this far from home."

"Or working as mercenaries," Kayden added. "Your classes are not something just anyone could just pick up. Your abilities, not something that you'd see from the average beast kind. And your weapons, not something you find a normal blacksmith for."

Milena pushed herself as deeply into the seat as she could. Which was most definitely not working, considering that she was taller than everyone else and the seat was made of wood. After realizing how futile it was, she spoke up.

"What do you want to know, exactly?"

"Why you're here, for starters. Do you really expect us to believe your tribe was happy to let you go?" Kayden asked. Rowan chose to remain silent, realizing he'd seldom heard the baron sound so cold. "Usually, there's only one reason that we see beast folk so close to the frontier."

"We weren't banished," Marcus hurriedly said. "I promise."

"And?" Camilla said. Rowan realized that the baron and baroness made an incredible tag team. They could apply pressure just by being in the same room together.

"And our tribe has long-held traditions and well-developed class paths," Milena said. "And here we are. I'm a shaman, while Marcus is a guardian."

Kayden gave the slightest of nods for Milena to go on.

"Life in our tribe came with certain expectations. Our home is harsh and unforgiving—the far north often is. Everyone has to do their part. Optimal, logical choices. The men are shamans while the women are guardians. Our physiques naturally make up for the short-comings in the classes. I can bridge the dexterity gap with my height, and Marcus can place fewer points into vitality due to his build. But neither of us was happy with our roles."

"Didn't like the idea of being a warrior?" Rowan asked, feeling a certain degree of kinship with the twins. After all, he hadn't exactly volunteered for the [Spearman] class, either.

His Heart Card had made that choice for him.

"I hated it. I hated the training, the expectations, all of it. Marcus felt the same way about being a shaman. And then we got our Heart Cards," Milena said. "Our clan has led the tribe for generations, and we found Heart Cards that confirmed and strengthened our bond as siblings. And they didn't bind us to something we didn't like."

"Exactly," Marcus confirmed, his own tail wiggling in happiness from where he still had it in a death grip. He gestured at his shield and Milena's staff. "So, we took our gifts and snuck away."

"Wait," Rowan said, looking between them. "That's it? You just swapped your weapons?"

Milena nodded. "That's our story. We ran away from home, and when they found us, we told them why we ran."

"And that put a lid on their desire to bring us back. The chief's children had deviated from the path," Marcus said. "Point is, no one's looking for me and my sister. And we didn't do anything all that wrong to end up where we're at."

"And you're okay with giving up your inheritance?" Kayden asked.

"An inheritance that neither of us is willing to pay the price for," Milena answered.

"Then we have no qualms with you. Rowan?" Kayden said.

"None. Welcome to the party, Marcus and Milena."

What Rowan didn't realize was how many details there were to iron out when adding official party members. Olivia had been a special case as the baron's daughter, and previously both of the beast kind were temporary members, which meant a simplified process.

But for the formal process, Kayden had rolled up his sleeves and begun negotiating on the finer details of party membership. The baron circled one of his territory's settlements where the twins would have a small plot of land. And he was halfway through the loot distribution when Rowan stepped in.

"I hate to interrupt this, but how long will it take us to get to the frontier town? Do the four of us need to start packing immediately?" Rowan asked.

"It will take us nearly the entire three weeks to get there, I'm afraid," Camilla answered. "Rest's Remorse is almost at the edge of the frontier. We'll need to hurry. I truly hate traveling that far."

Rowan paused. Something about the baroness's words sounded off to him.

"What do you mean, we?" Olivia asked. "And why does it matter if you hate traveling, Mother?"

"Come now, Olivia. Do you really think either of you is ready to handle this on your own? No, I'll be coming with. You need someone to help run the town until you learn how to do it."

"Oh no. No, no, no," Olivia squeaked out, obvious terror in her voice and eyes. "You can't come."

"Oh, I must. Besides, I wouldn't dream of sending out the two of you without a chaperone." Camilla's smile suddenly turned very sharp. "It would be a shame if you two were without supervision and made a mistake. I'm not ready to be a grandmother yet."

"Mother!"

CHAPTER TWO

Before the Road

A couple hours later, Olivia had gotten over the fact that her mother was coming along with them and had a huge smile on her face.

"Welcome, everyone, to the first official meeting of my party!" Olivia said. Though she was very much *not* the hero, Rowan let her language stand.

For one, the four of them were stuck in a small room with barely enough space for everyone to sit down. And more importantly, the hero was still lying in bed. He had been *planning* to get up and greet the day. But before he could conquer the warm confines of his bed, Olivia had barged into his room, chairs in hand and the twins at her heels.

"If you keep saying stuff like that, I'll totally kick you out of my party, you know," Rowan teased.

"You'll never kick me out. You like me too much." Olivia sounded very self-assured when she said that.

"I don't know. Try barging in on me a couple more times. See what happens," Rowan grumbled.

"All right. I'll make sure my parents know you made that offer," Olivia said, her smile growing in proportion to his dread. "I'm pretty sure my mother made her stance on grandkids known."

"Olivia!"

The gremlin cackled and collapsed on top of him, ignoring the fact that she'd gone to the effort of actually dragging a chair into the room. Rowan sighed, acknowledging that he'd definitely lost this particular round of squabbling.

"What exactly was it that you wanted to do?" Rowan asked.

"Well, I thought we might put our cards on the table. Literally and figuratively," Olivia said.

That made the two new party members stiffen a little. Rowan watched as they exchanged glances and decided to be the first to share.

Rowan Clairfont
Level 37 Reckless Spear
Mana: 50/50
EXP: 185,430/240,000
STR: 39*
VIT: 12
DEX: 39*
PER: 20
INT: 10
WIS: 12
Deck (5/5):
[Heart] Keen Spear (Epic, Passive)
[Class] Blood Siphon (Uncommon, Passive)
Ravaging Lightning Lance (Rare, Active)
Persistent Regeneration (Rare, Active)
Lavish Feasting (Rare, Passive)
Blessings:
Awakened Blessing of the Stalwart Hero

"That's . . . definitely a build." Marcus winced a little, reading over the class description and the details of Rowan's cards. "How is it that I'm the tank and you somehow managed to make a build more masochistic than my own?"

"Here, I'll go next!" Olivia offered.

Olivia Sutton
Level 41 Combat Alchemist
EXP: 1,258,252/9,000,000

Mana: 1,200/1,200
STR: 11
VIT: 14
DEX: 15
PER: 15
INT: 60*
WIS: 60*
Deck (6/6):
[Heart] Pursuit of Brilliance (Epic, Passive)
[Class] Stable Creations (Uncommon, Active)
[Class] Combat Conversion (Rare, Active)
Reduced Cost (Rare, Passive)
Flash Freeze (Uncommon, Active)
Waterlogged Abyss (Epic, Active)
Blessings:
N/A

Rowan choked a little when he saw the experience counter. And then he saw the mana pool. If he was reading things right, she was getting a whopping twenty mana for every single point she had in intelligence. He had known that she was dangerous, but he didn't realize exactly how much so until he saw her stats.

[Combat Alchemist]
Some alchemists content themselves with
peaceful research that extends a person's abilities.
That is not your path. You seek to directly inflict
dread and injury upon your foes using your
deadly arsenal of potions.
By picking the [Combat Alchemist], you will gain
a massive boost to your proficiency when crafting
combat potions. The mana cost of all combat-related
cards and activities will be significantly reduced.
You will also gain a keen instinct for how to best use
said potions to cause maximum damage.
Additional beneficial effects:

**A massive boost to the effectiveness of your
intelligence and wisdom stats.
A massive boost to the growth of your mana pool.
A large boost to your combat awareness.
Combat-class potions will be more potent and
much cheaper and easier to craft.
Class penalties:
A medium increase in crafting difficulty
for all noncombat-class potions.
A large increase in mana cost when crafting
all noncombat-class potions.
Attached card: Combat Conversion (Rare, Active)**

Did that class suit Olivia? Honestly, yes, yes, it did, and Rowan was more than willing to admit that it made her very, very scary. And whether it was an intentional choice by Olivia or by accident, he could see the descriptions of her class cards.

**[Heart] Pursuit of Brilliance (Epic, Passive)
The effectiveness of every unique alchemical item
you produce will be doubled, and the effectiveness
of items crafted from your original recipes is
boosted by fifty percent.**

**[Class] Stable Creations (Uncommon, Active)
Your experiments have taught you how to best
handle volatile reactions. You can pause or
outright eliminate any unstable reactions
during the potion-brewing process.**

**[Class] Combat Conversion (Rare, Active)
Leaving your safe laboratory fully behind you, you step
foot on the battlefield. So long as you have a sample
to draw from, you can duplicate the effects of
any combat-class potion in the form of a
spell by expending your mana.**

Olivia had apparently chosen to keep her **Stable Creations** class card in her deck, which, considering how often she grumbled about it, definitely surprised him. Other than that, she was running both **Flash Freeze** and **Waterlogged Abyss**. The two attack cards were a bit of a surprise.

Flash Freeze because he thought she'd replace it with something more alchemy-focused, but she seemed fond of the card. **Waterlogged Abyss**, meanwhile, was something she'd recently synthesized and was possible only thanks to the wraiths dropping enough copies. And Olivia had loved it the moment she laid eyes on it.

"That's a very impressive build," Milena admitted, eyeing the status windows in a bit of a daze. "I have to admit, the fact that we have a party full of Epic Heart Cards is a minor miracle."

A minor miracle or meddling from the divine? Rowan thought.

"Well, I guess I'll go next." Marcus grinned.

Marcus Murmurin
Level 41 Aura Guardian
EXP: 3,351,249/9,000,000
Mana: 225/225
STR: 15 (+5)
VIT: 74 (+5)*
DEX: 15 (+5)
PER: 15 (+5)
INT: 45 (+35)
WIS: 104 (+35)*
Deck (6/6):
[Heart] Twinned Nature
(Epic, Passive)
[Class] Assigned Protection (Common, Active)
[Class] Until the Last (Uncommon, Passive)
[Class] Aura Coverage (Rare, Active)
Rot Shield (Rare, Active)
Wrath of the Storm (Rare, Active)
Blessings:
N/A

Rowan was pretty sure someone was playing a very crude joke on him, because Marcus's stats were, frankly, *insane*. The sheer fact that he'd somehow managed to hit *one hundred and four* wisdom was enough to make him wonder what he was eating for breakfast.

[Aura Guardian]
You've shown a dedication to the well-being of others that few possess. So, let your soul unfurl and stand between harm and those you care about.
By picking the [Aura Guardian] class, you will gain the ability to protect large groups of people by covering them in your aura, blunting incoming damage and taking on any harm that manages to make it through you if you so choose. You will also gain a massive boost to your proficiency in wielding a shield.
Additional beneficial effects:
A massive boost to the effectiveness of your vitality and wisdom stats.

[Heart] Twinned Nature (Epic, Passive)
You were born as a part of a greater whole.
You share some of your stats and deck effects with your other half.

And there it was, the big reason behind why Marcus's stats were all inflated by a significant amount. **Twinned Nature** was so powerful that Rowan half wished that he could trade **Keen Spear** for the card.

But as Rowan looked through the rest of Marcus's deck, he realized how rare cards were for people who were not heroes or born to nobility. Marcus was still using his Common-tier class card in his deck and the only two nonclass cards, **Rot Shield** and **Wrath of the Storm**, were things they'd earned fighting together against demons. The former had been thanks to the scouting demon while the latter was from the flying demon mount.

Wrath of the Storm (Rare, Active)
Wreathe yourself in elemental rage to both protect
yourself and visit ruin upon your enemies. Your mana
expenditure is directly proportional to the range
and effectiveness of your defenses.

"That Heart Card, what do I need to do to get something like that?" Olivia grumbled, obviously sharing Rowan's own feelings on the subject.

Milena, meanwhile, was looking incredibly shy and hesitant. "Guess I can't avoid this now, huh? Just don't judge too much, okay? Shaman *can* be a little creepy as a class-upgrade path."

Rowan nodded, surprised that Milena seemed a tiny bit ashamed of her class in spite of how much she'd praised it earlier. After all, she *had* chosen to go against tradition just to pick it up.

Milena Murmurin
Level 41 Elder Shaman
EXP: 3,457,243/9,000,000
Mana: 1,480/1,480
STR: 15 (+5)
VIT: 45 (+35)
DEX: 15 (+5)
PER: 15 (+5)
INT: 74 (+5)*
WIS: 104 (+35)*
Deck (6/6):
[Heart] Twinned Nature (Epic, Passive)
[Class] Rotveil (Common, Active)
[Class] Curse of Weakness (Uncommon, Active)
[Class] Elder's Call (Rare, Passive)
Mirror Image (Rare, Active)
Chill of the Grave (Epic, Active)
Blessings:
N/A

[Elder Shaman]
You are a shaman elder of your tribe. You protect, heal,
and pass on the oral traditions of your people.
Do not let their spirit die.
By picking the [Elder Shaman] class, you will gain
access to the ability to cast and conduct greater rituals.
Your affinity with curses and malignant magics
will increase. You will also become capable of
forging a direct connection between yourself
and your tribe's ancestral spirits.
Additional beneficial effects:
A massive boost to the effectiveness of your
intelligence and wisdom stats.
A massive boost to the growth of your mana pool.
A massive boost to your rot, mind, death,
and blood mana affinities.
Class penalties:
To unlock and choose this class, you must meet
strict bloodline requirements.
Attached card: Elder's Call (Rare, Passive)

Rowan was a bit too tired of big numbers to really react to that mana pool. That, coupled with her mana regeneration, actually put Milena miles ahead of what Olivia could sustain in battle.

Though it did make him wonder how tiring and demanding shamanic rituals actually were. Milena was constantly taking mana potions, and even with the chance to prepare, she usually stuck to one or two rituals.

And her shiny new Epic card wasn't going to massively help with that.

[Class] Rotveil (Common, Active)
Cover yourself in a haze of rot mana that will
obscure your location and make you harder
to track through divination.

[Class] Curse of Weakness (Uncommon, Active)
Curse your foes, robbing them of their strength
and potential. The greater your mana investment
is, the greater the effects of the curse.

[Class] Elder's Call (Rare, Passive)
You have an innate connection to the ancestral spirits
of your tribe. Call on them, and they will answer.

Rowan had actually never outright seen her use the **Rotveil** card, though he now had a pretty solid idea of where all the floating skull clouds were coming from.

"I kind of feel the need to close my eyes and not think about anything for a while," Rowan muttered. "That was . . . a lot of information all at once."

"Well, it's a good thing not thinking comes to you naturally, then," Olivia teased, poking his side. "And that you're already in bed."

"Yes, well, the fact that I was *rudely woken up* isn't exactly helping anything here, you know?"

"You were already awake, and we both know it."

"Nuh-uh."

"Uh-huh!"

"Um, you two, not that I don't like sitting here watching you flirt and all, which by the way I don't, that would be weird, but should we finish our discussion first?" Marcus said. Immediately, Rowan and Olivia straightened up, and although they were blushing up a storm, they were at least acting like adults again.

"You know, we have a very solid party on our hands here," Milena ventured. "We have a damage dealer in Rowan, a damage sponge in Marcus, a versatile damage dealer with some utility options in Olivia, and a support debuffer in me."

"True, we cover each other's weaknesses rather well," Olivia murmured, shooting Milena a thankful glance for being acknowledged as a true combatant.

"We just need to touch up our builds, all of us." Rowan sighed, collapsing back into bed for the moment. "I, for one, am kind of in an awkward spot. I really want a better damage card, but I can't remove my regeneration combo."

"Well, you did get the **Ravaging Lightning Lance** card out of our fight with that flying cambion," Marcus mused. "But I unfortunately have to agree. Don't take this the wrong way, but if you're going to be our main damage dealer, yeah, you need more destructive potential."

"You can't ruin your combo." Milena stepped in immediately, partially because Olivia was starting to look cross, and partially because she actually believed that. "Besides, you'll be at the Rare tier soon. You might get a high-damage-potential class card."

"Maybe," Rowan said, feeling the effects of choosing the spear more keenly than ever. The lack of freely available high-damage cards meant he couldn't just ask the baron for spear-related cards.

"Hey, cheer up! Didn't you get a bunch of **Rapid Regrowth** cards from that last battle?" Olivia said with a smile, only for it to go plastic when Rowan groaned loudly.

"Yeah, but I fought a whole army of demons and monsters and I'm still Uncommon."

All three of his other party members flushed. It was often easy to forget that Rowan was a couple of steps behind them despite his combat prowess.

"Well, um, you'll get there soon, right?" Marcus tried, he really did, and Rowan was thankful for that.

"With where we're going, I'll be shocked if I'm still Uncommon for long. At least that's a good side of this entire mess. Still, what are you all planning with your own builds?" Rowan asked, trying to change the subject.

"I need more support cards for my build. Stuff that decreases damage taken, maybe even outright blocks a couple of attacks," Marcus replied.

"I need to look into replacing **Flash Freeze** and **Stable Creations**. I'll keep **Stable Creations** in my cardholder and swap it in when I'm crafting potions. Same with **Reduced Cost**. I don't really need any of them in my deck on the regular." Olivia sighed.

"I know it sounds like a lot, but remember that you're basically completely switching your class around," Rowan ventured, trying to get Olivia to cheer up a little. It was funny how seeing Olivia in the dumps immediately distracted him from his own problems.

"Yeah, I know, it's just a lot, and it's not like it's particularly easy to get a ton of high-rarity cards. Still, moving on, what about you, Milena?"

"I want some direct cards. I love my class and deck, but they're mostly passive cards and abilities so far. I need a way to more directly contribute to battle. Sometimes, I wish I had a more typical caster class, really," Milena said.

"What even is the real difference between 'typical' caster classes and shaman?" Rowan asked.

"Well, as you've seen, we mostly rely on rituals. We're really not that great at casting on the spot. But if you give us time to prep, and if we can work long-term on securing a territory, then we're powerful."

"Oh yeah. Back home, you basically couldn't touch any of the areas that 'belonged' to the shamans, be it of our own tribe or otherwise," Marcus confirmed.

Olivia was interested. "I've heard a little about how shamans fight. Magical creatures, summons, and traps, right?"

"Sounds about right. Traps are curses upon curses upon curses. You can watch a person wither away between two breaths if they venture into the lair of a powerful shaman. Summons and creatures mostly come down to undead and spirits."

Rowan wasn't one hundred percent sure he liked that. "Like necromancers?"

"Sort of. Except we deal more in souls than corpse reanimation." Milena shrugged. "I'm honestly unlikely to do much of that."

"Lack of means or lack of will?"

"Both. The answer is definitely both." Milena wrinkled her nose. "Do you have any idea how much undead creatures *smell*?"

"Probably worse than Marcus's socks," Olivia joked.

Rowan laughed, surrendering himself to banter between friends. They'd stress and plan and worry about things later. For just a little while, he just enjoyed the moment and got to know his new friends.

After Blake and Kayla, Rowan was glad that he had finally found his own community. And he'd fight like hell to keep them all together.

Roadside Blues

As clichés go, the day of a hero's departure should be wet, rainy, and miserable. It should reflect the inner mood of the heroes who are finally leaving behind their loved ones and heading toward danger.

Except the cliché didn't hold.

The day was perfectly clear with not a single cloud in sight. And Rowan wasn't leaving behind everyone he cared about. They were coming with him.

In fact, the road looked beautiful. It was like they were about to set off on a huge stretch of clay tile. Rowan was willing to bet reasonably large amounts of money that the baron had improved the roads at some point. It made practical sense, easing the transport of goods and information between recovering settlements. But it also made it so that this journey was going to be far smoother than it should be.

Before they could set off, however, they had to pay the parent tax. More specifically, Olivia had to pay the parent tax.

This was made even worse by the fact that she wasn't the only one leaving for the frontier. With Camilla going with them, the baron and baroness reenacted a scene straight from a soap opera. There were tears, flowers, and grand gestures that Olivia looked absolutely sick of as she stood to the side, forgotten for the moment.

The rest of the hero party were standing by their rides, firmly outside the magic privacy bubble someone had thought to conjure so the Suttons could be spared some dignity.

"You think she's going to ignite due to sheer anger?" Rowan asked, watching Olivia grow progressively more red in the face. Honestly, it was kind of impressive the way she managed to change color like that.

"I'm more worried about whether or not she's going to try to take out her own parents. I mean, we haven't even received our land deeds yet," Marcus said with a lopsided grin.

"Well, I think this is really sweet. They've obviously been together for years, and they still care about each other. The two of you are just mean, and Olivia is too embarrassed to be properly appreciative." Milena said that a bit louder than strictly necessary, making Olivia's head snap in their direction.

Olivia glanced between her parents and her party before shrugging and marching over.

"What are you lot arguing over now? Can I really not leave you for five minutes?" Olivia demanded, crossing her arms in front of her chest. Honestly, the effect was a bit ruined by how adorable she looked, dressed in something that wasn't battle fatigues.

"We're being good. Just waiting for your mother," Marcus said.

"Well, you need not wait any longer." Camilla's voice floated over. Somehow, without anyone noticing, Lady Sutton had ended up in the carriage they would be using.

"How?" Marcus asked in breathy awe.

Camilla just smirked, and Rowan realized in that very moment that he had absolutely zero clue what the baroness's class was. He knew Kayden used swords, but he'd never seen so much as a single indicator of what Camilla was all about.

"If I asked very nicely, would you tell me your class?" Rowan asked before his brain-to-mouth filter could catch up.

"Rowan! You can't just ask my mother something like that!"

"Is it really that big a deal?"

"Yes and no," Camilla supplied, looking amused. "Don't worry, though, I won't take offense. At least I won't if all of you are inside this carriage within the next five minutes."

With just one final pause for the baron to hug his daughter and quietly threaten Rowan with bodily harm if he hurt her, they finally rolled out of town.

* * *

The last time that Rowan traveled in the carriage, he had essentially no time or mood to enjoy the scenery. There was training, both physical and mental, and the fact that he had been summoned to the middle of a divine meeting and then literally dropped into a new plane of existence.

Not easy things to get over.

Now, though, there was extremely little to do. He could run after the carriage, but it was more mindless fun than exercise that could improve his stats. Unless he decided to do the whole trip by foot, Rowan was pretty sure that he wouldn't even break a sweat.

He hoped to find solace in his companions, but that was a no-go, too. Everyone knew what they were getting into and was busy preparing.

Olivia was tinkering with some kind of traveling alchemy kit. Her mother was lost in a pile of scrolls that looked very serious and official. Milena had an old leather-bound book in hand, and Rowan didn't want to think about what had gotten flayed for her to have reading privileges. Even Marcus was distracted, summoning and then experimenting with his protection aura. Rowan was pretty sure he was trying to make it as efficient as possible, since it occasionally grew so thin that it flickered out completely.

Frankly, Rowan wished Marcus would try the opposite, especially considering his mana regeneration. It'd be a much nicer world if he could constantly provide them with the magical equivalent of plate armor. Unfortunately, that idea was shot down as soon as Rowan brought it up. Marcus's mana was high but not infinite. And doing something like that had a ridiculous mana cost that even he could not easily pay, and definitely not for long.

All that meant that Rowan was well and truly *bored*.

"Tell me, hero, when was the last time you just sat and did nothing?"

Rowan jerked in surprise and found Camilla staring at him.

"Um, I don't know." He tried to think of a time when he'd sat still and nothing came to mind. Even back on Earth, there was constantly something to do. Homework. Watching countless TV shows he was behind on. Playing video games. Just messing with his phone.

True and actual relaxation and quiet?

Those were incompatible with Rowan's vocabulary. Or his ingrained behavior, really. As much as he liked being lazy sometimes, that was just a response to a long string of stressful days.

"You haven't," Camilla said. Rowan met her eyes and realized that the baroness was looking at him, or maybe *into* him would have been a better descriptor. He felt like she was staring beyond his outer shell and into the inner parts of himself. There was nowhere for him to hide. Sandwiched between Milena and Marcus, Rowan was sitting opposite Olivia and Camilla, who enjoyed the much more comfortable circumstances of only having two people in their half of the carriage.

"It's been a while," Rowan admitted.

"I see," Camilla said and began to pack up some of the documents she had been poring over. "Tell me, Rowan, how much have you done with card fusion so far?"

Rowan was learning just how quickly conversations moved with the baroness. "Well, we've done some of it, both to improve some of the cards we had and to avoid ending up with thousands of Common scrap."

"You made new cards?"

"Some. I don't really enjoy how it's completely random what card you get," Rowan complained, genuinely upset by the way that mechanic of the system worked. There were thousands, if not millions of cards that the fuses could create. Most of which were entirely useless. "Eventually figured it was just better to upgrade to higher tiers and wait. Better for future trades."

"Ah, but you still have some, yes? Common cards, or at least scraps of them?"

"Yeah?"

"Because I really don't think anyone's shown you how to use card fusion properly. We'll get to that in a second. My daughter also mentioned you're looking for some new spear cards. Mostly to replace your Common class card?"

"Kind of. I have **Empowered Thrust** in my cardholder at the moment."

"Do you mind if I take a look?" Camilla asked, but it was really more of a demand by the way she put out her hand.

Shrugging, Rowan complied. It wasn't like he had much reason to hide the card away. Unless Camilla was secretly a [Spearman], she couldn't use the card anyways. Truth be told, Rowan should have fused the card. It was the only Common card in his cardholder, and he had dozens of different Uncommon and Rare options. But, for some odd reason, he'd kept it.

"Okay, I see what we're working with here. Before we start, I suggest you take a close look at your card. Remember how using it felt. Read through its description. It'll all be very important," Camilla said.

Confused but unwilling to go against the mother of the girl currently eyeing him from the corner of her eye, Rowan did just that.

Empowered Thrust (Common) (Active)
Empower the thrust of your spear using mana,
increasing its destructive potential.

It wasn't a complicated card. Rowan could remember the joy he felt when he was first made a hero. And it had served him more than well.

With those memories was the feeling of how mana would move inside him when using **Empowered Thrust**. It would swirl around his chest, flow into his arms, and leap onto the spear. Rowan grabbed the spear next to him and tried to follow the same pattern without the card equipped. The mana was surprisingly obedient for the first two steps, but when he tried to pour it into the spear, there was only a shower of sparks.

Rowan couldn't help it. He scowled.

He knew he now had a stronger, higher-tier card. But the fact that he missed his old one didn't go away. It was just the way he was with things he liked. He clung to them and hoarded them until he was forced to give them up or they broke apart completely.

"I see that look in your eyes. What would you do if I told you that you can try and salvage that card from just languishing in your cardholder?" Camilla asked, and he saw the other three pairs of eyes in the carriage widen.

"What's the catch?" Rowan asked.

"Well, if the process fails, the card will be either ruined or destroyed. One shot at improvement or completely losing your card. I can explain how it would work and what to do, but you'll need to decide whether you want to do it on your own."

He mulled that over for a second. "Okay, let's do it."

"Splendid! Now, you have to understand one thing first. Class cards are special. The system operated on the assumption that you'd only get one and that it's special to your class in one way or another. Do you know why class cards don't evolve or disappear when you rank up?"

"Because no other cards do that?" Rowan offered.

Camilla laughed gently. "Yes and no. The main reason, as far as we can tell, is to give us room to experiment and find our own individual path. You see, unlike other cards, class cards don't need to be fused with only their own copies. So long as you can find compatible cards, you can use them to upgrade your class cards. But there's no guarantee you'll be happy with the fusion."

"So I could end up with a useless card regardless?"

"Of course. It's a science. What do you hope to upgrade your card to? What cards are you feeding into the upgrade? How do each of those cards interact with your class card? All these are things that will impact success."

"There's another problem," Rowan interrupted. "I don't have any other spear cards."

"And we will fix that. How many Common scrap pieces do you have?"

"A couple hundred?" Rowan pulled out a small sack that he had been using to carry the shards. "Maybe more."

"One thousand, two hundred, and thirteen," Olivia said.

For a moment, Camilla looked proud of her daughter. "Okay, take out eight of them. Put your hand in contact with the piece and then focus not just on the idea of starting up a fusion, but also about how it feels to wield a spear."

Rowan followed the instructions and found a new system prompt greeting him.

**Eight scrap pieces required. Initiate fusion with [Spear]
as the designated preferred trait?
Y/N
Emanation Spear (Common, Active)
Ignite an orb of mana on the tip of your spear,
illuminating the space around it.**

"It is possible to pay a gratuitous fee to the system for the sake of narrowing down the results of your fusion attempts," Camilla explained. "However, the results are not fully guaranteed and you're using many more scrap pieces for each fusion."

"That doesn't matter! This is incredible!" Rowan exclaimed, a radiant smile on his face. If that sort of thing worked at *every* tier, then the possibilities were nearly limitless.

"Oh, I'm afraid that very much matters." Camilla stared at the card that Rowan had just created, even though its back was turned to her. "You focused on the idea of a spear and got a card that just lights up the tip of your spear. Let's do another experiment. Try adding another variable. Try thinking about dealing damage."

**Sixteen scrap pieces required. Initiate fusion with
[Spear] and [Damage] as the designated preferred traits?
Cruel Spear (Common, Passive)
Your attacks with a spear deal more persistent
damage, which resists healing and treatments
by a minor amount.**

"Sixteen," Rowan muttered, quickly seeing where things were going.

"Yes, and you got only a moderately useful card. A passive one. Now, if you wanted to specify that the skill should be active, it would be another doubling in cost. If you want to specify it should use mana, *another* doubling of the cost, and so on and so forth. So long as you know the exact card you want and what characteristics to focus on, you'll be able to get it. It just won't be cheap or easy."

"At least it's not entirely random," Rowan said, refusing to give up.

"And you'd be right. A second bonus is that you have enough card scraps to test things out for yourself. So let's try fusing another eight spear cards. Do whatever attributes you think would be useful."

A couple minutes later, Rowan found his enthusiasm considerably dampened. When he tried getting more specific with his fusion requirements, it began to burn through scrap at a rate of thirty-two or even sixty-four scraps at once. And the results were still a bit more average than he hoped.

Cruel Spear (Common, Passive) × 3
Your attacks with a spear deal more persistent
damage, which resists healing and treatments
by a minor amount.
Mana Infusion (Common, Active) × 4
Infuse your weapon with mana and then deal
a much more devastating blow.
Piercing Spear (Common, Active) × 2
Imbue your spear with mana, allowing it to achieve
much greater penetrative power.

If anything, Rowan was learning how strong class cards were. **Empowered Thrust** was equal to the three spear cards combined. And instead of taking up three slots in his deck, the class card only took one.

"And now, it's time to upgrade your class card," Camilla said from the side.

For a few tense moments, Rowan didn't want to upgrade his class card. It twinkled in the sun as he held it in front of him. A second hand joined his, and when he looked up, Rowan saw Olivia giving him a small but supportive smile.

Do you want to fuse [Class] Empowered Thrust
(Common, Active) with the following cards:
Cruel Spear (Common, Passive) × 3
Mana Infusion (Common, Active) × 4
Piercing Spear (Common, Active) × 2
Y/N

Rowan hit the "yes" button, and like always, the phenomenon of fusing even the lowest tier of cards took his breath away. White transitioned to green as light erupted from the fusion, and Rowan let out his breath when the card appeared intact instead of destroyed.

And like **Empowered Thrust**, the new class card was simple and straight to the point. Honestly, the system was almost too straightforward with the class card descriptions.

[Class] Essential Thrust (Uncommon, Active)
Imbue skill and mana into your spear, improving its
damage output and its destructive potential.

"Congratulations," Camilla said. "Now you have an important decision to make. Do you risk everything for a chance to get a Rare class card? Or do you stop here? You have enough scrap cards, but if you fail, the class card is gone forever."

Rowan thought about it and then tucked the card into his cardholder. "I'll stop."

Over the next two and a half weeks, Rowan found ways to distract himself and even fell into a pleasant routine. He'd chat with his party members in the morning, learn various lessons about the cards from Camilla, and then round off the day with some quick training to keep his skills sharp.

He'd even managed to sneak a couple of quiet moments alone with Olivia whenever they stopped. Though every time he came back to the carriage, he always found Camilla eyeing them.

And then they were finally drawing close enough to the town to see signs of destruction.

Ironically, he could almost track the path that the demons had taken. To the left of the town was a swamp of black puddles that released their stench into the air. Either no one had bothered to do anything about the issue, or the puddles were so deadly that they couldn't be cleaned. Rowan had a suspicion it was the former.

The town itself was proof of that. At some point, it had been a sprawling, almost magnificent thing. The walls towered into the sky, wrought out of some gray-black stone that sparkled in the sunlight like a beacon. But half of the walls were now missing, and anyone could see the buildings within the town were in only slightly better repair.

At least that was the case for the outer sections of the town.

As the group entered the town, Rowan realized that there was more to Rest's Remorse than met the eye. Unlike the baron's village, someone had built the town with purpose. All the homes were laid out in a grid and the streets met at sharp, straight angles. There were grates at intervals along the road, which Rowan assumed meant some kind of sewer system. It was obvious that the city was the love child of some obsessive engineer and that they'd gone all out during the planning stage.

The inner sections of the town were mostly intact, with a rare bit of damage here and there. Fighting had definitely happened within the town, but it seemed that the defenders had mostly kept the demons to the outer parts. In fact, houses past a certain point were still in pristine condition.

As they wound their way through the streets toward the ruler's residence that towered over the rest of the town, Rowan was starting to feel cautiously optimistic. And then he saw the welcoming party.

In front of the carriage was a host of mercenaries. Or the most irregular army that Rowan had ever seen. The men wore an array of different armors, some blue and others red. It was definitely good metal, just not standardized. And at the head of the group was a giant, his hand already on his sword.

"Troublemakers," Camilla sighed when she saw the sight. She gently stepped out before the carriage even fully stopped. She held her head high as she faced down the mercenaries. "What, exactly, is happening here?"

The lead mercenary scoffed. "I'll tell you what's happening. What's happening is that you seem to think you'll just come around and chase me out of my brand-new home. Well, lady, that's just not how things are done around here."

Even without his speech, the way the mercenary spat the word *lady* clued Rowan in to the trouble they were in.

CHAPTER FOUR

Small-Town Politics

Camilla Sutton, former duchess of the kingdom, sighed.

"So let me get this right," Camilla said. She didn't sound angry or upset. Just resigned. "Do you believe that you should run the town? Or that we should share power with you? Actually, what is it that you want?"

For several moments, Camilla just stood there, her head tilted back slightly as if in silent prayer, and the mercenaries doing their best scary-face routine. Rowan hopped from the carriage to stand beside her.

"All of you, go back to where you came from," the mercenary barked.

"You want to do this as soon as I've properly stepped foot in this town?" Camilla asked, putting her hand in front of Rowan to stop him from responding.

"Oh yes. Why wouldn't we? We finally have a nice thing going, and nobles are showing up to ruin it like usual."

"The succession of leadership in Rest's Remorse was arranged and approved by the king. Hero Rowan Clairfont is the leader of this town."

"Listen, lady, you're here, we're here, the king ain't. He also never gave a rat's ass about this place before, so long as everyone paid up what they owe him. So I said that it's time for me to take charge. Now, is the king going to back up his words? Because my men will back mine up."

"Usually, when someone says something like that, there's an 'or else' in there. What's yours?"

The mercenary laughed and glanced around. Behind his band was a group of servants, obviously anxious about the whole thing. "Lady, you can either give up and leave, or else you can have a little demon-related accident like the last mayor."

Even Rowan could see the false bravado. Whatever the mercenary liked to pretend, the mention of the king did actually rattle him. But it wasn't like Rowan was entirely unfazed, either. The suggestion that the last mayor was murdered and hadn't died in combat? That didn't really sound all that great for Rowan's own long-term prospects.

"I see. Now here's my predicament. We're not in a position to leave, since that would be directly disobeying the king's orders," Camilla said calmly.

"Oh?" The mercenary leaned forward, mistaking the baroness's composure for weakness. "Heh, I guess you can stay. Haven't had any quality entertainment in some time, and if a fine *lady* such as yourself wants to accompany me, who am I to say no?"

"I see I've utterly wasted my words on you," Camilla snapped, her eyes blazing with rage. A pair of daggers appeared in her hands. They were wicked, curved weapons, chiseled out of some black material that swallowed up sunlight. The mercenary drew his sword. "You have exactly three seconds to prepare yourself."

"Three seconds? Lady, I don't need—"

From what Rowan could tell, the mercenary's stance was rock solid and his focus on point. He might not have been the most pleasant person, but his skills seemed to back the talk up.

Unfortunately, that didn't save him from the baroness he had managed to piss off.

One moment, Camilla Sutton was standing next to Rowan, and the next, she was inches away from the mercenary leader. Everything seemed to happen in slow motion after that. She stabbed one of her daggers forward and plunged it hilt-deep into the mercenary's chest. The man slowly tilted his head to look at the wound. Before he could do more, Camilla swiped up with her second dagger. As it made its arc from her side to the sky, the mercenary's hand slid off his wrist and flopped onto the ground. The man's lips opened, and he tried to gurgle something, but only blood leaked out. Almost gently, Camilla whipped her first dagger up, carving through flesh and bone and splitting the man's chest with a deep gap.

"You needed the three seconds," Camilla said casually. Behind the mercenary, none of the other men moved or even spoke. As the baroness looked them over, she had a hint of amusement in her forest-green eyes. "Now that he's dealt with, am I going to have to do the same with you?"

The mercenaries all sported deathly pale faces. If Rowan was a betting man, he would have put money or cards down that none of them could last more than two rounds at the hand of the baroness. They were beat.

It was a stalemate for a few seconds before one of the mercenaries stumbled back and then broke into a sprint. It was like a signal for the rest of them to flee. A moment later, there was a stampede of mercenaries.

Rowan even saw one of them trip and then get mercilessly pounded into the ground by the feet of his own comrades. Thankfully, people in his new world were made of sterner stuff, so the man managed to stand back up and then stumble off.

All that was left from the welcoming party were the servants.

"Well, that was eventful. Will you be showing us to our rooms now, or has this fool managed to delay that as well?" Camilla stabbed her finger downward like she might use it to skewer the mercenary again.

"No, my lady. The rooms are ready. We had them made up just this morning. The mercenaries taking over was a . . . recent development." One of the older ladies spoke up, stepping forward in spite of the tremble in her voice and body.

"Excellent. Lead the way, then. Before I forget, I will not be taking the primary bedroom. That would be for Hero Rowan." Camilla reached back to grab Rowan by the wrist, and the hero noted that the daggers were gone just as suddenly as they'd appeared. "This is one of the summoned heroes and your new mayor."

"Of course. It is a pleasure to meet you, my lord." The maid servant didn't miss a beat.

Rowan sent a confused, pleading look Olivia's way. His total experience dealing with maids was his time in the baron's household and getting trampled by the [Battle Maid]. He was much stronger now, but some memories died hard. Olivia realized the same thing as she giggled and strolled forward.

"The hero would like to see his room because he's tired," Olivia said with authority, and the servants complied immediately. It probably helped that she looked a lot like the noble they just saw butcher a man right in front of them.

"How did your mom do that?" Rowan whispered as he followed Olivia and the maid to his new accommodations. After giving it a bit more thought, he realized that Camilla could probably hear him with her stats.

"You know, my mother used to be a duchess. Do you know what a noble needs to do to hold on to that title long-term?" Olivia asked back.

"No?"

"You need to produce at least one Epic-ranked individual every two generations, and you would preferably have another marry into the family at the same frequency, too. Of course, my parents are overachievers. Both of them are Epic, it's just that most people focus on my father."

"And why's that?" Rowan couldn't help but ask, curiosity overcoming any fear he might have felt.

"Because my mom's whole thing is not being noticed. She's a [Spirit-Borne Assassin]. Very Rare class, elf-lineage exclusive. Amazing, right?" Olivia said that in a chipper way, but Rowan felt all kinds of unpleasant shivers down his spine.

That was a fact that he could have known earlier. The same [Spirit-Borne Assassin] had been teasing him about his relationship with Olivia. He was suddenly glad that he had mostly borne the words without much of a response. It really didn't seem like a good idea to get on the bad side of someone who could vanish a person as easily as Camilla just had.

"Yes, amazing. Very interesting, that." Rowan suddenly needed a couple glasses of water. His mouth was as parched as a desert and strolling arm in arm with the daughter of an extremely lethal assassin was definitely not helping.

I thought the danger would come from Kayden. At least the physical kind. Who knew that Camilla would be lethal in both her words and her actions?

It didn't take long for Olivia to realize how stiff Rowan was. Nor did she have any qualms against milking his sudden realization for all it was worth. She leaned into him, hugged his arm, and whispered nonsense words into his ear. With each motion, Rowan would tilt his head back slightly and see the baroness trailing behind them with a smug grin. It wasn't long before beads of sweat began forming on Rowan's forehead.

Why did I ever accept that sponsorship offer from Kayden?

Then again, it wasn't like Rowan regretted that decision, considering the fact that it had led him to his party with Marcus and Milena. And to one green-haired girl in particular.

Rowan realized that there was at least one benefit to being suddenly sent to the very edge of the frontier against the demons: an extremely comfortable bed.

The bedroom that Camilla had directed the maid toward housed an absolute monstrosity of a bed. It was larger than a king and probably even bigger than the fabled California-king beds that only appeared in mattress stores. And it felt like a cloud. When Rowan collapsed down, it practically swallowed him with its boundless softness.

He sighed in contentment. All his stress rolled off his shoulders. He was now alone, safe, and—

"Sleeping already?" Another person plopped down next to Rowan, breaking his relaxation. He glared at the intruder, but it seemed that nothing could stop the grin on Olivia Sutton's face.

"You aren't real," Rowan muttered as he closed his eyes back again. "I'm hallucinating."

"Can a hallucination do this?" Olivia poked Rowan's cheek. When he didn't respond, she started pinching it.

"See, this is the problem. I was trying to rest. But now I have this annoying alchemist, well, annoying me," Rowan grumbled.

"Tough luck, never had that issue." Olivia grinned wider, rolling over so that she landed right in the crook of his arm and stared right up at him with her big, adorable eyes.

Rowan slipped to the side. "You do realize where we are, right? And that your mother is just down the hall? Your *scary assassin* mother?"

"Is that really an issue?" Olivia stuck her tongue out at him.

Rowan's brow twitched. Enough was enough. It was time to go on the offensive. He half tackled Olivia and found himself looming over the petite alchemist.

"Tough luck?" Rowan whispered. Olivia's eyes started to widen with some emotion he couldn't recognize. But that only emboldened him. "Do you know what happens when you play with fire?"

Before Rowan could relish in his victory, the sound of someone knocking on his door rang out. It was accompanied a moment later by a voice full of dry amusement. "I hope I'm not interrupting anything."

Camilla. Just my luck.

Rowan's body was a second slower than his mind and Olivia made sure to take advantage of that. Her hands sneaked out and locked around his neck before Rowan could get away.

"No, Mom, you can come in," Olivia called out.

Rowan tried to buckle himself away, but the alchemist had apparently invested in more physical stats than he'd realized. So when Lady Sutton walked into Rowan's new bedroom, the first sight she saw was her daughter hugging the hero's neck in a rather suggestive position.

At least it was a semigood day to die.

"I see. Looks like I am interrupting after all," Camilla said in a neutral voice. "Regardless, you need to follow me, Rowan. You can come along as well, daughter."

"Yeah, sorry," Rowan said meekly. He tried to get up one more time and half dragged the alchemist into a sitting position. The stubborn girl just refused to let go. She was firmly affixed to his chest, looking as content as a person could be.

Of course she is. It's not like her mother is going to kill her. *She's going to kill me.*

"We need to see the chamberlain of this estate about the transfer of authority. You have the royal edict putting you in charge of this town. But you need to have it officially acknowledged and notarized that you're here as you were ordered," Camilla said. Rowan could have sworn that he heard a hint of impatience in her voice.

"Yeah, coming." Rowan tried to stand and Olivia did her best impression of a monkey clinging to his chest.

"Whether my daughter wants to be difficult or not, we need to get this handled as soon as possible." Camilla coughed. "If we delay and the deadline passes, then it will be interpreted as your refusal to cooperate. It doesn't matter what has happened, all that matters is what is officially acknowledged."

"Yup." Rowan looked at Olivia, who turned her head the other way. Somehow, she seemed ready to fully embarrass him in front of her parents. None of these hijinks were going on back when they were at the village and just enjoying each other's presence. In an attempt to stall for time, he tried to start a different conversation. "You mentioned a royal edict?"

"This." Camilla was suddenly holding the scroll that had started that whole mess. "This is an official missive and edict of the king. It has his crest and seal, denoting it as an official document of the state."

"So, we just need to show the . . . chamberlain that?"

"Correct, then we'll need to stick around for the reading of the will and the transfer of duties, and you'll be free to rest for the day."

That, at least, sounded good. Better than good, really. They hadn't done anything physically demanding, but Rowan couldn't properly put into words how utterly exhausted he felt. The nearly three-week carriage ride had taken a real toll on him. He really wasn't the traveling type.

Rowan brute-forced his way forward. And to her credit, Olivia released him the second they crossed the room's threshold. It was like there were two different Olivias, one for private time and the other for public areas.

One was a force of nature and also an absolute nuisance. The other was still a force of nature, but much more proper and noble-like. That wasn't much of a shock, considering she was a real noble.

In a few minutes, Camilla stopped in front of a massive oak door.

"Here we are. I had a chat with the man earlier myself. He's quite pleasant and dutiful, so just follow his directions." It wasn't exactly a glowing review, but upon second thought, that was one of the nicest things Rowan had heard Camilla Sutton say about anyone not directly related to her.

Rowan pushed the door open, strolling into a well-furnished study full of comfortable furniture. But the real feature of the room was the copious number of documents, scrolls, and more stacked on top of each other.

"Ah, Lord Rowan, it is a pleasure to finally meet you," the elderly chamberlain said, standing up without ruining his perfectly pressed suit.

"Likewise, sir . . . ?"

"My apologies, my lord, I am a rather well-known face around here and forgot my manners. Henry. My name is Henry, and I am your chamberlain from today onward," the chamberlain said.

"I hope this doesn't sound rude, but why do I need a chamberlain?" Rowan asked.

Thankfully, the man didn't take offense to that and instead offered a seat to Rowan. Both of them sank down into the embrace of the chairs.

"No offense taken. Feel free to ask me anything that comes to mind. But to your question, the frontier towns are under the control of the nobility. They pay for upkeep and, in return, receive most of the taxes and other profits they might generate. A small portion of that goes to the royal treasury," the chamberlain said.

"Can't say that I really approve of things, making money like that," Rowan grumbled.

"It's the way of life. The noble houses take a risk in building a town like this, and the mercenaries would never have been able to hunt demons on the frontier without having secured towns nearby. But I digress. What I wanted to say is that the royal family needs these towns to continue running and for them to be run well. This way, the kingdom's best interests are maintained. And for that, capable servants and town managers are required."

"I see. And that's your role? Someone who serves the king and is here to look after the town?"

"In a manner of speaking, all of us are pledged to serve the king. But I suppose you are correct, Hero Rowan. A long time ago, one of my ancestors was the chamberlain of this town. Since then, it's been a tradition and requirement for our family to take up a post as chamberlain or similar so we can assist the lord of Rest's Remorse. I've known most of the people who serve in this town since I was a boy."

"And now you're stuck with me, someone who doesn't know the first thing about town management." Rowan could see the man's predicament.

The chamberlain laughed. "You'd be surprised how many people don't know the intricacies of town management. I'm sure you'll see that most of us are quite happy with a change of leadership and happy to help make sure this town runs smoothly. We just don't have much appreciation for unreasonable demands."

That was about as plain of a negotiation as Rowan had ever heard. The staff would pledge their support to him as long as he didn't ask too much of them. Honestly? That was *exactly* what he wanted.

"Agreed. I'll hold up my end of the bargain," Rowan said.

"Great, and the town of Rest's Remorse welcomes you, Lord Rowan." The chamberlain tilted his head away from Rowan. "Lady Sutton, if I may receive the official missive?"

Camilla smiled and passed the scroll over. The man received it with both hands and brought it only mere inches from his face as he scanned over the contents. It took a couple long minutes before he was satisfied, but no one rushed him. Even Olivia remained quiet and respectful in her corner of the room.

"Everything is in order," the chamberlain said as he dipped behind his work desk, pulling out two sheets of heavy paper and a something that looked like a stamp. "Lord Rowan, may I please have your signature here and here?"

He signed both sheets.

"Excellent, now, if I could have just a single drop of your blood?" the chamberlain said in a polite tone, as if that was an entirely normal request.

Enough time around Milena had taught him of the importance of blood. Rowan paused. He glanced to Camilla for confirmation, and she gave a slight nod. Seeing no other choice, Rowan picked up his spear where it was resting by his thigh and nicked his finger on it.

"Where do you want it?" Seeing that Rowan was willing to bleed seemed to put the old man in a much better mood, and he quickly motioned to three circles on yet another three contracts before tilting the seal upside down and indicating one final place that needed his blood.

When Rowan put his lightly bleeding finger against that, electricity zipped out of the seal and burrowed directly into his chest.

Authority over Rest's Remorse obtained.
Do you wish to exercise your power?
Y/N

"What was that?" Rowan asked, feeling the spot on his chest that had been impacted by the electricity.

"You now possess a direct connection to the city's ward network, as well as the prison controls."

"Ward network? Prison?"

"Correct. One of the main duties of the mayor is to ensure the safety of the town, both from outside and from within. Wards will tell you if some threat is coming and give time for defense preparation. Prisons are . . . well, a bit more self-explanatory. You could throw the rebellious mercenaries in them. But while both of these things are important, they pale in comparison to your other duties."

"Okay, hit me."

"Hit you?" The chamberlain hesitated as he tried to make sense of the words. And then the older man nodded as if the hero had said something perfectly reasonable. Rowan hoped that the translation function of the system had kicked in. "The first two weeks are some of the most important for a new mayor. You'll need to find your footing and establish yourself in the town such that everyone defers to your authority. But once that's done, you are expected to lead an expedition into the demonic wastes every two months."

"Every two months? That . . . doesn't sound too bad," Rowan said.

"Two months includes the amount of time of the expedition. This isn't a one- or two-day trip. Even if everything goes well, you'll need at least a month for a round trip," Camilla cut in.

"Lady Sutton is correct. The primary goal of these expeditions is to clear out the buildup of demons that might threaten the kingdom. Many of these hordes are deep within the demonic wastes. But as a hero, you have a second goal. When you grow strong enough, you'll need to locate and eventually slay each of the Legendary demons that have made the wastes their home in anticipation of their master's arrival."

"Legendary?" Rowan repeated. "How am I supposed to do that? We only just won against a Rare-tier demon. And barely survived an Epic-tier demon. But Legendary? Pray that it starts attacking itself?"

Camilla burst into laughter, and even the old chamberlain let out a few chuckles. "Don't worry, Rowan. I promise it's not as bad as it sounds. You'll have support from the armies, and Legendary demons have only ever fallen to the unified assault by the heroes," Camilla said.

"You mean to say we'll be fighting them together?" Rowan asked.

"Correct. As a lone hero, your mission will just be to locate them. A hunt for a Legendary demon will then be organized and the heroes brought together to face the threat. That *might* change if one of you managed to rise to Legendary tier, but that's far in the future," Camilla said.

"Lady Sutton is right. Lord Rowan, heroes are one of the most important resources for our kingdom. Your safety is a high priority. Now, there are a couple other minor duties for a mayor to think about right now."

"Sure, anything that doesn't involve fighting a Legendary demon."

The chamberlain laughed, his eyes twinkling. "Of course, Lord Rowan. First, the people are going to be looking to you to enforce the laws and rules of this place. And second, the town's economy is still recovering after the last demon siege. Trade is the lifeblood of frontier towns. The more trade, the more people and the safer the town. And you also get more profits."

Seeing Rowan's expression, Camilla stepped forward. "Rowan, until you grow enough to protect yourself and my daughter, I will stay here. That's why I chose to join you to begin with. You need both advice and protection, and our family can offer both this time."

Rowan was quickly realizing how important both of those things were. Felton's Mill would have fallen in the first wave without Bron. If there was even the slightest chance that things could proceed smoothly and normally this time around, Rowan needed every bit of help he could get.

"Deal."

CHAPTER FIVE

Hostile Alliances

I can't believe how uncomfortable these clothes can get," Rowan grumbled. He thumbed the stiff collar of the suit he'd been forced into and tried to get more comfortable.

To be perfectly truthful, it wasn't the suit that was bothering him. It was the manifestation of his nerves. It was hard not to be on edge when he could hear a loud and boisterous crowd just outside his door.

Things were moving far too quickly for his liking.

After he'd been declared the official mayor of Rest's Remorse the day before, Rowan had thought that Camilla would handle everything else. He could be mayor in name only and keep doing the things that he had been, adventuring and heroing. Those hopes had been dashed as soon as the sun rose the next day, when he was informed that he would be attending a "gathering" with every notable figure in the town.

He wasn't quite sure why they would all decide to attend. He did have a strong suspicion that they were eager to scope out their new mayor and his abilities. The biggest problem was, Rowan didn't really have many abilities he was proud of.

"You're really saying that? Really?" Milena growled, making Rowan wince as his eyes went briefly to the wolfkin.

The unfortunate woman was stuffed into a getup even worse than his. She had first been given a dress, but when the maids of the mayor's manor saw the outcome, they dropped that idea faster than a hot pot. The suit that Milena wore now had a rather nice and flattering cut, but the way it made her fur puff out was a highly suspect fashion choice.

"They wouldn't let you attend in a plain robe, huh?" Rowan sighed, shaking his head.

Milena just growled at him, her fangs snapping.

"Easy now, we're all friends here," Marcus laughed, looking even better in a suit than Rowan did. Which was frankly unfair, since the man had required a hole to be cut into his pants for his tail to poke through.

Milena huffed and turned away from them.

Truth be told, Rowan didn't look too shabby himself. Despite how uncomfortable they could be, the suits for all three of them were about as high quality as one could hope for. They were dyed a classic black with golden swirls rimming the sleeves and had the baron's crest embroidered on the backs.

Rowan didn't begrudge Kayden for it. He *had* thrown in his lot with the baron, and this extremely blatant sign of his allegiance would hopefully go a long way in keeping people from pushing too hard on certain matters.

There was only a single person in the room who seemed entirely unfazed by the impending gathering.

"Relax, would you?" Olivia Sutton teased, green hair perfectly framing a face that bore just a hint of casual makeup. She was also dressed in black with gold accents and her family crest. Her dress, however, was much fancier than what the rest were wearing. The sleeves were puffy, trailing behind her as she walked, and the top of the dress had a luxurious amount of material. But as the dress came to her hips, it began to slim and accentuate her body before billowing out past her legs.

The dress was horribly impractical, and Rowan was complete certain there was no way Olivia could manage to fight in it, even if her only job was chucking potions. It also made her look ethereal and beyond beautiful, which was extremely distracting when she was attached to his arm, hugging it gently to her side.

Maybe this world isn't so bad after all.

"Easy for you to say. You actually look like you belong at one of these functions," Milena said, her tail curling around her waist like she was trying to give herself a hug. Marcus was hiding his anxiety much better, but it was obvious that he, too, didn't think he belonged there.

"It's not like we're going to be meeting nobles," Olivia sighed, looking the two over again. "They're just mercenaries and famous adventurers."

"Exactly. That's worse than nobility," Milena quipped, eyes narrowed.

"How does that make sense? Nobles are by far the more touchy, intimidating sort. No offense, Olivia," Rowan asked.

"Well, you see, we actually care about what these people think about us, unlike with nobles." Marcus jumped in. "They've all *earned* their power. They're respected because of who they are. What if they don't like us? What if they don't think we can make it in the profession? Especially the Mercenary King. If he doesn't like us . . ."

Just like that, Rowan felt a gulf open between him and the twins. Like them, he had been thinking about life after being a hero. The twins were probably going back to living as mercenaries and this was their chance to impress the celebrities of their profession. But Rowan, for the first time, wondered if his choice of going back to Earth was the right one. Could he really just forget everything that happened here and live a normal life again?

"If it helps, I think that once they get to know you, they'll be impressed," Rowan said before his mind could fully process all the words coming out of his mouth. "I mean, I bet that not a lot of them ever stood up to an Epic-ranked demon before. And even if they did, they kind of lost, considering *this* is where the demon army broke through."

That was a sobering thought and the group fell silent, staying that way until a side door opened, admitting Lady Sutton into the room.

While Rowan and the twins were obviously nervous and looked a little awkward in their clothing, Camilla's flowing silver dress accentuated her beauty and gave a certain air of nobility to her bearing.

Instantly, he felt more than a little unprepared.

"They might have lost," Camilla said as swept past them and positioned herself in front of the door like she was planning to protect them from what was beyond it. "But they have the men we need if you want to be the true leader of this town. Or to keep you safe when we venture into the demonic wastes. They're important. Of them, the Mercenary King is the most important. He's an Epic, the only one in this town that isn't on our side. We get him on our side and half the battle is won."

Rowan nodded seriously. "Sorry, I meant it as a way to cheer us up."

"But it's a good thought to have." Camilla's tone inflected upward. "These are the men who lost against the demons. They deserve your time because of their resources, but they don't deserve your respect yet."

"Got it."

"Good. It's time," Camilla announced, fingering a dagger and tucking it into her dress. "Prepare yourselves."

Rowan's hand twitched for his spear. Without it, the world felt a little more threatening, like it was closing in on him. Even his thoughts felt slower and more fragile. He settled for the next best thing and threaded his arm through Olivia's and relaxed when she patted his hand.

The door was pushed open, and the sounds of chatter and arguing intensified.

He took a deep breath and glanced at Olivia. With her there, he would make it through the gathering. Camilla stepped forward and pushed open the door.

"I present to you Lord Rowan Clairfont, his party, and Lady Camilla Sutton, their adviser and guardian," one of the servants announced.

The room they entered was large and well lit. Tables edged the walls, covered in food and drink Rowan thought looked expensive. The men and women, too, were dressed in quality clothes.

Still, he couldn't help but feel that the entire thing looked at least a little off. It *reminded* him of the reception he'd attended at the palace in form, but there was something missing from the spirit of the gathering.

When Rowan took a closer look at the attendees, the difference hit him.

All these men and women looked awkward in their clothing and finery. They held themselves stiffly or moved like warriors rather than the nobility Rowan had seen before. There was a certain aura nobles had that these people lacked.

And that difference was made plain when one of the attendants spoke up. "Well, well, well, we finally get to meet our new mayor. Shame what happened to the last one, of course, but I'm sure you'll do *much* better."

Rowan scanned the crowd and found the voice's owner, a mercenary surrounded by a cadre of other men. The mercenary wore a blade at his hip. The presence of weapons carried so openly threw Rowan off balance for a moment and he glanced at the baroness.

"Florin Zest. A pleasure to meet you," Camilla said with an inflection in her voice that made it obvious she didn't care much for the man. "I see that you're armed to the teeth."

"Oh, this?" Florin pointed at his blade. "It's nothing. Just a toothpick."

"Still a toothpick that you shouldn't have brought." Camilla looked the man straight in his eye. "Do you see me or the hero carrying weapons? If we had known this was supposed to be a show of force, we'd have brought in the army."

Florin's eyes flicked up and down. When he didn't see a weapon on the baroness, he relaxed slightly. "Apologies, Lady Sutton. But you know me—[Blood Reaver] isn't a class that deals in finesse."

Even though Rowan had personally seen Camilla playing with a dagger just moments before she entered the room, he didn't bother to speak up.

"We all have our flaws. I see you have your guild with you today. Your men have been causing trouble in the town. The townsfolk have been complaining," Camilla stated.

"They'd be harping about chickens not laying eggs if they could." Florin dismissed the concern. "We're right at the edge of the demonic wastes. Things happen."

"You should know that these days, a Rare class doesn't count for much," Camilla said flatly. "We live in tumultuous times."

Florin flushed red and gritted his teeth. Camilla smiled and turned away.

But before Rowan could celebrate the baroness's minor victory, a buttery-smooth voice greeted them.

"It's been a while since I've last seen you, Camilla. It's good to know you are still so very . . . pleasant."

Camilla paused, took a deep breath, and turned toward a woman in a wine-red dress who was trailed by two cloaked figures. "Tamara. It has been too long."

The other woman tittered, her black eyes sparkling with amusement as she swirled a goblet of some kind of drink. Rowan noted that, out of the entire gathering, she was the one who looked most at ease in the setting.

"My gods, I haven't seen you since I was last at the Mage Tower," Tamara purred. "It's a shame, really. The kingdom could really use my magic, especially for how destructive it can be. There's beauty in strength."

"I don't speak for the king or the kingdom," Camilla warned. "But I imagine that if you could control your class better, they might look favorably at your situation. Instead, you've been here, taking on apprentices."

"And deny the world my [Mage] class variant? Never," Tamara said in mock shock. "I must say, I'm surprised to see your family has managed to snag a hero. I thought that was reserved for *truly* powerful families."

"Well, I'm not surprised you're not well informed, considering the fact that the Mage Tower sent out a notice with the consequences if you or your apprentices so much as dared to step foot in the kingdom," Camilla retorted. "Say what you want, Tamara. I am a Sutton."

Rowan noticed how the baroness hadn't included mention of the woman's surname.

Seems like the mages weren't the only ones to disown her.

Now that she had vanquished the early troublemakers of the gathering, Camilla took a deep breath and turned toward the real power in the room. Situated near one of the tables and feasting at his leisure from a plate piled high with food was a man who looked like a miniature mountain. The man picked up a slice of meat from his plate and gingerly took a bite. It almost seemed like he was there to eat free food.

But Rowan's enhanced perception could see beyond the surface. For starters, a whole group of men and women stood just a few paces away in a vaguely circular formation. Second, the man was perfectly comfortable with his size. His formal dress shirt had a couple buttons unbuttoned, revealing a stretch of well-toned muscles. Rowan got the feeling that the extra weight wasn't a hindrance but rather part of the man's strength.

When Camilla and the hero party drew closer, he paused midbite and smiled. Instead of greeting or disparaging them, he nodded at the food along the edges of the room.

That seemed to do the trick of stopping the baroness in her tracks.

"Mercenary King," Camilla said coolly.

"Camilla, could I get a moment with the hero?" the man asked. "The roast here is absolutely delightful. We can talk after you eat. I'll be here."

Camilla stood still, taking measure of the man before her. The pressure built with every passing moment before her gaze swung to the food and she decided that the confrontation could wait. She glanced at Rowan and gave the slightest nod.

Marcus was the first to split, guiding his sister over to the food table and shooting the man a grin as he started to pile food onto a plate. Soon enough, his plate was almost as full. The living mountain laughed and nodded approvingly. Finally, both Camilla and Olivia stepped away, leaving just Rowan behind.

"So, you're our new mayor?" the Mercenary King asked.

Rowan didn't hear any hostility in the voice and took that as a good sign.

"Unfortunately." Rowan decided to go for honesty, even if he could feel the baroness's eyes digging into his back. "I'm here a bit ahead of schedule and the circumstances aren't the best, as you'll probably agree."

The man laughed, nodding along. "True. The old mayor . . . well, it's a shame what happened. I hear you're not even at Rare yet. Is that right?"

Rowan hid a wince. "Just a couple levels off. Turns out, beating two Rare-tier demons and surviving an Epic doesn't guarantee you'll earn all that much experience."

"Heh, don't I know it." The mercenary paused to shovel some more food into his mouth, looking Rowan over like he was searching for something. "At least you seem like a fighter. Got the physical build. Or the start of one."

"Start of one?" The comment threw Rowan for a loop. Frankly, he was in the best shape of his life. The stats and exercise had worked miracles, giving him a toned, well-muscled body that managed to look balanced and natural in spite of his bulky stature.

"Aye, start of one. You'll still need to exercise and work for it to get into the best condition, lad. Stats and fighting can do much, but they're not a replacement for hard work. You should always keep in mind that stats enhance what you have," the mercenary said.

Rowan could recall the baron giving him similar advice a long time ago. He hadn't thought much of it at the time, given how fond the man was of grueling training. But it did make sense.

"What would you recommend, then? What should I do to train?" Rowan asked.

"First, figure out what sort of workout is best for you. What are you trying to build yourself up for? Speed? Endurance? Strength? Once you know that, you can introduce the right routine into your day. I'd advise you to stick to it, lad, no matter what else is happening. You'll be able to push much harder than most with your stats and level. Especially when you hit Rare."

Rowan nodded, giving the man's muscles another look. He supposed the mercenary would know what he was talking about. "That does make sense."

"Might just save your life one day," the mercenary said. "Even being able to fight for a couple minutes longer can be the difference between life and death."

Camilla walked up to the two of them with Olivia in tow. "As much as I hate to interrupt, we do need to talk about other matters, Lucius."

"I suppose we do, Camilla. It's been a while since I've seen you, or Kayden."

Behind Camilla, Olivia stiffened slightly. No one had said anything about the Mercenary King knowing her parents. Though with how Camilla knew Tamara the uncontrollable mage, Rowan supposed that the baron's family was a bit more well connected than they let on.

"Yes, it has. I ate the food and waited while you had your conversation with Hero Rowan. Let's talk business." Camilla walked up next to Rowan. "You know why we're all stuck here, Lucius. We're going to need your help. I'm asking for your help."

The mercenary put down his massive plate of food to properly face the baroness. "You know I can't promise you that, Camilla. My oaths and my responsibilities lie with my men, first and foremost."

"Yes, and those men were, as I recall, hired on to bolster the defenses of the kingdom against the coming wave of demons."

"And that's exactly what we're doing. Why do you think the town didn't fall? We were hired to defend it, and so we did. The buildings on the outskirts might be a little damaged, but all the civilians were safe and the wave was diverted."

"It was diverted into my family's lands!" Camilla hissed, struggling not to let her voice rise even more, even though everyone in the room had been sneaking glances their way for a while. "They nearly broke through. Two villages. Gone. All lives lost. It would have been worse if it weren't for these children and the assistance of another hero."

"I'm sorry for that. I really am. But what was I supposed to do? Chase after the demons? Order my men to their deaths? We're only being paid to defend this town, Camilla. Not to venture deeper into the wasteland, not to guard the borders. Just the town," the mercenary said. His voice was soft but also determined.

For a few moments, Camilla stared at the man's face, her green eyes meeting his pale-gray ones. Even from the side, Rowan knew that the mercenary wasn't going to offer his men to help the expeditions.

"What about a job, then?" Camilla said, calming down slightly. "I'll hire your men. Or even you personally."

"We're already on a job. You know what that means. Until our pay dries up or we're dismissed, we will stay our course." The mercenary paused and glanced at Rowan. "If you want me to train them a little, I can do that. But that's the most I can offer. I'm sorry if it's not what you wanted to hear."

"Fine, Lucius." The baroness closed her eyes for a few quiet moments. She gestured at Rowan and the rest of the hero party. "We'll find someone else."

When they were far enough away, Marcus walked closer to Rowan. "So that was the Mercenary King. Scary."

"He seemed nice enough, even if he wouldn't help us," Rowan said. "By the way, why is he called the Mercenary King?"

Marcus almost tripped midwalk. "You haven't heard of . . . Oh, right, you're not from here. He's the most famous mercenary alive. When he was young, he was known as a madman who only took the most dangerous jobs on the frontier. He was a legend even back then. When he reached the Rare tier, he decided to form a company."

"The men around him?" Rowan asked as he shot the mercenaries a glance.

"Yeah. The Mercenary King isn't just a title. It's the name of his class. He single-handedly improved the status of mercenaries in the kingdom of Rhys," Marcus said. "Even his company takes after him. They do the most dangerous jobs."

"He's just a man," Olivia said from the side. "Mom? What are we going to do now?"

"The Mercenary King isn't the only one here," Camilla said. "Florin and Tamara are the second- and third-largest independent powers. But there are more mercenaries here than just them."

Over the next few minutes, Camilla must have realized that she had overplayed her hand. The smaller factions were more than willing to talk. They had nothing but praise and good words for their new mayor. But when the topic shifted to the expedition into demonic lands, the mercenaries immediately excused themselves.

After the fourth rejection, Rowan found Camilla staring at the far wall. There, both Florin and Tamara were lounging against the table and looking back with smirks. The man said something out of the side of his mouth that sent the mage into titters of laughter.

Camilla tried one more time. Even with her target pale-faced and stuttering, she couldn't get them to say yes to adventuring outside the town. The baroness let out a long breath.

"Should we leave?" Rowan whispered to her.

"This was put together in your honor," Camilla said wearily. Her eyes were duller than before.

"And I don't care. If we're not getting anywhere, I'd rather leave," Rowan said.

She turned for the door. None of them said a word until they were back in their temporary home.

"We need more men," Camilla said as she looked at the remaining town's troops. "A lot more men. A frontier town has a garrison of at least a thousand."

There were not a thousand men in front of them. Barely two hundred souls remained of the town's army. And each and every one of them suffered some kind of injury. Rowan could see several slings, too many bandages to count, and even a couple of people struggling to stand on crutches.

The only silver lining was that the town's training ground was remarkably undamaged. Racks of weapons stood arrayed on one side of the large courtyard, and dummies and all kinds of obstacles were clustered on the other. There was even a running track that stretched around the perimeter.

The stellar training ground was almost ironic compared to the men who now stood on it.

"Look on my Works, ye Mighty, and despair," Rowan mumbled. The quote seemed fitting. Not even Olivia bothered to ask him what that was supposed to mean. But as he looked over the ranks, he found a strange strength in the men in front of him. These were people who had been battered by demons and monsters. Yet they had chosen to stay, to fight again when they could have deserted or left the frontier.

Rowan cleared his throat and stepped forward. He could still hear Bron's voice in his head. *The mark of a good leader is someone who can inspire, and to inspire requires an inner courage to face the difficulties head-on.*

"Men. My name is Rowan Clairfont. You may know me as a hero blessed by Aristaeus, the god of soldiers. And that word, *soldier*, is exactly how I would describe you. I know you as the soldiers of Rest's Remorse. As the soldiers who didn't run when a group of demons and monsters were charging at you. As the soldiers who stood their ground and fought when things were at their darkest. As the soldiers who still continue to fight even when no one would blame you for retreating for rest.

"Our path ahead is not easy. I'm not going to stand here and down-play things. Until we slay the demon king, there will be hard fighting. I will be there with you every step of the way. We will bleed. We will sacrifice. But we will triumph. A long time ago, I was told that the measure of a person isn't what he does when things are easy but rather what he does when times are hard. Seeing you all here when the future is dim, I can say for certain that you all are heroes."

For a few seconds after Rowan's speech, there was just silence. A small bead of sweat began to form on the back of his neck.

Did I say the wrong thing? Did I just screw everything up?

A cheer rose from the front row. It was small but infectious. The other ranks began to add their voices to the cheer until the whole army was hollering for Rowan.

Nope. I said the right thing.

Rowan waved at his men and the cheering intensified. He felt a weight leave his shoulders even as a new one took its place. They weren't alone in the town anymore, but he now needed to figure out how to get the men back into fighting shape.

"Any chance you'll be able to heal them up?" Rowan asked Olivia quietly. "I know it's a lot of men, but every bit helps."

"Probably. Just not with the ingredients I have on me, though. We'll need to head out into the town and look for some, or maybe ask your chamberlain to order the ingredients."

"Sounds like a date," Rowan murmured before he remembered who was with him.

"A date, is it?" Camilla asked. "This is all you have left in terms of troops, and you're still angling to seduce my daughter?"

"No, it's—"

"No matter. After that speech, you get a pass. Your plan does have some merit." Some light had sneaked back into Camilla's eyes as she looked at the remaining army of Rest's Remorse. "Go on. Plan your outing with my daughter and make sure to procure enough materials for those potions. I'll need them and more."

Rowan shuddered. Something about Camilla's words reminded him of Kayden and the brutal training he had put Rowan through. The men weren't going to have a fun time under the baroness's care. The only question now was if that was going to be his fate, too.

CHAPTER SIX

A Simple Outing

As it turned out, organizing a day out on the town with a baron's daughter wasn't the simplest thing in the world. There was planning out which parts of town to visit, learning the town's power dynamics, and, more importantly, figuring out which outfit to wear.

"I can't believe the way this makes me look. I don't look *that* fat in it, right, Rowan?" Olivia grumbled, glaring down at her simplistic dress like it was at fault.

"Of course not." Rowan's answer was immediate and determined. He didn't know a whole lot about relationships, but he definitely knew the right response to a question like that. "You look great, no matter what you wear."

"That sure sounded sincere," Olivia laughed.

"Well, I did mean it," Rowan said calmly as he squeezed her hand, and, for the first time, it was Olivia who blushed first.

"Hero Rowan, Miss Sutton." The chamberlain's voice sounded from outside the carriage. "We're here."

Rowan opened the door and let Olivia out first. Although he had been joking, this was as close to a date as they'd ever had. It was just going to be the two of them. The chamberlain was just there to escort them to the right place.

"Thanks," Rowan said, ducking out of the carriage. "So, this is it?"

"It is. We're in the outer parts of the town," the chamberlain said. "Rest's Remorse isn't a big town but still large enough. I would imagine that the combination of you and Miss Sutton should be enough to handle any trouble that comes your way."

That was true. Rowan still had trouble remembering that he was only a few levels away from Rare while Olivia was already there. And having a Rare class wasn't something that happened to everyone. The other Rare-tier people in the city all had their own mercenary groups or companies.

"And this dress is absolutely necessary?" Olivia asked. "Not even the poorest commoners dress this badly in the barony."

The chamberlain had a sad little smile as he climbed back onto the carriage. "Rest's Remorse is on the frontier. Survival is a struggle here. When the two of you are ready, just walk up to any guard and let them know to admit you."

"This doesn't make any sense," Rowan said after just ten minutes of walking around.

There were two types of people in Rest's Remorse and zero middle ground. The first were mercenaries, fighters, and crafters. They looked well-fed, happy, and overall confident in their lot in life. They strode down streets with a sense of purpose and destination. The second, and far more numerous, were the downtrodden, people who looked so poor, weak, and starved that it turned Rowan's stomach to even catch a glimpse of them.

"It doesn't. Even a monster wave couldn't have done this." Olivia gripped Rowan's hand tighter. "This town isn't that poor."

Rowan realized that Rest's Remorse, at least on paper, was his. It was his responsibility to do something about the crippling poverty he saw.

"Let's keep walking. I want to see more of the town," Rowan said. He had to first figure out if this was an isolated instance of poverty, whether they were on the wrong side of town or if there was a wealth gap like this everywhere.

The two of them gradually made their way from the outskirts of the town to the center. While Rest's Remorse was not the most beautiful town Rowan had ever seen, the houses were still built in neat little rows. Every building built out of stone that was weathering the conditions of the frontier without any issue. Almost every home *looked* fresh and perfectly fit for habitation. But no matter where they went, they saw gaunt, haunted-looking people.

"Where are the children and the elderly?" Rowan asked. After a couple more minutes of wandering the streets, he'd noticed quite a few things different about Rest's Remorse. The most striking of which was the fact that most of the starving figures looked to be around his and Olivia's age, or slightly older at best.

"Hmm? Could you repeat that?"

"Children and elderly. I haven't seen many of either. I've seen maybe two kids the entire time. And the only older person I saw was that one man at the general store we passed."

"Frontier towns aren't exactly geared toward families or the elderly," Olivia admitted as her teeth worried her lower lip. "The people who come here are those looking to prove themselves."

"So, all these people . . ." Rowan trailed off, daring a glance at an alley where a man just a few years older than him sat, looking blankly at the wall across from him.

"Most likely combat-class commoners. A lot of people aren't happy taking up a crafting or lifestyle class. Even if they have a bad Heart Card for it, they still try to become fighters," Olivia said.

"Isn't that how mercenary bands grow?" Rowan asked. Rest's Remorse seemed to be half populated by mercenaries.

"Yeah. Still, they can't take everyone. It's not easy to take someone with a Common Heart Card to the Uncommon tier. Getting them trained enough to kill a higher-tier monster takes time and resources. Besides, if they don't have a good Heart Card, it's unlikely they'll have good cards in general."

"Why don't they leave, then?"

Olivia turned to Rowan. "Travel is expensive. The three-week carriage ride we took? That cost enough to feed an entire family for a year."

"So, the people, they travel all the way to the frontier, use up their savings if they had any, and end up like this?" Rowan asked, taking in the town with a whole new perspective. The shiny buildings and well-paved roads looked like death traps.

"It wasn't this bad in the frontier town my family ran," Olivia said. "Or most other frontier towns. There are usually safeguards in place. Work for those who failed or at least an opportunity to earn their way back to their families. What's happening here . . . I don't know."

"So, the best and the most promising get recruited into the established companies. And everyone else just slowly withers away?" Rowan asked.

"No." Olivia paused in her step as understanding dawned on her face.

"What is it?"

"Normally, people in a frontier town go out and hunt demons. They kill a few corrupted beasts and slowly build their strength that way. But that doesn't work anymore. No, it wouldn't. Not with an impending demon invasion. It'll be easy to find Uncommon-tier monsters, and a group can even find Rare-tier demons with a bit of effort. But Common-tier creatures? Those are scarce now."

That made a certain amount of sense. In essence, Rowan realized, without a group, strong cards, or a ton of training, an average commoner with a beginner fighting class was completely stuck. They couldn't leave unless they had money, and they couldn't make money unless they were willing to risk their lives finding the occasional Common-tier creature.

"Wait." Rowan picked up on something he had vaguely heard but ignored at the time. "You said that for them to get an Uncommon class, they had to kill a higher-tier monster. Why is that?"

"Because they have Common-tier Heart Cards," Olivia explained. "Advancing your class beyond your Heart Card's tier requires a catalyst. In this case, a Common class slaying an Uncommon-tier beast would be enough. That's why the [Blood Reaver] is still at Rare. He hasn't found an Epic-tier demon that he can defeat yet."

Rowan nodded along as dots began connecting in his head. "One more thing. When we left, Kayden told us to be careful of the monsters on the frontier. That they had different cards. Why did he say that?"

Olivia glanced around them to make sure no one was listening in. "Because some monsters on the frontier have killed not just their own, but people. We don't know if everything in the world has a system, but if a monster kills a person with a card they could use, it's added to their deck."

Rowan realized what Olivia was saying: The Common-tier combatants trying to forge their own path were literally feeding themselves and their cards to the monsters in the town's vicinity.

"We should get what we need and go back," Rowan said, feeling incredibly tired all of a sudden.

The idea of a date was gone from his mind, and the parts of town he'd been looking forward to exploring simply filled him with a quiet dread now. For her part, Olivia nodded, too, just as eager to put all the unpleasantness behind her.

That, unfortunately, did not work out.

"What do you mean, the apothecary is gone?" Olivia asked. There was a slight edge to her voice as she glared at the man who blocked their way.

"I mean, the old woman packed up and left after the demon invasion," the man drawled, looking far too nonchalant in the face of an angry Olivia. "She sold the store to me, and I don't deal in herbs."

"Then where can I find some? You can't tell me there was only one single apothecary in this entire town."

The man stared at Olivia blankly, shrugged his shoulders, and then closed the shop's door in her face. The Closed sign stared back at her as she fumed, and Rowan thought for a moment that she was about to bust down the door and drag the brand-new shopkeeper out into the street by his beard.

"Come on, he's not worth it," Rowan said, tugging on her hand.

"I can't believe this. Is there anything in this town that's the way it should be? Mercenaries don't care about hunting monsters, shopkeepers are leaving, and the standard of living here is little better than a slum," Olivia complained.

Rowan was coming to understand more and more that Rest's Remorse was nothing but trouble. The standing army was all but destroyed, the town filled with factions in a naked power grab, and no one seemed interested in actually improving things.

He dipped his head down and started walking back.

A man, or boy, really, stepped out of one of the many alleys, setting himself in Rowan's and Olivia's way. "Hey. I saw you were looking for the old apothecary, right?"

Olivia said nothing, simply eyeing the boy. Rowan didn't have the same tact. "Correct. We need some potion ingredients. You wouldn't happen to know where we could find some of those, would you?"

"I might," the boy scoffed, crossing his arms in front of his scrawny chest. "What's in it for me?"

"Let's skip the tough act," Olivia said, not thinking much of the boy's bravado. "Five gold and you take us there. I'm feeling generous and don't want to waste my time."

"Twenty," the boy snapped back, his eyes dipping to the coin purse hanging off Olivia's hip.

She snorted. "It's four now. Even here, that'll get you a solid couple of days' worth of food. Don't push it. We don't need to ask *you* for directions."

The boy began to protest, trying to make himself look bigger, but some of his self-preservation instincts must have twigged because he quieted down quickly.

"Fine, four." The boy didn't look pleased, but he did turn around and start striding down the street. "Follow me."

The two did, though they left a healthy enough distance between them and the stranger.

"You don't think he's leading us straight into an ambush, do you?" Rowan muttered, keeping his eyes fixed firmly on the figure in front of them. The boy navigated through the town like he owned it, taking them through side paths and slanted alleys. It didn't escape Rowan's notice that they were heading closer and closer to the town's wall.

"I don't think so. And even if he is, I wouldn't worry about it. He's what, fourteen? Look at him—whatever ambush team he can put together won't be able to do a thing to us," Olivia whispered before raising her voice. "I'm Rare tier, and you're almost there yourself."

Rowan was tempted to point out that he was without his spear, but Olivia's lack of concern did make sense. Doubly so since he knew she'd made sure to pack a few nasty potions when leaving the manor.

At the time, he had wondered if they were meant for him if the date went the wrong way. Now? He was glad she had done so.

"Fine, fine. We do need those ingredients. You really think a shop this far out made it through unscathed when it was this close to the wall?"

"Guess we'll find out."

Their guide didn't continue walking for much longer, slowing a little as he entered one of the last few streets that separated them from the wall.

Here, the destruction was even more pronounced.

The streets were in disrepair. The paving stones were cracked or missing entirely, and there were even a few deep furrows in the ground where combat had happened. Likely the handiwork of some massive beast.

The houses, too, were almost entirely ruined. A couple were gone entirely, with only the foundations there to prove that they once existed. Surprisingly, though, there were also some houses in okay condition. Rowan thought he saw faces peeking out of empty window slots, but when he took a second look, there was nothing. Then, he saw their destination.

Ophis Apothecary had definitely seen better days. The board with its name on it barely hung onto the building's façade, and one of the glass windows was cracked.

The boy shot them a glance and knocked on the door. The house exploded in noise. There was a clatter and cursing echoed out.

"Clarke? Is something wrong? Did someone else catch a fever?" A bedraggled-looking man rapid-fired his questions as soon as he saw who stood in front of his shop, his eyes searching the boy for injuries. When he didn't find any, he smiled in relief.

"No, Mr. Ophis, I just have some customers for you." The boy tried to put on a gruff front, but when he looked back at the duo that had followed them, he didn't look nearly as self-assured.

Olivia stepped forward, nodding at the man in greeting. "We went to Tasha's Cauldron, but the store's closed. She sold it and moved out of the town, and the new owner isn't open yet, or in the same business."

The man clearly hadn't expected her to be so up front with him, but he recovered quickly enough. "Ah, well, can't say I've got as good a stock as Tasha. Still, I should be able to help. Please, come inside."

Olivia paused long enough to hand off five gold coins to the boy who'd led them there. Rowan smiled when he noticed that her heart had softened after the tough negotiating tactics earlier. Surprisingly enough, the boy joined them inside the apothecary.

Rowan entered the shop last, taking time to examine their surroundings while Olivia chatted with the shopkeeper. The very first thing he noted was that it definitely didn't look like any store he was familiar with. Even the glimpse he caught of Tasha's Cauldron's interior was far more in line with what he expected. There'd been shelves and drawers that contained all kinds of merchandise.

Here, the front room was furnished with cots and sickbeds, some more comfortable-looking than others. The entire collection had definitely not been purchased at once, with different styles, colors, and even sizes.

More alarmingly, two of the beds were occupied, by a boy and a girl around their guide's age. Rowan shuffled closer to them and checked to make sure that they were still breathing. They were. Both were pasty, drenched in sweat, and shivering. But they were in a deep sleep, not even stirring from the commotion in the room.

Rowan refocused on the conversation between Olivia and the shopkeeper, Ophis, just in time to get an explanation for what he was seeing. "I'm not a trained doctor or anything, no. Don't have a class for it, either. Still, I am an apothecary, so I can at least provide treatment."

"I suppose this is because of the recent demon attack?" Olivia asked, eyeing the trio of teenagers. She likely wouldn't admit it, but Rowan suspected she regretted being so harsh with Clarke before.

"Oh, no. I've been doing this sort of thing for ages. Lots of young folk come through without enough money for proper treatment. As I said, I try, but I can't always help them all. Things have been worse since the attack, but they've always been bad," Ophis said. He didn't shy away from those facts, but his eyes did flit over to check on his patients.

"So, you make potions?" Olivia asked as she went to the far side of the room where it looked more like a typical shop. There were hundreds of small drawers that covered the space from the floor to ceiling. She looked back at the shopkeeper, who gestured that she was free to explore. Olivia opened one of the drawers and made a small sound of approval.

"Potions? I can't make those. Don't have the training or the recipes. Besides, my class lends itself more to salves and tonics. No instant effects for me, just slow recovery and boosting the body's natural processes," Ophis replied.

"Really? You can't make any potions, yet you've managed to keep a small clinic running?"

"Potions are nice, but you don't necessarily *need* them." When Ophis saw Olivia's affronted look, he seemed to realize who he was talking to. "Oh, it's much better to have them, of course! I'm just saying I'm doing my best regardless."

"Hmm," Olivia hummed. "You know, if you're willing to offer me a discount, or if we can come to some sort of an exchange deal, I'd be willing to brew some potions for you."

The man blinked, clearly not expecting the offer. "How good are you at potion crafting, young lady? That's not exactly a profession that's easy or cheap to get into."

Rowan let out a laugh, drawing attention to himself for the first time. When he realized everyone was looking at him, he launched into a quick explanation. "It's nothing. She's just a Rare-ranked alchemist."

Ophis said nothing. He glanced at Olivia's clothing.

"Ugh, these stupid clothes," Olivia grumbled. She dipped her hand into one of the small pouches she carried, bringing out a potion. "Here, you can try this out on one of them." She motioned at the two sleeping teens.

Ophis accepted the potion cautiously, and even uncorked it to sniff. "Excuse me for just a moment."

He went deeper into the shop, past all the drawers and into a different room, before coming back with two small beakers. Rowan noted that instead of following Olivia's suggestion, he chose to split the potion into two servings.

"The potion won't be as effective if you do that," Olivia said with a slight hint of disapproval.

"They've already taken several tonics. This will do nicely to give them an extra kick and will even boost their healing beyond their current injuries. It will work," Ophis replied.

Olivia shrugged in return, letting him work. Clarke, however, looked like he was about to try and stop the shopkeeper before the two exchanged glances and the boy reluctantly backed down.

The potion spoke for itself. After the liquid was painstakingly fed to the two slumbering teens, their cheeks grew rosy and their expression relaxed.

"Well, I have to say, you definitely weren't lying." Ophis sighed in relief, even as he stood to offer Olivia a bow with an apologetic smile. "I meant no offense, but too many people try to come in here making similar claims."

"They do? And what happens? What does your potioneering guild do?" Olivia looked genuinely taken aback.

Ophis laughed. "We don't even have a branch of the potioneering guild here. You'll find all kinds of false potions being sold here. Out here, laws are far more . . . lenient. And the consequences of a bad potion resolve themselves."

Rowan shuddered as he realized what Ophis meant. "What do people use for healing?"

"Still potions. Just that they're a scarce resource on the frontier. All the mercenary companies, not to mention the mayor's men, have a stranglehold on potions." For the first time, Ophis's words turned bitter. "It's almost impossible to get your hands on a potion without a connection to one of the factions that have taken root in Rest's Remorse. And they don't care about our lives."

Olivia frowned. She was about to say something when Rowan stepped forward and grabbed her hand. "You wanted to buy potion ingredients, right?" he asked.

"I . . . yeah," Olivia said as she turned to picking out the potion ingredients with Ophis looking on.

Rowan stepped back to the edge of the room and let his mind wander.

On paper, the system was designed in a way where anyone could advance. As long as a person put enough effort in, they could improve and better their station.

But the Heart Cards complicated that. Where some people would hit their limits early with a Common Heart Card, people like Rowan could rise all the way up to Epic unhindered. And the nobles exploited that complication, adding more and more layers until the promise of the system was a distant fantasy.

A commoner had to travel to the frontier to get a normal chance at fighting an Uncommon monster. But once there, they had to risk their lives without any potions or fallback options. It was either life or death.

Rowan remembered his own beginnings, when he'd struggled to even pierce the hide of a corrupted boar. Unlike most people, he'd had an Epic-tier baron teaching him how to fight. What did the commoners have?

As Rowan looked over the two patients still in their slumber, a question started to rise in his heart. What could be done about this? More to the point, what could *he* do about this?

CHAPTER SEVEN

A Much-Needed Upgrade

Over the next two days, as Olivia holed up in her new makeshift laboratory, Rowan had plenty of time to think about what he could do for the town. He didn't have any money, and a quick trip to the chamberlain confirmed that the town's finances were more or less in shambles.

But the chance to earn came when Olivia exceeded everyone's expectations by putting the army back on their feet in two days and Camilla sent the whole group out on a hunting expedition.

Out in the wild, any apprehension that Rowan had had about the demons quickly disappeared. After the wave, the monsters left behind were mostly the runts. Perfect for an army looking to rebuild its confidence and for a hero who needed some real combat for his new deck.

"Hold the line!" Rowan roared. He sprinted forward against the wave of monsters charging at them. Lightning swirled around Rowan's spear as he thrust forward recklessly, trusting in Marcus's aura protection. That trust was rewarded when the monster's counterattack slammed into Rowan's stomach and failed to pierce through either skin or armor.

That didn't mean the strike did nothing. Rowan's stomach ached and his lungs fought for breath. But that was nothing compared to what the monster experienced. The spear buried itself in the monster's flank and a discharge of electricity locked its muscles in place. As

Rowan poured more mana into the attack, the lightning began to wreak havoc on the monster from the inside.

Rowan got the experience alert a few moments later and ripped his spear out of the carcass with perhaps a little too much force, almost flinging blackened monster pieces into one of his soldiers.

The man was thankfully too busy to notice, contending with his own nightmare monster. The army was facing a very specific type of monster, one that had writhing limbs resembling human hands and a stubby torso lined with maws. Luckily, appearances weren't everything. The soldiers were holding the line.

"Push!" Rowan yelled, but only some of them stepped forward for leverage. Even with Camilla's training, the Rest's Remorse soldiers were neither as disciplined nor as skilled as the baron's troops had been. What kept them together was their number as well as the fact that every last one of them was in the Uncommon tier.

"Press the attack!" one of the officers commanded from behind Rowan. His unit moved forward and split the monsters into two groups.

Rowan looked around to find that the rest of his party had joined him. Olivia and Milena were raining explosions and curses down upon the enemy while Marcus led the soldiers' charge. In moments, Rowan was surrounded by soldiers with spears. They worked in concert, waves of strikes impaling and grinding down the monsters.

Thankfully, the creatures weren't endless. After another fifteen minutes of chaos, the last one fell, and heavy gasps for air briefly reigned over the battlefield.

"Everyone, rest up. We'll be moving on in half an hour," Rowan shouted, stalking through the throngs of soldiers and checking on their injuries. Despite the hard fighting, all the soldiers were more or less okay. Reassured that no one needed emergency treatment, Rowan found his way to the officer who had pushed his men earlier. "Thank you."

"Happy to serve under you, Hero Rowan." The officer bowed.

"You're a spear class?" Rowan pointed to the spear in the officer's hand.

"Me and my men all started as [Spearmen]," the officer replied. "All ninety-eight of us."

Rowan remembered Camilla mentioning that the spear division of the army was the largest out of the 212 surviving soldiers. "It was a good formation that you used to break the monsters into two groups. What's your class?"

"[First Spear], Hero Rowan. My class revolves around commanding, leading, and fighting alongside men who have placed their trust in me."

"Rare?"

"Rare," the officer confirmed. Although Rowan's army was far smaller than it should have been, there was the beginning of a core cadre among those still alive. The average soldier was Uncommon, while some of the officers were starting to reach Rare.

"Got it. Keep up the good work and you'll have my trust, too," Rowan joked. "But good job today."

"Thank you."

Rowan patted the officer on the shoulder before stomping his way to his party members and out of earshot of the soldiers.

"We can't keep doing this," Rowan said in lieu of a greeting, collapsing on a massive, gnarled branch of a tree that had been knocked down by Olivia's potions. "If we go deeper into the wasteland, they're all just going to die. Those were monsters that we would have brushed off in Felton's Mill."

"It's not that bad, Rowan," Olivia said. "Every army needs a bit of time to train."

"I get it, I really do," Rowan sighed. "But they're supposed to be professional soldiers. A standing army of a frontier town. I guess I was hoping for . . . something more."

"It's why one of the strongest mercenaries on the continent was put in charge of defending Rest's Remorse. Give the army a bit of time. They're used to steamrolling everything as a thousand-strong force, not fighting individually. They're not like the Sutton guard, trained for group combat from day one."

"'Trained' is putting it lightly," Rowan grumbled. "You give your guard optimized decks. Together, a couple Sutton soldiers could take down an entire platoon of equal rank."

"And you can build the Rest's Remorse army to the same quality," Olivia countered. "It won't be easy, but it wasn't easy for Father and Mother, either."

Rowan thought about that. He had no idea what cards his army had, but they weren't very standardized. Almost every soldier fought for themselves or in small groups with people they knew. The only exception was the spear division, but even there, the only common denominator was their weapon.

"That's not the thing really bothering you," Milena said from the side. Rowan met her eyes. "I've never seen you this upset over other people before. Not even the villagers back at Felton's Mill."

Rowan froze and deflated. "You're right. I'm being unfair and unreasonable."

"We're here to help." Surprisingly, Marcus beat Olivia in making the offer.

"Thanks, but it's not something that can be helped. It's my card. **Ravaging Lightning Lance** is strong. It's one of the best cards I have. And yet . . ."

"You don't like it?"

The frank question from Marcus made Rowan realize what he had been trying to avoid. "Maybe, yeah. When I use it on my spear, it's almost like it's forcing me to charge. Like I have to be in motion for it to work. Does that make sense?"

When neither Marcus nor Milena responded, Olivia took up the conversation. "It's more common than you might think. Starting at the Rare tier, cards aren't exactly just things anymore. They have their own quirks, their . . . personalities. Like a tiny bit of whatever they originated from still lives on."

Rowan shuddered, thinking about some of the urges he sometimes got when he overused his **Lavish Feasting** card. Or the fact that he was still trying to deal with **Keen Spear** in a healthy way.

"It's that, but it's more. The card scorches whatever is unfortunate enough to be in its path." Rowan thought back to the fight, where he had wanted only to poke at the monsters and push them back. Instead, he'd killed one of them in a single blow. "It's a good problem to have, but it forces me to change my entire fighting style. **Blood Siphon** is almost entirely useless when the wound's cauterized thanks to **Ravaging Lightning Lance**."

"That's tough," Olivia commented. "We can try looking for a card to trade for back at the town. You don't have to get every single card on your own. It's fine to get it through a trade, or even as a gift. Like **Inspect**, if you ever bothered to use it."

Rowan grinned. The baron had gifted him **Inspect** to help keep him safe and give him an advantage outside of combat, but Rowan found that it was much easier to rely on Olivia's inspections, especially when his mana pool was so much smaller.

"Yeah, I know." Rowan stood back up. "And guys? Thanks for being here. I was letting my emotions get the better of me. The Rest's Remorse army might not be the best, but I shouldn't have blamed them. They have us and we have them."

While the rest of the hero party encouraged him on with smiles, Rowan went back to rallying his beleaguered troops. As he watched them stumble about and reluctantly rise to their feet, he wished the baroness was with them. She had elected to stay back and organize the financial recovery of the town. That and also keep an eye on the other players around.

If anyone caused trouble because the army was gone, they were in for a painful lesson that Lady Sutton was an army by herself.

Rowan took a few minutes to confer with the officers before deciding to risk things and dive deeper before heading back to town. The spear division officers put it best: An army was like a knife that became sharper with each grind.

On paper, Rowan agreed with those words. But in practice?

"Who came up with the name *demonic wasteland*?" Rowan asked Marcus as they struggled to make progress through the blighted landscape. "I was thinking a plain of barren dirt and enemies that we could see coming from a mile away."

"And instead you got a jungle," Marcus joked. "That's demonic mana for you. It doesn't kill things, just warps them into something unrecognizable."

"'Unrecognizable' is putting it lightly. Those monsters earlier were nightmare fuel. And the mosquitoes before that?" Rowan was referring to the disgusting, puppy-size mosquitoes whose bodies were mostly just wings, a massive, bulging blood sack, and a wickedly sharp proboscis. When poked, they burst into a shower of diseased-looking blood.

"Welcome to the frontier." Marcus shrugged.

Over the next few hours, the army burned down three separate copses of trees. It wasn't because of how the trees looked, though they were withered and gnarly. It was something much worse.

When the trees spotted the army, they began to wail while their roots lashed out like spears. Even their trunks bulged and disgorged waves of short humanoids with bark for skin that attacked with no regard for their own safety.

Rowan was just a hair away from calling it quits and heading home. But the worst monster they had encountered was barely at the start of Rare. It hadn't been fun fighting so far, but they hadn't been in any real danger. And the army was getting stronger with every fight.

It was only several minutes after the last torching when Marcus suddenly froze.

"Wait, do you hear that?" Marcus whispered, his ears twitching and shifting like a wolf's would when trying to catch a sound.

Rowan shook his head, looking around in confusion. Other than the wind rustling through the leaves and the incessant sound of things *slithering* around, there was nothing his ears could pick up. "What is it?"

Marcus frowned, focusing harder, then pointed to the right of where they were headed. "That way. I hear water, and . . . a voice? It's singing, or maybe sobbing? I can't tell and that's creeping me out."

"Do we check it out?" Rowan asked.

"Honestly? No clue. I'll one hundred percent bet you that whatever it is, it's not a person."

"You know what? Let's do the smart thing here."

Rowan waved the girls over and shared the issue with them. Predictably, Olivia rewarded him with praise.

"We can't ignore it," Milena said. "If it's somehow a person, we need to find them. And if it's a monster or a demon, it's probably alone, which means that we get an easy chance to take out future invaders."

"Mother mentioned that there aren't any demons in the area that we can't take on as long as we're careful. She'd know if there was an Epic-tier demon in the area—the last one changed the weather," Olivia added. "Plus, if we go back with the news that we cleared out a demon, that goes a long way in convincing the rest of the town to support you."

Rowan didn't disagree. It was going to be a good deed or a nice chunk of experience. Either way, he had a whole army with him. After communicating his plans with the officers, they set out. This time, the entire hero party was at the front, not least because they were some of the strongest people in the entire army.

Five minutes later, Rowan heard snippets of what Marcus had. Rowan was impressed. The shield bearer had focused stats in vitality and wisdom but somehow still managed to hear the sound earlier than anyone else.

Looks like there are some things that the system doesn't account for. One point in strength does not equal someone else's point in strength.

The sound that floated through the air was the definition of eerie. It was a siren song, carrying feelings of grief and pain, especially when the creature broke its aria in favor of sobs or wails. Now that Rowan had heard it, he couldn't unhear it. The sound crawled into his ears and nestled in his mind.

The only hint of what they would see was the sound of water, and they soon caught sight of a river. The water, like everything else in the demonic wastes, was an unclean thing.

Bobbing along on the river's surface were corpses of fish, globs of some black matter, and unidentifiable splotches of color. The smell alone threatened to make Rowan lose his breakfast, and the twins looked even worse.

The army traced their way along the river and found the singer.

Lounging beside the river, her fishtail languidly bobbing on its surface, was a mermaid straight out of Lovecraft's nightmares.

She had four arms, two of which were bracing her against the ground, but they were thin, anemic, spindly. Her skin was somewhere between pasty gray and purple, with large patches of diseased flesh that looked maggot-infested.

Her face was caught between a rictus of pain and a snarl. Milky-white eyes spun in their sockets. She had hair, after a fashion, but it was missing in patches and it was so filthy and clumped up that it looked more like rags torn into strips.

Oddly enough for what Rowan thought was a freshwater creature, jutting out from her forehead was a lure much like those on an angler-fish, and it glowed softly in the partial darkness of the forest.

Rowan wasn't entirely sure what was the worst part about the creature.

Was it the fact that she was an approximation of a female form, fully bare and looking like she was at least ninety years old? Or was it that every single inch of her flesh writhed like there were things trying to burst out of it?

Either way, Rowan wanted to back away and call the whole thing off.

On the other hand, his troublesome card was, for once, looking promising. This was not a fight he wanted to take his time on and slowly bleed his opponent to death. This was a fight where the quicker he could scorch the mermaid from the world, the better.

With one final deep and nauseating breath to steel himself and a quick few gestures at his companions to prepare, Rowan moved.

Deciding not to spare his mana pool, he pushed nearly everything he had into **Ravaging Lightning Lance**. Four lances formed from pure lightning flashed into existence around him and surged toward the creature alongside his own blazing spear.

The mermaid noticed immediately, yet didn't pause her song. If anything, the appearance of enemies made her voice swell harder, and for just an instant, Rowan felt like he was seeing double. Then Marcus's aura snapped around his body and he was free of whatever effect that was.

The next moment, he was close enough to strike, and the tip of his spear sank into the creature's side with no resistance or attempts to dodge. He knew then that something was wrong, but it was too late to try and abort his assault.

Ironically, it was the arcs of his lightning that saved him when the creature's skin burst where he'd punctured it and disgorged a tide of blackened blood and what looked like demonic maggots on steroids.

The mermaid seemed to carry a whole river inside her as a wave of blood washed over Rowan's legs, carrying the tiny critters along. But the gaping maws of the maggots were too busy spasming from the combined might of five lightning strikes at once.

"Corrupted Naiad Cambion, level thirty-six!" Olivia yelled.

"Get away from it! There's something weird about the water. I'm half out of mana," Marcus yelled as he ran forward a few steps, thought better of it, and stopped.

Rowan was already backpedaling, spewing out curses as he got a good look at the wound he'd dealt and saw that the entirety of the mermaid's body was filled with just black blood and critters.

"Hit it! Hit it with everything you've got!" Rowan shouted at the top of his lungs, even managing to conjure a much smaller lance of lightning and sending it spiraling into the creature.

From there, the fight devolved into chaos. The mermaid staggered and twitched as she fought to get closer to them. Her wriggly passengers began to jump into the river and use that as a way to close the distance against the army. Luckily, Marcus's protective aura prevented any serious damage.

Rowan had no idea what success would look like, and he was eternally thankful that by the time every last one of her spawn was dead, the mermaid also faded to ashes under a particularly strong fire potion from Olivia.

Exchanging a glance with the spear division officer, Rowan marched his army away from the creature and the disgusting stream of water. After fifteen minutes of near-sprint pace and finding a patch of safe ground, he practically collapsed while people did the same all around him.

Olivia snuggled into his side, ignoring the way his pants and the lower half of his chest armor stank of fish and the sea. "Whatever that thing was, I hope we never see anything like her again."

"I solemnly promise that from now on we're going to stay far away from any large bodies of water if we can at all help it," Rowan agreed, hugging her a little closer and feeling immensely better with her warmth so close to him.

"Your card worked out this time, though." Somehow, Marcus could find the positive.

"True." Funnily enough, that still wasn't enough to make Rowan feel better about it. Whether it was his own aversion or some influence from his class, he didn't want to keep using it.

"How close are you to Rare?" Milena asked. "Let's go back when you get there." A single look at the woman told Rowan that she was definitely eager to be done and on her way back to the relative safety of the town already.

He couldn't blame her.

"Level thirty-nine, almost there," Rowan sighed, wishing he could hurry the leveling process along.

The fact that he was the only one lagging behind the rest of them upset him. Everyone else was already Rare, and even some of the officers were a tier higher than him. It was true that he had climbed to near their heights in months when the others had spent years to get to that level. But he still felt behind.

"Just thirty-nine, he says," Marcus teased.

Rowan took the words in stride as he reached for his pack. "Hey, guys. I have a bit of a request. Two things, really. The soldiers deserve some kind of a reward. It doesn't feel right for me to have thousands of card scraps when they're still struggling for cards. And . . ."

"Go on," Olivia said.

"And I want to try and upgrade my original class card again. I have it up to Uncommon now, so it's still worse than the **Ravaging Lightning Lance**."

"You really don't like that card, do you?" Olivia sighed, thumping her forehead against his shoulder. "Even though we worked so hard to get it from that thing's mount?"

"Yeah, sorry, it's just *not* a good fit for me. I might be spoiled, but I just can't make it fit."

"No, it's fine, really. Everyone comes across a card like that eventually, at least according to our mother." Milena's voice grew quiet by the end, but she soldiered on. "You should do it. Both of them, I mean. I'll contribute my scraps as well."

"And mine," Marcus added.

"Of course you can use mine." Olivia smiled.

With the go-ahead, Rowan shrugged off his rugged backpack and carried half the scraps to the officer. He had originally doubted the wisdom of carrying such valuable card scraps earlier when Olivia told him to do so, but it was all coming in very handy.

"For the men," Rowan said as he handed the pile over to the spear division officer. "All of the men. I promise there will be more."

The officer saluted back. With that out of the way, Rowan began rolling for the right cards. It took more than a few tries, but he eventually had a set of nine good candidates to try the fusion with.

Grim Spear × 4

**Imbue your spear with the intent to cause harm, making
your mana take on the properties of a minor curse.
Your foes will be sapped of their strength with
every successful blow you deal.**

Mighty Spear × 2

**The strength of your spear grows overwhelming, crushing
the defense of your enemies at the cost of your mana.**

Greater Mana Infusion × 3

**Infuse your weapon with mana and then
deal a deathly blow.**

In a way, the selection reminded him of the cards he'd chosen when he got **Essential Thrust**, especially the greater version of **Mana Infusion**, which in his head meant his chances of success were better.

With just a moment of hesitation when asked if he wanted to fuse the cards, he hit yes.

The cards floated up and coalesced into a green light, coruscating and wavering for several long seconds. When the light grew unstable and almost broke apart, Rowan's heart leaped into his throat. He was suddenly regretting all his life decisions that had led up to this point.

Thankfully for his sanity, the entire thing froze, surged together, and took on a blue sheen just a moment later.

Finally, a brand-new card was revealed, hovering in the air before dropping down into his hand.

[Class] Reaping Spear (Rare, Active)
This card allows you to alter and channel your mana in
a way that will make your spear an implement of death.
Each of your blows will enfeeble your opponents and
each inflicted wound will linger, filling with death
mana that will make it more difficult to heal.

Rowan's breath left him in a relieved whoosh, and a smile slowly stretched across his lips. He didn't even have the presence of mind to feel embarrassed when he whooped in triumph and snatched Olivia up to spin her around in celebration.

"It worked! It worked, it worked, it worked. And it's absolutely *perfect*."

Rowan was still grinning when he finally put her down, switching out this new card with **Ravaging Lightning Lance** and letting out a breath of relief when he felt it settle into his deck.

It fit there perfectly, like it was always meant to be a part of him. The lightning lance card, meanwhile, had always made him feel like there was a small electric charge buzzing in his chest.

A howl ripped through the air. It was joined by another, and another, until the infernal forest was echoing with howls and the sound of trembling plants.

Rowan sighed, running a hand through his hair in resignation. "Sorry, I shouldn't have been so loud."

"Nah, it's fine." Marcus simply chuckled, hefting his shield again. "Besides, this is going to give you a chance to test out your new card!"

Rowan grinned. "Men of Rest's Remorse. Form up on me!"

* * *

The fight ended just as quickly as it began. The wolflike creatures that erupted out of the forest were strong, but they were no match for an army two hundred strong and newly invigorated by the promise of card loot.

For the first time since the expedition, Rowan could say that he actually enjoyed the fighting. Where the lightning lance had fought him for control and practically jerked his body around to suit its preference, **Reaping Spear** flowed easily and effortlessly.

He could summon the effect with a mere fraction of his mana, as little as a single point, yet it made his spear as sharp as a Legendary blade. Nothing could block his attacks. That wasn't all. Rowan could feel the way his opponent's vitality was sapped away into his spear with every blow he made. He was even vaguely aware of the patches of death mana his strikes left, allowing him to track the movement of every enemy he struck.

The effect was thanks to some combination of his class, his Heart Card, and the new class card. And he was only capable of hanging onto the movement of the mana for up to a minute. In the middle of combat? That was practically an eternity.

As the final foe fell, Rowan felt a chime in his head. He opened the system window immediately.

Class evolution requirements met.
Classes available for selection:
Spearmaster, Dark Spear, Lightning Lancer, Sacrificial Spear, Curse Adept, Berserk Spearmaster, Acolyte of Blood, Siphon Adept

Oh. These don't look all that friendly.

CHAPTER EIGHT

To Deal a Blow

Rowan?" Olivia asked, her voice breaking Rowan out of his thoughts. "Yeah, sorry." Rowan spun around and offered her a guilty-looking smile. "I hit Rare, but there's a problem."

"Problem?"

"The options are a bit, um . . . grim?" Rowan said and decided to explain things by sharing the system tab that listed all his class-upgrade options.

It took several very long seconds for the rest of his party to read through Rowan's options. And then they all broke into laughter in unison.

"It's not funny. Why are you all laughing? Keep it down," Rowan hissed, looking around again to see the soldiers sending funny looks their way.

"Are you worried that your class choices sound evil?" Olivia tittered, only worsening the hero's embarrassment. "Oh, Rowan. It's not like that."

"Then what *is* it like? I mean, look at those options and tell me they're *normal*."

"Oh, they're *not* normal. At all. They're one hundred percent Rowan-flavored," Marcus laughed, shaking his head at the window Rowan had shared with him.

At this point, even the densest person in the world could see that Rowan's worries were unfounded. Rowan himself relaxed, too. "What are you guys talking about?"

"Oh, come on now. You choose to constantly throw yourself into danger, you go for the most dangerous and risky builds, and you enjoy using two cards that are practically cursed. Now you're wondering how you ended up with these choices? They're almost as bad as mine," Milena joked.

"I'm not that bad."

"Yes, you are. Ask anyone," Olivia said as she ticked through the options again. "Class upgrades come from notable achievement or performing the right set of actions for the system to label you as compatible with a class."

"You're saying that I'm a dark, cursed hero type?" Rowan asked, his shoulders slumping a little.

"Have you looked through the descriptions for these classes? A lot of classes have weird names and they're perfectly fine. These? They're on a different level," Olivia said.

Before Rowan could go back to his system screen, Milena agreed with Olivia with a mumble. "My choices when I hit Rare were pretty suspicious-looking, too. [Dread Shaman], [Marrow Lord], and [The Repository of Curses]."

"Wait, time out," Rowan said. His head felt like it was about to explode with all the information being thrown at him. "You're saying that class names don't mean that much? So if I picked [Acolyte of Blood], I'm not going to get hunted down by an inquisition or something?"

"Of course not," Olivia exclaimed. "Why would you think that? If anyone was going to get hunted down, it'd be the [Blood Reaver]—if Mother hasn't already gotten to him."

"Okay, okay." Rowan took a deep breath. "Sorry, I got ahead of myself there for a bit."

"I don't think anyone ever told you. No one knows how classes are named besides the system," Olivia explained. "There are some pretty self-explanatory ones, which are just basic profession names. But then you have the infamous examples, like [Herald of the Pink Dawn], which has absolutely no logic to it."

"Huh, what does that class do?"

Olivia blinked. "Oh. Um. Well. Milena?" Her cheeks turned a rosy red.

"You brought that one up, Olivia. You get to explain it," Milena cackled, taking inordinate joy in seeing her friend flustered.

"It's a specialized class," Marcus said. "Rather popular in the less reputable parts of town."

"Less reputable?"

"A bagnio." When Rowan still showed no signs of recognition: "The cathouse."

"Ah." Rowan wasn't too sure how to respond to that. He escaped into his system menu for individual class upgrade options.

[Spearmaster]
You have proven your mastery of the spear, allowing
you to further advance the spear path.
By picking the [Spearmaster] class, you will get a large
boost to the strength of all cards and attacks related
to the spear. You will also master and improve
all spear-based combat skills much faster.
Additional beneficial effects:
A large boost to the effectiveness of your dexterity
and strength stats.
A medium boost to combat maneuvers and synergy
with other spear wielders.
Class penalties:
N/A
Attached card: Spear Mastery (Rare, Passive)

It was the most basic of the basic upgrade options, and Rowan dismissed it.

"Look sharp!"

Rowan closed his window and ducked as a soldier sailed over his head. Marcus's aura billowed out and enveloped the soldier, saving him from a painful reckoning with the ground.

In front of the army, far too close for comfort, was a ridiculously muscular gorilla. As Rowan watched, the colors of the jungle shifted and dozens more beasts appeared, all apparently in possession of some kind of camouflage-based card.

"Defensive formation!" Rowan called out. "Spearmen on the flanks and in the back."

If there was a benefit to the constant fighting, it was that he was learning how to command an army. At the start of every engagement, the soldiers instinctively looked to him. Every word that he said mattered. After that, the officers could take over and give more granular instructions.

"Olivia?" Rowan asked.

"Uncommons. A couple Rares—nothing we can't handle. Stay there and wrap up your class advancement. We've got this," Olivia said, her self-assured tone bringing a grin to Rowan's face. "It's time we got some experience for ourselves."

"Fine," Rowan said, quickly scanning and dismissing the some of the options so he could join them sooner.

[Lightning Lancer], [Curse Adept], and [Siphon Adept] were all quickly thrown out of the equation. If his experience with the lightning card he owned was anything to go by, he wouldn't appreciate having a class that focused on lightning. And the latter two choices seemed to be more suited for solo fighters.

There was a roar in the background, and Rowan risked a glance.

Marcus was tanking hits from two larger-than-normal monsters, while the soldiers were holding back the regular variants. Milena was building up her wall of miasma again, and Olivia was recklessly chucking potions left and right, as usual.

The army was working.

Rowan almost dismissed [Acolyte of Blood] as well, but a secret part of him liked the sound of the class name. Besides, while he was often thwarted by various odd physiques, his bleed effects came in handy more often than not.

[Acolyte of Blood]
You have made your enemies pay the price of offending you in blood and wrestled control over this primal element of mana for yourself.
By picking [Acolyte of Blood], you gain the ability to cast a variety of blood-based spells and enchantments

**that will enfeeble your foes, bolster your allies, and
make your weapons far more deathly. You will also
gain an innate understanding of mana manipulation
and the use of blood arts in battle.
Additional beneficial effects:
A massive boost to the effectiveness of your
intelligence and dexterity stats.
A massive boost to the growth of your mana pool.
Debuffs, poisons, and other debilitating effects
will be less effective against you.
You become capable of sensing and tracking every
entity with blood flowing through their veins
within a certain limit.
Class penalties:
Part of your spell-casting costs will be paid in blood.
Buffs, healing, and boosting effects will grow
much less effective when used on you.
Attached card: Blood Rite (Rare, Active)**

Rowan closed the class description.

If I was a spell caster, this would have been amazing. But it doesn't even mention using a spear.

So [Acolyte of Blood] was out. Rowan checked on his friends. They were doing okay, and one of the larger monsters had fallen. The soldiers still left something to be desired, but no one had died or gotten seriously hurt. Their teamwork was strong enough that they could pull the wounded back but not enough such that they could reliably bring down their opponents.

They need more training on how to attack. Not marches through the wastes and fighting whatever comes up. Individual, specialized training.

Rowan dipped his head down to read the last two class descriptions.

**[Berserk Spearmaster]
You will not fall before your foes.**

By picking the [Berserk Spearmaster] class, you gain the ability to imbue your body and weapon with the unbridled power of rage. You can maintain your boosted state and delay the effects of exhaustion and injuries as long as you have a target in sight. If you fail to designate a new target within sixty seconds, your boosted state will wear off and all the delayed effects will be applied to you simultaneously. The berserk state cannot protect you from the loss of limbs.
Additional beneficial effects:
A massive boost to the effectiveness of your strength and dexterity stats.
A grand boost to the power of your combat cards.
All fear and debilitating effects are rendered useless against you.
Class penalties:
Your reasoning capacity will be reduced for the duration of your berserk state.
Attached card: Rage (Rare, Active)

[Sacrificial Spear]
You are willing to sacrifice your very self for the destruction of your foes.
By picking the [Sacrificial Spear] class, you gain the ability to trade mana and vitality for massive boosts to your damage that will grow in proportion to your offered sacrifice.
Warning: Be wary, lest you burn yourself out.
Additional beneficial effects:
A massive boost to the effectiveness of your strength and dexterity stats.
A massive boost to the effectiveness of your damaging or debilitating effects.
You grow much more capable of ignoring injuries and negative effects during battle.

**You gain an extremely accurate innate understanding
of your current condition and an instinct for
the impact of using various cards.
Class penalties:
External attempts to help you heal or recover from the
damage caused by your sacrifices will be ineffective.
Attached card: Blood for Blood (Rare, Active)**

Rowan grimaced. Both classes were great options. The hard part about decisions wasn't when you had a bunch of bad ones, it was when you had two good ones.

For most people, the berserker option was lethal. Accumulated damage applying at once was more or less a death sentence. The harder they fought, the more likely they'd die. Rowan actually had a chance to survive the damage, especially in combination with his two recovery cards.

On the other hand, the sacrificial option was equally attractive. It was a bit of an assumption, but the wording on the class penalty meant that his recovery combination didn't count as an external healing attempt.

It came down to the question of preference. Did he want to keep fighting for a long time or dish out a massive amount of damage at once?

A roar ripped through the air and Rowan found the army now fighting against a monster that was twice the size of the other gorillas. It almost made the others look cute.

"Need help?" Rowan asked as he jogged a few steps forward.

"You read all your class options?" Olivia asked back.

"Not yet."

"Then no. We'll handle this."

The new gorilla stomped on the ground, and a miniature earthquake rippled through the army. It scanned its opponents before settling on and charging at Marcus.

The shield bearer managed to angle his shield so it dissipated most of the power from the charge. But the blow still rocked him back. In the change of momentum, Milena stepped in with a thick fog of miasma while the spear division flanked the monster.

They had things under control.

[Dark Spear]
You have slain corrupted foes and your spear has
been quenched in their blood.
By picking the [Dark Spear] class, you gain the ability
to turn the power of corruption against your foes.
With every corrupted monster and demon slain,
your strength grows.
Additional beneficial effects:
A massive boost to the effectiveness of your
strength and dexterity stats.
A massive boost to your affinity with corruption,
rot, and disease mana.
You gain the ability to bind a spear to you so
you may grow alongside it.
Class penalties:
Your mind grows more fragile and prone to instability.
Your chances of succumbing to corruption increase.
Attached card: Corruption Wielder (Rare, Passive)

Truth be told, Rowan almost chose [Dark Spear] after he read the beneficial effects. It was like the class had been designed for him. The stats were in the right place, and the specialization was perfect. After all, he was about to fight the demon king. Plenty of corrupted and demon opponents in the future.

But the class penalties were almost too high for him to accept. It wasn't just the fear of his mind growing more fragile. It was the cascading effects that would have with **Keen Spear** and other cards. Olivia had mentioned that Rare and higher cards had their own spirits. [Dark Spear] meant that he'd be more susceptible to their effects in the future.

"Don't panic! Stay collected!"

Rowan closed his system window to find a completely different world. The giant gorilla had somehow beaten attempts at containing it and was now rampaging through the army. No one seemed to be in terribly serious trouble, but Marcus was looking paler by the second.

And then his aura broke. For the first time, Olivia looked scared. She paused her potion throwing as the gorilla smacked away the officers trying to maintain order. And then the monster focused on one specific officer. It ignored everyone else as it closed its paw on the spear division officer.

In that instant, Rowan knew what class to choose. It was an odd feeling. A moment ago, he had been unsure of his choices. And now, when his hand tightened on his spear and his intent sharpened, he knew that he'd made the right choice.

The new class slipped into place around what Rowan imagined was his soul, and power surged through his body. When he dug his heels into the ground and rocketed forward, the exhilaration he felt was just barely tempered by the seriousness of the moment.

The anger at the beast for hurting someone was there. But it was a quiet, mastered thing. The emotion that Rowan really felt was one of desire.

His spear lit up with the crimson glow that had been his trademark since reaching the Uncommon tier. But the red color began to intensify and darken until it was pulsing a red-purple. Rowan felt energy leave his body, his attack sapping away at some vital part he didn't even realize existed. He didn't care. New strength surged into his limbs, assuring him of his eventual recovery.

When Rowan landed in front of the monster, poised for a strike, the Stalwart Hero's frame was almost gaunt.

The lack of muscles did nothing to mitigate the power of his strike when the spear dug into the monster's flank.

Power exploded out of the spearhead, surging into and tearing through the demonic gorilla's belly. The creature had barely enough time to attempt a pain-filled roar before the sound was aborted.

There was a head-size hole starting at the front of the gorilla's stomach and exiting out its back. A shower of blood sprayed over Rowan, but that was the gorilla's last hurrah.

The monster released its grip on the spear officer and looked down in shock. It swayed, stumbled, and collapsed in concert with an experience ping from Rowan's system.

Through a haze of shock, Rowan noted that the monster had just given him almost as much experience as the demon mount. That meant it was a high-level Rare. And he had just slain it with a single hit.

Then reality reasserted itself, and each and every one of the smaller gorillas surged at Rowan to avenge their leader.

Unfortunately for the monsters, they had the entire Rest's Remorse army in their way. It was a slaughter, and Rowan joined in as soon as **Lavish Feasting** rebuilt enough of his muscles.

Rowan began to understand what it meant to have a Rare class. He danced around blows that would have required serious dodging before and dealt near-lethal blows almost casually.

Hell, Rowan realized, he was having a ton of fun.

The way he could feel his body more intensely than ever before blew him away. He could feel every single source of his power, his mana, his blood, and even the vague, ephemeral concept of "vitality" that his class had described.

By the time the final gorilla monsters fell, he was back in top condition, a grin almost etched on his face.

"What was that?" Marcus was the first to reach Rowan, and the awed quality to his voice made Rowan's grin grow, if that was possible.

Seeing the rest of his party gathering around him, Rowan simply shared the description of his newest card in lieu of an answer.

[Class] Blood for Blood (Rare, Active)
Offer up your mana, blood, flesh, and vitality to fuel
a strike that will fell your foe. The power of this card
grows exponentially with the size of the offered sacrifice.

"All of those options, seven or eight of the classes available to you, and you pick the one that gave you a card that has an actual, solid chance of killing you if you overuse it?" Olivia asked, exasperation obvious in her voice.

Rowan resolved, then and there, never to share his class description with Olivia. It was the only class he'd ever seen with an honest-to-god red text warning attached to it. Some things were better held close to his chest, especially when they could result in a lengthy lecture from his favorite alchemist.

"I guess so?" Rowan said.

"Only you, Rowan, only you."

Rowan smiled. [Sacrificial Spear] came with its problems, there was no denying that. It cut into his survivability, but he'd also just felled a Rare-tier enemy *with a single blow.* If they ever encountered another demon mount, or even an Epic demon, he wasn't going to be useless anymore. Even if all he managed to do was deal one single good blow, he could make them bleed.

And that, more than anything, was what had guided Rowan's next choice.

"Officer? I never got your name," Rowan said as he joined the spear division officer.

"Bryson. My name is Bryson," the officer replied. "And thank you, Hero Rowan. I wanted to gather my men first, but I owe my life to you."

"It's my job," Rowan joked. When the officer didn't understand, Rowan cleared his throat. "But I need your help. I just made a mistake."

"A mistake?" Bryson asked.

"I killed the monster."

"And that's a problem?" Bryson said slowly like he didn't want to offend Rowan by not understanding things.

"It is," Rowan said. He turned to the soldiers and saw starry-eyed faces. Not a single one of them saw fit to feel bitter over the fact that he'd dragged them all out of the town, constantly killing off all the Rare-ranked monsters and the majority of the Uncommon ones to level up before them. "Can you ask everyone to come closer?"

"Men, form up," Bryson yelled. His voice cut through the air like his spear had cut through the monsters, and the troops tensed before springing to comply.

"How many of you are at the max Uncommon level? Raise your hand if you are," Rowan called out.

Hesitantly, at first, then with much more gusto, hands rose into the air. A full tenth of the soldiers had their hands up.

Ever since arriving at the frontier, Rowan had had a nagging question at the back of his mind. He could understand how the rest of the kingdom was stuck at Common levels. It was hard to find opponents to fight. But that logic didn't apply to the soldiers stationed on the frontier.

"How many of you have fought and killed something higher rank than yourself? I mean something at the Rare tier," Rowan asked.

The hands went down. No one had, which made sense since they were all at the Uncommon rank.

"How many of you could have killed something at the Rare rank?"

This time, a few hands went up. Rowan noted the people they came from and realized that he knew a couple of them. One was an extremely quick swordsman who'd rescued his comrades when they slipped into an unfavorable condition in battle.

Another of the soldiers, a woman with a pair of axes, tackled each battle with ferocity that outshone even Rowan's own, and she'd actually avoided sustaining a single wound the entire day.

"Why didn't you kill the Rare-ranked opponent?"

No one responded.

Bryson was the one who answered Rowan. "Army policy states that higher-rank kills are reserved for the highest-ranking officer."

"Do you agree with that policy?" Rowan asked.

"Different policies make sense in different eras. We're entering a new one," Bryson said.

It was a diplomatic answer, and Rowan's estimation of the officer rose.

"Okay. Hands down, everyone." Rowan turned to look at Olivia. "How much more time do you think we can spend out here today?"

The question earned him a soft smile and a fond shake of her head. "One, maybe two hours at most. It's too risky to spend the night outside the walls without a larger force and a lot more preparation."

"I can work with that." Rowan nodded, then faced the troops again. "Listen up! We're staying out here for as long as we can today, and we'll be hunting down every Rare-tier creature we come across!"

His voice carried over the gathered crowd, and Rowan immediately saw most of them slump just a tiny bit. A few of them, though, brightened and looked at Rowan with something very closely resembling hope. They were the ones who'd put two and two together.

"We're going to hunt them down and teams with the largest number of max-level Uncommon members will get priority for the kill. It's not going to be a perfect system, but let's try to get as many of you to Rare as we can today, okay?" Rowan didn't need to yell those words. The dead silence after his first sentence meant they naturally carried across the army.

As one, the soldiers erupted into cheers. Rowan could feel the tides of morale changing. They weren't just willing to fight, they were excited to do so. And the number of unhappy faces could be counted on the fingers of one hand.

Ironically, most of them were the officers.

Rowan quietly noted the ones that seemed to disapprove of his actions and was glad that Bryson wasn't among them. If they continued to feel that in a couple of days when he had more than a few of their peers to pick from as replacements? Well, he didn't know any of them, nor did he know why they were elected to their stations.

Familiarity wasn't something a person could count on when a new ruler rolled into town.

"Bryson, can you get the men ready for marching in five minutes? We're going to hunt as much as we can until we need to head back," Rowan asked.

"Yes, Hero Rowan," Bryson said.

Rowan walked over to Olivia and slipped his hand into hers as they watched the army reorganize itself.

"So I have a question," Rowan started. "Why does the army have that policy? Doesn't it make sense to help people rank up higher?"

Olivia giggled. "You did all that on instinct? Remind me to never bet against those instincts. But now that you're Rare, the only way you can progress is to kill monsters at the Rare or higher tiers. The same applies to the officers. Why would a commander let soldiers advance when they can climb the ladder of power themselves?"

"Am I making a mistake?" Rowan asked softly, looking over the gleaming faces of their troops.

"No, Mother would have abolished the policy, too. Father prefers to keep his troops as highly ranked as he can, and the officers hold power through personal courage and intelligence instead of raw power. That's why his army was the first thing he was stripped of when he was demoted."

"Just how influential *was* your father when he was a duke?"

"Influential enough that if he so chose, I'm pretty sure half the kingdom would have backed his rebellion." Olivia's voice was flat and a tiny bit frustrated.

"You know, Olivia?" Rowan said. "If I get close to really making you mad, please remind me never to upset you instead of immediately chucking potions."

Surrounded by the racket of happy troops, Olivia Sutton offered the hero a wide grin, slipping her arm around his. "I'll consider it."

CHAPTER NINE

Growing Pains

Over the next hour, the army managed to hunt down six Rare monsters, a rather stunning number made possible only by one explanation.

"Am I a monster magnet?" Rowan wondered.

"Maybe," Olivia laughed. "Just enjoy it."

Although only six Rare-tier monsters had been taken down, the army had gained an extra twelve Rare-tier soldiers. Everyone's spirits were high as they marched back toward home.

It was a start. But it wasn't enough. Nor was it perfect. Rowan was quickly realizing that the solution to his army's strength wasn't as simple as helping some of them reach Rare. It helped, but even if all the soldiers managed to reach Rare in the next few hours, it still wouldn't be enough to really change things.

Most of the soldiers had taken the basic [Spearmaster] or equivalent Rare classes, which meant they got a new card and a nice boost to the effectiveness of their stats. But in terms of actual combat, it was only a marginal improvement. It would probably take two or three full parties of four to fight a Rare-tier monster that Rowan could slay with a single spear strike.

They needed more training, better decks, and simply more experience against enemies. Even at the most basic level, the makeup of Rowan's party was far superior to even the best party that the army could put together. Most of them were bog-standard melee fighters, and although a division of spearmen was a scary thing to face on flat ground, there were dozens of ways that a demon army could tear them apart.

As the men joked with each other on their way back, Rowan slunk to the back of the march, where he was joined by Olivia.

"Hunt wasn't to your liking?" Olivia asked.

"No, not that. We're going to need so many more soldiers if we want to have a fighting chance," Rowan groaned, rubbing his face in frustration.

"Mother will help with that. She might grumble and complain that we need to learn, but she'll help. I'm sure she'll manage to browbeat the mercenaries into helping out eventually," Olivia tried.

Rowan didn't see things that way. If there was one thing that Rowan's limited historical knowledge taught him, it was that a reluctant ally was way worse than an insidious enemy.

"We still need strength that we can call our own. We need more men in our army," Rowan said. That was his best short-term solution. What they couldn't achieve in skill or cards, they would make up for in bodies.

"Or you could reach Epic." Olivia's face paled. "Sorry, that was a joke. Please don't try to do that."

Rowan opened his mouth to tell her even he wasn't that reckless, but snapped it shut with a click when he realized that his past two classes were called [Reckless Spear] and [Sacrificial Spear]. There was good reason for her to worry.

The army made its way back into town without problem. Once again, Rowan was glad for the officers who could handle the logistics of moving and settling so many men. He was free to head straight back to the mayor's manor.

As Rowan passed through the streets, he suddenly swung his head in a particular direction. The [Blood Reaver] stood in the shadow of a half-collapsed house and met Rowan's eyes. The mercenary had a bottle of something dark in his hand, which he raised up to Rowan.

For a second, a small voice in the back of Rowan's mind wondered what would happen if he ordered his troops to attack. It'd make his life easier, and a show of force would bring the other mercenaries in the town to heel.

But then the moment passed and Rowan kept walking.

The next few days passed by in a haze. While Camilla worked the mercenaries, Rowan led the army into the wilderness. By the end of it, all the soldiers were either at the upper half of the Uncommon levels or new owners of Rare classes.

As the sun set on another day of training, Rowan made his decision. It was time to be a ruler.

He had an idea. It wasn't a good idea. It wasn't even necessarily feasible. But it was one that could be the answer to his problems.

The meeting room, once a symbol of the town's prosperity, now felt cavernous and cold. Maps littered the table, each marking a reminder of their precarious situation.

"Thank you all for coming," Rowan said. Sitting around the table were Camilla and the chamberlain. In some ways, this was the first meeting they'd had since he became mayor.

There were dark circles under Camilla's eyes betraying nights of difficult negotiations. "Not a problem," she said, looking at Rowan with a glint in her eye. "I'm surprised, though. You haven't been very interested in what happens in your domain."

"My domain? The kingdom takes back the town when this is all over, right?"

"Of course not, why would they? It's in their best interest to look after and make things more convenient for any heroes that choose to stay."

"I just assumed . . . well, never mind. That's not why I brought everyone here." Rowan took a moment to organize his thoughts again. "Do we have extra equipment? Besides the ones that are currently assigned to the soldiers."

"We do," the chamberlain said, his weathered hands fidgeting with a quill. "Most of the equipment from those who fell or left was salvaged."

"Okay, then. What are our finances like? Can they support the current army comfortably? What if we double those numbers? Or even a full one thousand soldiers again?"

"Full thousand?" Camilla said as she pursed her lips. "I'm afraid not. The town has simply suffered too much damage for that. There's too much to fix and too many businesses to rebuild. And the real costs of maintaining an army comes from the price of feeding them. Five hundred, though? That would be manageable."

"Okay, one last question. How exactly do people recruit potential soldiers?"

Camilla traded a glance with the chamberlain. "The process is slightly different depending on which noble house you're talking about. For the Sutton house, anyone with an Uncommon Heart Card that's combat or combat-adjacent is welcomed. As well as someone with a Rare or higher crafting, support, or lifestyle-type Heart Card. Past that, we give tests to anyone with a Common Heart Card that's focused on combat and select the best."

"Okay, perfect. This is what I'm thinking: We put out a recruitment notice. We accept every applicant that passes our fitness tests until we have five hundred soldiers employed."

Camilla sighed. "That won't work. Heart Cards aren't just indicators, Rowan. They're the essence of a person's potential. I heard about what you've been doing with the army. I think it's a good idea to boost morale right now, but you've noticed the problem with it, right? The soldiers have trouble fighting higher-tier monsters." Camilla waited for Rowan's nod before continuing. "Adding more recruits would stop you from raising champion fighters. The officers would be weaker, which means that when they can't stop a demon, it's a massacre."

"All we need is to give them a chance." Rowan pushed on. "A chance to level up to Uncommon or even Rare. It won't matter what their Heart Card is at that point. It won't be easy, but we can have some of the new Rare-tier soldiers lead them on leveling expeditions. A whole army of Uncommon or Rare soldiers has to count for something. We defended Felton's Mill with less."

"It's different." Camilla frowned. "Do you have any ideas how many people you have loitering around the town with delusions of becoming a combat class in spite of having Heart Cards or conditions that even the mercenaries didn't want?"

"A lot of them," Rowan answered, thinking back to his outing with Olivia. "Most of them stuck and starving. This is a beacon of hope for them."

"It's not hope if you fill your army with useless chaff and drag the whole town down," Camilla hissed.

Rowan leaned back, stunned by the baroness's vehemence. The chamberlain stepped in to explain things. "What Lady Sutton meant is that swelling your numbers by drawing in raw recruits is how armies fail. The breaking point for any army is around ten to fifteen percent losses in a single battle. No matter how well trained a soldier is, when his friends start dying, his will to fight plummets."

"Even mercenaries, known for their independence, make sure to only recruit those with Heart Cards that have potential. Our problem isn't quantity. It's quality. We need trained men, and only the mercenaries have them at the moment."

"But?" Rowan could hear that there was something Camilla wasn't saying.

Camilla calmed down enough to lean back into her chair. "My apologies, Rowan, I didn't mean to snap at you. The mercenary companies are proving more uncooperative than I anticipated. The last few days have been trying."

"Apology accepted," Rowan said immediately. "Is it Florin and Tamara?"

"I don't think so," Camilla said slowly. "They have something to do with this, but they don't have anywhere near the influence to unite all the mercenaries. It almost feels like the whole town is in on a plan that we were not informed of."

Rowan's thoughts immediately turned to Kayla. He swirled the idea around briefly before dismissing it. She had no reason to do something like that. Curiously, he never doubted that she *could* do it.

"So, what do we do?"

Camilla looked like she had swallowed a lemon. She turned to the chamberlain. "When the previous mayor of Rest's Remorse fell, what happened to the army?"

The chamberlain paused. "The army retreated to the inner walls and held the town there. They performed bravely."

Camilla turned back to Rowan. "As much as I think this will probably end in tragedy, I don't think I have a better alternative. Any more time spent on the mercenaries at this point would be foolish. They've chosen to remain stubbornly independent."

"Lord Rowan." the chamberlain had a twinkle in his eye as he addressed Rowan. "What do you need from us?"

"I don't have the first idea about how to recruit or train an army," Rowan admitted. "But I think the soldiers can be more than a cleanup crew. What we need is probably a combination of training, levels, and equipment."

"Lord Rowan, I feel like it would be a mistake if I didn't say this. What you are proposing will tax the town's treasury to the limit. We won't have enough funds to hire one of the mercenary companies if we proceed down this path."

"I believe it. Let's try recruiting more soldiers from among all the interested commoners and we'll go from there."

"Very well. It will take a few days to organize the recruitment. We need to clear a testing area, prepare criers and notices, and more," the chamberlain said.

"Rowan, is this really what you want?" Camilla asked one last time.

"It is."

"Then I'll help. I just hope this works out."

Rowan didn't reply, but he hoped so, too. He prayed for it to every deity that would deign to listen, including Aristaeus.

As it turned out, anxiously awaiting the start of a new recruitment experiment wasn't ideal for one's nerves. Rowan managed to hold up well the first two nights, but on the third evening, he didn't even bother trying to sleep.

Instead, he attempted to sneak out to the mayor's private training courtyard as soon as darkness fell. Attempted, because there were more than enough servants walking the halls, even at night, to notice him. Rowan discovered that nothing ruined a good sulk quite like running into a maid who immediately insisted on asking if he required assistance.

On this particular evening, his failure to sneak about was doubly pronounced. A voice rang out into the still night air, mere minutes after Rowan started mindlessly thwacking away at a training dummy.

"Somehow I knew I'd find you here."

A part of Rowan had expected Olivia to find him eventually. Or perhaps her mother, who seemed to walk without sound. Out of everyone, though, the last person he'd expected was Marcus.

Yet there he was, a light smile on his lips and a mischievous twinkle in his ice-blue eyes.

"Can't sleep, either?" Rowan always reached for deflection whenever he was caught off guard.

"No, I'm good. It's you I'm worried about. You've been off for days, even before you organized that meeting with Olivia's mother. Come on, why don't you join me and explain what's bothering you? I promise I won't judge."

The wolfkin easily folded his legs under him and plopped right down on the dirt of the practice yard, patting the spot next to him.

Rowan wasn't given to grand emotional outbursts. He didn't even know how to express his emotions most of the time. There was, however, something appealing about the offer. So, eventually, the hero sat.

"Marcus, do you think I'm messing it all up with my plan? That it's not worth trying to recruit commoners?" Rowan asked quietly, avoiding the wolfkin's eyes in case he immediately said yes.

"I don't know, Rowan. It's not the kind of question members of my race ever have to confront."

"Wait, it's not? Then how do you even organize your armies? Do you have a way to manipulate the Heart Cards people get?"

"Hardly. You're just forgetting that our society is much more tight-knit than human culture. You don't just ignore when a member of your family is hurt or suffering. Most people have the chance to pursue their interests because we want to keep everyone happy."

"Why can't it be like that here?" Rowan wondered, keeping his eyes trained on the plethora of stars in the night sky. He hadn't really gotten a chance to admire them since that fateful ride from the capital with the baron.

"Numbers, I imagine. Our tribes are much smaller. A strong tribe doesn't even rival this town in size. We do have grand chiefs who rule over a series of tribes, but that's different. There's still some blood link between the grand chief and the people under their protection."

"I'm not sure whether our future recruits will make things better or worse. I don't want to get attached if some of them die or fail, but still . . . I don't even know how I could possibly help them succeed."

"Rowan, have you ever heard the story of the Thorn Knight? I know it's unlikely, considering your origin," Marcus asked.

The sudden pivot threw him off, but Rowan eventually shook his head. "I'm afraid not."

"Well, it's one of the most popular stories out there. We don't know her name anymore, or whether she was rich or poor. We only know she desperately wanted to be a knight, but her Heart Card was extremely poor."

Rowan scoffed, shooting the wolfkin an unamused look. "You're trying to make me feel better with a fairy tale."

"It's not that. We know the Thorn Knight existed. You see, when her system awakened, she didn't get a damage card or a buff card. She got a true damage reflection card, the Thorn Guard. At Common tier, too."

"That doesn't sound great."

"It wasn't. The card could only bounce back five percent of damage taken by the cardholder. So, to use her card, she had to fully tank all damage coming her way."

"Unpleasant."

"Except she didn't let that stop her! She left home, honed her build, and eventually became an immortal juggernaut that would grind all attackers down to nothing. I'm skipping parts, obviously, but the point stands."

Rowan sighed, letting himself fall back to stare at the stars again. "That Common cardholders can grow and become amazing, too?"

"Exactly. Everyone agrees the Thorn Knight got her happily ever after. Some say she settled down and started a family. Others say she became a queen and started her own bloodline. Some claim they know her real name and what she became: Locke, the goddess of knights and valor."

Rowan smirked a little. "I can't imagine her church likes that idea much."

"Actually, her church doesn't mind. It's the other followers of high gods that get uppity at the implications. Still, no one can deny that Locke's priests, paladins, and followers use a lot of thorn- and damage reflection–themed miracles and incantations."

Rowan laughed, feeling a little better. It wasn't some revolutionary tale, and it hadn't made his problems go away. But having a friend willing to miss sleep just to hang out with him lifted his spirits.

"Hey, Marcus?"

"Hmm?"

"Thanks for coming to find me."

The man was silent for an uncomfortably long stretch. When he spoke, Rowan could hear the smile in his voice. "Nothing to thank me for, Rowan. Nothing at all."

They sat there awhile longer in companionable silence. When Rowan returned to his bed, he actually managed to get some sleep.

CHAPTER TEN

To Pick a Soldier

Rowan looked out over the sea of suspicious faces. His recruitment campaign had taken the town by storm, first met with doubt, then derision. Nearly everyone seemed to have a thing or two to say about the idea of recruiting commoners that even the mercenaries had passed over. Now, as he prepared to open applications, the air thrummed with tension.

"Those of you who want to support your families, fight for your home, climb up the tiers—you're welcome here," Rowan declared, his voice carrying across the square. "Today, some of you will get the chance to pursue your ambitions. We will be picking out a total of three hundred new recruits. As a recruit, you will be putting your life on the line. Every day. It'll be painful and it'll be dangerous. But it'll also be a chance for you to change your life. And no, your Heart Card's quality doesn't matter."

A murmur rippled through the crowd. Some cautiously stepped forward, others back. Years of mistrust had taught these people to look for angles, for ways they'd be exploited.

Sadly enough, even if he did have bad intentions, Rowan couldn't see a single reason someone would scheme against these people. Most of those who had shown up looked several stages past desperate. Thinning frames, unkempt appearance, and clothes that were falling apart.

The second half of the gathered crowd was the polar opposite of the first. Curious and bored mercenaries were watching the gathering and snickering.

Well, most of them were snickering.

Rowan noted that those bearing the insignia of the Mercenary King's company fixed their attention on him. What exactly they were looking for he did not know.

"Applications are now open," Rowan announced, gesturing to the waiting clerks. "Step forward if you'd like to join our army."

Rowan ran his eyes over the crowd one final time and stepped back to join the rest of his party. The stage had a little sitting area with some basic refreshments. This was done at the insistence of Rowan, since he was planning to stay right there and oversee things.

If he simply left and someone caused trouble, his entire recruitment plan would fail.

"You did well," Olivia whispered, offering him a smile as he got seated.

"Doesn't really feel like it. No one is even moving forward."

People hovered just far enough away from the awkward-looking clerks to not be perceived as approaching them. Some looked tempted more, but ultimately, it seemed like the word of their new mayor, hero or not, wasn't enough.

Then, a determined teenager pushed through the crowd. "My name is Clarke. I'm a level-one [Swordsman]," he declared, voice wavering slightly. "My Heart Card is **Gullible Thoughts**."

The clerk got to work as soon as the young man opened his mouth, expertly filling out the application form. "May I know what your Heart Card does?"

Now that he had admitted his card's name out loud, Clarke was remarkably more willing to discuss its effect. "It's just a Common tier. It slightly improves my chances of catching someone when they're lying to me. It's pretty obvious as a feeling I get when it works."

"Excellent. Now, can I ask you to do fifty push-ups for me, please?"

The young man looked more than a little embarrassed, but complied anyway. Rowan felt for him, but he was the one who'd insisted on at least testing that much. He needed able-bodied recruits, and even in their dilapidated states, fifty push-ups were possible through sheer force of will.

Clarke didn't even struggle with the task. The clerk pulled out a smaller form, filled it out, and stamped it. "Here you go, young man. You are to report to the military training field next to the mayor's mansion tomorrow morning."

Looking more than a little shell-shocked and stuck staring at the slip of paper, Clarke nodded and then wandered away from the clerk. Instantly, two more people stepped forward and found their own clerks.

Rowan looked over the crowd once more. They were starting to stir. He could almost sense the thoughts percolating through the crowd: There was still doubt, but he could feel the embers of hope rising. The doubt wouldn't disappear in a single day, but he could fan the hope some more. Rowan nodded to a couple of the Rare-tier soldiers, who went into the crowd and began advertising as the living embodiment of what was possible.

"That was nerve-racking," Rowan admitted as he sank into his seat a little more easily. It was ridiculously soft, and he was more than a little happy at being able to enjoy it properly.

"Were you worried no one would apply, oh mighty leader?" Milena teased, but Rowan wasn't fooled. The beast folk was just as nervous as he was initially. Her tail was practically fighting her to poof out.

"Yes, yes, I was. If no one applied after all this, it would have been more than a little embarrassing and a waste of time and money. Can you imagine what Lady Sutton would have done to me?"

"Isn't it a bit much to be so afraid of your mother-in-law?" Marcus drawled, though he quickly shrank into his seat when he was nailed to his chair by a sharp glare instead.

"That's extremely rude, Marcus. Rowan isn't terrified of my mother!" Olivia, eyes twinkling with cruel delight, turned her attention to Rowan. "Isn't that right?"

This time, Rowan definitely blushed.

As the day dragged on, the recruitment proceeded mostly without a hitch. Though Rowan was worried one of the other town factions would try something to mess with them, the worst they had to deal with was the threat of heatstroke.

The sun beat down relentlessly, and Rowan ordered chilled water for the crowd. It was another expense on an already overtaxed budget, but if a little bit of ice could build a positive image of him in the town, he'd take the trade any day of the week.

The other hitch in the recruitment process came at the very end.

The problem presented itself as a small, malnourished girl. Her size wasn't the issue. Nor was her health, since almost every one of the new recruits was malnourished or weak.

The problem was that she was rather loudly arguing that her age shouldn't disqualify her application. The clerk kept his voice calm and immediately flagged one of the people in charge of water distribution so the girl could have a drink.

That only made her argue harder.

"The hero mayor said that our Heart Card doesn't matter! We only need to do fifty push-ups, right? Well, I can do that!" To prove her point, she did them, then pouted up at the man. The effect was rather ruined when she could only barely see above the edge of the desk he worked behind.

"The quality and effect of the Heart Card doesn't matter, no. However, the implication is there that you need to have a *Heart Card*," the clerk repeated, for about the fifth time. "You're only eight. Why don't you come back in a couple years?"

Rowan was just about to intercede when Olivia sighed and stood up.

The girl didn't notice her at first, too busy arguing, but the onlookers sure did. They opened up a path, allowing Olivia to slip up behind the girl and plop her hand on her head.

"You are an awfully determined little thing, aren't you?"

"I'm not little!" the girl protested, pushing away Olivia's hand and spinning around, only to falter when she caught sight of the alchemist. "Oh. Um." Just like that, her courage fled her, and she drew in on herself like she was trying to make for a smaller target.

"Tell me, can you help with cooking? Carry things around? Any experience with past work?" Olivia asked.

Having something to latch on to, the little girl immediately launched into a reply. "Yes, yes, and yes. I used to help out in the tavern near where we lived." She paused, then, as though she was afraid that wasn't enough, rushed to add, "Everyone said I was super useful!"

"Well, I suppose we'll see about *that*," Olivia said haughtily, but Rowan could see the spark of delight in her eyes. She waved to one of the water distributors. "Can you please take her back to the manor? Tell whoever's in charge of the kitchen that she'll be assisting with meal distribution for the new soldiers."

"I didn't want to—" The girl's words came out rushed and angry before the fight left her. "I mean . . . thank you." She obediently trailed after the man who was put in charge of guiding her.

Ironically, Olivia seemed a lot less sure about her decision after making it. She sneaked a few glances at Rowan as she made her way back. "You don't mind, do you? I mean, I know it's your manor and all, but when I saw her, I just . . ."

"It's fine," Rowan said, placing his hand on hers. "I was about to do something similar myself. Not going to just let a kid run around if she's desperate enough to apply to be a soldier." Olivia offered him a smile, and Rowan realized he would have approved her request just to see that expression. That made all kinds of feelings squirm in his chest. "In spite of everything, I really don't think we're going to hit the numbers we were going for."

Plenty of people had come to see what all the fuss was about, but far too many were still milling around. It was obvious that only a fraction of the total number intended to apply.

"Honestly? That's fine. It's not like you have a battle to fight tomorrow. Give it time. None of them know what you're planning to do with the new recruits, so it's natural for them to be skeptical," Olivia replied.

At the end of the day, Rowan walked away from the square with 213 new recruits. Not quite the three hundred he'd wanted, but it did effectively double the number of souls under his command.

The thought both thrilled and terrified him.

*   *   *

The next day dawned sunny and pleasantly warm. For the first time in days, Rowan actually got enough sleep the previous night and managed to outrun his troubles for a few moments.

The baroness was still doubtful about the success of his plans, but even she had congratulated him on the number of new recruits when they returned the day prior.

Now, he basked in the sun as ten new officers surrounded him.

Behind them were rows of tables, holding literal piles of bread and similarly robust food items. The food wasn't anything special, just stuff that wouldn't spoil while sitting out in the sun for a couple of hours. Still, for the recruits who had been struggling at the very bottom of the local society as recently as yesterday, it was a veritable feast.

"They should be here soon, my lord," one of the officers, a woman named Rayne, said. She looked as eager to get her hands on the recruits as he was. "They're currently receiving their new gear and some basic instructions on how to care for it at the barracks."

"Wonder what they'll think of us later today," another officer, Trevor, said. "I must admit that your plan for them is quite something, Lord Rowan." He, unlike Rayne, sounded worried for the recruits.

Rowan looked to Bryson, who had remained quiet through all the chatter. In designing his army, Rowan had taken direct inspiration from Kayden. The men all reported to Bryson, the spear division officer that Rowan had promoted. In fact, the training program was also copied from Rowan's time under the baron.

"It's good to have compassion for the people under your command," Bryson said. "But too much coddling will only get them killed on the battlefield. Better to sweat in training than bleed in a fight."

Rowan hadn't picked out the most powerful or talented combatants to lead the new troops. Instead, he'd picked out the most patient and detail-oriented ones. In the time the baroness and chamberlain were preparing the recruitment drive, he had spoken to the army's officers at length and even interviewed some of the potential officers himself.

Finally, the recruits started to trickle in.

They came alone or in pairs. No real groups had formed just yet. Some looked uncomfortable in their new armor while others were right at home. It was a ragtag army, one that would need to be trained. Which was just what Rowan intended to do.

"Okay. Now that you're here and you're properly equipped, we can start. First, I want you to meet your superior officers."

One by one, the officers stepped forward and loudly announced their names before falling back. Most of them were quite young, something the recruits had noticed, too, judging by the considering and greedy gazes of some.

If they thought they'd be getting a quick and easy promotion out of joining up, though, Rowan was eager to disabuse them of the notion.

"Excellent!" Rowan gave his most bloodthirsty, unhinged smile. "Now that's over, let me make one thing clear. As you are now, you are useless to me. Most of you are barely in good enough shape to recruit to begin with. So, from today, we'll work on fixing that. In other words, I want you to run."

Confusion was apparent in the ranks of the recruits, even if several of them were quick to head for the running track that circled the training grounds. Rowan noted those immediately and subtly signaled for Trevor to note down their names later.

He wasn't upset when most of the recruits didn't follow to do the same. After all, motivating them and building up good habits was why he'd promoted new officers to begin with.

Still, when Rayne stepped forward and cracked an actual whip, he did wince a little. "His Lordship said to run, little recruits. So, you'll run."

The recruits got the message. But on the track, they were pitiful. They were slow. Their stamina was so ridiculously low that Rowan wondered if he had ever been that bad himself.

Still, they tried. And when their bodies faltered, his officers were there, hounding, prodding, and threatening them to continue. It was mostly Rayne who was doing the last part, but Rowan had to admit he was reluctantly impressed.

By the time a mere half an hour was over and they were allowed to stop running, Rowan's recruits were a sweaty and exhausted mess.

Then the officers pounced, once again shouting instructions and beginning the next set of exercises.

He'd had the foresight not to give them a hearty breakfast before training began. But that didn't seem to be enough when some of the recruits began throwing up. Rowan stayed in his place even as the smell of the training grounds grew progressively worse.

"You can leave any time you want," Rowan said, his voice echoing above the heavy breaths. "I'm not here to chain you to this army. But neither am I here to run a charity. If you want a purpose, then you'll first build yourselves into a force. Hearty meals don't come cheap."

Once the allotted time for torment ran out and the recruits were reduced to quivering messes, an army of servants marched onto the training grounds. Much to Rowan's amusement, the little girl whose name he still didn't know was among them.

As they went about forcing a pair of potions down each of the recruits, Rowan had to stifle a sigh. This was the most expensive part of his whole plan and easily the riskiest one. He had assurances from Olivia it would work, and she'd done her best to minimize the costs, too.

As the potion effects took hold, he watched as the recruits' condition visibly evened out to something approaching functional. Then, of course, a monstrous hunger took hold, and Rowan suspected that even without instructions from the servants, they wouldn't have hesitated to head for the food.

"Impressive and horrifying," the hero muttered, watching with wide eyes as his new recruits descended upon the food like a host of ravenous demons.

There wasn't even a crumb left by the time they were done.

"Okay, you sorry lot," Rayne commanded. "Now that you've eaten, you are to return to your assigned barracks. You have two hours of rest time, so use it wisely. If any one of you doesn't show up here after that time is up, I'll come to drag you out here myself."

With that ominous warning, Rayne allowed the weary crowd to shuffle off in search of shelter. Most of them looked incredibly drowsy, and Rowan sighed as he realized that a number of them would likely get to see that the woman wasn't making idle threats.

Rowan didn't enjoy torturing the recruits, but this was something that they needed. Camilla had done her best to teach Rowan about the basics of running an army, and discipline was a core tenet in every fighting force. Everyone had to know the rules. That was the only way to command hundreds of men in a single direction.

But with the potions Olivia had brewed, the recruits would actually survive the process.

It was a special recipe, one that was inspired by Rowan's own **Lavish Feasting** and **Persistent Regeneration** combination. One potion made digestion ridiculously effective, allowing the body to take in far more energy than normally possible. The other used that energy to heal and build muscle.

In other words, Rowan was putting them through a cardio and recovery regime from hell. So long as they could complete what was coming at them, his recruits would at least be in acceptable physical condition. Olivia had warned that it wouldn't be effective once they had a decent number of stats, likely around ten, but it was more than enough for his current purposes.

Especially since the cardio program was only half of the equation. Once the morning break was over, it was time for the recruits to start combat and weapons training.

If he was being honest with himself, Rowan felt more than a little depressed at his recruits' pitiful class variety. There were so many [Swordsmen] there that he was absolutely certain that the only thing that had guided their decision-making was youthful exuberance. For some reason, the [Swordsman] classes were the epitome of honor and power in the kingdom he now called home.

But it did simplify things somewhat. Even with a couple of more unusual classes, standardizing the training regime for the new troops wasn't difficult. The officers all had extensive experience with the weapons they were teaching, and he could always temporarily pull others from the original army.

Rowan was reluctant to do that too much, especially since those troops could dedicate their time to hunting monsters and boosting their levels.

In fact, he would be joining them soon. He insisted on being there for the recruits' first day, but there was absolutely no reason to idle away watching them train. He wouldn't let himself fall for the pitfalls the baroness had pointed out to him.

His troops needed to be strong, yes.

But the hero party had to grow, too.

It was absolutely amazing what two short weeks could accomplish, Rowan reflected as he watched the recruits train.

Just a short time ago, the basic exercise would all but crush them. Now? They were breezing through it, even with a heightened level of difficulty.

"I have to say, I know I provided the potions for it and all, but this is . . . impressive," Olivia said, looking inordinately proud.

And she had more than enough reason to be.

"I don't think I say this as often as I should, but you're amazing, Olivia," Rowan said. She giggled, bumping him with her shoulder. "You think they're ready for heading outside the town?"

"Oh yes, I should say they are," Milena said approvingly, eyes roving over the recruits and looking for signs of weakness. "Honestly, I can barely even recognize them. I watched them get recruited and this is an incredible transformation."

In a way, Rowan was extremely flattered to hear her say that. He'd picked up a bunch of half-starved, hopeless men and women.

Now?

Well, no one would mistake them for starving peasants ever again. Each and every one of them looked healthy, and the corded muscles they sported hinted at their profession.

Of course, the fact of the matter remained that they were untested. These troops had received the best training he could offer to them. But they were still mostly Common classes. They needed experience.

And they needed to be put under a real stress test.

"I am extremely proud of your progress," Rowan announced. "I still remember the way most of you looked that first day after your initial training. But look at you now! However . . . I'm afraid this is not enough." He could see their faces fall at his words. He'd started building them up, only to snatch further praise away. He had to admit that the baroness's advice was quite effective most of the time. "Now that your foundation is set, it's time to deliver on my promise to you. I promised you levels. I promised you that you would rise through the tiers. So, it is time that my promise is kept. Tomorrow, you will accompany my party into the wastes. Tomorrow, you earn your first levels."

His new troops didn't disappoint him.

He could see the hunger in their eyes, the desire to grow and become better. As cheering rose up around him, Rowan smiled.

CHAPTER ELEVEN

The Proving Grounds

Before anything else, Rowan broke the recruits into four groups. It would be unruly to march two hundred fresh soldiers into the demonic wastes where the weakest monster was at the Uncommon tier. They needed to lessen their footprint.

The leaders of the other three groups were Olivia, Marcus, and Milena. Although Rowan had known for days now that he would have to temporarily dissolve the party due to system rules, it didn't make things any easier.

The fact that he couldn't easily check their statuses weighed on his mind, but there was something else to cheer him up.

"Stick with me and you'll never go hungry again!" Rowan muttered under his breath, chuckling a little and humming along to the *Lion King* song echoing through his head.

If pressed, the Stalwart Hero could honestly say that he was in a great mood.

He had doubled his troops, the general affairs of the town were in order, the baroness was doing a predictably stellar job of running the financial recovery projects, and his own little initiative was working out great. After all, with an abundance of Uncommon creatures to hunt, the recruits were very quickly getting leveled up.

"Isn't this too easy?" one of the recruits whispered rather uselessly. Rowan's perception stat wasn't for show, and his ears had always been quite keen even before getting boosted by the system.

"I mean, maybe?" another recruit said.

"Would you two prefer to fight a full-health Uncommon-tier monster instead?" their final companion, who had much higher intelligence if Rowan was the judge, piped up. "I'd like to remind you that we're still in the low Commons."

Rowan wasn't just force-feeding them levels. He was also making their lives much better, and their effort was bearing fruit that much quicker.

Some people got advantages. Rowan was just of the opinion it was finally his poor recruits' turn.

Being at the edge of the wilderness, it took a while before a group of monsters was willing to attack them. But when they did, Rowan, like the other Rare-tier soldiers and officers, jumped into action. He picked one nasty-looking beast in particular.

With his stats and cards, the Uncommon monster could do nothing to stop him from dismantling its defenses. However, right before his carefully aimed attacks would render it useless, Rowan pulled back.

This left a bloody, enraged beast on its last legs against three fresh-faced Common-tier recruits. It was a fair fight, perhaps a bit too fair. The recruits were soon fighting for their lives.

Rowan circled around the fight, ready to step in if things went wrong. But he also had enough time to chat with his subordinates.

"I have to admit, Hero Rowan, that this is highly unusual. It's usually the other way around, crippling monsters for our officers instead of the lowest recruit," one of the officers said after finishing up his group's fight.

"That's the hope, Jacob. With any luck, we'll have them up to the basic Uncommon tier in record time. After all, it's not that hard to drag someone out of the Common tier." The admission made Rowan briefly feel horrible, but he discarded those feelings quickly enough.

The world wasn't perfect, but he was working on it one step at a time.

By the time his chosen three recruits had barely downed their enemy and broken into a celebration, Rowan was smiling alongside them.

"Rayne, what's the current status report on the recruits?"

"Sir, we've got two parties up to Uncommon already, with another three very close to the early double digits. The rest are still leveling at an expected rate."

Rowan nodded, reassured. That lined up nicely with what he'd seen in the last few fights. The recruits under the leadership of the more experienced or talented soldiers and officers were advancing swiftly with relatively little trouble. The trick was to weaken the monsters enough that they wouldn't be a danger to the recruits but were still strong enough for real combat experience. It was a fine line to walk.

"That's excellent news. Keep up the good work, and we'll be done with this much sooner than any of us expected to be," Rowan said.

It wasn't an exaggeration. Rowan had expected to spend weeks training all the recruits into shape. Rayne had accelerated things so much that Rowan wondered if he should just put her on new-soldier training from now on. While it was true that pretty much all the recruits had nightmares about her, the results were undeniable. Her party was the only one besides Rowan's that had advanced to the Rare tier.

"Yes, Lord Rowan," Rayne replied as she went back to her own group of recruits.

Rowan looked back at his own group members, who had finally taken down the beast and were now celebrating in their own ways. Funnily enough, the experience wasn't only beneficial for the recruits. Back when the baron was teaching him, Rowan sometimes relied on rote memorization instead of truly understanding the instructions. Combat had taught him the meaning behind some of Kayden's instructions, but teaching the recruits and skillfully weakening a foe had Rowan reexamining his understanding of the spear.

So far, because he was fighting opponents that were often a tier or more higher, Rowan had been all aggression and no tact. His fighting style was to overwhelm an opponent in the first few seconds with a flurry of card combinations. It wasn't a bad thing per se, but it meant that he didn't have a lot of answers for defense or deflection if the battle started to slow down.

The baron also had a hand in this. The maneuvers he'd taught Rowan were the basic foundation, but the forced training meant each of these moves was sharpened to maximize damage instead of skill. All that meant Rowan's style was uncomplicated and damage-heavy.

There were two solutions to that. The first would be to slow down and train with an actual spearmaster on technique. For the moment, that was about as likely as the demons retreating. So the second, and more promising, solution was to minimize the drawbacks of fighting with wild abandon.

I really need to upgrade that card already, Rowan grumbled to himself, inordinately annoyed that **Persistent Regeneration** was still stuck at Rare. One single Uncommon-tier **Rapid Regrowth** card or another Rare-tier **Persistent Regeneration**, and he'd be able to get a full set of ten, netting him his second Epic card. But the card just stubbornly refused to come, even with card-scrap fusing.

Before Rowan could spiral too far into contemplating his build, a commotion started up to his left. Knowing that's where one of the forward teams was sweeping through the corrupted jungle, he immediately led his party of recruits toward the noise.

To Rowan's delight, he found a large, brown-golden viper with rows of eyes running down its sides. The monster was vicious, churning up earth with every strike of its tail. It made a perfect excuse for Rowan to get some exercise.

He streaked forward, leveraged his upgraded dexterity stat, and buried his spear deep into the monster's side right through one of its blinking eyes. It screeched and thrashed in pain.

"You three, what are you doing? You're fighting this thing," Rowan commanded. His recruits paled, and he hoped that they had enough trust in him to follow his orders. Luckily, they stepped forward.

The following battle was a blur of action, one that pushed Rowan's limits in an entirely different way. He wanted the three to have experience with fighting something vastly beyond their own limits, but he also needed to keep them alive.

This meant a fancy dance of Rowan flitting around and getting in front of every blow he could, diverting them while minimizing the amount of mana he used to hurt the monster.

"Keep your wits about you! Aim for the areas I've already damaged, or go for the eyes. For the love of all that is holy or unholy, please stop trying to pierce its scales on your own!" Rowan yelled.

The recruits were starting to understand, some faster than others. Once they were back in town, Rowan decided he needed to set up lessons on combat, especially since one redhead seemed fond of metaphorically bashing his head against a wall.

With most of the monster's body gradually accruing wounds, it became obvious that it was flagging. Its defeat was apparent to both parties. So, when its eyes suddenly firmed up and turned vicious, Rowan knew what was about to happen.

He pushed his dexterity stat to its utmost and became little more than a blur as he slammed into the recruits, knocking the breath out of their lungs but pushing them far enough away from the battle to be unaffected by what was about to come.

A second later, the viper erupted into a red haze, a thick blood mist that swallowed Rowan, instantly doing horrible things to his flesh. The viper then unhinged its jaws and a stream of black liquid shot out, tingeing the cloud black.

The reason the monster hadn't used the card before was obvious. Its body grew more emaciated, its remaining scales grew dull, and even the flow of blood from its wounds slowed as the vital liquid was consumed and converted into an attack.

It didn't feel good being at the center of the monster's attack.

But Rowan's pain resistance had been tempered by the demon's mount and nearly getting eaten alive. Even as his skin sizzled and his muscles corroded, he moved.

His spear briefly *blazed* with ominous colors, and this time, when it impacted the creature's head, the monster was blown apart, bits of flesh, bone, and brain raining onto the jungle away from Rowan.

Then he was speeding away even as his regeneration card kicked in, allowing him to exit the cloud of death looking a bit more like a person and less like a melted monstrosity.

"Lord Rowan!" One of the soldiers rushed forward, already fishing out a healing potion. "Here, hurry, you must—"

Rowan laughed and waved the man away. The recruits watched as the hero's body restored itself right in front of their eyes. Rowan thanked the soldier before addressing the gathered crowd.

"Now, I hope what happened will be a lesson to you all. Never assume that your enemy can't do anything to take you down with them. The monster used a card that was practically suicidal. But it was backed into a corner. There, even the faintest glimmer of survival is magnified."

Some of the braver recruits began to ask questions about the fight. Rowan answered them as well as he could. Though he did gently steer away any questions about his build. As much as he was loath to admit it, he didn't fully trust the people in his army yet.

Plus, the lack of conclusive proof of what his build actually was would hopefully work to keep people on their toes and more hesitant to do anything unwise.

Rowan tried not to show any favoritism during the training. But eventually, he upgraded his party of recruits to the Uncommon tier and found his way to commanding Clarke, the boy who had led him and Olivia to the apothecary at the edge of town, and his two friends who'd been treated by Ophis.

He hadn't really done it much with the other recruits, but here, he struck up a conversation almost immediately with a smile. "So, how's the army treating you so far?"

Rowan enjoyed the way Clarke squirmed a little. "It's been good so far, sir. Rough, but good," Clarke said meekly, clearly unsure how to act around the hero.

"You know I don't hold our meeting against you, right? You did nothing wrong back then, and we were trying to remain anonymous for a bit longer while exploring the city. So, relax. I'm not going to feed you to a monster," Rowan joked. "Or maybe I will. Gotta stay on your toes."

Clarke relaxed, or at least tried to. His muscles remained tense and his eyes were constantly sweeping over the jungle surrounding them. That, Rowan could understand. Even for someone who'd been desperate to become a combat class, venturing into the wastes was likely nerve-racking.

Especially since the boy was still level nine, and that was five levels higher than he'd been in the morning.

"You were the one who helped us, right, sir?" one of the others, a girl whose name Rowan still didn't know, asked cautiously.

"Not really, no. We made a deal with the apothecary that your friend guided us to, but he was the one who fed you the potion. And the one responsible for said potion was Olivia. I was just along for the ride. What are your names?"

"Flora, sir."

"Oliver, sir."

That made Rowan pause for a moment, and shoot the boy an amused look that clearly unnerved him. It was somewhat ironic he shared such a similar name with the baron's daughter, and Rowan made a mental note to mention it to her.

Then, a thought came to Rowan and he decided to do something vaguely rude that was only slightly tempered by his standing and status as their employer. "Tell me a bit about your classes?"

All three of them flushed and looked a little reluctant, but Clarke eventually spoke up.

"I'm a [Swordsman], sir. Plain as bread, absolutely nothing interesting about my deck. I did manage to get a card that suits me. I got **Sturdy Body** from one of the Uncommon monsters we fought today."

Just a single extra card? Somehow, Rowan had forgotten how difficult it could be for commoners to get a decent deck cobbled together. Even those who advanced to Uncommon often had only their class card in the correct rarity. In a very real way, the presence of the wastes was a blessing in this regard. So long as they could survive venturing into it, the recruits would eventually get something good.

"What about you two?" Rowan asked.

"I—I got the [Mercenary] class," Oliver said.

That caught Rowan's attention. "Explain."

If he was a little brusque, he didn't care. If memory served Rowan right, the only way to unlock that particular class was to do a job as a mercenary. Or to get hired on by a mercenary company as one of their recruits.

Rowan had some serious doubts about the boy's ability to do the former, especially on the frontier. The latter? Well, it felt a bit too on the nose for the mercenaries to be sending someone with such an obvious class to spy on him.

Noticing Rowan's sudden intensity, Oliver hurried to explain. "You must have noticed I'm taller and sturdier than I should be at my age, sir." The boy motioned at his body. That much was true, since he had filled out much more quickly and impressively than most other recruits.

"What about it?"

"I have some dwarf blood on my mom's side of the family. Makes my muscles denser and my frame bulkier. My father's family are all extremely tall. They say we have some ogre blood, but that's nonsense, obviously."

Maybe it wasn't all that nonsensical, seeing that Oliver had chosen a pretty massive maul as his weapon.

"And how does that tie into your class?"

"So, I was always bigger than usual for my age. And my family owns a smithy, so I was working there as an apprentice. But I wanted adventure, to become famous. So, before I got my full system access and my Heart Card, I came up with a plan. Because I looked tougher and older, I lied to a merchant."

"What was your Heart Card again?"

"**Metallic Instinct.** Perfect for a smith, even at Common. It lets you sense flaws in metal and correct them more easily. For someone who lied his way into escorting a merchant to the frontier wanting to be a mercenary, though? Not as great."

Not as great was definitely a gentle way of putting it. The boy seemed genuine enough and more than a little upset by his own story. Rowan chose to put his mistrust aside for the time. "I see. Well, thanks for sharing your story with me. And what about you?"

The last question was directed at the girl in their party, who briefly squirmed under the scrutiny. Rowan noticed that she seemed generally averse to attention of any kind. Even with her friends, she preferred to blend into the background.

"I'm a [Ranger]. **Plant Identification** Heart Card. Not much of a nice story to tell. I was born here, like Clarke. My dad was a scout for the town, and he even took me out to the shallow wastes a couple of times. Nothing like now, but it was enough for me to unlock my class."

Rowan nodded, having known a bit more about her than the other two. Rayne had mentioned her in passing earlier. Ranged and support-oriented classes were a priority in any army, his included.

"That's impressive. We can always use a bit more ranged coverage. How decent are you with that bow?"

Flora unhooked the bow from her shoulder, nocked an arrow, and pinned a leaf to the trunk of a tree.

"Lethal," Rowan complimented.

"Thank you, sir."

The following period was genuinely enjoyable for Rowan, if for no other reason than getting to see the coordination between three people who were familiar with and trusted each other. That alone put them a step above average.

Whereas some of the recruits frequently checked on their fellows and refused to commit to an attack for fear of no one guarding their backs, the three had no such compunctions. Each blow was dealt with near-wild abandon, and more than once they placed their trust fully in the hands of their companions.

Or maybe it was Rowan's presence bolstering their courage?

When he decided to hang back farther and tell them he'd only interfere if things became dire, this assumption was proven false. They definitely did trust each other and work well together.

Honestly? Rowan was a little worried about their future. They'd eventually get a more permanent fourth party member, and he wasn't sure how well they would take to the new member. If that particular choice was made badly, the group could fall apart.

Of course, the same risk held true for every single trio running around following their assigned soldier or officer right now.

"Excellent work. However, Clarke, please stop trying to get yourself killed. I know you want to be more useful, but please learn to dodge or block." Rowan didn't miss the irony of that particular statement, seeing what his fighting style was.

Hells, there was a decent chance the boy had picked up the recklessness from watching *him*.

"Yes, sir," Clarke said reluctantly, eyes downcast.

"Oliver, please, for the sake of my sanity, stop swinging so close to your allies. Also, keep in mind that some creatures have acidic, poisonous, or corrosive blood. If you keep splattering them like that, you'll have to deal with the consequences eventually."

The boy looked sheepish, but also more than a little enthusiastic about splattering more enemies. Rowan just sighed and moved on to the sanest member of their little group.

"Flora, amazing work. You supported the two of them with cover fire, didn't put an arrow into either of them, and jumped into melee when you had to. Just make sure not to lose track of how many arrows you have again. You know who to talk to about replenishing those, so do it."

She squeaked out a thank-you and then bolted toward a bored-looking party absolutely buried under a ton of bags, a massive backpack, and even a few rolls that held various smaller weapons strapped down and secure for easy transport. They'd get their chance to train and be subbed by a different party soon enough.

When Flora finally came back with a half-full quiver, Rowan sighed. There was still some more work to do here.

He shook his head and stalked forward, heading for the nearest source of noise and combat. "Come on, let's get you all to Uncommon today so you can actually defend yourselves out there without a chaperone."

By the time they were forced to head back to town, Rowan was content. As it turned out, it was kind of easy to force people up to Uncommon if you dedicated an entire day to power-leveling them in a place with nothing but higher-tier enemies.

Since he remembered the baroness's advice, Rowan had even taken all the Rare-tier enemies for himself, too. In a way, at least it made sense. His blessing meant that the experience was used to its utmost, boosting his party far faster.

The day had even yielded one final, glorious surprise, and Rowan couldn't stop grinning as he eyed the card he held. A copy of **Rapid Regrowth** had been dropped by a particularly nasty giant lizard monster, which had actually given him some trouble despite being Uncommon.

Not because it threatened his safety, of course.

It had the unnerving ability to detach its tail like regular lizards did, except the detached tail then grew a maw at the stump and tried to munch down on anything living around it. Rowan had barely managed to keep the party accompanying him at the time from getting chewed on.

But the reward was worth the effort and Rowan was loath to keep waiting. He fished out the extra copies of **Persistent Regeneration** and **Rapid Regrowth** and started fusing them together.

The light show caught the attention of the soldiers, who seemed uninterested when the green light turned blue. But when Rowan unequipped his regeneration card to complete the set of ten, they started paying attention.

Purple light far brighter than any of Rowan's previous lower-tier fuses lit up the surroundings. Briefly, everyone was blinded, and Rowan blinked away stars to see his brand-new card.

Natural Renewal (Epic, Active)
Your body yearns to restore itself to its natural state no matter the damage dealt to it, drawing on mana, energy reserves, and muscle mass to achieve this quickly. Part of this cost is offset as the body intakes ambient mana. This trait allows lower-level regeneration to be active at all times as a passive effect.

Rowan felt the change the moment he equipped the card. Each and every one of his cells yearned to be whole, to be flawless. They sucked down ambient mana, and Rowan felt minor aches, pains, and inconveniences that he hadn't even known existed disappear.

Well, isn't this nice? Rowan's smile grew, and it was bordering on malicious as he started to cackle.

If his soldiers stepped farther away from him, well, he was too busy feeling happy to care.

CHAPTER TWELVE

Heartache

Once the excitement of the new card faded slightly and Rowan no longer felt like he was over the moon, he realized that he had messed up.

Fusing the card on the spot was an impulsive decision made out of his desire to avoid delaying the moment. It also meant that each and every one of the soldiers and recruits now knew that the hero had a brand-new Epic card added to his deck.

Put simply? The baroness was probably going to kill him when she heard about this.

Well, she'll try, Rowan thought smugly as they approached the ruined town gates, whose repair still hadn't started. *My new card is going to make dying a whole lot more difficult.*

The fact that his new card actually drew partially on mana, not to mention *ambient mana*, was a game changer. If he could master the use of the card, he could still boost his regeneration while sparing its draw on his own mana and bodily resources.

It would be nowhere near the full extent of what the card could do, of course. Still, in a battle? Especially a prolonged one? Any amount of completely free regeneration was invaluable. And with Rowan's build? He could keep a low-level sacrifice running near indefinitely with **Blood for Blood** while using **Natural Renewal**'s ambient mana regeneration to restore his body without dipping into **Lavish Feasting**.

Once he was inside the town, Rowan caught sight of the rest of his party and their respective groups. Out in the wastes, he had pushed a little harder and stayed a bit longer, just so that the last of the recruits could hit Uncommon.

He sped up, leaving the soldiers a short distance behind him, as he went to rejoin his Olivia and the rest of his party.

Rowan was so caught up in his happiness and desire to brag about his new card that he never even saw the attack coming. There was no warning, no sudden dramatic surge of bloodlust that would alert the hero and allow him to react.

One second, he was happy, healthy, and whole. The next, Olivia's eyes had widened and a long, wickedly curved blade was sticking out of Rowan's chest.

The next second, the blade's twin flashed in front of the hero and dug deep into his throat, opening it up with ridiculous ease.

Blood burst from both wounds as Rowan gasped, the instinctive reaction doing nothing but filling his lungs with blood. If he wasn't so used to pain, Rowan would probably have collapsed there and then. His throat and chest were gushing blood that his ravaged heart, with a blade in it, pumped through his body.

Instead, with a near-silent hiss replacing the roar Rowan wanted to make, the hero spun around with his spear.

His refusal to drop dead and the sudden movement forced the assassin to let go of the weapon in Rowan's chest, but the hero was far more thankful for the way his assailant instinctively backed up, creating some distance between them.

It would have been tricky to skewer the assassin with a spear if the man had chosen to stick close to him. As it was, fueled by his anger and his sacrificial card, Rowan drove his spear toward the man's left arm, which still gripped a weapon.

Even in his trance, Rowan knew to not fuel **Blood for Blood** with that much energy. He could feel his reserves plummeting as they struggled to repair his body. Still, what energy he did use was more than enough to cause a miniature explosion that blew the man's arm off at the elbow.

The assassin screamed, eyes wide with pain and fear as he backpedaled farther. Rowan snarled out of his healed throat and took a determined step forward, only to falter when the blade in his heart sliced new wounds.

His regeneration was doing its best, but the blade hadn't been removed, and when the flesh tried to seal over it, the weapon *reacted.*

Rowan wasn't sure what the exact enchantments on the thing were, but it was apparently sharp enough that it was slowly sliding its way down his body by sheer virtue of its honed edge.

He fumbled at his back, but his hands were too slick with blood and the blade's handle was at too awkward an angle for him to grip it.

The assassin took the distraction for the opportunity that it was. The masked man dashed for one of the alleys that went between relatively intact houses. Rowan's soldiers and the twins gave chase, but the man was far too swift, managing to keep ahead of them even with a bleeding stump of an arm.

"Rowan!" Olivia's voice let Rowan smile in spite of everything, and the relief that followed when she gripped the blade and ripped it out of his chest was indescribable.

He tried to take a deep breath but broke into a coughing fit instead. Each heaving cough was accompanied by flecks of blood as his body purged the liquid that was never meant to find its way into his lungs.

A part of Rowan found the whole thing humorous. There he was, in another world, coughing blood like a cultivation protagonist.

The weary chuckle must have worried Olivia, because she clasped her hands around his cheeks roughly and forced him to look her in the eye. She'd obviously never had first aid training. "What's wrong? Are you not healing right? He didn't even hit you in the head."

Rowan flinched before he realized that she wasn't joking. There was an undercurrent of worry and fear in her voice. He leaned back in and dragged her into a short hug. Olivia hissed something about getting blood all over her, but judging by how hard she hugged him back, she didn't mind. Probably.

"We need to catch him. We need him alive," Rowan grunted after a second, letting go and bending down to pick up the spear he'd dropped in favor of holding her without even meaning to.

Calmness swept through him, and he pointed at one of the recruits who had lingered, horrified and confused.

"You. I want you to take these blades and get them to the mayor's manor as quickly as you can. The rest of you, follow and protect him." Rowan gave his orders swiftly, eyeing the hand and part of an arm still gripping one of the blades. "Take the arm, too."

Rowan swirled around and stared at the commotion in the distance. The assassin and the pursuing soldiers had moved surprisingly far from them in the time it took for him to fully recover. Without thinking more about it, Rowan sprinted.

It was exhilarating to draw on his dexterity for the first time since his second class evolution, and Rowan realized with a start that he wasn't nearly as limited in his options to pursue as he thought he was.

Instead of heading for one of the alleys that zigzagged between the crumbling buildings, Rowan ran straight at one of the ruins.

One of the walls had partially collapsed, leaving a jagged splinter of stone that resembled a very dangerous set of stairs. But when Rowan's feet landed on the stone, they did so with surety and balance the hero still marveled at.

He ran right up to the peak of the collapsed wall, then leaped. He came down on the partially collapsed roof of the next house, and the chase was on.

It was glorious.

Rowan had done exactly zero parkour in either of his worlds. He was sprinting off pure instinct and the keenness of movement afforded to him by his stats and body awareness.

He vaulted over a collapsed portion of a roof. He slid down the cracking shingles, leaving them clattering in his wake, then launched himself off the roof's edge and onto the next in a move that caused the wall of the ruined building to shudder and collapse.

It was an obstacle course straight out of a video game, and Rowan loved it. What he loved even more was the speed at which he was gaining on the fleeing assassin.

Finally, he was just a few rows of houses away from the action, and he even caught a glimpse of the battle through the breaks between them.

The assassin was faster, better trained, and clearly at the high end of Rare. Rowan's soldiers and the twins weren't missing an arm and losing a ton of blood, though.

Rowan took a special kind of vindictive pleasure at the sight of the damage. And when the assassin reached into one of his pouches and pulled out a potion, Rayne's whip cracked through the air.

It struck the potion perfectly, sending the liquid and glass shards down onto the road.

The assassin tried to retaliate by drawing a throwing dagger from somewhere, but the blow was effortlessly stopped by Marcus's aura of protection, and the delay allowed the cloud of miasma pursuing the man to finally catch up, clinging to his clothes and further sealing his fate.

That's when the angry hero made his final leap, eating the impact damage and the havoc it would wreak on his knees in favor of dramatically appearing just a short distance away from the fight.

Rowan had to admit he loved the flare of fear he saw in his assailant's eyes and the way even his soldiers flinched. Marcus just grinned, of course, and Milena rolled her eyes.

"You're trapped and without a weapon. If you value your life at all, you will surrender now and be taken into custody," Rowan declared, rubbing his neck as he did. The regenerated skin was still a little tender, even if the tingling feeling was rapidly fading.

The reminder of the assassination attempt did make him wish the assassin would refuse to comply, though. Even with **Keen Spear**, anger was blazing through Rowan. He would have been dead if it weren't for his card combination. A price had to be paid.

For some reason, the assassin just stood there, his eyes slowly scanning over the hero party and their arrayed troops. Olivia caught up to them.

"There's nowhere for you to go," Rowan growled. "Surrender now."

The man must have reached the exact same conclusion as Rowan, because his shoulders slumped. Relief was just about to enter Rowan's body when the assassin suddenly collapsed, face buried in the ground.

Olivia cursed as she rushed forward, and shoved the assassin onto his back. She didn't even hesitate as she quickly ripped the mask off his face, but by then, it was too late.

The man's face was *melting*.

His features were far too damaged to ever make out what he used to look like, and the copious amounts of blood leaking out of his mouth would have been reassurance enough that he was dead all on its own. Its black color and sludge-like quality was only further confirmation.

"Poison," Olivia spat, looking incredibly angry. "Potent and fast-acting. He was dead before he even hit the ground. Probably had a suicide pill in his mouth the entire time."

Rowan didn't respond.

What was there to say after someone had stabbed him in the back, slit his throat, and then committed suicide?

The man was clearly a professional instead of some opportunistic idiot who got paid a couple of gold coins to take out the annoying new mayor. That only left one question: Who?

Rowan assisted Olivia with trying to find the assassin's identity. The man's skin was spotless, his pockets empty of everything but the tools of his trade, and even those were rather nondescript.

Hells, even the potions were bog-common, the only hint that there was something special about the man being the fact that he had them at all. Since not even the town's apothecary had them, that cast suspicion in the direction of the mercenary companies. But this could have just as well been an outsider sent by some noble to carry out the assassination mission.

The final clue was the blades, but those had been sent ahead. Still, no matter how useless the corpse was, Rowan wasn't about to leave it behind.

"There's very little useful information I can offer you about these weapons," Camilla Sutton said, handling the two short swords gently.

"Nothing at all? There's no assassin order that exclusively uses blades like it or something?" Rowan sighed, knowing that it was absolutely a ridiculous long shot after how prepared the assassin had been.

That coaxed a smile out of Olivia's mother, but she shook her head nonetheless. "I'm afraid not. They're obviously enchanted, and enchanted well. Honestly? These are nearly on par with blades I'd feel comfortable using myself. And I'm at Epic."

"Isn't there a chance we could use that to learn more? People capable of crafting weapons like that aren't common," Olivia pointed out, somehow angrier over the assassination than Rowan himself was.

"They might not be common, but every serious noble house has one in their employ. The only thing this tells us is that your would-be assassin was well connected. The weapons don't have a crafter's mark, for obvious reasons, so hunting down the person who made them is very much a bust," Camilla said.

"What about finding the person who sent this guy? I mean, I know that security hasn't been the best in the town since its near destruction, but I don't think someone this powerful and high level can just operate out of town without being noticed," Rowan asked.

"What makes you so sure he was unnoticed or that he wasn't a native?" the baroness countered, sounding tired. "I am unfortunately fairly certain that he was both known and a local."

Rowan leaned forward immediately, eyes glowing hungrily. "You know him?"

"Know him? Hardly. However, you might remember that I've mentioned a ton of problems in the town, mostly in the form of illegal activity. This place is rife with it. Frontier towns are prone to problems as it is, but this . . . I honestly don't know what the previous mayor was doing."

"It's that bad?"

"It's that bad. Managing this town has been a headache. Black markets operating in open air, contraband that was banned kingdom-wide, disregarding of laws, including protection of commoners and lower-tier individuals, and so, so much more."

Olivia went around the desk and offered her mom a hug.

"I apologize," the baroness sighed. "It feels like a lifetime since I came to Rest's Remorse. Anyway, for your question, Rowan, I'm pretty sure there are underground guilds and a couple of black companies operating in this town."

Rowan had no clue what she was talking about, but judging by the gasps and concerned faces, it was pretty important.

"Care to clue in the guy who's not from your world?" Rowan asked.

"Right, sorry. Underground guilds and black companies are, as their names imply, illegal gatherings of people who cannot afford to appear openly in view of both local and international laws."

Camilla paused there, but Olivia was thankfully ready to fill in. "They have banned classes. Some of their members are also wanted criminals, traitors, and fugitives. But the biggest problem is definitely the banned classes."

With a flicker of unease, Rowan recalled what Olivia had said when she reassured him that no one would try to kill him just because his class name sounded edgy. "What are those, exactly? I've already seen some classes that sound . . . sketchy. Including my own."

"Oh, not yours," Olivia said as a look of understanding dawned on her face. "Banned classes are those that are either outright malignant or whose unlocking requirements are so vile no one will tolerate their holders. The most relevant of those, for you, are demonic classes. They belong to those who accept demonic Heart Cards and use them to replace their own."

While Olivia explained things, the baroness moved off to one of the cabinets that lined the walls of her temporary office and pulled out a tall bottle of wine and five cups. Rowan raised an eyebrow as Camilla distributed the drinks before collapsing back into her chair with a weary sigh.

"What Olivia is missing is that once a corrupted or demonic Heart Card is accepted, the process warps the user's class, too. These classes are often extremely powerful but come at the cost of the person's sanity or humanity. All the people who use them either go mad or gradually transform into demons themselves. Any time we find one, they're immediately placed on cross-kingdom bounty lists and hunted on sight."

Rowan nodded. "Checks out. What about examples of banned classes? Is it stuff like [Necromancer] and the like?"

It was Milena who made a noise of disgust, rolling her eyes so hard that Rowan swore she almost lost them. "Oh, please. People always say stuff like that, but necromancy is a perfectly valid and innocent profession. Just because they handle corpses doesn't make them evil."

"True," the baroness interceded. "The classes I'm talking about are much, much worse. [Plague Adherent], for example. To unlock that particular evolution of [Apothecary], you need to purposefully infect at least two hundred people with a deathly illness. Then, there's the other vile classes, like those that let their users steal stats through torture and other depraved rituals."

Rowan shuddered, suddenly realizing that he definitely didn't know as much about his new world as he likely should have. But his mind made the connection to something more immediate. "What about [Blood Reaver]? That definitely doesn't sound like something you'd get for behaving lawfully."

Unfortunately, the baroness just shook her head. "The class has had negative connotations historically. Most earned it through pillage, rape, and slaughter. However, it *is* possible to unlock it through particularly vicious culling of monsters, which Florin claims he's done."

"I doubt that," Marcus muttered, wrinkling his nose. "He smells like he takes regular baths in blood and then rolls around in the corpses afterward."

"There have been aspersions as to the veracity of his claims, but nothing was ever proven," Camilla said. Rowan had noticed some time ago that the baroness had a tendency to fall back on formal language when upset.

"So what's our best option?" Rowan asked. "Is there anything that we can do? I mean, I'm the mayor, and he's in my town."

"Not many like Florin, but many rely on his services. He's been building connections to various nobles for decades. The only reason he isn't at Epic already is because, even for him, paying for or earning access to an Epic-ranked dungeon under noble management is highly improbable. That's the safer option, and he's enough of a coward to continue working toward it instead of looking for a proper fight out in the wastes. Too risky for him."

The answer was clear. Florin, whether he was a monster or not, was out of their reach.

"What is he even doing here, then?" Rowan asked. "The wastes are right next to us, and this place was recently invaded by an army of demons. If he hates risk so much, why stay? Why come here in the first place?"

"Good question. The simple answer is, I don't know. I've written to my husband and some of my contacts, but it will take time for any replies to get to us. This *is* highly unusual, however. I thought the Mercenary King was the only major player in town, only to find Florin and *Tamara*, of all people."

Rowan noticed the slight emphasis that Camilla put on the name Tamara. He sneaked a glance at Olivia, but his friend's face betrayed nothing but concern for her mother. The baroness had history with the mage. But Rowan wasn't about to go poking his nose into her business, seeing as he had no interest in losing it.

"So what do we do?" Rowan asked.

No one had any answers. Thankfully, the silence was interrupted by a knock at the door. The chamberlain strolled into the room, looking unflappable as ever.

"Please tell me you have some good news for us," Rowan said.

"I'm afraid not, Lord Rowan. I've done as you asked and checked the body after organizing a search in the area where you were attacked. The results, though, are less than ideal," the chamberlain said.

"Let me guess, no discernible proof of affiliation on the body, and absolutely no clues on where this guy came from?"

"Well, that is close enough, my lord, yes." The chamberlain hesitated. "However, it appears that the man who attacked you *was* spotted before."

Instantly, the old man became the center of undivided attention in the room. "Don't keep us in suspense," Olivia said tensely, and Rowan didn't like the way her hand twitched toward her potion bag.

"The assassin was seen hanging around the city gate you were regularly using for the last few days. He did nothing of note, loitering around and occasionally purchasing some food. He never spoke, never took off his mask, and would vanish after purchasing a meal."

Rowan cursed quietly and paced in the confines of the room. The information made him feel stupid.

He knew there were people unhappy with his presence in the town. He also knew that they might eventually try to do something about it.

In spite of that, he'd happily traipsed his way into the wastes and back on the same route every single day. Frankly, it was a bit of a wonder that he hadn't been attacked earlier.

It wasn't that Rowan was still angry over the fact that he was attacked. That was unpleasant and it hurt. Still, out of the entirety of their party, he was uniquely suited to surviving the ordeal. Even Marcus, if he was caught off guard and the right weapon and poison combo was used, would die more easily than him.

It was the thought that others could have gotten caught up in the mess that got to him.

What if Olivia had been right next to him and the assassin decided to slit her throat instead of his? After all, most of the time, stabbing someone through the heart was more than enough to keep them down.

I haven't taken enough precautions. I haven't organized the army right. I even broke them all up into groups, increasing the odds of an attack. I—

"Rowan!" Olivia's voice snapped Rowan out of his daze, and he froze, rooted to the spot. "Are you back with us now?" Olivia was standing right in front of him and looking him in the eye.

Rowan swallowed thickly and looked away. "Yes. Sorry. Did you say something?"

"We were just talking about increasing patrols and boosting the numbers of guards and soldiers traveling together at the same time. It might not do much, but it might discourage something as blatant as this."

"I also believe it would be a good idea to have them on the look-out for anyone suspicious," the chamberlain supplied. "If we'd known about someone watching the gate, then we could have acted earlier."

The baroness disagreed. "No. That would be a waste of time and manpower. How do we even define suspicious? With the number of homeless and destitute in this town, we'd be shaking down every poor soul that dares loiter in place for too long. They don't deserve that, and it would be pointless besides."

"We should offer a reward," Rowan said, eyes sparkling as he happened upon the perfect idea.

"A reward? For reporting suspicious activity?" The doubt and disapproval in the baroness's voice were more than enough to communicate her opinion on the matter.

"Not that. We should offer a reward for every actionable piece of information people can give us on the assassin. Even if he was loitering around the gate for the last few days, where was he before that? He's not a wraith. He must have traveled through the town to get there. He *lived* here."

"That . . . could work, but, my lord, I'm afraid we don't exactly have a lot of resources to pull on for this," Henry said, sounding more than a little apologetic.

"Then don't. Offer a meal to everyone who comes to report something and tell them that they'll get an Uncommon card if their words lead to anything. I have more than enough of those for now. I bet we get something useful out of all the reports before I run out."

"You might just get a bunch of fake reports," Camilla said.

"But it could also work," Rowan insisted.

"True. Do it, Henry. Leave the cards you are planning to use for that with me, Rowan," Camilla said.

Rowan turned over the stack of cards he'd earned that way and looked at the chamberlain again. He had been so absorbed with his own problems that he didn't even remember the man's name. Rowan had always thought of the man as the chamberlain instead of his real name.

"This will certainly be helpful. Any cards that you're not planning to use, scrap, or trade, I suggest handing over to me. Not just as rewards but in general," the baroness advised them all. Then, apparently losing patience with them, she motioned toward the door. "Go rest. There's nothing else we can do today."

They complied.

Rowan headed straight for his room, having taken a quick bath to get rid of all the blood when they arrived. On the way there, however, he had his hand stolen by a certain alchemist.

When she followed him into his room and cuddled up into him, he didn't protest. That had stopped back when her parents arrived at Felton's Mill, but that night, Rowan slept better than he had in weeks.

CHAPTER THIRTEEN

To Track an Assassin

When the first day passed without any results, Rowan thought that the assassination attempt was going to meet a quiet end. He obviously didn't know Camilla Sutton, the woman who had once struck fear into the minds of all who opposed her family as duchess, well enough.

As day after day passed with little information, Camilla's dormant coals of frustration grew into a bonfire of anger. She began taking actions that she probably would have otherwise avoided.

Suddenly, businesses were hit by fines and legal trouble, mercenary companies found their services rebuffed, and certain key establishments, especially those under the mayoral office's purveyance, were refusing to service outsiders entirely.

The last point became a pretty big deal, especially in a town where everyone was at least nominally loyal to the mayor. The mercenaries would soon find themselves running low on supplies, and when that happened, it was anyone's guess as to what would happen.

"Still no information?" Rowan asked as he signed the latest orders drafted by Camilla that imposed even more restrictions on the mercenaries. The baroness was playing a dangerous game, but it was one Rowan supported wholeheartedly.

"Nothing useful. But with more pressure, someone's bound to step forward," Camilla answered.

"Do we really need to keep staying inside?" Olivia hissed. "Unless they bring an Epic, no one's going to be able to touch us."

"Olivia, you do realize there are people who want you dead out there, and there are more ways to kill a person than in straight combat. Especially when you're going to be parading in front of them willingly?" Camilla countered.

In moments like these, it was easy to see that the baroness wasn't just worried about Rowan's life. There was a very real fear that next someone would go after her daughter, who was nowhere near as well equipped to survive having her heart destroyed as the hero was.

"People have wanted to kill me my whole life." Olivia tried a different tack. "You can't tell me otherwise! The first time someone tried to poison me, I was two years old. I know that for a fact because you keep reminding me of it."

Rowan choked a little on the tea his chamberlain had handed to him.

"Exactly. And I've kept you alive through all that. Don't you think I am keenly aware of what it will take to keep you breathing?" Camilla brushed off Olivia's argument with ease.

"Mother, I love you, but I will not abandon the people I consider friends and the responsibilities I've taken on in favor of sitting pretty and safe in my room."

"You are also free to sit in this office. Maybe finally take the time to learn about governance for once. Seeing as you seem to be keen on eventually marrying a hero, it's only fair to learn how to act as a lady in your own right," Camilla said, her words finding their mark with deadly accuracy.

Olivia sputtered and Rowan gave a sheepish grin. He noticed that she didn't actually protest. It was sort of hard to argue the fact that they'd spent the last three days going to bed together. They hadn't done anything but cuddle and sleep, of course.

"We've already increased the security around the town," Rowan said. For the time being, he resolved to put his feelings on the subject aside and help sort out the argument. "We'll alternate our routes out of and coming back into Rest's Remorse. But we can't very well abandon all the plans we have, both for the sake of personal growth and the growth of our troops."

For just a moment, the baroness's eyes flared with something cold and wrathful. Fortunately for Rowan, she took a moment to breathe before speaking up again.

"If I find out you took unnecessary risks, any unnecessary risks at all, you won't need to worry about demons getting to you. Do you two understand me?" Camilla said.

In spite of her mother's anger, Olivia looked nothing short of ecstatic as she bounded over to give her a hug, with quiet assurances that she would be fine, before fleeing the room to resume her regular preparations for the next day's hunting.

Rowan could have just fled himself. However, curiosity got the best of him. "Why? I mean, I'm glad you agreed, but why?"

"Because she's not just my daughter anymore," Olivia's mother admitted, pain in her voice. "She has her own goals and responsibilities now. If I continue pretending that's not the case, she'll just grow to resent me eventually."

Rowan couldn't find the words to respond to that. He nodded solemnly and managed a quick sentence before he left.

"I'll do my best to take care of her."

"We're almost done with the basic prep." Rowan's eyes glided over the rows of soldiers marching back to town, and there was no denying the surge of pride and happiness in him.

Within a week of starting their live training, the recruits were already showing remarkable results and becoming real soldiers. However, higher levels only told part of the story, and a very incomplete one, at that.

All the new soldiers were now at Uncommon. One very rare and very valuable class had even been dragged up to Rare. In the spear division, one of the soldiers had managed to land [Standard Bearer] at the Uncommon tier. In its Rare form? It was a game changer.

"Only the basics, hmm? Not going to declare us ready to explore the wider area and even launch an expedition of our own?" Olivia teased, but Rowan could detect a hint of underlying seriousness.

He hesitated. "We might be able to, honestly. We have a lot of Rare classes, which is rare enough in any army, apparently. The additional recruits we just got would make things a whole lot easier, too. But if we bite off more than we can chew, the whole thing could collapse," Rowan said. "We can't afford a defeat. Not yet."

"Then we'll stay the path," Olivia declared. "We have time. We don't need to rush into any decisions yet."

"We have some time. Which is slipping away from us already." Rowan sighed and took a moment to look around.

Thanks to Camilla, the town was in a better state. Most of the rubble had been cleared, while the collapsed houses had been demolished and scavenged for any and all useful material. In other words, the town looked cleaner, and the plots of land where houses once stood showed promise of a better future.

"You're worried about the expedition?" Olivia guessed.

"Yeah," Rowan admitted. "It's better if we face the challenge head-on, like we've been doing."

"You mean I'll be forced to watch while you do something borderline suicidal?" Olivia quipped, and Rowan's face twitched slightly. Recently, Olivia had begun using comments and other little things to remind him when he stepped too far out of line.

It happened when he did or said something stupid, just like when he charged an odd-looking Rare-tier mud-crab monster that almost bisected him with its claws. Learning what exactly would happen if he took damage like that wasn't in his plans for the day, so after a quick use of **Blood for Blood**, Rowan emerged victorious and in one piece.

That did get him thinking about the limits of **Natural Renewal** combined with **Lavish Feasting**. Knowing what he could survive was important in judging the risks he could take for the future. But that experiment would have to wait.

"I'm not sure I want to wait until the kingdom forces the issue. If we leave early, we can decide what to do instead of having to follow their demands," Rowan explained.

"That . . . makes sense, I suppose. Our king hasn't been very sensible or reasonable as of late," Olivia grumbled, no doubt thinking about her father's political position. Rowan knew he didn't have the full picture there, and whenever he tried to subtly ask, she would rebuff him.

Politely, but firmly.

"Do you think we could have everything ready to go in a couple of days? I realize this might not be the ideal timing, but then again, it might be useful to get out of town while your mother figures out the assassination attempt," Rowan asked.

"Possibly. You do remember that you asked me to prepare a whole lot of different, often highly situational, potions, right?"

"I know."

Rowan tensed slightly as he noticed a few pairs of eyes watching him. At the moment, they were too far to be a threat. Ever since the assassination attempt, they were giving assailants no easy opportunities.

For starters, the hero party stuck together, no longer disbanding to optimize the army training schedule. That meant Rowan was under Marcus's meticulous aura protection at all times. The shield bearer's ability to use his aura as a damage sponge was prodigious. His own vitality stats allowed him to shrug off damage that would take his sister's or Olivia's life.

Second, Rowan had his own healing combination. He made sure to never overtax **Lavish Feasting** during normal fighting. The extra energy from the card might be the difference between life and death.

And third, the group was in the middle of an entire army. Around them were rows of soldiers, all looking ready for war and pretty pissed at the prospect of someone trying to kill their mayor. Rowan's soldiers, new and old, really did seem to love him. A part of that was self-interest in that Rowan was willing to share experience and card drops. But there also seemed to be a deeper loyalty; they were following a hero who genuinely had their best interests in mind.

"I just hope something happens soon. Mom is going to be absolutely enraged if we fail to discover anything in the end, and trust me, no one wants to deal with her when she's like that."

Olivia's words were nearly prophetic, since the baroness's mood dipped lower and lower the longer they went without results. This, in turn, resulted in harsher treatment for the guilds and companies in the town.

Finally, it got bad enough that Camilla won a Pyrrhic victory.

"They're finally starting to crack. I knew they would, eventually, but I was really starting to think I'd have to do something drastic to bring them to that point," Camilla explained to Rowan and Olivia after they returned from their latest leveling trip.

Rowan didn't want to imagine what *drastic* meant to the baroness. Half the taxation documents he had stamped were severe enough that the town's own income was suffering.

"What did they say?" Olivia asked.

"That two-bit mage and the Mercenary King messaged us. The latter to show support and deny any and all involvement in the attack. The former to express her condolences and apologies over not being more useful for our investigation. The problem is, I think they're being sincere," Camilla said.

"That's a good thing, right?" Rowan asked, failing to see the reason why the news was making the baroness frown so much. "I thought we wanted more allies."

"Yes, but we're never going to have that . . . mage on our side. The same applies to the Blood Reaver. They'd both sell us out in a second if they could. The Mercenary King is different, of course, but . . ."

But he was also the Mercenary King. The man had already stated that he wasn't going to help in the expeditions. Short of a miracle, nothing was going to budge the troops under the Mercenary King.

"What about the Blood Reaver? Has he contacted us?"

"No." Camilla looked conflicted. "It's pretty obvious he knows something."

"So he's our main suspect?"

"Not yet. There's something here that I'm missing. Something that explains all this."

It was another day before a letter from Florin arrived, expressing his regret over the attack and the difficulties they were facing due to the less scrupulous members of the mercenary profession. He didn't share any relevant information about the assassination attempt. Just a bland letter for the sake of sending a letter.

Just a couple hours after Florin's letter, a second one, from Tamara, arrived.

Rowan and the rest of the hero party were summoned to Camilla's office and found the baroness stalking around the room in short, frighteningly controlled steps.

Taking the letter, Rowan's eyes caught on the relevant paragraphs quite easily in spite of the rambling nature of the text itself.

It has come to my attention that certain less trustworthy members of my new profession have taken residence in the Rose's Delight inn. Their activities have been growing increasingly rowdy as of late, which is why my apprentices heard about them.

I've taken the liberty of looking into them, at least superficially. I have to say that they are worryingly well equipped, and that it seems like they won't be running out of funds any time soon.

They certainly don't seem to think so, if the way they're acting is anything to judge by.

The rest of the letter, before and after those lines, was useless.

"What does this mean?" Rowan asked. "'Well equipped.' 'Won't run out of funds soon.' Does that mean there's a noble backing them?"

"Most definitely," Camilla answered. "I bet she knows who. But she's dangling that information in front of us as bait. She'll never tell us. She just wants to know how much we know."

"And what do we know?" Rowan said.

"Not enough."

Rowan resisted the urge to frown. These days, his emotions didn't bubble up to his face as often. It had started back at the village when Bron taught him about what it meant to lead men. Slowly but surely, Rowan was getting better control of his emotions, even without **Keen Spear**.

The current situation was sorely testing his patience, though. If there was another faction backed by nobles in the town, that just made the whole situation a lot more complicated.

"I say we hit first," Olivia said. "Honestly, I can whip up some kind of fire accelerant. More homes around here are made of stone, but it's not impossible for them to catch fire. Have them meet us on our territory."

Rowan looked at Olivia blankly for several moments before her suggestion caught up with him. "Olivia! We're not committing arson. Especially with bystanders in the building."

His slightly murderous alchemist sighed. "You're right. It would be awfully hard to get any evidence if it all went up in flames."

The baroness had the inn watched while Rowan put things in place, soldiers strategically moving into the district in pairs of twos and threes.

It was a hard task. The Rose's Delight inn was too central on the street where it was located, and soldiers didn't make for the best spies. Still, by some miracle, the enemy group didn't notice them. People came and went from the inn, armored but not jumpy.

For the last two hours, Rowan decided to watch the inn himself. At first, things looked normal, but as time went on, fewer and fewer people began to exit the somewhat large building.

They know. I don't know how, but they know we're here. And now they're preparing a counterattack, Rowan thought. He signaled for the rest of his party to be alert.

As the minutes passed and nothing happened, Rowan began to doubt his judgment. He started to develop a slight headache. One second he was staring at an innocuous person crossing the street, and the next, he was blinking stars out of his eyes. He forced himself to relax, and when he finally unclenched his shoulder muscles, the pain in his head eased, too.

"We should go," Olivia whispered.

"Everyone's in position? Perimeter is set up? I don't want any of them escaping," Rowan asked.

"Not even a mouse can slip through undetected," Olivia confirmed.

"Then let's do it."

Rowan gave the signal, and soldiers popped up from their hiding spots. One more hand movement and everyone was charging toward the inn.

The hero party was in full fighting formation as it burst through the door of the inn. Marcus was in the lead with Rowan just behind. Olivia and Milena were side by side in the back, ready to give support if they encountered a foe.

They didn't.

Rowan slowed down his steps as he took in the inside of the inn. It was a charnel house. There wasn't a single surface that wasn't stained in blood in some way.

The teams of mercenaries, oddly well equipped but otherwise unremarkable, were sitting around the tables. Most of them still had half-full drinks in front of them. Some of the mercenaries had managed to react and died with a weapon in hand. It didn't seem to make a difference, seeing how they'd still died in the end.

Near the back of the room was the person Rowan assumed to be the leader. She was a head taller than everyone else and had been nursing a pint of lager when she died. Her killer had somehow dealt a lethal blow before she could even put down her drink, and she bled with the tankard still in her hand. Blood spooled out of her wounds and dripped onto the table and floor below.

The worst, for Rowan at least, were the staff.

One of the terrified waiters was nailed to the wall by an ax that had been driven through his stomach, handle first. A waitress lay on the floor, her apron the only thing distinguishing her from the mercenaries. Another waitress and what he assumed was the matron of the establishment were slumped over the counter that served as the divider between the tavern and the kitchen.

With morbid curiosity, Rowan noted that the attacker had broken off the leg of a chair and driven it through the matron's eye as the killing blow.

No one spoke, for a little while.

"How? We were all out there. We saw some of these people enter the inn!" Marcus whispered. "We should have heard or seen something."

The slaughter had happened right under their noses.

Rowan glanced back at the soldiers still crowding the doorway and realized they needed to control the situation.

"Officers only. Everyone else, stay back. Spread out. Look upstairs. Actually, scratch that, we'll take the upper floor. Stay here and don't let anyone else come or go," Rowan commanded.

Now that his hasty instructions were given, Rowan led the way up the stairs, cautious and angry. Marcus followed second. The formation felt instinctive. Marcus had a defensive aura, which meant that he could provide protection without encumbering Rowan's attacks. More importantly, the shield bearer in the second spot meant he was closer to the girls and more readily capable of helping them.

The second floor was more of the same.

Every single room had a corpse or two, save for the ones that were completely empty.

The trend continued until they reached the final room and realized that it had once been a mix of bedroom and study. Rowan used the word *once* because the room had been entirely ransacked.

Papers were strewn all about the floor, furniture was broken and shattered, making the floor a minefield of splinters, and, Rowan noted, there were a few dying embers in the room's fireplace.

"Shit, they burned everything," Rowan cursed.

"What about these papers?" Marcus bent down to pick up some of them.

"Probably useless." Rowan crouched down to look. Most were blank, and the ones that had writing on them talked about mundane things. It was a dead end. Someone had beaten them to the inn and made sure that nothing, person or paper, could give Rowan a clue about who'd been here. "Shit."

Rowan sent some of the officers still on the first floor to pick up the papers and comb through them for any hints of who the mercenaries were or what they were doing in Rest's Remorse. On instinct, he called in a couple of the soldiers and pointed at the corpses.

"Search them. If you know anyone who has a Heart Card good for this kind of stuff, bring them. Anything goes," Rowan said.

Almost as soon as his voice fell, a hand near the back of the crowd of soldiers shot up. Rowan motioned the soldier to the front and was surprised to see Clarke.

"I found this in one of the bodies near the door. I thought he looked funny. He had this in his mouth," Clarke said as he offered a bundle of fabric forward.

Rowan took the fabric and gently unfurled the strands to reveal what it held. After a few passes, he found that the fabric had a pattern and held a signet ring. Both had the same symbol—an eye, rays of sunlight forming lashes, and a crown hovering at the top.

"How did you think to look there?" Rowan asked.

"Um, you met the doctor. Before I became a soldier, he had me helping with all sorts of things while we took care of these two." Clarke motioned at his party members. "Lots of the little ones used to try and hide meds in their mouths, and especially under the tongue. So, I guess I picked up a thing or two. His face just looked . . . off."

"You certainly did. Thank you," Rowan stated honestly, still eyeing the crest before turning to Olivia and arching his brow.

"Can't help you much here, I'm afraid," Olivia answered. "That doesn't belong to a noble, but that's all I can tell you. I'm not exactly up-to-date enough with illegal guilds and mercenary companies to be of help. What I can tell you is that what we found was put there by the man himself."

"So, you mean, he wanted someone to find the crest? That why he stuffed it in his mouth?"

"Judging by the torn and desecrated bodies of some of these corpses around us, yes. It seems like every shred of their affiliation was removed and carefully destroyed. He probably wanted someone to know at least a hint of truth about this place."

Now that she pointed it out and Rowan looked more closely, it was true. Lines that were far too pale around people's fingers showed where they used to wear bands just like the one in his hands. Patches of clothes where an insignia should have gone were also missing.

Rowan just stared at the trinkets the man had so desperately wanted to safeguard and promised that he would get to the bottom of everything. No matter what it took.

CHAPTER FOURTEEN

A Moment of Levity

The aftermath of the massacre was enough to disrupt the whole town for days to come.

Someone had slipped under the nose of the army, including the hero party, and slaughtered a whole inn's worth of people before slipping out unnoticed. All Rowan had for his efforts was a symbol hidden by a dead man.

"Why did I have to open my mouth and suggest a festival?" Rowan complained, dodging yet another thorn-covered vine on his way out of the wastes.

"Because you're worried and you like to do nice things. To be fair, though, the jury is still out on the topic of your intelligence," Olivia teased, light on her feet and words because she wasn't contributing to the transport of their hunt's haul.

"I thought your mother was going to order a massacre," Rowan protested. "I said the first thing that came to my mind."

When Camilla Sutton had heard about what happened, she was absolutely livid. The fact that someone had ventured into their town and done such a thing? She was ready to flip the town upside down to find the culprit. It was beyond the fact that someone had tried to assassinate the hero. It implied that someone or some force had strong, durable roots in the local settlement and that no one was safe in the long term, from mayor to maid.

"She wouldn't have done that," Olivia said, serious now. "Someone who could do all that while we were outside would have to be either a very strong Rare or Epic. Even if we turned Rest's Remorse upside down, we wouldn't find them."

"Either way, I'm glad we're having a festival instead of some kind of austerity," Rowan said. He had suggested the event to alleviate the mood of the town.

The only silver lining of the massacre was that Rowan had positioned the army to stop bystanders from wandering into the street, which meant that news hadn't spread throughout the town. As far as most people in Rest's Remorse knew, their mayor and hero had suffered an assassination attempt and this was a triumph against the enemy.

An exciting, *positive* public event was just the sort of idea that Rowan's tired brain could come up with to turn the mood of the town around.

That was why, for the first time since their training outings into the wastes, the army was hauling monster parts back to the town. They had elected to leave corpses behind in the past to stay nimble. But today, they needed to show their progress in more substantial forms.

The only ones spared from having to lug dead monsters were the support classes with the wrong stat distribution to meaningfully contribute. At the moment, there were exactly three of those in the army, a shaman, an alchemist, and a standard bearer.

"Are you sure I can't help out somehow, my lord?" the anxious-looking standard bearer inquired.

"You get to sit out today, Burke. Just be quiet and happy for it. Trust me, you don't want to be carrying a bunch of meat around in the humid confines of a jungle," Rowan said.

Burke was, like Rayne, one of Rowan's unexpected finds in the army. Even when nothing wrong was happening, the man looked vaguely worried. Burke claimed it was his eyebrows. They did, admittedly, give his entire face a complexion of quiet concern. Rowan thought it was more than that. The eyebrows didn't help, but Burke had a permanent slouch, like he was expecting a blow at any time, and would wring his hands like something was on his mind.

But appearances were deceiving. The man was one of the bravest and most loyal soldiers of Rowan's army. Burke had received the class and embraced it about as well as anyone could have. Although his physical stats were far behind his peers, he would charge ahead of the army, inspire bravery, and offer buffs to the men and women behind him.

"Maybe we should get you some more monster meat to carry, hmm, Rowan?" Olivia teased.

Rowan ignored her. If it wasn't for the fact that they'd be heading to the square immediately after their return for the planned festivities, Rowan would have liked to spend a solid hour straight washing himself.

Thankfully, it wasn't long before they broke through the cover of trees, and today, the outline of the town in the distance was practically glowing.

The people under Camilla had gone full out on the preparations for the day. In spite of the approaching night, the town was brighter than ever. The sounds of song and music even carried all the way to the army.

As the army drew closer to the gate, they were greeted by a myriad of happy and hungry faces. Rowan's soldiers fanned out and surrounded the hero party, keeping them firmly in the middle of the press of bodies.

Rowan waited until they were close enough that he could see the eyes of the town's residents and hear their words.

"People of Rest's Remorse," Rowan called out. "Your army has returned. We've slain the monsters plaguing this town and taken the best cuts. The meat is for you. Only by sticking together through thick and thin can we rise above the demons. Enjoy."

In less than a few minutes after entering the town, most of the soldiers were relieved of their burdens. The citizens, like an industrious line of ants, quickly funneled the meat toward the town center, where bonfires blazed. The group of soldiers with Rowan's party in the middle of the army moved slower, but that was mostly owed to Rowan refusing to relinquish his own pile of monster parts.

Part of that came down to him wanting to finish the journey on his own. Part was guarding his party's portion of the upcoming meals, since an assassin could easily find a chance to apply poison. Finally, a very frustrating chunk of this came from Camilla's advice.

She wanted people to see their hero working and sweating to provide for them. Even if none of them personally ate the meat he brought in, it would leave an impression that said their new mayor was doing his best to help the town. It was more than a little manipulative, but Rowan saw no legitimate reason to deny her request. Town management, he was learning, was full of these small tricks that chained together to something greater.

Once they finally made it to the square, Rowan dropped his burden and fully appreciated what Camilla Sutton had been able to organize.

The festivities weren't overly ostentatious, or even a true festival at all. However, the baroness had sourced chefs to cook all the meat and there was plenty of drink to go around. That appeared to be all the people of Rest's Remorse really needed.

After making sure that his meal was well guarded, Rowan made his way toward Camilla. Ironically, the baroness responsible for the festival stuck to the stage that had been erected for recruitment and kept herself separate from the celebratory mood. Rowan watched as she nursed a drink and scanned the crowd, pausing only on the mercenaries who were enjoying the atmosphere.

"You think they'll cause trouble?" Rowan asked.

"Hmm?" Camilla blinked before refocusing on the hero. "Oh no, they wouldn't dare. But it's good for them to know that I'm watching them. Metaphorically and literally."

"Got it. Remind me never to cross you," Rowan deadpanned.

A slight smile graced Camilla's face as she turned away from Rowan and stood, pulling herself to her full height above the crowd below.

"A moment of your attention, please!" As always, Camilla's voice carried easily, seemingly with no real effort on her part. The festival slowed to a halt as conversations quickly disappeared. "I would like to take a moment to thank Hero Rowan for helping organize this event. Your new mayor has both graciously provided the food for this gathering . . . and offered up the cards he and his party have fought and bled for in order to make the event more exciting!"

Of course, every single soul, from the most hopeless commoner to the most excited mercenary, knew what she was talking about. The festival wasn't just about food and drink. They had attached an opportunity to the event: the card-trading market.

"As you may well know, for the next twenty-four hours, everyone is invited to relax, feast, and browse the cards on offer. We have an excellent collection of cards up to and including the Rare tier, as well as a significant number of scrap cards of every rarity for purchase.

"If you're lucky, you might just have the opportunity to set yourself and your family up for life! So, please, be merry and enjoy yourselves. I hope this will be a day you fondly remember for a very long time."

A deafening applause and roars of approval answered Camilla's speech, and Rowan let it push him into one of the plush, comfortable seats that had been set up on the stage.

Camilla walked back from the edge of the stage and saw Rowan's expression of content. "You look like you just avoided a fatal disaster."

"I really thought you were going to make me join you and give a speech," Rowan admitted. The prospect of talking to hundreds, even thousands, of people didn't terrify him quite as much as it used to, but if the goal was to relax and enjoy the day, he definitely didn't want to kick things off that way.

"Not today." Camilla had a small smile on her lips. "Rowan, you know, you've been nothing but surprises for me. At first I thought that you were just going to be another hero who came to our world for a quick trip. But you weren't. So today, you get to spend time with my daughter and simply enjoy yourself. Next time, though? It'll be you giving the speech instead of me. You know that you're at the center of all this."

Rowan knew. He really did. With everything that was coming, he could hardly afford to pretend that he could stay by the side forever. The different clashing spheres of influence, desire, and thirst for power all had him in the middle. So far, he'd even taken some of the power for himself, even if it was only to protect the people he cared about.

"I think I'll ask Olivia to take a walk with me," Rowan tried, giving Camilla another look.

"Just remember what I told you about security. You can't very well be of use to anyone if you're not around anymore."

Rowan didn't reply, but he did subtly motion at some of the soldiers who were still on-duty for the current shift to follow at a respectable yet actionable distance. Quite frankly, though, he didn't see as much point in it as Olivia's mother did.

The two of them were stronger than most soldiers. So if anyone could protect Olivia, it would be him. In spite of that, it was better to keep the baroness happy.

Rowan found Olivia easily enough. She was just a short distance away, chatting with an older lady who was roasting the meat they'd brought in. She was using a custom blend of spices, which he figured was the reason she'd caught Olivia's eye in the first place.

Rowan paused. He watched the way Olivia's face flickered in the firelight, the way she was relaxed and at ease for the first time in a considerable time. Some of that underlying tension was still there, but for the first time in a while, she wasn't thinking about how to kill monsters or practice chucking her combat potions.

I should do more events like this. If only for what it does for Olivia.

A few moments later, Olivia somehow felt his eyes on her and looked around. Their eyes met. Rowan's feet took him closer to her.

"Would you like to walk around with me? Just the two of us? As a date?"

Rowan waited. He could feel each beat of his heart in his ears. He wondered how he could possibly be so bad at the whole thing. It wasn't his first experience with dating, but it sure *felt* like he was doing it all anew. For the first time, Rowan wondered what his intelligence and wisdom stats were doing.

All they seemed to do was make his mana pool bigger or speed up his mana regeneration.

"I'd absolutely love that," Olivia chirped. Before Rowan knew what was happening, they were strolling down the street, each with a skewer of meat in their hands.

Rowan took a tentative bite and remembered the day he'd first tried the corrupted squirrel. There was no question that Olivia had good taste. The skewers with the lady's special spice blend were scrumptious. He tried to commit the seller's face to memory, but it kept escaping him. He was just happy to be spending time with Olivia, alone.

"What's your favorite memory?"

"Hmm?" Olivia gave him a confused look, like the route he was taking through their conversation didn't fit her expectations.

"We've been training and fighting ever since we got to know each other. It's been nonstop." Rowan lifted his hand and brought Olivia's with his. "But this is nice. I really like this. Right now is probably one of my favorite memories since I came to this world."

Olivia's face went blank as she took a moment to think. "Before all this. Back when Father was still a duke. Everyone was always busy, Mother, Father, and my brother, but one day, they took a break. It wasn't even a holiday or a birthday or anything. We just spent the time together and went on a picnic at a lake. It wasn't just us, but I remember how happy I was. I remember how wonderful the lake looked."

Halfway through the description, Rowan stiffened slightly for two very different reasons. The first was Olivia herself. She wasn't quite like him. Rowan never had a ton of friends, and for the most part, he was okay with that. She, on the other hand, thrived in the company of others. Sought it out. The second reason was because like Olivia, Rowan had a family. It was easy to forget that sometimes when fighting monsters with a spear, but he had been in this world for months now, alone. He also couldn't fully commit to staying. Not yet. So if their relationship progressed and one day the demon king was defeated?

Rowan shook his head, refusing to think about that.

"What about you? Favorite memory?" Olivia asked back.

It took a while for Rowan to shake his thoughts back into place. When they did, he dug through them for a cherished memory. "It was when I got my own apartment for the first time. Think of a castle, but a different person lives in every room. I was in college and I couldn't wait. Wait, do you know what college is?"

"Some kind of guild?" Olivia guessed.

"Close enough. Anyways, I had a terrible time at college before. Then I moved out to my own place and I got a pet cat. It was bliss. All alone with a nice warm drink and a feline friend. I was happy."

"That's fun," Olivia said as she shot him a grin and pulled food from a vendor and shoved it in his direction.

Rowan was about to warn about poison before remembering who he was with. If Olivia's experiments were anything to go by, she was an expert in all things toxic.

Fifteen minutes later, Rowan was regretting not stopping things sooner.

"This fruit juice. I haven't had it since I was a kid," Olivia said, radiant as ever. "You should try it."

"I'm going to puke if I eat anything else," Rowan tried.

"Juice doesn't count." Olivia thrust the drink forward again. "Come on. Just try a little sip."

Rowan took the fruit juice and drank it down. A small part of him hoped he would throw up on her shoes. To his chagrin, he both liked it and didn't puke.

It was the little things that made his evening. The way she smiled at him when she thought he wasn't looking. The way she grinned when she knew he was. And the way she pushed him out of his comfort zone and tried to get him to try as many things as possible.

Rowan could honestly say that he was having more fun with Olivia Sutton than he ever did with Blake and Kayla or their . . . final, half-forgotten friend who hadn't needed to go through the horrors of being summoned to another world.

Olivia knew it, too. She was gradually homing in on Rowan's tastes. At first, he liked about sixty percent of the stuff she was handing him. By the end, everything she gave him was wonderful, and each time, Olivia had a tiny smile on her face to go with the food.

Can I really go back to my own world when this is all over? Work a normal job and forget about the time I was a hero and fighting for my life? Or Olivia?

In that moment, Rowan wished desperately that he could take Olivia with him when he went back. But, even if that were possible, he'd be stealing her from everyone she knew and placing her in a very, very confusing society.

Olivia ran off to one of the food stalls to the side and bought a mountain of food. Before Rowan could protest, she took a giant bite, leaving cheap sauce all over her left cheek.

Olivia belongs in this world. And maybe, just maybe, so do I.

That kind of resolution felt like it should be accompanied by a sufficiently dramatic gesture. Rowan leaned in. Somehow, Olivia intuited what he was about to do. He could almost taste their last dish on her lips, even though their lips hadn't touched yet.

"I am so very glad that I could find you, Mayor Rowan." The cool voice of Tamara cut through the refreshing evening air, and Rowan jerked away from Olivia as quickly as he could.

Olivia spun around and glared at the disgraced mage with such vitriol it could have spontaneously turned into a deadly spell, or at least a potion recipe she could brew and poison the woman with later.

"Can I help you?" Rowan asked brusquely.

"Do I come at a wrong time?" Tamara asked, suddenly wary and a bit confused. She seemed to genuinely not understand what had almost happened before she arrived, so Rowan decided to cut her a bit of slack.

"No, it's fine. What did you want to say?" Rowan said.

"Hero Rowan, I want you to know I had nothing to do with the assassin. If you tried, you could probably dig up some kind of link between us. That's also true for every mercenary in this town. Not everything is as clean as people would like to pretend it is," said Tamara.

"And why are you telling me this?"

"Because, as far as I'm aware, we have common enemies, you and I."

"Who?"

"The person who believes she's the mayor."

"Really? What makes you think I'm against the parents of the girl I am honestly extremely fond of?" Rowan said, his anger coming back again.

"I'm not strictly opposed to your in-laws."

Rowan didn't even bother with the correction. "I'll note that you very carefully didn't say you're not opposed to me. That's a bit of a concerning start for an alliance, isn't it?"

The mage arched a brow as Rowan smiled back. *That's right, I'm a relatively quick study, and Camilla is scary when she wants you to memorize stuff like picking out hidden meanings in words.*

"I understand," Tamara said as she relaxed her shoulders. "Let me say this, then. I'm not directly opposed to you. I have my goals, yes, and have to represent the goals of certain interested parties. However, there's very little you have to worry about from me."

"And why should I believe you?" Rowan asked.

"Because I'm here."

"What about your fellows? The Blood Reaver and the Mercenary King?"

"I'm not sure, at least when it comes to Florin. The Mercenary King is, was, and always will be loyal to the letter of the law. Even if he's sometimes reluctant to follow through on the spirit of the agreements he's signed."

"The Mercenary King?" Rowan was really enjoying the use of these questions. He didn't need to offer any new information while extracting the maximum possible from the woman.

"It's a small thing. Unless you go around kicking kittens and puppies for fun, he won't bother you. He's rather fond of animals."

"And Florin?"

"Ah, yes, Florin. Good old Florin. Don't trust the snake, hero, no matter what he offers you. People tend to just die or disappear when it's convenient for him. Can't say too much on the subject of morality, because I'm not much better myself. But, if he lives by any kind of code or believes in loyalty, it's only to himself. First and foremost, always."

Rowan frowned. None of this was new information, but it almost sounded like she was sincerely trying to warn him of something. He took a second look at her. For a second, he wasn't sure if he was still talking to Tamara. This woman was far more open. Far easier to see through. Flecks of her emotions seeped through the facade like she was a novice at the art of negotiations. This didn't seem like it was the same woman he had met at the gathering.

Before Rowan could ask his next question, he was distracted by his spear. The weapon was turning cold and there was a cool stream trying to sneak up his arm. He looked down and noticed that it was struggling against something.

When the stream shattered against something strong and resilient, Rowan was suddenly the recipient of a mild headache. He looked to find Olivia stumbling slightly, slipping on the slight indentation of a sewer grate.

Rowan turned to face the mage. She was gone.

"Well, that was something. Suitably creepy. What was Tamara even trying to do?" Rowan muttered, drawing closer to Olivia.

"I think we need to talk to my mother about the whole thing," Olivia said, looking around to see if the woman was still next to them.

"You think it can wait?" Rowan asked.

Olivia shrugged. "It can wait. Whatever she or the Reaver wants to do, I doubt it'll happen tomorrow. We have better things to do today."

Indeed, they did.

The mood, after their near kiss, was far better. Rowan knew she was interested. And now, she knew Rowan was, too. From there, there was no reason to rush things.

They toured the celebration, checked out the cards people had traded, and even looked at the cards the mercenaries were peddling alongside the main attractions.

The selection wasn't great, and it catered mostly to Uncommon and Common classes. Still, it was something, and it definitely helped broaden Rowan's horizons on what cards made possible in his new world.

That evening, the two were once again together, and Rowan couldn't help but notice that for all the teasing, Olivia's family had never actively gotten in their way of exploring their feelings.

But with Olivia's warmth in his arms, that hardly seemed to matter.

He didn't even notice the ease with which he left his weapon by the door.

CHAPTER FIFTEEN

Duty

The next morning, Rowan realized that it was time.

He had dragged his feet the past few days with the festival and everything. He was as ready as he would ever be. It was time for him to do his duty, to lead expeditions into the waste.

With Olivia, he slipped into the meeting room with the chamberlain and the baroness and shared the good news.

"The preparations are mostly complete. The old army is now entirely at the Rare tier, and several of the most promising new recruits are starting to bump up against that tier as well," Rowan stated proudly.

Unfortunately, Rowan seemed to be the only one who was excited about that. The chamberlain was still doubtful of the effectiveness of putting so much experience into the hands of nonelites, while Camilla had grudgingly accepted Rowan's strategy. He still hoped that the results would win both of them over.

"I've also prepared enough potions to support an expedition, too," Olivia said, though the slight bags under her eyes showed she had pushed herself to accomplish that.

Of course, Rowan would have looked the same if it weren't for his regeneration card. After all, he woke up with her and watched her work, keeping her company.

"And you think you're ready?" Camilla asked. Rowan shook his head. "We only get one chance at this. We still have two weeks from when we need to make an expedition. You don't want to use all that time?"

"This is the best time," Rowan answered. "With the festival being a success, we need a show of might. If we wait and go out later, we risk new variables entering the equation."

"Fine," Camilla agreed, surprisingly easily. "But we can't do this quietly. Not when the whole kingdom is watching and waiting to see how you perform."

"I can't just slip out with the army without anyone knowing where we're going?" Rowan sighed, as he knew the answer to that. "Won't a big announcement open us up to ambushes? We still don't know who ordered the assassination, but that hardly matters when they can strike against us directly out in the wilderness. Especially if they know that we're going to be gone from the town for a while."

"Whoever they are, they're clearly worried about getting caught. This implies they at least can't risk publicly being seen as responsible." Camilla dissected her learnings. "They won't be able to act out of the ordinary, either. We haven't found them because they've entrenched themselves in the city. If they suddenly try to change their behavior, we'll notice it."

"That . . . makes sense," Rowan allowed, then asked the question that had been bothering him for days. "Any news on the insignia we discovered at that inn? Or the ring?"

The baroness looked like she'd bitten into something sour, and the expression made her face look far more severe than it usually did. "No. I reached out to some of my acquaintances, but the underground guild was clearly started and based in Rest's Remorse. There's still something bothering me about that eye motif. I'll keep digging."

Rowan nodded, pleased that there was some news for once, even if it wasn't exactly positive. "Then let's make the announcement tomorrow and handle things as they come."

The announcement was a mess.

Some things were good. The town, still high on the embers of the festival, wholeheartedly approved the expedition, even though failure would rob the town of its army. The soldiers, still settling into their new classes, were thrilled at the chance to further prove themselves.

But the mercenaries, who had been standoffish the whole time, changed their tune.

All of a sudden, every two-bit mercenary in town was thrilled about the idea of applying to accompany the expedition. It was the most extreme change in attitude Rowan had ever seen. There were people who just a day or two earlier were sneering at him who now believed their chance for glory was in the expedition. They must have had whiplash from how hard they'd pivoted.

Even two of the three largest mercenary companies had contacted them with offers of troops and supplies.

Rowan and the baroness rejected each and every one.

"You know, if this had happened when we just got here, I would have pushed for us to accept them all," Rowan muttered, eyes narrowed as he glanced over the latest letter asking that a minor company be allowed to join the army for the duration of the expedition.

The baroness scoffed. "Yes, and I would have likely allowed it. I don't know if this is going to work, but our inspection yesterday showed that your troops are reliable. More than I can say for these mercenary companies."

Rowan was inordinately pleased with that admission, even if he tried not to show it. Camilla Sutton wasn't someone who gave out compliments lightly.

"Anyway, we're rejecting all of them, right?" Rowan asked.

"Of course. The change in attitude alone is worrying. You know yourself that none of them were willing to support us before," Camilla said.

"Do you think it has something to do with our accomplishments, the assassination attempt, or the celebration we put on?"

Rowan strongly suspected this had something to do with Tamara, but after the mage had blatantly admitted that she was against Camilla, Rowan held the information back. The woman had seemed eager to clear her name of the accusations against her, even if Rowan didn't understand why. It wasn't like he was in a position to take on an entire mercenary company at the moment.

"This is probably a mix of wanting to get some of their people into your army so they can spy or try something more malicious," Camilla said. "There's probably also some good-intentioned people. Now that people know you better, they feel safer following your lead. Still, not a good enough reason to just accept them."

Rowan agreed with that sentiment. If he accepted mercenaries who wanted to join up simply because they felt safer now, there was every chance they would abandon him when they felt the opposite. It was much, much better to take only the people he could trust with him.

Of course, his army was still untested. But the hero felt that the time they'd spent together was enough to at least give them the benefit of the doubt.

There was one final thing Rowan had to do before his troops were fully ready to set off, and it wasn't very pleasant. As he stalked in front of the rows of soldiers, he struggled to open his mouth.

He was a hero, though, and even more importantly, he was their leader.

"As you well know, we will be heading out on our very first expedition together soon. I would love to say it won't be dangerous. That all of you are guaranteed to make it back. I can't do that."

Rowan took a deep breath, then looked at his soldiers, pausing to lock eyes with a couple of them. None of them seemed cowed by his words. If anything, they just looked more determined.

"This is why I want each and every one of you to write a will. You can find the paper and writing supplies at the administrative office attached to your barracks. You can also have one of the clerks pen a will for you, if you don't know how to write yourself. In the will, you'll need to designate a beneficiary, or beneficiaries, if that's what you prefer."

Once again, Rowan paused, letting them absorb his words.

"Your designated beneficiary will receive all personal effects, wealth, and whatever we can recover and bring back to them should you fall. They will also receive monetary support from the mayor's office."

There wasn't much he could do for those left behind if their loved one didn't come back. Still, he could make sure they didn't starve or immediately slip back into poverty. After all, his new recruits had just improved their own standings.

"That will be all. Prepare. Spend some time with the people you love. We will be setting off tomorrow, marching against the demons."

That evening, Rowan found himself standing in front of the baroness's study.

She had requested to see him, but the way she had phrased the message had him hesitating before the door.

Odds were, she wanted to talk about Olivia.

While he was busy building up courage and dreaming up a thousand and one silly scenarios for how things might go wrong, he was suddenly embraced from behind.

"What's got you worrying so much?" Olivia's voice was low and teasing, and Rowan immediately relaxed. The idea of facing down her mother with her by his side was nowhere near as terrifying as doing it alone.

"Camilla asked you to come, too?" Rowan asked, turning around and leaning against the door.

She let him pull off the maneuver but kept sticking to him in a way that made him blush.

"Yeah. I was wondering what it was about. Want to keep her waiting a bit?" Olivia asked in her special voice that Rowan found very hard to say no to.

Before Rowan made the cardinal mistake of saying yes to Olivia, the baroness's voice emanated from beyond the door and brought everything to order.

"I really don't know whether you're bold or stupid to flirt in front of an assassin's door. Just come in, the both of you."

At least she sounded more resigned than angry, Rowan thought as he rearranged his clothes and pushed the door open. He ignored the way Olivia was pouting at him.

"How can we help you this fine evening, Lady Sutton?" Rowan noticed that he was picking up the same speech patterns as Camilla, resorting to formality when uncomfortable.

"I have a couple of things for you before you set off." Camilla gestured at two packages on her desk. One was long and thin, all wrapped up in expensive leather. Next to it was a smaller package, something Rowan identified as a box wrapped in paper. "I was also going to leave you with a couple warnings, but I don't really think that's worth much at this point. I strongly suspect my daughter will be the danger, rather than vice versa."

Rowan had just managed to improve his composure, but now it was in tatters once more and his cheeks were scarlet. Olivia managed to keep her reaction down to a very smug, catlike grin. She didn't even bother to reply to the accusation.

"Go on, then, take these," Camilla said. "The smaller one's yours, daughter."

Olivia complied, and Rowan fought down his mortification long enough to do the same.

The second he picked up his package, he knew exactly what was inside.

A spear.

Rowan's eager fingers were surprisingly clumsy as he struggled to undo the leather straps holding the weapon hostage. In spite of that, he had to admire the overall quality of the packaging. The leather was dark, ridiculously soft, and oiled. The straps were about five inches from each other, and they kept the spear secure within its protective covering.

When Rowan finally unfurled it, he even discovered there were smaller straps attaching the spear directly to the roll of leather.

Of course, what caught his attention far more was the weapon itself. It was a work of art.

The body of the weapon looked like it was forged out of a single solid piece of metal. The metal itself was dark as night, with flecks of color that resembled stars strewn throughout. Subtle grooves marked the spear's length, making it easier to grip it more firmly.

What really made the weapon stand out was its front half. The head of the weapon was jagged and vicious. The spear tip was made to sink into flesh and savage its target. The blade was a little over a foot long, which was perhaps the best indication that this was a monster-slaying tool instead of one meant to be used against other people.

Just before the sharp edges of the spear tip melted into the shaft, there was a bloodred crystal icosahedron. Each edge promised misery, sharp and gleaming under the light. In fact, the crystal wasn't forged into the spear. Instead, what looked like veins of scarlet emanated from the crystal and merged into the spear.

Frankly, Rowan was terrified of even touching the spear, not because he thought it was cursed, but because of the sheer value he imagined it had.

"Stop staring at it like that," Camilla laughed, clear and clean and thoroughly amused. "I can't tell you how much that cost. Actually can't. My husband handled it and called in a ton of favors to get it done besides. Favors that were owed to him from when he was a duke. So, take it."

Finally, Rowan did. And the second his fingers brushed against the spear, a status window popped up.

You have come in contact with an unbound soul artifact.
Do you wish to bind to the item and reveal
its properties?
Spear of the Blood Well
This spear was forged from the remains of a vicious
ancient artifact that once grew mighty enough to
threaten even the gods. Its wielder was slain, its spirit
crushed, and its body broken. All that was left behind
was a mere spark. That spark was enough to birth
the seed of a new legend.
This spear will feast on the blood its wielder spills
and grow alongside them.

Oddly, when Rowan's fingers firmed up on the weapon and the familiar chill descended on his thoughts, he felt complete. It felt like a piece of him was finally slotted back in. When the link took hold, it improved some innate quality he didn't even know he possessed. His nose felt stuffy all of a sudden.

With a shuddering breath, Rowan raised his eyes to meet Camilla's. "I can't possibly do enough to repay you for this. Thank you."

The woman seemed to think little of his thanks. "Don't. It's our duty as your patrons. However, if you must repay me somehow, use that to skewer anyone who goes after my daughter."

"I was already planning on that."

"Hey!" Ignoring the distraction of her own gift, Olivia felt the urge to intervene. "You know, it's a bit weird to hear the two of you bonding over the idea of killing people."

Rowan grinned. "Sorry, what did you get?"

Olivia held up a very odd, long armguard, more of a vambrace, really, with slots in the leather.

"It's neat," Olivia gushed. "See here? I can slot in potions, and they'll stay connected to my skin. This way, I can just keep copying potion effects for my attacks without having to grip one with my left hand."

Rowan made some noises about how smart the item's design was and watched as Camilla seemed to puff up out of the corner of his eye.

They spent the next few hours together talking about the expedition and what to expect. Even without getting a new spear, Rowan would have enjoyed spending that time bonding with Olivia and her scary mother.

It paid to have a good relationship with one's potential in-laws, after all, and Rowan only freaked out a little when he realized that he now considered the baroness as a potential in-law.

It felt like the entire town had turned up to see them off on the day of their departure. Most of the mercenaries had slight scowls on their faces, on account of being turned down. The regular townsfolk, at least, had no such compunctions.

They cheered, they waved, and some would occasionally surge toward the marching soldiers to offer a bundle of food or trinkets.

Rowan saw more than one teary-eyed goodbye, but did his best to ignore those. A part of him wondered how many of his soldiers would never return from the expedition. He knew that it was a twisted way of looking at things, that these people were likely going to have a much worse life filled with poverty without him, but he still despised himself a little for recruiting new soldiers.

He was, knowingly and willingly, asking people to die for him in defense of a town that did very little for them.

Rowan gripped his spear, leaned into the cool confidence it instilled in him, and focused on the world passing him by instead.

Like before, it was misleading to call the area beyond the frontier "wastes". There was plenty to see. In a strange way, Rowan was even starting to enjoy the odd coloring of the jungle. It was like a child had been told a story and decided to paint it without ever seeing the real thing.

He soon grew tired of it.

In their past outings, the army stuck to the relative outskirts of the wastes. The trees were large and overgrown, and things were out to kill them. Every so often, the two problems became one. Some trees had thorny roots that whipped out of the earth when someone passed too close to them. Why those roots also had thorns when they were buried underground most of the time was a biological mystery.

But these were threats that Rowan could understand.

As the army ventured deeper, the threats became more varied. For one, their surroundings grew brighter from glowing fungal growth on the ground and nearby trees. Their enchanting glow was genuinely pleasing to look at.

"Masks!" Olivia yelled. "Find a piece of cloth and breathe through it, take slow breaths. Only exceptions are if you have a Rare class or above forty points in vitality."

The army slowly complied. Rowan looked back in confusion. Olivia answered by pointing at the root of a tree. There, Rowan saw the body of a small creature, fungi bursting out of every inch of bone or rotting skin. It was easy to understand Olivia's panic now. Around them, masks were already looking a little stained blue.

"You sure I don't need a mask?" Rowan asked.

"You'll be fine. Just a few spores," Olivia said lightly. Rowan didn't think a few spores was something to ignore, especially with the corpses of animals around them. His face must have left a clue, because Olivia continued on, "These are a Common-tier creature. They can't infect anything more than one tier higher than them. Even if everyone breathed it in, they'll only feel more tired and lethargic."

At least the fauna was less tricky to deal with.

Throughout their march, various Uncommon monsters would leap into their ranks before being put down by the Rare and Uncommon soldiers. There were only two notable exceptions.

The first had been a bit of a scare, but ultimately little more than a nuisance.

A small hummingbird, wings moving so quickly they were invisible, was suddenly just *there* in the middle of the troops. When it charged into the nearest soldier and rebounded off his chest armor, everyone laughed.

It then stabbed its proboscis-like beak into the man's neck and the laughter stopped.

The frightened soldier gurgled and batted at the bird, but couldn't get it off. It was only when one of his party members stepped forward and kicked the bird with the grace of a professional footballer that he was finally freed.

A squirt of blood shot into the air out of his wound, but his fellows descended upon him immediately, feeding him a healing potion.

The bird, meanwhile, was entirely unharmed. It just buzzed louder, wings fluttering more quickly in anger, and tried again with a blood-smeared beak.

Chaos broke out from there, with people striking at the bird using everything from someone's pack to fists to proper weapons. The little bugger was stunningly resilient, and when someone actually tried to trigger a card effect, their strikes somehow went *through* it.

In the end, it took Milena working with Rowan to bring it down. Her curse slowed the bird's erratic movements and Rowan got the chance to skewer it with his brand-new spear. It was alive for a few moments before the spear went to work, feasting on the bird's blood. With such a small body, it only gave a few twitches before going limp.

Before Rowan checked his loot screen, Marcus was already yelling.

"I didn't even know you could have something like this! Do you realize how many possibilities this opens up? It counts as a *shielding* effect."

To be fair, Rowan understood the fuss once he saw the card.

Ethereal Reprieve (Rare, Active)
Shield yourself from harm by temporarily turning your
body incorporeal. The duration of the effect depends
on the amount of mana invested. The cost of
upkeep increases based on the amount of enemy
mana trying to interfere with the effect.

Essentially, it was a battle of mana. Against mages or incorrectly built alchemists, the card wouldn't be of much use. But against Rowan, who had a low-three-digit mana pool? Marcus would be nearly invincible. The card went to him, replacing one of his class skills.

Their second battle of the day was much harder and explained why people didn't just head into the deep wastes every other day for experience and loot.

It had been a few hours since the hummingbird. Scouts were sent farther out to secure the perimeter, but everyone was in a pretty upbeat mood. Rowan could almost hear the soldiers thinking that the demonic wastes weren't that bad.

And then one of the soldiers started screaming.

Near the front, a female soldier frantically swiped her weapon around her and hit absolutely nothing. The claw marks perilously close to her jugular were proof enough she wasn't delusional. Before they could help her, a second wound opened up on her throat and she collapsed to the ground.

"Close rank. Form up," Rowan yelled. "It's an invisible enemy. Stay alert. Keep close to your party and form up on me."

A few seconds later, another soldier collapsed with half of his side missing. Then a soldier lost a chunk of his arm. The invisible attacker was somehow everywhere. A spurt of blood erupted from a soldier whose lost a chunk of his thigh. Somewhat fortuitously, the spray of blood also left a few flecks of the liquid on the attacker, and a keen-eyed ranged fighter pointed out where it was.

"Melee, stay back. Ranged, attack."

A whole barrage of strikes hit the area, but instead of bringing it down, they made the monster angry.

The army suddenly found themselves staring at a short, vaguely humanoid weasel with a crazed look in its eye.

It smirked, shoved its bloody claws into its mouth, and its eyes started to glow red. The downed soldiers started screaming. Their veins bulged and squirmed like there was something wiggling inside.

To Rowan's mounting horror, Marcus's aura shielding was helpless. It didn't save the soldiers from the attacks earlier and couldn't bring an end to whatever the weasel was doing now.

Rowan tried to push forward but found his earlier orders working against him. Everyone was clumped together and he couldn't get to the front quickly enough. In his desperation, Rowan threw caution to the wind. He filled his weapon with as much mana and life force as he could afford and launched it.

With his dexterity and strength stats? His throw more than rivaled any ballista from his old world.

He didn't quite manage to nail the monster head-on, its instincts and dexterity helping it jerk to the side, but when the spear buried itself into the tree behind, the wood exploded in a shower of plant bits.

Luckily, that was enough to break the monster's concentration and its ability's effect.

It also provided the time needed for four Rare-tier soldiers to step forward and attack. The first of them led with a sword, edge shining and aimed straight for the monster's heart. The dazed monster managed to dodge, slip between the man's legs, and savage his ankles on the way out.

The second soldier wielded a spear and was one of the few solo users of the weapon in the army. His strike buried deep in the forest floor when the monster made a little hop, landing on the shaft of his weapon and scurrying up it. Before it could do damage, the third soldier launched some kind of close-range mana attack that launched the monster away.

The final soldier was the best of the group. She drove her dagger at the thing, weapon shining black. However, when the monster hopped to the side, face lit up in malicious glee, the soldier accelerated and drove the dagger into the monster's shadow.

When the monster moved to strike against her, it suddenly found itself incapable of moving even a single muscle.

The third soldier returned to finish the job with a single heavy strike that would have been impossible without the others' teamwork. It worked. The monster lost its head and the screaming subsided.

"What in the world was that?" Rowan asked, half paying attention to the trees around them for more attackers and half watching Olivia heal the wounded.

"That was probably a fully maxed-out Rare. And . . ." Milena trailed off, sounding distracted. Rowan didn't have to guess what she was doing, since he knew exactly what could stop a conversation like that. "And my new card."

A couple minutes later, the card that had caught her eye was in her deck and the rest of her party was admiring it. The delay mostly came down to the fact that they needed to calm down the wounded soldiers, and Rowan personally commended and rewarded the four soldiers who'd stepped forward first.

Blood Boiling (Rare, Active)

Draw on malice and anger toward your target to cause their blood to boil within their veins. You can designate up to four different targets for this spell effect. The spell effect will fail if the targets are behind wards or other magic defenses. However, once the effect is in place, it will only stop if you lose concentration or run out of mana. If you have drawn or tasted the target's blood, the curse can bypass all magical defenses and its power is strengthened. The curse is also more effective when performed through an appropriate ritual.

It was, hands down, one of the most complicated cards Rowan had ever laid his eyes on. It was also one of the most exciting ones, since it was basically a checkmate as long as they got the target's blood and had more mana than an opponent.

Pulling himself up, Rowan scanned his army. After a day of basically hiking and fighting only, the men were getting tired. He ordered a quick march to create some distance from the last battlefield before they would set up camp for the night. For the first time, Rowan got to see the value of having so many followers.

Tents were set up in record time, neatly and to exact specifications. A group of soldiers broke off, building a cooking area from scratch and settling in to prepare a simple meal. Meanwhile, other soldiers formed a perimeter, went scouting, or even tried to chop down a tree or two for firewood.

In contrast, if the four of them had been alone, even just setting up sleeping shifts would have exhausted them.

As Rowan settled into a tent with Olivia that night, he was still patting himself on the back for his recruitment initiative.

CHAPTER SIXTEEN

Forewarned

Fighting deep inside a jungle was a whole new ballpark compared to what Rowan was used to. In spite of the danger, he was actually enjoying the experience.

Putting his enhanced dexterity and strength to full use was sheer joy.

As he dodged the thorny vines of something that could only be described as a walking sunflower with an undulating jaw in place of its mouth, Rowan launched himself halfway up a tree's trunk, pushed off that to somersault forward, and aimed his spear from midair straight down into the creature's face.

This conveniently let him avoid the shower of plant matter and uncomfortably sticky juice that followed. Marcus was not that lucky, and the whine he let out was heartbreaking.

"Why? Why must you do this to me? My poor tail. My poor, poor tail," Marcus growled, looking at his formerly fluffy, now matted-down, tail.

"Sorry. Next time I'll bring along a professional [Groomer]," Rowan teased. Predictably, it did nothing to improve the forlorn wolfkin's mood, but it did provoke a reaction from his sister.

"We honestly should. Look at him, complaining when his *tail* is the only real point of contention for him. What about me? Do you know how hard it is keeping my fur spotlessly clean in these conditions?" Milena grumbled.

Unlike the two frontliners, Milena and Olivia both looked spotless. Staying in the back and pelting enemies with curses and potions had its own benefits.

"Marcus, your aura defense didn't stop things?" Rowan asked.

"No," Marcus sighed. "It's not like the aura is going to stop everything. Especially when what's happening is thanks to my sister's new card."

Blood Boiling was a perfect card for Milena. She now could do direct damage against enemies, and even though it wasn't as effective when she didn't draw or taste the blood of her opponent, just regular use was more than enough to bring the combat power of the party up a notch.

"I didn't know that was going to happen. No one said anything about the target exploding," Milena said.

"You know the card is very literal, right? The blood is literally boiling. It's really hot," Marcus complained. "You're buying my [Groomer] visits next time we're in town."

Rowan would have indulged in the friendly banter for longer but reality had other plans. One of their scouts, a man called Dale, a [Forest Wraith] if Rowan was remembering right, stumbled out of the tree line looking pale as a ghost.

The troops showed remarkable improvement, recruits and old guard alike, when all turned focused and battle-ready in less than a second.

"Report!" Rowan barked, cutting through the man's panic and dazed state.

Dale's eyes found Rowan. "We—we did as you asked, sir. We went as far as we could last night, just to see if any powerful beasts or demons made a lair along our route. But, sir, there's chaos out there."

The man broke into coughs, sputtering and wheezing. Rowan realized just how drained he was. He looked ready to collapse, and even with all his levels and Rare class, the man's legs were quivering like jelly.

Rowan unclipped an emergency health potion from his belt, striding over and pushing it into the man's hands. "Drink this. It'll help."

The potion did its job swiftly. The man's complexion eased the second he'd finished drinking and he cleared his throat experimentally before giving his full report.

"There's a monster, probably a demon, rampaging out there. It looks pretty badly hurt, but it's still ripping right through all the local Rare-tier monsters that have claimed territories in the vicinity. It looks, well, it looks like some kind of flightless bird monstrosity," Dale said. "The other scouts are keeping watch over it, but I'm not too sure how long they can hold out."

The news, Rowan realized, was both good and bad. On the one hand, the thing was clearing out the monsters and doing their job for them, even if it was "stealing" their experience points. On the other, from what the man was saying, Rowan guessed the creature was Epic tier. And so far, Rowan had only seen one Epic-tier nonhuman, a demon.

"How are the local monsters reacting?" Rowan asked.

Dale looked confused.

"Are they all defending their territory or pulling back?" Rowan clarified.

"I think only the first few monsters fought it. The fighting died down when I left," Dale answered.

"Shit," Rowan cursed.

"What's wrong?" Marcus asked from the side.

"The monsters—they'll either flock to the new creature's side or they'll flee. Some of them are going to be going in the direction of Rest's Remorse. If they hit the town while we're out here, it's going to mean trouble," Rowan said. He held back the worst news of all. The scout had reported that the monster was already badly hurt. There was something out there that was strong enough to badly wound an Epic-tier monster that, even weakened, could tear through local Rare-tier monsters?

"It's also an opportunity," Olivia pointed out. "It's already wounded, and we're a lot stronger than we were before. It'll be different this time."

Rowan knew what she was referring to. The Epic-tier demon at Felton's Mill had been like a massive, unassailable rock that hung over everyone's head. They would have all been corrupted or died if it wasn't for Kayla coming to help. As Rowan looked at each of his party members, he saw their fighting spirit. They wanted to prove themselves.

"We also know it's there," Milena added. "We're not going to be the ones surprised this time. If we ambush the monster just right, we'll have a shot."

"And it's not just us anymore," Marcus said. "We have a whole army to kill the damn thing."

Rowan considered their words. The stated goal of the expedition was to just venture out into the demonic wastes, cull the local monster population, and return to town at the end of the month. They were only eight days out. Could they go back earlier if they defeated the Epic monster? Probably. But was it worth taking that risk when they'd already finished a third of the expedition?

"It's a risk," Rowan said slowly. He glanced over at the soldiers huddled around Dale and watched their expressions change as the scout relayed his story, from hopeful to fearful. As Rowan watched, Dale struggled free of their care and came back to Rowan.

"Sir, I'm sorry. The monster. It came from deeper in the wastes." Dale paused and took a dry gulp. "This is my theory. I think the monster is coming in our direction."

Rowan digested the scout's words. "Does that mean it's going toward Rest's Remorse?"

The scout hesitated before giving a slight nod.

"Okay," Rowan said, showing outward calm when his inner thoughts were anything but. The risk pendulum had just swung in favor of fighting the monster. With his decision made, Rowan went on to his next task, convincing the army to follow him. "Men. I've just received news that in our path is an Epic-tier monster. The good news is that it's hurt. The bad news is that it's coming toward us and likely our home, Rest's Remorse. Now, we could turn tail and run back to the town, praying that the monster changes course. Or we can strike, deal damage, and kill the monster before it ever threatens our families."

Even as Rowan spoke, his mind was spinning with alternate possibilities. There were two Epic classes in both the baroness and the Mercenary King back at Rest's Remorse. There were also mercenary companies that would be forced to help the defense. But he shoved all these thoughts aside. They came with their downsides. What he needed right now was faith.

"Even if we don't succeed in taking the monster down, we will persist. The monster is reported to already be hurt. Every bit of damage we deal on top of that will make life back home a bit safer," Rowan called out. "For now, bunk down and rest. Tomorrow, we'll bring the monster down together."

Rowan could see some soldiers were still unsure of things. The newer recruits were, on average, in the latter half of the Uncommon tier. Impressive, for sure, but insufficient to fight an Epic monster. He needed to find a way to make the monster seem mortal, to bring faith to the rest of the army, to make it easier to fight than the desert.

A thought occurred to Rowan as he turned to his party.

"I have a plan."

Rowan's first order was to send someone toward Rest's Remorse to give them warning and time for preparations. Strong enough to trek through the demonic wastes alone but also with good organizational skills, Rayne proved perfect for the task.

The second task was sending Dale back to coordinate with the other scouts and keep information flowing.

Dale's words still echoed in Rowan's mind. The scout had described the monster as a flightless bird, which meant two possibilities: Either the bird had been injured and couldn't take flight anymore or it never had the ability to fly in the first place. Both cases meant Rowan could start the much less glamorous third part of his plan, digging.

The army didn't have too many shovels, but with enhanced stats and surprisingly soft ground, they were able to make do with their weapons.

"Olivia, different task for you," Rowan said. "What's the biggest potion you ever brewed?"

"Biggest in terms of effect?"

"Yeah, like if you made ten potions and poured them together, does that create a bigger effect?"

"I think so?" Olivia said slowly. "It should work in theory, but only for combat potions. Usually, if I needed a better potion, I'd just make an upgraded version of it."

"We don't need the best potions you can make, just a whole lot of them," Rowan said and gestured at the water barrels that the army had brought with them. "Can you fill them with combat potions?"

"All of them?"

"All of them," Rowan confirmed.

As Rowan went to grunting and using his spear to help dig a giant moat with the rest of the army, Olivia poured one potion after another into the empty water barrels, dropping an occasional herb in while doing plenty of weird stirring motions and incantations.

About half an hour later, Rowan's curiosity got the better of him. It definitely wasn't because his vitality stat was lagging behind his strength stat, making blisters an actual possibility due to the mismatch.

"So what are you making?" Rowan asked as he straightened his sore lower back.

"Lightning potions," Olivia answered without looking up.

"Why lightning?" Rowan asked, genuinely curious. "Why not normal explosion or fire potions? Those would probably be pretty effective."

Rowan noticed the twins were listening in on the conversation, too, so at least he wasn't the only one confused. But they were forced to wait for her answer a little while as Olivia finished another round of chanting over the potions.

"Two reasons. One, we have no idea what kind of monster we're dealing with here. So I made something as general as possible. Lightning is pretty hard for most monsters to deal with. And second, most of the monsters in this area are plant-based. They're not necessarily afraid of or weak to it, but they all dislike fire. If we go around chucking fire potions, we'll piss off more than just our target. Trust me, we don't want that."

"Indeed we don't," Rowan grunted as he went back to work. A part of him was genuinely impressed at the speed the army was excavating the clearing. The hole they were digging was already a couple yards deep and the officers were now leading men to fell trees and sharpen them into stakes.

Every couple minutes, one of the scouts would pop out of the woods and report the latest progress on the monster. It was still heading their way, still ripping through everything in its path, and still a threat.

Once the pit was big enough, Rowan ordered the stakes pounded into the sides. They were secured together by vines, tough enough to serve as very prickly rope.

By the time they were done, Rowan was looking at a pit large enough to temporarily inconvenience even a small dragon. It was less of a trap and more of a way to change the environment to one that was actively beneficial for the humans. The front of the pit facing the jungle was a bit higher than the rest, forming a slight funnel that would hopefully drive the monster onto the uneven terrain, where they could keep it down.

The trees, sharpened on both sides, were driven into the dirt and bound together in three rows along the side of the pit. Would they kill the monster on their own? Probably not. But if the monster was already hurt when it attempted to climb out or attack someone? Every little bit counted.

It was just in time. The explosions and cacophony rising from the jungle far ahead were keeping everyone on edge. With most of the preparation done, it was Rowan's turn to give his army one final pep talk.

As Rowan stood in front of the hole they'd dug, tired, dirty, and a little cranky, he first took the time to assess the state of his army.

They were, overall, in much the same state as him. Still, their spirits hadn't faltered yet. They stared at him with quiet determination, and not a single one of them looked like they were about to run for the proverbial hills.

Rowan felt proud.

"We have done as much as we can to prepare. Look at what you managed to build with the power you now wield." Rowan motioned to what was once a narrow field, and the change was stark. "Even without all this, I would rate our chances against the monster highly. It is wounded. We are not. It has rampaged for days, whereas we are about to rest and recuperate for the fight ahead of us. We could face it head-on and win. So, why did we work so hard, then?"

Rowan let the silence stretch and build until he noticed some unease appear on the faces arrayed before him. Finally, he smiled and decided to break the awkwardness.

"We worked hard so we can all get through this ordeal. If we fight it directly, we will win, but some of us will be lost. This way? This way, we can do our very best to eliminate casualties. This way, all of you get to go back home alive and well."

That finally stirred up their feelings the way he'd intended, and the cheer that went up brought a sincere smile to Rowan's features. These were his soldiers, his responsibility. He really meant every word he said. He wasn't the kind of man who would be content to waste his life helping people advance just to sacrifice them in one fell swoop.

Of course, even his hoping for the best would likely not be enough to prevent casualties. But that was a reality he selfishly refused to acknowledge.

"Now, please, do your best to rest. Take the time to prepare any way you can so that we can all get through this together. I will, however, be calling out names. When you are summoned, please come up so we can boost our chances of victory even further. When it's time for formations, I'll let you know."

Rowan turned away and walked over to his party, letting out a huge breath of relief. From the latest scout report, they still had an hour or two before the monster would arrive. It was far too early to get into formation. The last thing Rowan wanted was an army half-tired from waiting.

"Not much of a public speaker, huh?" Marcus asked.

Rowan just grimaced and nodded. He *was* getting used to it, but if he was being honest, it was highly unlikely that he'd ever feel fully comfortable with that sort of thing. He preferred to fight rather than lead.

Olivia had somehow already set up a couple of collapsible chairs and even had a table in front of her. A small, relatively fragile table, but a table, nonetheless.

The baroness had been insistent that they take along as many amenities as possible that would make their life in the field more comfortable. At first, Rowan scoffed at that. Now, though? He was looking forward to giving the woman a hug when he got back to Rest's Remorse.

Her suggestion of a half-decent bed was better than any divine blessing at the end of a long, tiring day. And the extra luggage was easily absorbed by the manpower in the army.

"How many cards do we have? I wasn't keeping track, beyond just checking if there were enough duplicates for fusion or if one of us could use the cards for something," Rowan said.

Olivia instantly understood what Rowan wanted to do. "One hundred and forty-four at the Rare tier, which are the most useful right now."

After the first day of the expedition, the hero party had further divided responsibilities. Rowan was in charge of talking to the soldiers and keeping their spirits up. Marcus worked with the officers, Milena helped the scouts, and Olivia snatched up the role of treasurer. She managed all the army's loot.

There were some benefits to being born into nobility. Olivia had a far keener sense of what should be kept, what counted as a unique Rare card, and what they should scrap as quickly as possible. Some of those cards she'd even set aside and labeled as rewards.

These were separated into what classes would find them useful, and then she handed them off to Rowan. In her own words, it was up to him to reward, discipline, and generally manage the troops.

Judging by the increased interest in performing well and the way soldiers would puff up when personally handed a reward by their heroic mayor, Rowan figured her logic was sound.

Now, Olivia pulled out a sheet of parchment, unfurled it, and revealed a thorough list of all the soldiers and their classes, as well as their latest recorded level. She was meticulous about updating the list, too.

"Adam, [Scorchflame Swordsman]," Olivia said.

Rowan repeated the name, calling for the soldier. His voice carried across the army thanks to a very basic mana-manipulation trick for addressing large crowds. Though it was called basic, Rowan had gone through twelve healing potions before learning how to pull it off without shredding his vocal cords.

As the soldier approached, Olivia quickly shuffled stacks of cards in front of Rowan, then pretended to be absorbed in her list. Rowan sighed, knowing the message she was trying to send.

"Good, Adam, you're here. We need everyone at their best, so we're distributing additional cards for this coming battle. You know what you need most for your build, so go ahead and pick." Rowan gestured at the cards laid on the table. "They're free."

The soldier obviously hadn't expected that but quickly did as he was directed, shuffling through the cards until he found the one he liked, thanked them for it, and then left.

The stacks of cards were separated into debuff, body enhancement, offense, defense, movement, healing, and support categories. The healing, debuff, and support stacks were tiny. Adam picked his card out of the movement stack.

The mood in the camp visibly improved when they realized cards were being distributed, and Rowan took the opportunity to ask a question that was bothering him while another soldier headed toward them.

"How are you picking people, exactly?" Rowan muttered quietly to Olivia so they wouldn't be overheard.

"By tier, class rarity, and contribution. I want people with powerful classes, preferable at the Rare tier, but who haven't had much chance to distinguish themselves and earn cards on their own to get a bit stronger. We don't have enough cards to cover everyone," Olivia said.

"And you've been keeping track of all that?"

"You haven't?" The judgment in Olivia's green eyes was obvious, so Rowan just shut up and looked away.

The process of handing out cards seemed to drag on forever, but it really didn't take that long. It was only a bit over an hour and a half later that the final card was given away. The man who picked it up didn't look all that thrilled, but he took it anyway.

The further into the process they got, the more Olivia started gouging the leftover cards and guessing at who might want or need them. It wasn't perfect, but Rowan was genuinely blown away by how she was planning everything out.

And then they had given away all their cards, which meant there was now nothing to do but fret.

The monster was still coming. The latest report from the scouts said thirty minutes, and Rowan made sure that when the scout went back to the team, he had a truly prodigious number of potions.

Their mission was simple: manipulate the route and progress speed of the Epic monster. They were instructed to find every high-level Rare monster they could and draw it into its path, and even provoke it from time to time by throwing potions at it directly.

Wounded as the monster was, he had little doubt that it could overwhelm Rare and Uncommon-tier humans who were trying to annoy it.

Higher-tier monsters are smarter. It might have already realized what's going on. Rowan suddenly thought perhaps he had made the wrong choice.

"It'll be fine." Olivia's voice cut through his thoughts as her hand fell on his knee. He realized he was bouncing his leg, something he'd been instructed not to do during lessons with the baroness. It was apparently in poor taste to let his soldiers know he was terrified of the possibility that he was leading them all to death.

Rowan let out a long breath. He gathered himself and stood up. He had made his decision hours ago. This wasn't the time to question things—it was time to act.

"Men, to your formations. We're fighting this monster. And we're going to win."

CHAPTER SEVENTEEN

Grisly Duty

Dale's life used to be a whole lot more dull. That was before an army of demons destroyed his chosen home, his lord died in battle, and they were left out to dry until a new and confusing mayor rolled into town.

Somehow, between the time when he was expected to just put in the minimal amount of work and the present, he found himself with a Rare class, an actual army of peers, and his abilities finally appreciated. The consequence? He was getting chased by an oversize chicken from hell.

Frankly, he still wouldn't trade with his past self even if he could.

An explosion jerked Dale out of his thoughts, sending him shooting forward and safely out of reach of the rapidly approaching jaws of the Epic monster.

It wasn't the right moment to get distracted, but when you were moments away from death and incapable of personally affecting the outcome, Dale found that people got introspective.

"Thanks!" Dale managed to grunt out, his mana refilling just enough for him to get off another use of his movement skill.

His body immediately unraveled.

Every inch of his being turned into plant matter that then sank into the tree he was touching. He was transported into a world both infinitely familiar and utterly alien.

He could feel the sun kissing the tops of his leaves. He could feel the corrupted ants eating through the uppermost layer of his skin, even as a number of them fought off other intruders that would have caused more grievous harm. Most importantly, he could feel his roots deep within the earth and where they touched upon the roots of a different tree. He slipped his consciousness down, and suddenly, he was a different tree, then another, and another.

Within mere seconds, he teleported hundreds of steps away, melting out of a beautiful corrupted pine tree and gasping for breath that rushed to fill his newly recreated lungs.

A grimace marred his features when Dale realized that he'd traversed barely a bit over half the distance he should have managed. This deep in the wastes, every tree was at least partially sentient, and each and every one distrusted his intrusion enough to resist his passage.

"I thought you really were a goner, old man," a young voice quipped from above him, but Dale didn't have the energy or time to argue with the newcomer.

A tiny part of him was bitter at the way the boy had progressed from a recruit to one of the most promising scouts in the entire army, force-fed enough experience to climb all the way to Rare in a matter of weeks.

For a soldier who had languished in the frontier army from the tender age of twelve all the way up to forty-two before finally being allowed to advance, it was practically an insult. Though a bigger part of Dale understood he was blessed to be in that position at all.

The new mayor was a little odd and a bit inexperienced, but many owed him their new stations in life, and Dale would throw away his life if the man demanded it. Not because it was his duty to, but because it was something truly required if the hero went as far as to ask.

Not that he wasn't doing something very close to that already.

Chucking a potion in the face of an Epic-tier monster before fleeing was a bit like suicide.

Around him were the other scouts. Young Ilsa would have been out for the count entirely if it wasn't for the top-quality healing potions they were supplied with. Losing almost the entirety of one's thigh tended to be rather permanent and traumatic.

As it was, she was just limping along behind them. So long as no monster discovered her, she would be just fine.

Thankfully, they were drawing closer to their destination, all while miraculously managing to steer the Epic monster in the right direction.

Lesser monsters had already been riled up or scared away in a direction that *wasn't* Rest's Remorse well before the arrival of the Epic monster. Any Rare-tier forest dwellers, meanwhile, were enraged and led straight into its jaws.

This had done the job of both slowing down the terror and preventing a monster tide.

Everyone understood exactly why neither one of those should be allowed to happen, so every scout willingly risked their lives for the cause. This was the sort of thing they'd signed up for in the first place, even if it came almost three decades later.

"We're almost there, old-timer—don't give up on me now!" the infuriating youngster shouted, making Dale grit his teeth.

That's what he got for acting as a mentor and helping the young man unlock a particularly potent class.

Besides, Dale wasn't flagging. He was just . . . conserving some strength by moving a tiny bit slower. Leave it to the youth to overlook the importance of such important strategic details.

He could tell it was true, however. Just ahead, when he briefly vaulted over the treetops, he could spot an unusually large break in the jungle's trees.

When Dale lost to the pull of gravity, caught one of the trees' branches and swung ahead, he also caught sight of the few monsters they hadn't managed to deal with.

Well, a few was more like fifty or so possum-like critters that chittered angrily as they fled.

Nonetheless, a smile tugged at the ranger's face. They'd done an acceptable job over the course of more than twelve very intense, very painful hours. They had all pushed their bodies as far as they could go, but soon, they'd get to see a brand-new legend in the making.

Or witness their heroic mayor get eaten.

Either way, Dale was ready for a bit of rest. If he was going to die, he wasn't going to die tired.

Rowan was glad that he had assembled the army slightly earlier than necessary. The Epic monster's arrival was preceded by a wave of frightened enemies, fewer than Rowan had expected but enough to have been a threat if they crashed into an unprepared army.

At the front, Rowan dealt with most of these monsters. Handling Uncommon-tier enemies had turned into a somewhat boring routine. Rowan would thrust and the monster would die. There was no technique or elegance to the fighting. It was just repeating the same motion over and over again.

It was only when he finally caught the sound of trees crunching in the distance and felt the faint tremor under his feet that he got serious.

"Incoming! Everyone, get ready!" Rowan yelled, and it had an immediate effect.

Soldiers scurried away from him, racing to the other side of the pit, where they wouldn't risk getting between the hero and his quarry.

Rowan just gripped his spear tighter, a smile on his lips and eyes yearning to catch any sign of the monster's approach. His spear lit up, too, energy in it already building and straining against his control.

Moments before the encounter, he realized they had miscalculated slightly and hopped on top of the barriers, moving to make himself a bigger target to greet the arrival of his foe.

The confirmation of what was approaching came when a group of nineteen battered scouts shot straight out of the jungle, one of them almost falling into the pit himself and laughing the entire way.

The hero's stomach squeezed when he realized one of them was missing, but the screech-roar of the Epic monster distracted him from worrying further.

"Get to cover! You have health and stamina potions waiting for you! Be ready to run if something goes south!" Rowan commanded.

Rowan couldn't help but note how his voice sounded, calm and ready. Back at Felton's Mill, the mere sound of an Epic-tier demon's voice had left him frozen and powerless. Now, while the screams of rage did unnerve him, they didn't affect his ability to function.

It wasn't just because of Rowan's higher tier, either, since a glance told him the Uncommon soldiers behind him were shaken but fine.

Is it because we're facing a monster and not a demon? Or am I more ready for a battle now? Rowan wondered, then shoved the line of thinking down as the battle literally barreled toward him.

The monster burst out of the trees like a wrecking ball. If it weren't for Marcus's aura of protection, Rowan would have been forced to evade or be skewered by large wood splinters. Still, in spite of the physical protection, the mental hit Rowan took almost cost him when he stood there blinking instead of attacking.

The monster looked like a dinosaur.

It was majestic, without any of the regular signs of demonic corruption, and if it weren't for trying to bite him in half, Rowan would have gladly just stared.

Rowan launched himself forward, choosing to catch the big thing by surprise and ramming his spear against the inside of its lower jaw. Over the past few minutes, Rowan had slowly but steadily channeled a ridiculous amount of energy and life force into the weapon, and if it wasn't for **Lavish Feasting**, he would have been reduced to a skeleton twice over.

Thanks to that, the strike was the strongest he had ever dealt.

The explosion that ensued rocketed him backward, into and then *through* the barricades they'd set up. He tumbled end over end, once, twice, thrice, and then he ran out of earth. Rowan's final impact with the ground all the way down in the pit drove the air out of his lungs and left him blinking stars out of his eyes.

In spite of that, as he gingerly moved his body, he realized nothing was actually broken. Standing was merely a matter of will. His badly bruised muscles protested, but Rowan managed the feat just in time to see an enraged dinosaur with murder in its eyes diving for him.

He tried to curse, but he didn't have the breath for that. He jumped aside, only for the creature's head to shoot forward unnaturally quickly.

Rowan should have died then and there. The monster's head was big enough that its jaw clamped around Rowan's lower body. Even though the regeneration combination was powerful, Rowan doubted it could fix an entire detached lower body.

Luckily, he didn't need to test that. His initial blow had done enough damage that the monster couldn't fully close its jaws. Its lower jaw dangled, connected to its face by a single, glistening string of something. Blood vessel? Muscle? Skin? Rowan didn't know and didn't care.

The monster's teeth met Rowan's midsection from the side and he was launched once again, this time straight into the stakes. Luckily, Rowan was small enough that he bounced off the side of a tree instead of getting impaled and staggered to his feet quickly enough to avoid the next attack in favor of the dinosaur ramming into the stakes itself.

Its shrieks of pain and anger tore through the air. The monster staggered a few steps back, revealing a stake fragment partially lodged in the ruin of what was once its lower jaw.

Finally, Rowan had a chance to get a real look at his opponent.

The monster was majestic, yes, but it had also definitely seen better days. There was still blood dripping down from its mangled face. Minor wounds crisscrossed most of its body, with even a couple of chunks missing from its legs and back. Its wings, short feathers jutting from its front legs, looked completely broken and burned.

But the most grievous injury the monster had suffered was on its chest.

Two massive cuts met in the shape of a cross, revealing the monster's cracked ribs and internal organs. The edges looked seared. In places, the intensity of the heat that had accompanied the blows was intense enough that its bones looked warped and cracked.

And yet, the thing still stood, screeching for Rowan's blood.

The monster blurred forward, awkwardly trying to sink its claws into something vital. Rowan met the strike with one of his own, but the force of its blow overwhelmed his own and drove the shaft of his spear painfully back into his ribs.

Again, he was sent flying, and this time he could feel the broken ribs poking into his internal organs. Ruptured liver, collapsed lung, and nicked heart.

He desperately heaved for breath while his regeneration inflated his lung again, and only managed to barely catch sight of the charging Epic in time to attempt another dodge through blurry eyes.

Much to his shock, he succeeded.

Suddenly, attacks from above spared him the need to immediately scramble again. Arrows, beams of light, Milena's miasma, and even a couple of potions rained down on the monster.

So, the hero took just a second to think.

The lessening pain and the lesson he'd paid for in blood finally made him realize something crucial. The Epic monster was not faster than him.

The thing hit like a truck, and he was willing to bet any number of his renewable limbs that its vitality was utterly insane, but he didn't think it had more dexterity than him.

Finally, a chance.

As his body finished fixing itself, Rowan launched himself into the fray, heedless of the potential to become a victim of his own allies.

The hero focused on his dexterity like he never had before. He wove between grasping claws, he dodged the kick from the monster's back leg, he lunged away from its desperate attempt to use its jaws again.

All the while, his spear danced too.

He couldn't damage its skin or feathers much with casual attacks. Even the ranged assault was doing minimal damage against those. He could, however, aim for previous injuries.

The tip of Rowan's spear found shallow wounds, deepening them. The serrated edges of the weapon slid along the rips in flesh, widening them. Each time, a burst of blood responded, prompted by the Uncommon **Blood Siphon**.

As he set about the grisly work, Rowan could feel his weapon vibrating subtly in his hands. Somehow, a part of him knew the weapon was luxuriating in the combat. It relished every drop of Epic blood that it came in contact with. And in spite of all the mess and visceral combat, the weapon remained spotless.

Not everything could work out in his favor, of course.

An arrow missed its original mark when Rowan and the monster switched places, sinking into his arm. The explosion of a potion singed his hair and the skin of his face, rendering his right eye blurry for a time. A particularly vicious streak of sword energy even bit into his leg, making him falter and almost literally eat a tail strike from the bird monster.

Finally, the moment Rowan was waiting for happened.

The dinosaur paused, stumbled, and then released an unearthly screech. Its carefully aimed attacks turned into a flurry of blows that were aimed at every direction without pause, and its eyes reddened before suddenly exploding right out of its head.

The blood curse had taken root. Milena had finally tracked down the blood from his initial altercation with the monster and started her ritual.

Empowered as the card was by both the requisite catalyst and a proper method of use, it was wreaking havoc on the monster's internals. So, Rowan limped his way over to the wall of the pit as far from the monster as he could, then hollered at the top of his lungs.

"Now!"

Up above, a carefully selected pair of soldiers stepped forward. The only feature they shared was the bulk of their bodies, and only in the sense that they were both ridiculously muscled.

The two giants hefted a barrel of distilled potion each, and then, leveraging their prodigiously high strength stats, they threw.

They weren't the most proficient at aiming, but with the size of their target, they didn't need to be. One barrel landed right on top of the monster's back. The other landed at its feet.

Both instantly exploded.

Rowan huddled up right against the wall and covered his head as best as he could. In spite of that, the sheer force and heat of the ensuing explosion left him shaking in pain.

A whole section of his armor was charred and partially sealed with his skin, every hair on his body was probably gone, and he felt more than a few bones snap when he was flattened against the stakes he'd been so proud of just a little while ago.

Unseen to Rowan, Marcus had gasped, doubled over, and collapsed onto his knees, only to throw up on the spot. No damage was immediately obvious on his person, but he was in just as much pain.

His state only eased when Olivia finally just drenched him in two bottles of healing potion, having given up on trying to pry his clenched jaw open. To her credit, the area she targeted first was his face, and the small amount of potion the wolfkin inhaled was probably helpful, too.

After relaxing his muscles, Marcus found a potion bottle getting stuffed into his face. It took another two and a near choking before he became cognizant enough to beg the alchemist to stop.

By contrast, Rowan was very much aware of the damage. His body's most pressing issues had fixed themselves quickly enough, but his energy reserves were all but fully gone and he came to the unfortunate conclusion that healing his skin would be . . . difficult.

The heat had fused it with his armor, and while his healing was angrily buzzing at the wound, it wasn't making the problem go away, either.

Every time he moved, the shifting of his body tugged painfully on the affected area, making him grunt.

He refused to fixate on that.

Rowan straightened, desperately eyeing the cloud of dust and smoke for any sign of movement. To his mounting horror, he found it.

The next moment, a mournful keening cut through the air, and the hero let out a shuddering breath as he staggered forward to charge at his fate.

If he couldn't somehow finish off the monster, he didn't want to imagine what would happen when it got out of the pit.

Closer and closer he went, relying on a mere dusty silhouette as his weary feet dragged him on. Each step was an agony, but at least his ability to attack wasn't all that impaired.

His life force could feed the sacrifice card entirely on its own, and he wasn't dead yet.

A twitch alerted him that he was quite close to his target, and the gradually settling dust let him make out more detail a few moments later.

The monster was alive, but only by the barest of margins. A massive chunk of its body was missing, including both of its front legs, a good portion of its chest, and its left hind leg. It had been driven against the edge of the pit, too, and its defenses were weakened enough for the stakes there to pierce into its flesh.

Blood, still somehow seeping out in spite of how much it had lost already, hissed and bubbled where it fell, Milena's ritual holding strong.

It was in pure agony, and even then, at the sight of Rowan, it tried to twitch toward him and attack.

He couldn't even respect its drive and determination. This was a monster with no intelligence; its eyes were dull and full only of unbridled bloodlust. Whatever this creature's mind was, if it wasn't entirely demonic to begin with—it had been reduced to a puppet of the demons' desires.

The Stalwart Hero raised his spear, aimed, and drove it through one of its eyes. He couldn't even afford to collapse on his back when he got the notification that signaled that the deed was done.

That sort of luxury was reserved for people who weren't leaders of an entire army.

Rowan opened his mouth to announce their victory, then faltered and broke into a coughing fit. The dust bothered him and his throat felt raw and scratchy after the heat wave he had just endured. He did accomplish it, in the end. "The monster is dead!"

Rowan even managed to keep his voice from faltering or cracking, and when the cheer broke out, he was immensely proud of himself.

Proud, eager eyes soon pierced the settling dust, landing on the hero, who was casually leaning on his spear stuck into the carcass of their foe. Rowan looked remarkably untouched by the entire battle, in spite of the way his **Lavish Feasting** was dull and colorless in his chest.

The card had never been run that low before, and it was crying out in anguish to refill its reserves. He did his best not to think about how appealing the half-cooked flesh of the monster suddenly smelled.

"Drink this immediately." Naturally, Olivia was the first to make her way to him. The rest of the army seemed to be too caught up in their celebration to notice, and the twins were busy fussing over each other. She, however, had noticed that his casual demeanor and stylish pose against the spear was actually a desperate attempt to stay upright.

Rowan eyed the potion, but shrugged. Or at least he tried to do that, before pain shut down the attempt. "I'm afraid I can't really move my limbs right now."

The alchemist growled, glared, and finally huffed and uncorked the potion. Rowan figured she would just do her best to feed it to him somehow. His eyes shot wide-open and then fluttered closed when she downed the potion, dragged him forward, and sealed her lips to his instead.

He ended up only getting a very small dose of that particular potion and was blissfully unaware of the renewed cheering and quite a bit of happy laughter. However, when the kiss was over, he did feel more capable of functioning.

"Maybe I should get grievously hurt more often," Rowan breathed, refusing to wilt when she nailed him with another glare.

"Just drink this, you reckless idiot." This time, Olivia brought the new potion vial up to his lips. "Why did you stay down there? You could have jumped out. I *know* you could have jumped out. You had a whole army waiting to help you."

"It seemed like the smart thing to do at the time."

"You're not capable of smart ideas in the middle of combat. That's been proven, time and again. Next time, just stick to the plan that doesn't require you, a damage dealer, to tank the stupid Epic monster and get caught in a death trap."

Olivia was hissing and making some good points, but she was also hugging him. So, who was really winning that argument?

"I really hate to upset you more, but I'm going to have to make a weird request," Rowan warned her, then when he got a concerned look, resigned himself to clarifying. Not fully, of course, because that would be boring. "I need you to skin me."

Olivia froze first, then her eyes fluttered down to his ruined armor in understanding. "You know, I really thought that the first time you asked me to undress you would go very differently."

The hero just sighed and kissed the alchemist again.

Several days' journey to the northeast, a different pair of emerald eyes was fixed on a missive. "Make sure everyone on the list gets this, immediately."

The old man who had spent decades of his life struggling against the various hostile factions trying to steal the authority of the mayor's office grinned and happily accepted his task.

The hero had sent word of a wonderful opportunity, and his chamberlain was not about to fail him.

Likewise, Camilla Sutton, the baroness of the frontier, was nearly giddy with anticipation. An ill-fated relationship was likely to draw to an end soon, and she would relish every second of the chaos and her former friend's grisly demise.

It would be grisly. She would make sure of that herself.

CHAPTER EIGHTEEN

To Catch a Mockingbird

The town of Rest's Remorse was on full alert. Unfortunately, that really didn't mean as much as it should have, seeing that its mayor and standing army were both away in the wastes.

Officially, the reason was that a minor monster wave might attack the town. Normally this wasn't much of an issue. But with the incomplete repairs of the town's wall? Potentially deadly.

Hence, the mercenaries.

Unofficially? Every single mouth in town was gossiping about the messenger who had rushed into the settlement and then stumbled over to the mayor's mansion. The messenger who'd brought news of another Epic-tier demon driving their army toward Rest's Remorse.

An attack they couldn't possibly survive.

The town had almost as many mercenaries as when they faced the original threat. They even had two different Epic tiers, the hero's mother-in-law and the brave Mercenary King. What they didn't have was an army to man the defenses, or the defenses themselves.

This meant that the very first wave of monsters would be enough to form cracks in the perimeter—and then the slaughter would start.

Every single soul that could afford to tried to buy or organize passage out of town the second they found out. At the gates, they were met with a heavy rebuff and ordered to stay, "for their own safety."

There was even grumbling and whispering among mercenaries that they should abandon the job and just flee. Surprisingly, it was the big three who stepped forward and announced that the citizens would have their protection and that battle would be done no matter what.

The Mercenary King's response was expected. He and his would fight to the last, no matter the odds, once they accepted a request. The other two mercenary companies raised a lot of eyebrows with their newfound resolution.

After all, the Blood Reaver was known for abandoning all but the wealthiest and most influential of his clients if things went bad. The mage didn't have a much better reputation.

Camilla Sutton, of course, had expected that reaction.

"The spies we posted next to their headquarters report that there've been no changes, my lady." Henry, ever efficient and loyal, delivered the news.

"I expected as much. What about the underground guilds and companies we have discovered?" Camilla's eyes were busy scanning over the town map in front of her, briefly pausing over the areas marked in red.

"They've accepted more deliveries in the last two days than in the last three weeks. You and the hero were right. They're not choosing to flee. Our spies have also noticed a number of them setting up inside the sewers, most of them here, here, and here." The chamberlain deftly pointed on the map.

The baroness scoffed. "Really? How is it that supposed professionals are so pitifully predictable?"

"They expect us to be on high alert and fully focused on our defenses. You even declared you would take to the field yourself if need be."

"Still . . . this feels . . . too easy. Are you sure they haven't managed to get to the officer? Rayne, was it?"

"She's currently in the former mayor's own secret chamber. No one but me knows where it is located." The chamberlain looked proud of that.

"For now, I'll content myself with being thankful for such a room existing at all," Camilla said. "But we do have a problem."

The chamberlain nodded gravely.

When the baroness first heard about the hero's plan, she ran a simple test. She put out an official notice and left the details of the real situation sitting on a scroll in her study.

When she went to meet with the mercenary leaders the next day, everyone but the Mercenary King seemed to know what she was going to tell them ahead of time. They did their best to feign shock, and Tamara was almost passable at the charade. But Camilla saw through them. She didn't survive as a duchess for decades to be laid low by the paltry acting skills of two ambitious idiots.

While there was no direct threat to her life, Camilla was still uncomfortable with the notion that they could spy on her private quarters in some way. She knew that the failure of the greatest dams started with a single leak. Even if she was one of the strongest people in the town, the situation could quickly spiral out of control.

"We need to do something about it," Camilla stated. It wasn't a question. Where Kayden often joked about Olivia's obsession with potions and research, Camilla was the same way. Except she focused on ferreting out secrets that could threaten her family. It was a wonder that she wasn't blessed by Ziraela.

"We should consider training up some classes that can counter such interference, my lady. I will share the suggestion with Lord Rowan, but he might find the process a tad distasteful."

The baroness grimaced, knowing that the man was right. Even her own husband preferred to rely on artifacts, wards, and enchantments for security. Classes that could counter spies, infiltrators, and worse were exceedingly difficult to acquire. The worthwhile class upgrades were even more hellishly difficult to unlock.

"I don't think he would forgive either of us if we recruited twelve-year-olds just so we could mold their classes into *that*. And that might impact his relationship with my daughter. What I'm trying to say, Henry, is to do nothing of the like without permission," Camilla said.

"Which I am unlikely to get, Lady Sutton."

Camilla refocused on the task at hand. "Be that as it may, it's not like the potential recruits would become immediately useful. We'd need months, years perhaps, before we could rely on them."

The old chamberlain inclined his head, conceding the point.

"Are there any new orders I should relay to our agents?"

"No, and I don't expect any to be needed. Now we simply wait. They should be here any day." Camilla's voice betrayed her eagerness, and the two of them exchanged excited grins.

After finishing his fight with the Epic-tier monster, a fight that had been significantly easier than expected, Rowan received word from Camilla about her plans.

Rowan had fun with it. Marching on his own town and faking the impression of a monster wave was a nice break from fighting and almost dying to an Epic-tier monster.

Rowan pointed at a tree.

"Marcus, I think that tree is looking at you funny," Rowan said.

"On it," Marcus laughed. He charged straight into the tree with his shield in front of him and leveled the plant.

The two of them laughed at the destruction while soldiers around them all generally made noise amid the destruction of the jungle that had given them so much trouble just a few days ago.

"I can't believe you're wasting energy on things like this," Olivia grumbled, looking away from the havoc the hero and his army were inflicting on the nearby scenery.

Rowan kept laughing until he choked on a combination of dust, leaves, and splinters.

"Oh, come on, you know why we're doing this. It's not my fault that you can't contribute because it would be too obvious," Rowan teased.

Pretending that an Epic tier was advancing on the city was relatively easy when most of the scouts that could potentially see through the ruse were on your side and the mercenaries were too busy gearing up their defenses for thoughtful probes. It also helped that Rowan had a couple of the scouts setting up a perimeter and stopping anyone from seeing that it was a human army marching on the town, not a monster one.

For that reason, all the strength-based classes in the army, and even a few others with particularly destructive abilities, joined in on the fun.

Some of the destruction was intentional. They had to make a path for the massive body of the Epic monster, which was being transported on a travois cobbled together from the remains of the barricades and more thorn vines.

After making sure that Rowan was all right, Olivia began the process of chewing out both him and Milena. Rowan for destroying some of the creature's teeth, and Milena for literally boiling its blood away. As it turned out, the thing's proper name was [Corrupted Dragon-Blooded Bird of Zearnash], and while the name didn't mean much to Rowan, Olivia practically had stars in her eyes at the potential of getting her hands on any creature with the remnant blood of dragons running in its veins.

The fact that said blood was missing was a point of great anger for her, but she eventually contented herself with its body. She assured them it would be more than worth hauling it back to the town and even threatened physical harm to Rowan when he suggested just eating it. So, there they were.

Rowan's good mood couldn't keep his worries at bay forever, though.

"Just a couple more hours," Rowan muttered, worrying at his lower lip.

The plan was sound. The baroness had riled the town up with news of a supposed Epic demon driving an army toward them. Then, if any of the mercenaries or underground guilds took the bait and attempted to backstab the defenders, they'd purge them from the city.

This was going to be their best shot at rooting out Rowan's enemies and figuring out their intentions. Rowan seriously doubted they would choose to skip out on such a good opportunity when they'd tried to publicly assassinate him already. After all, with the demons as the excuse, they couldn't even be blamed for any deaths in the town. As long as no survivors made it out, they could brush the whole thing under the rug.

"You're not getting worried *now*, are you?" Olivia asked quietly, doing her best to keep any such discussion out of the ears of nearby soldiers. "This was your plan as much as Mother's."

She was referring to what he had told Rayne. In a fit of overconfidence, Rowan had sent her back with word that he was sure to defeat the monster and that the news could be used as an opportunity to root out their lurking enemies.

"I know, I know. It's just . . . We're bringing the fight to the town. The people there don't deserve to get caught up in pointless political conflicts or whatever's actually going on. We killed an Epic without losses, and now there's a decent chance my army will die fighting other humans?" Rowan did his best not to sound bitter, but there was no keeping the anger and disgust out of his tone. If only he could get his hands on whoever was responsible for the mess and stop all this from being necessary.

"They'll be fine. You helped them advance and they've got levels backing them up now. A ton of the recruits leveled up to Rare on our way back, too," Olivia said.

She was right, of course. In spite of the hero party hogging most of the Rare enemies, when recruits slowly maxed out their Uncommon-tier levels, they helped them advance.

The hero party was also growing at a rate all three of Rowan's party members praised as prodigious thanks to taking down the dinosaur monster. Rowan himself had already passed level fifty.

"They can still die because of a stupid mistake or a lucky shot," Rowan sighed, giving voice to his worries once more.

Olivia said nothing more on the subject, choosing to just grab his hand in a silent show of support.

Rowan walked the rest of the way with her, his appetite for wanton destruction thoroughly soured.

"Go ahead. Make sure you don't run straight into the monster wave, though." Rowan gave the order, earning a wan smile from the young scout before the scout launched himself ahead.

Rowan couldn't remember the man's name and would take steps to remedy that, especially since he had made amazing contributions in the fight against the Epic, saving the lives of several other scouts in the process. Right then, however, the scout looked more like a beggar than a rising star of the hero's army. His clothes were stained, ripped, and even bloody.

In other words, they were perfect for putting on a show of warning the town of an approaching beast horde that was supposedly fleeing a demonic army.

The irony of the situation was that the beast horde was actually real. The wanton destruction of the jungle had flushed out hundreds of monsters that called the wastes their home. But instead of being a serious threat, the wave was a harmless flood of weak enemies that the baroness alone could slaughter to the last.

The scout was dispatched and the monsters were driven out and, finally, only one last stretch of trees separated Rowan from what would soon, hopefully, be a town cleansed of internal enemies. When the final tree fell, Rowan looked at Rest's Remorse with anticipation.

Of all the things Rowan had imagined, his plan working *too well* was not on his bingo list.

The town was on fire, multiple plumes of smoke grasping for the skies.

"Shit," Rowan cursed. "Leave two parties to guard the corpse. The rest of you, with me, charge!" Rowan paused only for long enough to sneak his arm around Olivia's waist before he broke into a sprint.

The alchemist gave a squeak of surprise, but didn't protest. She wasn't fast enough to keep up, but Rowan could tell just by the way her body had stiffened that she wasn't about to be left behind.

His dexterity was thankfully enough to eat up the distance quickly enough, past the blood-soaked dirt and the bodies of the Uncommon monsters, beyond the crumbling walls, and right into the bedlam the town had turned into.

Already, groups of mercenaries were fighting in the streets, people were screaming, and the fires were growing.

Thankfully, some of the men had the blue ribbon tied around their upper arms, just like he'd arranged with the baroness.

"Can you do something about the fires?" Rowan asked.

"Yes, but—"

He didn't wait to hear more and left Olivia behind, out of harm's way. Then Rowan let his body move the way it wanted to.

In an instant, he was in the middle of the first melee. He twisted around the blow of his ally, swept aside an attack that would have landed on the same ally's back, and buried his spear right through the throat of an enemy.

Rowan didn't let himself hesitate, didn't let the realization that he was no longer fighting monsters take root.

Out of the five enemies in the skirmish, he claimed the lives of four, and then he was moving on again. Running. Picking out targets.

Up ahead, there was a swordsman with a large cleaver-like sword who was capable of sending energy slashes through enemy and ally alike. Rowan managed to sneak up on the man, poured a bit of his regenerated energy into **Blood for Blood**, and took care of the enemy.

It was utter chaos.

Rowan's next target was a skilled whip user, demolishing a whole line of houses on his own when his glowing weapon simply passed through stone like a knife through butter. He met Rowan's charge head-on and Rowan had to push his dexterity to the utmost. Rowan slipped right and sacrificed a couple fingers to redirect the whip before he was close enough to skewer the man.

An arrow pierced through Rowan's thigh. He looked up to see a female archer on the roof of a nearby house. Another arrow went through his left shoulder before he closed the distance. The final present from the archer was taking Rowan's ear off before he made sure she couldn't shoot ever again.

Those were just the most notable of his enemies. The most dangerous ones. Rowan lost track of the fighting soon afterward. He had no idea how many mercenaries he came across and dispatched when moving from one skilled enemy combatant to another.

He didn't want to count, anyways.

The town was in complete chaos and the mercenaries were much tougher fighters than Rowan had expected. Almost every encounter left him with a new wound that **Natural Renewal** struggled to heal. However, by and large, they wore the insignia of the Blood Reaver's company.

Tamara's men were nowhere to be seen, and that filled Rowan's stomach with more than a little dread.

The attackers were also not exceptionally well armed. Their equipment *was* of high quality, but it came nowhere near the level of what the slaughtered underground guild had had in their possession, let alone the enchanted blades of his would-be assassin.

"Out of my way," Rowan roared. As he got closer to the mayor's manor, the fighting thickened. And in the frenzy, no one listened to him. In spite of knowing just how deadly the baroness was, a part of Rowan feared for her safety. Gritting his teeth, Rowan charged forward with his spear.

Before he could get far, a body was launched through a wall just to the right of him, and a mercenary with a blue armband tumbled to the ground, broken and unmoving. Out of the hole stepped Florin, looking worse for wear but still very much alive.

"Florin!" Rowan screamed. The mercenary leader looked dazed, absentminded, even. He stepped forward and buried one of his twin sabers into the man he had downed. The weapon pulsed, and blood streamed out of the corpse before settling on the blade, making its red color a tad richer.

Rowan screamed again, this time to express his anger. He went at the [Blood Reaver] from the side and made use of his dexterity to slide right into range, his spear's tip trained at the man's throat.

The spear was batted to the side. Then, with a smidgen of life returning to his eyes, Florin looked at Rowan.

"The hero. Of course. Let me guess, there's no Epic demon coming our way at all?" The man laughed, and stopped abruptly. "Abandoned. Me. Think they can just use me and discard me, do they? I'll shit on their little cult once I'm through with slaughtering them all."

As unstable as the man looked, Rowan couldn't let that pass. He paused. "What cult? What's going on."

"Failed? Piss you. I'll piss on all of you. I'm going to become an Epic today, you hear me? I'm going to rip the power out of that bitch's chest, and then I'm coming for *all of them*," Florin yelled.

A slash passed right by Rowan's nose. Rowan hadn't even seen the strike and was saved by an instinctual flinch. He tried to retreat, but the Blood Reaver pressed on the assault, sticking close to the hero.

Flash after flash of Florin's blades lashed out, and Rowan was only barely keeping up, stopping the wounds from becoming cuts that could cripple him. He didn't want to admit it, but Florin was both faster and more skilled than him.

The dance the Blood Reaver wove with his sabers should have left him open to assault. Wielding two blades with such proficiency went well past the human limits. And yet, his arms moved completely independently of each other and could both attack and defend at the same time.

Rowan realized, even as he earned another nick on his cheek, that Florin was using *two different types of swordsmanship at once.*

Rowan was starting to pant, his chest heaving in air. His feet landed on something slick, and he had to commit to a dash to the side just to avoid falling. The maneuver cost him when Florin's blade sank deep into his thigh, sliding right through the muscles and weakening his left leg to the point that he could barely stand.

Of course, the flash of pain made another thing become painfully apparent.

He was bleeding, and not just a little.

A wide-eyed glance showed that his clothing was absolutely bathed in blood, and that he'd painted the area where they fought in red.

His cuts weren't healing.

Rowan didn't even feel them.

"How are you standing?" Florin asked, sounding genuinely confused. "You've lost enough blood to kill three people. I know. Trust me."

Rowan refused to rise to his bait, taking the chance as the man idly twirled his weapons to run his mana actively through his body.

It was hard. The mana that typically flowed easily through the ethereal channels within him stuttered and dragged, like invisible obstacles were in its way. Obstacles that Rowan couldn't even detect without serious effort. Pushing his mana a step further, he forced it through the blocks, only for each of them to resolve into a wound.

It was only then that his regeneration card latched on to the injuries, quickly remedying the issue.

Until that point, it was only struggling along to replenish his blood.

The Blood Reaver blinked, eyebrows climbing as he watched the wounds seal up and disappear, leaving unblemished skin behind. "Well, I'll be. Guess heroes aren't for show after all! Wish I could keep that card once I'm done ripping it out of your heart, but eh. Not worth dying for. Can you heal from this?"

Florin twirled his right blade one last time, then gripped it tightly, raising it above his head.

All the blood in the vicinity, be it on the ground, on their clothing, or even *inside Rowan's body*, trembled. Then, all the red fluid lifted off and floated right into the Blood Reaver's saber.

There was a rumble in the distance, too, and with a start, Rowan realized that a tidal wave of blood was rapidly approaching them from every side.

The Reaver's weapon rapidly increased in size and volume, and that was just from the blood immediately around them. If the rest of the blood tide reached the man, Rowan wasn't sure how he could win.

There was only one chance for victory. A slim and dangerous one, but a chance nonetheless.

One of Florin's swords was busy accumulating blood, leaving only a single blade for the mercenary leader to use. Rowan swiped aside the man's first blow and waited. Although Florin used two different sword styles, he never switched styles between arms. As expected, the man's next move was a vicious stab, threatening to skewer the hero.

Rowan didn't even try to dodge the attack.

He shifted his hold on his spear, gripping it close to the tip with both hands and allowing the saber to slide right into his rib cage. Once there, Rowan immediately trapped the blade with his elbow and drove the tip of his spear into the underside of the Reaver's jaw.

Florin didn't even get to look surprised. He experienced a brief moment of pain, and then the power inside the spear blew the entire front of his face off.

Rowan wasn't in a much better state himself.

He coughed, and flecks of blood landed on the ground before he stumbled back, the motion and the dead man's grip on the saber ripping it out of his chest. Rowan glanced down and grimaced at the sight.

Florin's blows had clearly been empowered in some manner. The area around the wound was ravaged in an odd, concentric pattern that had sliced through the nearby flesh. In a way, it reminded Rowan of a flower. But the odd beauty of the wound wasn't enough to distract Rowan's body from the fact that his organs had almost been turned into mush, and he collapsed to his knees.

The wound, again, wasn't healing on its own.

With a snarl of anger on his lips, Rowan fumbled at his belt, grabbing the healing potion there and quickly swallowing it down while trying to marshal his mana into breaking the card effect messing with his regeneration.

The potion barely kept him aware long enough to succeed.

It did work, though, and with one final disgusted glance at Florin, Rowan began making his way forward again. He was just a few streets away from the mayor's manor, and the explosions he was hearing from that direction weren't very encouraging. Thankfully, he only ran into another two groups of enemies on the way there. Both were surprisingly powerful and well trained, but still nothing compared to Florin.

And then, finally, Rowan laid eyes on the place that was slowly becoming home.

The building was a mess. The entire front facade was charred, and the majestic doors were nowhere to be seen. The source of the explosions also quickly became apparent.

A man wielding a massive great sword was currently engaged in combat with the baroness, the Mercenary King, and, of all people, Tamara.

The baroness flitted between the massive mana slashes the man was launching, while the Mercenary King calmly and methodically dismantled them using his sword-and-shield combo. Tamara, meanwhile, was pelting the stranger with blue fireballs that were wreaking absolute havoc on the street.

The battle had already extracted a grisly cost. Corpses were strewn all around, most of them ripped to shreds like someone had patiently cut them apart slice by slice. Some, however, were charred black or even lay dead with no easily discernible wounds.

As Rowan took in the scene, the combatants also noticed him.

The stranger immediately pivoted, sword lighting up brighter still as he triggered some sort of movement card. His impressive bulk came barreling right in Rowan's direction, and his feet were ripping apart the street with every step.

The trio reacted just as quickly.

The Mercenary King *blinked* right in front of Rowan, a dome of energy erupting out of him and inserting itself into the path of the stranger's sword. The two forces clashed and cracks developed on the barrier before someone else broke the deadlock.

A bloodred bolt of lightning shot down from the sky, the heat and force of it collapsing the barrier entirely while also turning the ground into glass.

The stranger, on the other hand, took the lightning bolt head-on. He locked into place, muscles steaming and spasming.

Finally, the baroness appeared behind the enemy, and her hands became a blur Rowan couldn't follow. A second later, a cloud of blood erupted from the man, and the energy haloing his blade guttered out. He slumped down to the ground like a doll.

"Could you learn to actually aim that bloody thing?" the Mercenary King bellowed at the top of his lungs, eyes firmly fixed on the mage.

"I was just making an opening for dear Camilla," Tamara said huskily, sending the baroness a wink that was answered by a glare. "Not my fault you were just standing there."

"I swear, I'll drag you down and—"

"Enough. We need to check on our troops and make sure all the enemies are down. You can argue later. You know where to go," the baroness snapped, stopping the argument before it could devolve into actual combat.

And Rowan could tell it would have happened, too. The Mercenary King was obviously angry, and Tamara had a look in her eyes that reminded Rowan of a dangerous cat looking for her next prey.

The two obeyed, both moving quickly in different directions. That left Rowan with the opportunity to finally voice his confusion.

"Why isn't she dead?" Rowan asked.

"Trust me, I'm wondering that myself. Tamara struck at the traitors before even we could," Camilla said, relaxing her shoulders now that the stranger was dead. "She's why you're not coming back to an empty town."

"I'm really going to need to ask you to elaborate."

"We knew where they were massing. Or, well, where most of them were massing. The second the monster wave showed up following the warning from your messengers, they were poised to strike. Tamara ambushed them first, before they even made their move."

Rowan just shook his head and grimaced. "Why?"

"I have my guesses, but I'm currently more thankful than annoyed. They had two Epic-tier fighters, Rowan. And more troops than we could ever have guessed. If she hadn't sided with us, things could have been much worse."

"We won?"

Camilla nodded. "We were winning even before you came. But that was the final nail. We've won."

Rowan glanced down the street, where more people were dead or dying.

They'd won, but was his scheme actually worth it?

CHAPTER NINETEEN

The Spoils of a Burning City

In spite of Rowan's fears, the town was actually in relatively good condition. The fires had broken out in several places, but the fact that most homes were built almost entirely out of stone did a good job of preventing the flames from spreading.

Olivia's intervention had also played an important role. She had single-handedly extinguished the worst of the blaze.

The swift arrival of the hero's army was another thing that changed the whole event from catastrophe to inconvenience, and Rowan was extremely proud of each and every one of them.

Marcus and Milena chose to stick with the army, supporting and overseeing their advance, and their unified front shattered all enemy groups they encountered. Other than some injuries, they didn't even suffer losses.

But it wasn't all good news. The mercenaries, especially those under the Mercenary King, had suffered heavy casualties. The number of enemies and the intensity of fighting both surpassed all their expectations. They had won but had taken a real risk of defeat in the process.

Then there was the matter of Tamara. The woman was entirely too helpful, enthusiastically leading her disciples in rooting out every last enemy hiding within the town.

She even used scrying to locate hidden caches, rooms, and even a whole covert production facility that catered to underground guilds and companies by using enslaved crafters. Privately, both Rowan and the baroness were convinced that she knew about all those because she'd used the facilities herself.

It was hours later, in the baroness's study, that they finally had a chance to chat and complain.

"At least the civilians are mostly okay," Rowan grumbled, holding a cup of chilled wine to his chest. Henry had shown up with a whole pitcher as soon as they sat down, then made himself scarce.

"They shouldn't have been involved at all to begin with, but it's not exactly easy to control the spread of chaos and damage when you have Rare and higher combatants fighting in the middle of town. The evacuation and fear of the incoming horde did help," Camilla said.

"I saw what some of them could do when they don't care about collateral damage." Rowan grimaced, mind immediately drifting to the whip-wielding mercenary whose weapon had sliced through the nearby homes with remarkable ease.

"We did win, though. Mostly. I wish our victory didn't come at the cost of putting even more power in the hands of that insane mage," Camilla sighed, sinking deeper into her chair.

"Wait, what?"

"We formed a party while we fought," Camilla explained. "It's easier to coordinate that way. So, when we killed those two Epic-tier combatants . . ."

Rowan just stared at her blankly. "Are you telling me that the dangerous and unstable mage you hate is now Epic tier as well?"

"I can still kill her. The Mercenary King can, as well," Camilla countered. Rowan didn't like how defensive she sounded. "And she's unlikely to try anything now. Unfortunately, I know her. She figured out the winning team, so she'll stick with it for the time being."

"I . . . really don't like how little that guarantees."

"You and me both. Now, why don't you go work on getting my daughter to forgive you? Leaving her behind while you charged into a flaming town isn't the romantic gesture you think it is," Camilla said as she closed her eyes. "I still have a lot of work to do to tide this over properly."

That was definitely a fine suggestion, and Rowan even had a solid idea of how to make that happen.

If there was one thing war was good for, it was apparently experience and cards. Rowan had, over his time fighting various mobs, received a ton of unique and interesting drops. However, the cards he'd earned by slaughtering fellow humans were both of overall higher quality and more useful.

He wasn't sure how to feel about that.

What he *was* sure about was the best way to make use of those cards.

"Olivia? Can I come in, please?" Rowan knocked on her door. He could hear her moving about inside. But no response came back. He signed and got ready for a wait, awkwardly adjusting the straps of the bag he had over his shoulder.

It was another ten minutes before the door opened.

"What do you want? Why haven't you run off again?" Olivia scowled.

"I'm the hero," Rowan said. As soon as the words came out of his mouth, he knew that he had said the exact wrong thing. "My **Lavish Feasting** was recharged. It was kind of reckless, but reckless is sort of my whole thing."

Olivia scoffed and turned away, but she did leave the door open, so he followed her.

"What do you want, Rowan? I'm not in a good mood right now," she grumbled, hesitated, then added, "Maybe in like an hour or so."

"I wanted to talk to you about something else. I want you to use these to build a deck for yourself," Rowan said, taking the bag off his shoulder and dangling it in front of the alchemist.

Olivia took the bag from him, opened it, and stared. "Rowan. I can't just take all of these! Do you realize how many cards are in here?" she whispered, slightly awed.

He couldn't blame her. There were a little over three hundred Rare cards in the bag, the sum total of everything they'd earned on the way back to the town and in the slaughter within it. Some of the cards were potentially useful, but if sacrifices had to be made, they were willing to make them.

"We talked about it," Rowan said. "Me, Marcus, and Milena. We just want you to have a decent deck. All *our* cards more or less synergize with each other. Marcus has his insane buffs, I have my combo, and Milena is, well, Milena. Not entirely sure how her class works, to be honest. I don't mean to insult you, but your cards are a mess."

"Well, then, thanks for the vote of confidence!" Olivia replied.

"It's not . . . I can't seem to say anything right today, can I?"

"Nope, not at all."

"Then I guess I'll say all the wrong things at once. Half of your cards are for crafting or identification and the other half are for fighting. I get why, but that's why I left you behind. If you want to fight on the front lines, you need to be able to hold your own. So, use those cards, please?"

Olivia hesitated, and for a long few seconds, Rowan thought she would decline. Finally, she let out an exhausted sigh and nodded. "Fine."

Instantly, Rowan was in a much better mood. "Great! Here, take a look through these—I think they might have something useful." He pulled out a whole extra bundle of cards, handing them over. These were the cards they'd found in the underground workshop, presumably stolen from or collected for some of the alchemists there.

Olivia took the cards, quickly cheering up as they worked on putting together a true battle-alchemist build. With each new card that they found, both of them got more and more excited. In the end, they only had to scrap about half the cards Rowan had brought.

Olivia Sutton
Level 59 Combat Alchemist
Deck (6/6):
[Heart] Pursuit of Brilliance (Epic, Passive)
[Class] Combat Application (Epic, Active)
Caustic Presence (Rare, Active)
Alchemic Fire (Rare, Passive)
Alchemist's Reach (Epic, Passive)

The first win of the day was Olivia's decision to throw caution to the wind and attempt an upgrade of her class card. Luckily, **Combat Conversion** improved to **Combat Application**, which further boosted the power of any copied potions and even made it possible for her to create multiple ethereal potion copies at once.

From there, things only got more interesting with her two new cards.

Caustic Presence (Rare, Active)
Shield yourself in an aura with alchemical properties
by copying a material or potion in your position
to both protect yourself and attack.

Alchemic Fire (Rare, Passive)
Sense and boost the power of all alchemical fires,
explosions, or caustic reactions in your vicinity
at the cost of mana.

Alchemic Fire was an odd combination of passive and active effects, somewhat reminiscent of Rowan's own new regeneration card. Even more impressive was the fact that it was so versatile at Rare when Rowan's card was at Epic.

Speaking of Epic, of course, there was Olivia's final new card—an actual find from the underground workshop rather than a fusion.

Alchemist's Reach (Epic, Passive)
Manipulate the range of your potion and alchemical
reactions as well as the tolerance range of various
concoctions and materials during brewing,
at the cost of mana.

Rowan didn't fully understand the card, but Olivia assured him that it was amazing. The obvious part of it allowed her to either minimize the effects of her attacks to one area or spread out their destructive potential.

The second half was production-focused and could apparently make it easier or harder for ingredients to tolerate things like temperature, pressure, and more. Olivia said something about the card making a ton of new recipes viable, but again, not Rowan's field of expertise.

All in all, Olivia was over the moon with all the new improvements she got, and Rowan was right there with her.

Thanks to the new cards, she was a whole lot more deadly, and even capable of handling herself in a one-versus-one scenario somewhat. **Caustic Presence**, at least, would serve as a nice way to buy time and make some distance from any attackers.

They ended up spending time together much later, but with how much fun they'd had going through the various cards and options, Rowan didn't mind.

It was almost a foreign concept, but Rowan was actually told to rest and do nothing for a couple of days. Rather firmly, at that.

The rest of his party and even Camilla were worried about his mental health and well-being. Apparently, most people didn't go from battle to battle like he was doing. The fact that Rowan was a hero or that he literally had a card that was meant to keep him in peak physical condition? Apparently irrelevant.

So Rowan found one of the many empty rooms of the mayor's manor and set himself to go through some casual spear forms. The spear felt so natural in his hand at this point that practicing forms was perfect for clearing his mind while thinking through what he wanted to do with some of his new loot.

In the past, loot had always been something that Rowan could equip or scrap in hopes of fusing a better card. This time, part of his gains included things that didn't cleanly fit into either category.

Heart Cards, to be exact.

The hero knew exactly how much people valued those, and why. With a single good Heart Card, a family could set itself up for generations. Entire fortunes were even built around a single Rare Heart Card.

Epic Heart Cards? That's the stuff *noble* families were often started with.

And now Rowan had one of those, along with two separate Rare-tier Heart Cards.

[Heart] Terror Hound (Epic, Passive)
Detect and track all sources of fear and unease in your
vicinity. When those feelings are directed at you,
you receive a minor boost to your two highest
stats for every source.

Rowan wasn't exactly sure whom he killed for that card to drop, but if he was a betting man, it was probably Florin, the Blood Reaver. Of course, the Heart Card had some slightly disturbing implications. In spite of that, it was invaluable for a scout class, and fighters of every kind would relish having the thing in their deck.

The other two Heart Cards were a lot humbler but just as powerful.

[Heart] Sharpened Edge (Rare, Active)
Imbue your weapon of choice with a cutting aura that
will enable it to slice through creatures and materials at
the Rare tier or lower with ease. The effect is reduced
when used against higher-tier enemies, and its
effectiveness depends on mana consumption.

[Heart] Eyes of a Predator (Rare, Passive)
Your eyesight, dynamic vision, and hand-eye
coordination are all significantly improved. You will
also have a much easier time tracking prey, no matter
the environment you find yourself in.

These two, at least, were rather obvious when it came to who dropped them. The whip mercenary was responsible for **Sharpened Edge**, and the archer was likely the former owner of **Eyes of a Predator**.

What it all came down to was simple: Rowan could easily start three brand-new families, which would likely be eternally grateful to him. Well, grateful to him for the next few generations, at least. The problem was, he had no idea where he could possibly find the right candidates to receive the cards.

He briefly toyed with the idea of tracking down the little girl who'd managed to weasel her way into the hearts of Olivia and most of his mansion's staff, but the idea of forcing her down a path of combat didn't sit right with Rowan.

Of course, after stressing over the question for a while, he sighed and resolved himself to finally face the real reason why he was brooding.

Rowan leaned his spear against his shoulder and pulled a card out of his pocket. Its border was purple and the image at the front was a slavering maw.

Gluttonous Banquet [Epic, Passive]
Gorge yourself on every available source of sustenance, breaking it all down using mana and storing the energy away to be used at a later date. You are limited to storing energy equivalent to thirty times your body weight.

The card was, on paper, amazing. It had also come straight from the Epic-tier monster they'd killed. Almost as soon as it showed up, Rowan had plucked it out of his loot screen and placed it in his cardholder. But he hadn't equipped it or mentioned it to anyone else.

Deep in Rowan's chest, there was a quiet feeling of dread when he read the card's description.

His hesitation was not entirely logical, but neither was the feeling of hunger that constantly lurked just underneath the surface of his thoughts. Ever since his rise to Rare granted him an increased awareness of card effects, he could feel **Lavish Feasting** lurking. Waiting. Pushing him to eat more.

And the description for that particular card was "food." The card often took certain liberties with the interpretation of the word, especially with the way it acted up around corpses. **Gluttonous Banquet** came with no such promises and only claimed it would draw on "every available source of sustenance."

Would he feel tempted to take a literal nibble out of his friends if he equipped it? What about other, less desirable sourced of "sustenance"? It turned his stomach just thinking about the question.

There was also the fact that his current, Rare version of the card would mentally scream out when it wasn't given full charge. And that one was limited to three times his own body weight. **Gluttonous Banquet** was ten times more demanding.

Of course, Rowan knew that he couldn't exactly run from a useful card. He'd just need to be prepared.

A couple hours later, Rowan found himself in the mansion's empty dining room, all the servants sent away and a feast fit for a king laid out on the grand dining table in front of him.

Rowan looked around the room. He was alone. Around him were stone walls and metal ornaments. Both inedible. Even the table was a heavy marble, while the plates were porcelain. All impossible to bite.

Before Rowan began, he thought back to the strange life he was now living. Just a few days ago, he was at the head of an army, marching through a demonic wasteland where they were besieged on all sides by monsters and corrupted plants. And now he was sitting at a table, holding his fork like a proper noble. The juxtaposition was jarring.

More than that, the list of things that should have been driving him insane as someone used to modern comforts was extensive. Yet, he could quickly identify all of these, put them aside, and deal with the important things on his agenda without getting distracted.

Truly, his **Keen Spear** was more than pulling its weight.

The one thing that his Heart Card couldn't do, it seemed, was help him commit to the task he needed to do.

For the first time since Rowan had laid eyes on the card, **Lavish Feasting** left his deck, and he gasped, as it felt like a part of his soul had just left him. Almost instantly, he felt more tired. Then, before he could second-guess himself, **Gluttonous Banquet** went into his heart deck.

The feeling that immediately assaulted him was intense. A deep, gnawing hunger rooted itself into the center of his stomach, demanding he do something about it.

The hero obliged.

One by one, the many dishes arrayed in front of him vanished down his throat. He couldn't taste the food at all, and he was barely stopping long enough to chew.

By the time he'd swept through the entire feast prepared for him, the card's reserves were barely half-filled, and it was demanding more.

With a near-manic gaze, Rowan's eyes flicked between the tastefully arranged plants, the many cloth covers, and even the nearby chair. He hadn't even thought of these things as edible before. Now? He was almost drooling to eat them.

Desperately, Rowan's hand shot to his left and grasped his spear once again, fingers still sticky from his feeding frenzy.

Instantly, some of the intensity to his urges fell off, and he could think somewhat clearly again. That was an instant relief, but he couldn't very well spend the rest of all his time with a spear in hand, could he? And it wasn't like it was comfortable to live with a constant gnawing pit at the bottom of his stomach.

If he couldn't find a way to ease the effects of the card, it was as good as useless to him. Rowan opened his system screen and was about to remove **Gluttonous Banquet** when he paused.

It confirmed something Rowan had long since suspected. Cards could be dangerous, whether they were inherently "evil" or not. Some seemed to suit his nature perfectly and just slotted into his deck with no fuss at all. Others had to be wrangled, managed, and carefully monitored.

Gluttonous Banquet definitely belonged in the latter category, yet was a pretty central part of every "optimal" build he could think up. With the increased energy-storage capacity, he wouldn't have been nearly wiped out in his battle against the Epic-tier monster. With the increased storage capacity, he could keep fighting well beyond the limits of nearly every mortal creature out there.

He needed to find a way to use it. He had to.

Keeping a tight grip on his spear, Rowan called out to the people in the hallway for two more rounds of food and tried to look away from the plants in the meantime. After two more hours, his card was finally sated.

He could feel its frustration that it couldn't fit any more energy. It desperately *wanted* more. It was a near certainty that as long as he consumed even a scrap of power, the card would be back at it again. However, for the time being, it was a price he was willing to pay for security.

"You know, for someone who claims he'd rather not be in the middle of constant trouble, you're being awfully mopey that Mother won't let us out of her sight yet," Olivia drawled, shooting Rowan a grin from her position on the bed. She had her feet up against the headboard, and her head was somehow dangling off the edge, watching Rowan where he sat reading a history book on the floor next to the bed.

"I'm not being mopey! I just think it's unreasonable that she's stopping us from leveling up. We're so close to finally getting to Epic, and yet we've had to spend the last three days since our return just lying around."

"It's called rest, Rowan. Also, you know why this is necessary. Mom's not sure yet whether there are still more people hiding and preparing to cause trouble. Sure, Tamara is helping, but that's part of why Mother is suspicious to begin with. The army's doing fine on their own."

"I know, I know! I just . . . Is it weird that I feel anxious? We did an amazing job, and we can obviously manage some of the Epics now. But, it still feels like I should be capable of . . . more. That *we* should be capable of more. And we're so *close* to that."

"Rowan? Take a deep breath and remember for a second how far you've come in these few months. You caught up with years of hard work and then surpassed that. And yet, here you are, complaining that you think you're not doing well enough?" Olivia teased, reaching over to muss his hair.

Rowan just groaned, throwing his head back and resolving himself to his fate. He knew better than to try and get her to stop. It just encouraged her.

"When's the last time we did nothing? Really did nothing? Because, even in that village, after my parents came, we were more recuperating than relaxing. Maybe when we went on that outing together?"

Olivia was clearly trying to get under his skin, but it worked. His face flushed.

"Still, this feels suffocating." Rowan closed his book. He wasn't the most well-adjusted hero, but Rowan really didn't feel that he could be blamed. Everything he'd been through since his arrival in his new world had definitely left its mark. Now, he was a constant ball of tension and desire to do *something*.

The only time he felt at peace, the only time he really relaxed, was when he was with Olivia. But that could only go so far.

It isn't right to so completely depend on someone, Rowan thought. He had come to the realization that there was no stopping the affection he felt for the alchemist. *But it's only a matter of time until she gets tired of me. And then a good thing will have turned bad.*

Rowan felt arms wind around him. "What's wrong? What's really bothering you?"

The hero hesitated, worry, anxiety, and worse all swirling in his chest. He was never the best at expressing himself. Social anxiety and self-doubt and even creeping depression always got in the way when it mattered.

"I'm not annoying, am I? Or too . . . pushy? I don't bother you when you'd rather be alone?" Rowan asked quietly, looking as far away from her as he could.

Olivia didn't answer right away, instead slipping off the bed and pushing herself into his side to gently catch his hand between hers. "Rowan, what brought this on?"

"I mean, every time I'm upset or feel off or whatever, I immediately go looking for you. That's . . . that's not okay. I should, I don't know, be able to deal with it on my own."

Olivia groaned, tugging on him insistently until he finally fell over, scooting back as he did so he ended up with his head in her lap. "Rowan, I guarantee that you never bothered me. I like spending time with you. And I look for you when I'm down, too," Olivia whispered, running her fingers through his hair.

Rowan's heart was threatening to burst out of his chest, but with a deep breath, the hero finally spoke. "I think I'm in love with you, and I have no idea what to do about it."

To his shock, her answer was a giggle. "And you think I know what the right thing to do is? I'm in love with a clueless hero whose bed I climbed into and who still thinks he bothers me!"

Rowan blushed and covered his eyes with his hand. She continued to laugh, but he couldn't really say he minded much when she leaned down and kissed him.

As it turned out, rest days went by much faster when the hero could spend a decent portion of the time kissing his chosen princess.

CHAPTER TWENTY

March of the Inexhaustible

Nothing really lasts forever. That was especially true of Camilla Sutton's desire to keep her daughter and potential son-in-law out of trouble at all costs. Five days after the fire, when the entire town had been appropriately swept through, cleaned up, and restored to relative order, she organized a meeting between the most important local figures of authority.

In practical terms, that came down to her, the Mercenary King, Tamara, and the hero party.

"Thank you all for coming. I know we've had a rough few days, what with all the chaos and the cleanup, but I want to start by thanking all of you for what you did." Camilla's voice was still colder than strictly necessary whenever her eyes swept over Tamara, but not even the mage could complain about the level of cooperation and goodwill the baroness had shown with her actions in the last few days.

"Of course. It's only fair that we help out the town we live in," the mage said happily, lips tilting in an almost taunting smirk as she stared at the baroness unblinkingly.

The Mercenary King just grunted, looking distinctly uncomfortable. "I owe you. My job is to keep the town safe. If you two hadn't been there, they would have managed to bring the town down. Then I'd fail my contract."

Rowan wasn't really sure what that said about the man, who was more worried about the potential failure of his contract than about his own death, but it sure said something.

"No one could have guessed there would be two Epic tiers just waiting to strike." Tamara, oddly enough, spoke up first. "I'm sure you could have managed regardless."

"Doubt it."

If Rowan was occasionally dim when it came to emotions, then the Mercenary King was an outright stone.

The baroness's smirk and Tamara's grimace at being rebuffed were amusing, but Rowan felt it was best to push things along. "Yes, to summarize, Rest's Remorse is safe now. That means we can focus on pushing for things to get better around here."

"Oh? And what suggestions do you have for that, hero?" Tamara purred. Rowan could feel Olivia bristle beside him. He was pretty sure that the mage wasn't flirting with him, but she seemed to enjoy getting a rise out of everyone.

"Schools, for starters. I know we don't have a whole lot of very young children around here, but we do have a surprising number of young adults who have not yet awakened their classes. More knowledge and experience will help with getting better class offers, right?"

"What exactly do you mean when you say schools, hero?" Tamara asked. "Because I assure you, if you're planning to teach them how to become [Scholars] and [Scribes], you'll fail. You can't even find teachers for classes like that around here."

Rowan sighed, knowing she was right even if he didn't strictly like it. "No, nothing like that. Just basic combat lessons, along with some reading and writing. Most of them want to be combat classes, anyway."

Rowan still had those Heart Cards burning a hole in his pocket.

"That *could* work, I admit. At least it's likely to produce some slightly more useful classes than the usual rabble we get this far out on the frontier with no proper schooling. Let me tell you, recruiting disciples is harsh out here when most are completely illiterate," Tamara said, making a complete reversal in the span of a couple of sentences.

That brought Rowan up short for a moment, and the way he looked at the woman changed a little. It was true enough that she was unpleasant, but he sometimes forgot she was running a mage cabal all her own. If anyone had experience with getting frontier children up to snuff, it would be Tamara.

"Do you maybe have any suggestions? Even when it comes to setting up these initial bare-bones schools?" Rowan asked earnestly, making the mage shoot him an odd look.

"Well . . . I suppose I could contribute, a little. Got plenty of apprentices who would love a chance to teach snot-nosed brats. They're fond of gutter rats, for some reason," Tamara said dismissively but, oddly enough, without any real malice or judgment. Once again, Rowan was quite confused about who, exactly, Tamara was. He was starting to suspect he didn't have the full picture.

"Yes, well, that would be wonderful," Rowan said. "My other idea are public projects, like we've been doing already. People need jobs and some basic security in their lives, and we need people willing to work on fixing up the town. They're not perfect for it without the right classes, but every bit helps."

This, too, easily passed muster, even if the Mercenary King wasn't really contributing much to the conversation. In fact, his first time chiming in was when Rowan asked for more ideas on how to help people and improve the town.

"Need to recruit more mercenaries. Bunch of my men got maimed or killed this time around. Will take care of them, but need new blood, too. I'd like permission to do it," the Mercenary King said.

Rowan was briefly confused before memories of some of his recent lessons with the baroness resurfaced. Before a major recruitment drive, the mercenaries needed direct permission from their local mayor, lord, or similar.

Naturally, Rowan had no real reason to decline. "If you can find enough people for it, go ahead. I had a rather rough time of it when looking for soldiers."

"They didn't know you. If you try again now, you'll have a lot more applicants. Still, plenty of people want to join my band. Got a reputation," the Mercenary King said.

Rowan's smile turned a little wooden, but he couldn't deny that made sense. He was a new, untested mayor, practically asking for their lives. "Well, with that little tidbit, does anyone else have—"

Before Rowan could finish his sentence, a creature of light and fire burst through the open window. What happened next was ordered chaos. In spite of the fact that no one openly carried weapons into the meeting, everyone was equipped to kill in mere seconds. Daggers and short swords were aplenty, and Rowan had *no clue* where Tamara got the glowing magic orb that suddenly orbited around her.

Ironically, Rowan seemed to be the only person without a weapon. But he had something better. Olivia already had a whole pile of potions arranged on her arm, ready to throw.

Thankfully, before violence could break out, the fire bird started to speak.

Hero Rowan,

I am sorry to inform you that Hero Blake is currently in grave danger. He has ventured much too far into the frontier, and he and his party have been separated from their army. We have a way to track them down, but the closest reinforcements of notable strength are still months away.

You and Hero Kayla both are, therefore, charged with finding and retrieving the hero. Should he be dead already, then you are to retrieve his Heart Card. It must not be allowed to fall into the hands of demons.

Attached here, you will find the item that will lead you to your fellow hero. Make haste—and make sure you don't fall prey to the same hubris.

Sincerely,
The King's own seneschal,
Patrick Rubeus

The construct's odd, echoing voice came to an end as it erupted into flames even more intense than before. When the light show finally ceased, two items drifted down to land on Camilla's desk, showing an unsealed letter and a compass-like item made of some odd black material.

Rowan immediately picked up the latter, finding that its pointer was stuck pointing far north. By the content of the letter, it didn't take a genius to figure out what it was.

"How did they make this thing?" Rowan asked quietly, deeply disturbed. "Do they have one of these attuned to me? Can they track me wherever I go?"

The messenger construct had, after all, tracked him down quite well. Rowan suddenly felt more than a little sick.

Tamara just scoffed. "No, they don't have one for you, stop looking so pale. Unless you willingly gave a drop of your blood. I'm guessing they just asked your fellow hero for one, seeing how close he is to the king."

"Tamara is right, Rowan," the baroness reluctantly agreed, crossing her arms across her chest. "And that was just a messenger summon—they can find their targets wherever as long as they have the right name. I'm much more worried about the hero."

"Great Hero Blake," Tamara spat out with a bit more venom in her words than Rowan expected. "How did our paladin get separated from his army? How did they even let this sort of thing happen? And why are they sending *the other* heroes to risk their cards, too?"

"Of course you're worried about the cards and not about the lives of the heroes," Camilla snapped.

"Oh, come off it. If Hero Blake charged straight into the wastes, that's on him. I'm just worried about what will happen if he dies and that card makes it to the demon king," Tamara said.

"Wait, what happens if the demon king gets a hero Heart Card?" Rowan jumped in, suddenly more than a little alarmed.

All the older generation in the room suddenly looked distinctly uncomfortable, while the other members of Rowan's party looked as confused as he felt.

"It's a conversation for later. Let's just try and prevent that," Camilla rushed to say. "Good thing you trained up your army, because you'll need more than a little support to pull this off. I really can't believe this is happening."

For a second, silence reigned. "Do you think they'll be enough?" Rowan asked. "I know we fought and beat an Epic recently, but it was quite badly hurt, and we're not quite at Epic yet ourselves."

"Doesn't matter. I'm coming with you. I know there's plenty to be done around town, but I can't just let you venture out there on your own. It's too much," Camilla said.

"No." The Mercenary King spoke up.

"I'm sorry? It sounds like you're against me supporting the hero's party, which, might I remind you, contains my daughter."

"Exactly. I'm saying you should stay. There's much you need to do here still. I'll go."

The baroness's anger changed into shock.

"You? You're going to get off your behind and finally do something that's not just sitting in this town all day long?"

The Mercenary King sighed as he stood. "Yes. You are an assassin. In combat such as this, you are out of your element and you know it. I should go. My entire skill set is based around leading armies into war. Monsters or humans, it doesn't matter what we're fighting."

"I'll follow the army as well," Tamara offered before the Mercenary King could make his exit. "None of you have mages under your employ. Having the support of me and my disciples is going to be invaluable."

"That's . . . not my decision to make. Actually, none of this is my decision to make," Camilla admitted. "Rowan, would you prefer I accompany you? Or would you like the Mercenary King and Tamara to come with you?"

The hero didn't respond immediately. Instead, he took a moment to gauge the reactions of everyone in the room. The Mercenary King looked indifferent, if a little bored. Tamara was the perfect picture of subservient innocence, and that was nearly enough to turn his stomach. However, he wasn't stupid enough to turn away a mage, even one with strange intentions.

"Lady Sutton, you should stay in the town. These two should be plenty," Rowan said, despite the grimace he made.

Tamara shot him a winning smile, and the Mercenary King simply grunted.

The next day dawned bright and early, the first rays of the rising sun illuminating quite the procession on its way out of town.

An army, a thousand strong, was marching.

Rowan's soldiers were naturally there, but the addition of another five hundred troops under the Mercenary King's banner was more than welcome. They did wonders to calm Rowan's flip-flopping stomach.

Of course, he was entirely uncertain how to feel about the groups of mages floating well above the army, observing the march with boredom or indifference. Tamara's disciples apparently preferred to spend their mana so they didn't have to walk. But Rowan noticed the fact that she had a full fifty apprentices under her.

Rowan bitterly wished they could use horses or any other mount to speed up the journey ahead of them. Unfortunately, the only thing they had was the odd tracking device and their own feet. No regular animal was going to survive within the wastes for very long without getting corrupted, and even tamed beasts would be driven insane in no time.

"Hey, I know things aren't exactly in our favor, marching deep into the wastes, but we'll be fine," Olivia whispered, nudging Rowan with a playful smile.

Rowan couldn't exactly reciprocate. "It's not that. It's . . ." He trailed off, terrified to even share the fears that had gripped him upon the announcement of the danger Blake was in. The Stalwart Hero was nowhere near as indifferent to the whole situation as he pretended to be.

"You can tell me, you know? I keep telling you that."

"He's my friend, Olivia. My best friend. I have no clue where I'd be without him, and now he's stuck somewhere in the middle of the wastes with hordes of monsters after him."

It was true that Kayla had changed. Rowan wasn't sure how or why, but the woman he'd met only had a vague resemblance to the person he'd once called friend. Blake, however, had gone out of his way to warn him of approaching danger with his letter.

Even if he'd changed, it wasn't to the extent that Rowan would struggle to recognize the man anymore.

"We'll find him. If a hero dies, trust me, the kingdom will know," Olivia said. At a questioning glance from Rowan, she clarified. "I did a bit of reading yesterday. The previous mayor didn't have an amazing library, but it's satisfactory enough. When a hero dies by demons, there's some kind of an oracle."

"Do you know why they were so worried? About the demons getting Blake's card?"

Unfortunately, Olivia shook her head. "There's only mentions of a 'calamity' that typically follows the death of a hero when it happens at the hands of demons. There weren't mentions of the event outside of that. It's like the authors didn't want to write it down."

"Well, at least we know it's extremely bad, then. Maybe we can press the Mercenary King or Tamara for an answer, or—"

"Lord Rowan." The Mercenary King's deep, booming voice cut off the hero, and the pair looked up to see the man approaching.

"Yes? Is there already a problem with the troops?" Rowan asked. That would have been a really impressive feat, if for no other reason than that they were only starting to approach the wastes proper.

"I would like to formally request both to be included in your army and that I be granted the right to stand in as the acting general of the troops until you are ready to step in yourself," the Mercenary King said. Rowan felt like there was more at play than it seemed. He hesitated to reply but eventually nodded. "I need you to verbally acknowledge my request, Your Lordship."

"Why? Why is it so important that I need to officially and verbally approve it?" Rowan's eyes narrowed, and he was already scanning for ways to put distance between himself and the Mercenary King if the worst happened and combat broke out.

"A lot of my class effects and cards are tied into empowering and leading an army. However, I can only affect those who are officially under my command," the Mercenary King explained.

"Are you telling me the system stops you from using your cards if you don't have official authority over the troops? How is that even possible?"

"I do not know. All I know is that's how it works. I suppose it's the solution to being able to affect more people than just your own party."

"But Marcus has a defensive aura ability, and he can use it on anyone he wants to?"

"I am not a system scholar, Your Lordship. I cannot give you the answers you want. If there's a difference, it's due to both my monarch-style class and the fact that I don't have a defined range at which I can buff my troops. They just need to be marching under my command."

Rowan sneaked a glance at Olivia, who gave him a little bit of a nod.

"Okay then. Lucius Orgrim, I *officially* accept you as part of my army and name you general of my troops whose authority is second only to my own." Rowan paused. "Would that work?"

The man grinned, some of the tension falling off his shoulders. "Well, let's find out, lad, shall we?"

It was Rowan's turn to grunt in dissatisfaction. "What happened to 'Your Lordship'?"

"Eh, I'm technically under your employ right now, lad, but it's bad for business to act too unfamiliar. Still, seeing as I'm your right-hand man right now, let's get this started. **March of Heroes.**"

The Mercenary King's voice echoed through the air, and every soldier and mercenary gave a little jolt. The mercenaries seemed used to it, most of them grinning, but Rowan saw the way the soldiers were suddenly glancing around in confusion.

He couldn't blame them. A well of energy seemed to be opening up in the center of his being.

"Forward, march!" the man barked, and Rowan's eyes widened to the size of saucers when his leg lifted without him even meaning to do it.

Rowan had a feeling that he could fight off whatever was happening, but when his strides took him much farther and much more steadily across the terrain than he could have managed without seriously engaging his dexterity stat, he didn't.

The sheer ferocity of the march and the unified movement of the army should have been an impossibility. A glance at Olivia revealed that she was effortlessly keeping up with the more physical classes.

"How? How are you doing any of this?" she asked, barely paying attention to the ground she was covering in record time.

"First time seeing a true commander or ruler class at work?" the mercenary teased, a huge grin on his face. "Why do you think I'm stuck out here on the frontier, lass? Because I'm utterly indispensable for the defense of one of the shabbiest frontier towns? No offense, lad. It's just the truth."

"Why *are* you here, then?" Rowan's curiosity got the best of him, even if he did feel like he might regret asking the question.

"Can't have two monarchs in one kingdom. Thankfully, [Mercenary King] is not a class that demands territory or the like. But it's still a monarch class. No king is going to let me take root in their domain. But I'm too useful to just get rid of. So demon duty it is for me."

Rowan considered the man then. In spite of the grim things he was saying, he felt that Lucius was still perfectly relaxed and even satisfied with his lot in life.

"Why take such a class, then?" It was Olivia that asked the question, but Rowan was just as curious.

"I needed a way to lead and protect my men. They put their trust in me, count on me to help them secure a good life for their families. Why shouldn't I take the best class to help me do just that? Consequences be damned."

Rowan could respect that. The man looked gruff and guarded most of the time, but with all the new information, Rowan couldn't exactly blame him. It was probably hell navigating the politics of having a ruler class without any land or legitimacy for such a claim.

"Thank you for telling us," Rowan said.

The man gave him a look before breaking out into a small smile. "No problem, hero. You know, I wasn't sure what to think at first. Especially when you took a bunch of hapless civilians into the wastes. Still, you're all right, lad. Keep it up."

With those words, the Mercenary King rushed ahead, taking a position at the head of the army. Amazingly enough, the effect they were under got an additional minor boost, and Rowan scoffed.

He didn't mind being "supplanted" as leader, as long as the benefits of that were apparent. Plus, even a temporary reprieve from his duties was welcome.

If anyone had tried to explain the gulf between powerful Epic classes and their lower-tier counterparts before their march, Rowan likely would have scoffed. Sure, the difference was supposed to exist, but describing it as "insurmountable" was surely false.

Unfortunately, the actions of the Mercenary King proved the true strength of Epic classes quite thoroughly.

Two days. Their march continued, unhindered by any sort of breaks, for two days. Two days of no food, drink, rest, or sleep. Just mindless marching to the will of the Mercenary King.

They didn't even run into any trouble. The hero's army had done an amazing job pacifying the region's more powerful monsters, and the leftovers took a single look at the overwhelming mass of humans and booked it.

And Rowan couldn't even tell where the time had gone. One second he was still falling into the rhythm of the march, and the next, they were finally being told to slow down and recuperate. The funny thing was, he wasn't even excessively tired.

His legs ached a little, and he could go for a hearty meal, but there was no gnawing hunger, muscle pain, or his new energy-storage card going wild with desire for sustenance. Just a gentle easing out of the march.

Needless to say, all the soldiers began to look at the Mercenary King in a different light.

"I hate seeing him use that card. He tried to use it on me once, too, and I threatened to burn him for it. I won't have anyone using mind-control effects on me, no matter how mild or benign," Tamara proclaimed. The mage jumped off her traveling platform, landing on her feet, and then grimaced, looking at the dirt with the kind of disdain typically reserved for one's worst enemies. Considering the fact that she was still wearing an expensive, beautiful dress, that wasn't necessarily far from the truth.

"Not everyone has a floating platform to use. I'm surprised you decided to come down to join us lowly mortals," Rowan said, a bit more coldly than he necessarily needed to.

"You really don't like me, do you?" The mage sighed, rolling her eyes. "I'm not surprised, not with Camilla acting as your mentor, but I'm really not your enemy, Rowan. Is there anything I can do to prove that to you? Anything at all?"

Rowan was about to thank her for the offer when a thought came into his mind.

"There is one thing. How fast is your flying construct, exactly?"

"If you want me to fly ahead and try to reach Hero Blake before the rest of the army, I'm afraid I'll have to decline. If he's been cut off from his own army, the number of monsters there is not negligible. Nor are they likely to be weak."

"Oh, no, don't worry," Rowan assured her. "I have something slightly different in mind."

CHAPTER TWENTY-ONE

Breaking Into Traps

You advanced into an Epic class," Rowan stated.

Tamara hesitated a split second before she nodded.

"Do you have a way of finding other Epic-tier monsters?" Rowan asked.

"I do."

"Then all I ask of you is to help me hunt them. My party's close to the limit of the Rare tier, and if we can advance into Epic classes, then everyone wins."

Seeing Tamara's reaction, Rowan wondered if he was about to be attacked on the spot. Her face went through a whole gamut of emotions before settling into a wry smile.

"Fine," Tamara said. "Get your party together. We'll hunt while the army rests."

Fifteen minutes later, they were all slowly lifting away from the ground, making Rowan's stomach plummet with a curious mixture of primal fear and excitement. Amusement park rides had nothing on the spell mages used to get around.

"What was so important that you got the mages to give us a lift?" Marcus wondered, staring with fascination at the ground that was growing ever distant.

His sister was taking the whole thing much worse, and Rowan was truly starting to worry that she would empty her stomach all over the unfortunate mages.

"Tamara has graciously agreed to help us," Rowan explained. "With Lucius taking care of the camp for the night, we can take our time tracking down an Epic-ranked monster. If we can all rise to Epic before we get there, we'll be much safer."

"Tamara? She wants to help us get to Epic rank?" Olivia didn't outright call him out for being a liar, but her tone of voice strongly suggested what her true opinion of the subject was.

"I wouldn't say *want* is the right word. She offered to help me with anything, and I took her up on it," Rowan quipped, managing to avoid sounding smug. It wasn't his fault that she hadn't bothered specifying what was on the table.

"The woman was stuck at the peak of the Rare tier for years, and now she's helping someone else with advancing into Epic?" Olivia muttered relatively quietly, but the violent mage was close enough that Rowan could tell she was listening in.

As her facial muscles twitched, Rowan hurriedly minimized the damage. "It is her innate generosity at play, I'm sure."

At least Olivia caught on relatively quickly, rolling her eyes but finally falling silent.

When he was brought before it, the beast was already on the verge of death. Reluctant or not, there was no way to deny that Tamara had followed through on her offer.

The once-majestic snake was missing a large chunk of its tail, its body was riddled with lightning scars, and its eyes were blinded. Even the weak flickering of its tongue betrayed its current state. Yet, strangely, staring right at the incapacitated Epic-tier monster, Rowan wasn't feeling particularly happy.

"There it is, boy. Isn't that what you wanted?" Tamara's voice was still somewhat husky, but it came out with a flat inflection that betrayed her true feelings.

Rowan could sense her desire. She wanted the Epic monster for herself, and she'd definitely earned it, if the few traces of blackened cloth on her chest were any indication.

Her apprentices looked rather tired as well, with more than a few sitting on their floating platforms in meditative positions. Those who were still fully aware were busy glaring at the hero and his party, though they looked away when their mistress swept her eyes over them.

"Truly, I can't thank you enough. This will go a long way toward assuring that our mission is successful this time," Rowan said, stepping forward with a spear in hand.

Is this what Blake and Kayla went through? Having monsters literally served up to them on a platter? Rowan wondered. Then he brought down his spear.

As it was, Rowan finally got the message he'd been looking forward to for so long.

Class evolution requirements met.
Classes available for selection:
Flawless Spearmaster, Spear Marionette, Spear of Unity,
Monarch of Blood, Fragment of Brilliance,
Consecrated Spear, Herald of Ennui

Rowan sighed and closed his eyes, allowing himself just a single moment of quiet relief and victory. Then, he turned to his dazed companions, no doubt dealing with their own slew of notifications and options.

"It's about time we caught up, isn't it?" he asked playfully, ignoring Tamara's gritted teeth.

Rowan was more certain than ever that the master mage was not following them out of the goodness of her heart. Her decision to team up with Camilla and Lucius had been suspicious from the start, but giving up on an Epic-ranked monster when she could either hog the experience or potentially ascend a student?

Rowan would be a complete fool if he bought any of her excuses at that point.

He went back to the army first. Then, it was only when the Mercenary King accepted his request to guard them while they fiddled with their systems that he relaxed and sank into the many class upgrade options offered to him.

[Flawless Spearmaster]
The peak of humanity's spear mastery is defined by you.

By picking the [Flawless Spearmaster] class, you will get
a grand boost to the strength of all cards and attacks
related to the spear. You will also achieve an innate
mastery of every spear style you come across.
Additional beneficial effects:
A grand boost to the effectiveness of your dexterity
and strength stats.
A large boost to combat maneuvers and synergy
with other spear wielders.
Improved combat instinct and spear style application.
Class penalties:
N/A
Attached card: Flawless Spear (Epic, Passive)

Once again, while not necessarily horrible, the base class upgrade
version was lackluster. The very next option he viewed more than
made up for it, though.

[Spear Marionette]
Some people fear the loss of their humanity;
others embrace it.
By picking the [Spear Marionette] class, you fully
invest your soul, mind, and essence into your
spear. Your former body will become a mere
shell for you to showcase your mastery.
Warning: This class will trigger a racial change from
[Human] to [Cursed Armament].
Additional beneficial effects:
A grand boost to the effectiveness of your strength,
vitality, dexterity, perception, intelligence,
and wisdom stats.
You may choose to possess any creature capable
of wielding a spear and transform them
into your shell.
Immunity to all mind-altering, debilitating,
and debuff effects.

As long as your true body persists, you can replace
your shell as many times as required.
Class penalties:
Your shell cannot venture more than ten yards
away from your true body.
The loss of your shell renders you incapable of acting
independently until you acquire a new one.
Attached card: Cursed Spear (Epic, Passive)

The sheer implications of the class were more than Rowan was willing to deal with. For one, he wasn't exactly ready to give up on his humanity and become just a weapon. In fact, the idea of that sort of terrified him. It might have worked if he was fighting by himself and without any attachments. But even though the class was appealing overall, it was a step too far for who he was now.

[Spear of Unity]
You fight for them, as they fight for you.
By picking the [Spear of Unity] class, you will gain
the ability to designate eight [Knights] who will
fight by your side as your companions.
Additional beneficial effects:
A grand boost to the effectiveness of two chosen stats.
You will gain an innate understanding of your [Knights].
Your [Knights] will be able to select and duplicate
the effects of one of your cards at will, though
the selection can only be made once.
You will gain ten percent of the stats your [Knights]
possess, and thirty percent of their experience
gain will be shared with you.
Class penalties:
A [Knight] must willingly accept their designation.
If a [Knight] breaks their connection to you or is
dismissed, you cannot elect a replacement for a year.
You can draw on the power of your [Knights],
but be wary lest you harm them.

Rowan was tempted by the class, especially considering everything it promised. It did not, after all, specify what tier the knights had to be.

Then there was the promise of stats, and even the ability to select which stats he wanted to improve. Still, he wasn't going to make his choice without considering every option.

[Monarch of Blood]
You shed blood for them. That blood now protects them.
By picking the [Monarch of Blood] class, you will gain
the ability to imbue your weapon with the power of this
origin element. All your subjects will benefit from
your affinity, and related classes will be both
stronger and easier to acquire.
Additional beneficial effects:
A grand boost to the effectiveness of your
wisdom and intelligence stats.
An innate sense of your subjects' condition, general
sentiment, and even the location of notable subjects.
A grand boost to your affinity to the blood element.
The ability to store blood and blood mana
in your weapon.
Immunity to blood loss.
Class penalties:
An increased affinity for slaughter.
A growing urge to amass blood and blood mana.
Attached card: Blood Banquet (Epic, Active)

Rowan was really not sure how to feel about the fact that he'd been offered a class like that. On the one hand, his affinity for blood-related cards was, at that point, not really something he could deny. On the other, which of his decisions had led to the unlocking of that class?

Was it his slaughter of demons and demonic beasts? His willingness to take human lives in defense of Rest's Remorse? Or was it the fact that he was willing to potentially plunge the town into chaos just to identify the hidden rebellious elements?

He moved on before his mind could spiral any more.

[Fragment of Brilliance]
You burn like a dying star.
By picking the [Fragment of Brilliance] class, you
will gain the ability to imbue the power of your
strikes with the totality of your being.
Additional beneficial effects:
An ascendant boost to the effectiveness of your
strength and dexterity stats.
The ability to channel every force that makes
up your being.
A grand boost to your mental resilience.
No one strike can fell you.
Class penalties:
Life span reduction.
Attached card: Moment of Brilliance (Epic, Active)

Nope. Nope. Nope. Nope. Just . . . nope. Rowan was a lot of things. Reckless. Somewhat willing to sacrifice pieces of himself if that meant everyone would come out the other end of a conflict alive. What he wasn't willing to do was outright commit suicide on the battlefield.

That, of course, left him with two final class choices. And just by looking at their special effects on his status screen, he was already not a huge fan.

So, he resolved to go through both of them quickly.

[Consecrated Spear]
Your will aligns with that of your god.
By picking the [Consecrated Spear] class, you will
gain abilities that conform to the portfolio
of your divine patron.
Additional beneficial effects:
An ascendant boost to the effectiveness of two chosen stats.
The ability to channel the might and presence
of your divine patron.

**A minor inheritance of your divine patron's portfolio.
An innate sense of and the ability to command
all of your divine patron's followers at or
under your own tier.
Class penalties:
Diverging from the will of your divine patron will
render your class unusable.
Attached card: Divine Descent (Epic, Active)**

**[Herald of Ennui]
They fear you, as is your right.**

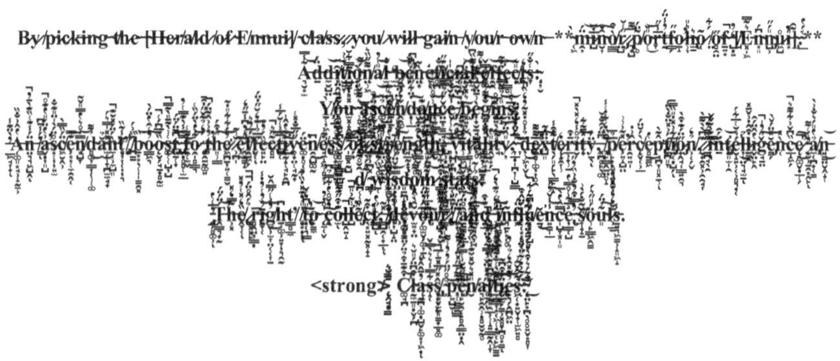

Right . . . Rowan just quietly closed out of that particular status screen window, silently promising to himself never to open anything marked in red again.

That still left the matter of picking his new Epic class.

Except, there's really only one acceptable choice, no? Rowan thought, with lots of conflicting feelings.

The monarch class was powerful, but a horrible fit for him overall due to the stat emphasis. The two classes he checked out last were out because neither of them was something he was willing to risk. He was Rowan Clairfont and not anyone's puppet or sacrifice or whatever.

Speaking of puppets, he would be lying if he said that [Spear Marionette] didn't appeal to him. It was powerful, it came with some rather insane benefits, and it would even make any future worry about his physical body a moot point.

Of course, there was the small drawback of forever abandoning his humanity and essentially becoming a magical parasite.

Feeling more resigned than happy, Rowan navigated his way back to [Spear of Unity] and hit accept.

"I can't believe how good this feels!" Marcus was all smiles, his hands constantly balling up and unclenching as he kept testing the new-found power within his body. Somehow, the excited wolfkin was forcing his way past the mind-numbing effect of Lucius's card and chattering away. It probably helped that he was the same tier as the Mercenary King now.

The others seemed just as thrilled at their advancement, each and every one brimming with newfound confidence.

All of them except for the hero. He was caught in a bit of a dilemma.

For his new class to work properly, he was expected to find and select [Knights]. Ordinarily, the hero would say that his party members were the perfect candidates for that. What stopped him was the instinctual knowledge of how to use his class.

More importantly, it was the "innate understanding of [Knights]" benefit that was giving him pause.

Did he want to have that kind of power over his party members? He considered them all friends, and Olivia more than that, but did he want to be in their heads at all times?

The simple answer to that question was no, he didn't. People kept secrets for a reason. They didn't share each and every emotion they felt for a reason. And while there was no guarantee that his class effect would be that intrusive, Rowan wasn't willing to bet on something like that. Especially when a test of the class feature would render him unable to elect a new [Knight] for a full year.

The worst part of the whole thing was that he knew the twins wouldn't really mind. Olivia would definitely choose to opt out, but he'd never ask her anyway.

Still, the doubts, the fear, and the desire to maintain their friendship kept the hero silent.

The march continued on.

* * *

The first inkling Rowan got that something was afoot was when the tracker keyed to Blake took them right past the battlefield where they'd fought the dinosaur monster.

There was a feeling, then, that he knew where the whole thing was leading. When a mere day later they came across another battlefield, that feeling crystallized into certainty.

The ground was churned up, trees were scarred and toppled, and all throughout the battlefield, scorched scars were present. There were remains of beasts, monsters, and even something Rowan strongly suspected was a true demon.

The thing that had hurt the Epic-tier monster enough for them to kill it was most likely his old friend.

"How far are we from the other hero, lad?" The Mercenary King had chosen to fall back so he could address Rowan.

For some reason, all of them refused to even consider carrying the odd compass around themselves. Only Rowan held it, and he had already taken it out. Over the course of the last day, the magical device had started to glow and even shake lightly. It was entirely guesswork and his own intuition, but Rowan gave it his best estimate.

"Another eight, nine hours of marching, I think. In that direction." Rowan pointed, but he really needn't have bothered.

The damaged jungle practically formed a path for them to follow. Rowan could even make out tracks where the boots of countless soldiers had trampled down the dirt.

"I'll have everyone get ready, then." Lucius sighed before his gaze turned stony. Rowan watched as every bit of the man's joviality evaporated, and in its place emerged the perfect ruler of the battlefield. Rowan briefly wondered which of the two was the actual personality of the Mercenary King. Either way, he was glad to have the commander ready.

As the army continued its march and scouts were dispatched ahead, Rowan expected trouble. For that reason, he and his party found themselves at the head of the procession, right alongside the Mercenary King. Tamara, too, started flying lower, ready to react to any ambushes or similar trouble.

Contrary to these preparations, however, the only thing they found were corpses. Human corpses.

Unrest swept through the troops, but it was quelled quickly enough when the Mercenary King's Epic-ranked aura suddenly swept over the entire army.

Rowan found that it reminded him of the day they faced the knight demon. But instead of panic and helplessness, the Mercenary King's aura steadied the army's spirits and repressed any sign of doubt. Rowan could feel the aura try to seep into his own skin before being blocked by Rowan's mana. For the first time since his advancement, Rowan reached out for his mana, and what he found stole his breath away.

His mana had shifted, turning from something light and ethereal into a viscous, persistent force. He felt like a single thought would allow him to impose his weight, his very existence, onto the world around him. That he could force everyone to acknowledge the fact that he was an indelible piece of reality.

For the very first time, Rowan *understood* exactly what the Epic-ranked aura was.

That understanding also led to more questions than before. What was the difference between his aura and the Mercenary King's? What about the Epic-tier beasts he had killed, with or without assistance? The dinosaur monster was just a stronger version of Rare beasts, and Tamara's fight with the snake monster had been tough but not impossible. Neither monster showed an aura.

Regardless, Rowan pushed his thoughts aside. The number of dead humans in their path was rapidly multiplying. More interestingly, he could also tell that most of the people had been killed while trying to run.

Some had died clawing their way forward, and some were left in pieces, clearly torn apart by a massive beast of some kind. Some even appeared entirely unblemished, save for the looks of agony on their faces. And when the scouts made their way back, he was almost shocked to see them alive.

"Lord Rowan, Chief," one of the scouts said, stepping forward. The others, Rowan noted, all looked pale and struggled to catch their breath.

"Report, lad. This isn't the time for formalities," Lucius scolded lightly, eyes still fixed on the ravaged forest and the corpses ahead of them.

"There is a large gathering of beasts ahead, sir. A few demons, too. Five in total, that we could see. The hero is still alive."

That was a relief, and a sigh escaped Rowan before he could even think to stop it as his eyes fell briefly closed. "How can you be sure? Did you see him?"

"No, sir. However, the beasts and demons are all gathered around a massive barrier. I suspect it's some kind of miracle-based spell, because of the mana color. Golden," the scout reported.

The Mercenary King sighed and nodded, then immediately gave his order. "We advance, at top speed. We need to recover the hero as quickly as possible. If you agree, of course, Lord Rowan."

Rowan didn't need to think about that one. "Yes, I agree. We should proceed as quickly as possible."

"Very well. Tamara, you caught all that, right?" the Mercenary King shouted up at the mage, who snorted and nodded her head. Rowan hadn't even noticed when she'd drifted lower to listen in. "Good. In that case, advance ahead of us. I trust you won't have trouble with laying down cover fire?"

The way the woman grinned was positively malicious. "Indeed I won't. I'm looking forward to really letting loose for the first time since my advancement."

She didn't wait for further instructions. The platform lifted, taking her into the sky along with her disciples. Rowan sighed. He still wasn't sure he could trust her, but time would tell. They had bigger things to worry about, like breaking into a trap meant for Blake. If it was a trap at all, and not a result of his recklessness.

"Very well. Let us advance," the Mercenary King bellowed, and another card effect swept over the troops.

Rowan felt the attempted intrusion and allowed it to happen this time. When the Mercenary King broke into a sprint, every soldier in the army joined him in perfect unison, power coursing through their bodies. Even Rowan felt a minor boost, though it was clearly not as effective on him as it once used to be when he was keeping a Rare class.

It didn't take very long for them to spot the barrier in the distance. A massive, glowing dome rose over the trees, groups of mages hovering above it as flames and lightning rained down from the sky.

Then, the monsters were in their sight, too, and Rowan felt the army lurch and then speed up even more. The Mercenary King was pushing hard, but when they slammed into the backs of the monsters, Rowan was convinced that it was worth it.

Soldiers that would typically struggle to face a single enemy at their own tier fought like they were possessed. Weapons flashed out with unerring accuracy, slicing and striking with a truly exquisite ferocity.

Rowan contributed, too. His weapon moved faster than he could ever manage before, scything down one Rare-tier beast after another in his rush to reach the barrier.

The Epic-tier monsters and demons had responded to the appearance of mages and were clustered near the far side of the dome. Ranged abilities were flying through the air like they didn't cost mana, but so far, Tamara was holding.

And the distraction meant that he could cut his way through right up to the barrier, his party and the Mercenary King right by his side. Already, Rowan could see vague shapes of people on the other side, but the opaque nature of the spell didn't let him glean much more than that.

"Go! We'll distract them for now. Regroup with the other hero," the Mercenary King shouted, pivoting to face the horde of monsters.

Rowan surged forward, hand reaching out for the barrier experimentally.

His fingers slipped right through.

The hero party stumbled, expecting the barrier to pose at least *some* resistance to their entry and entirely unprepared for what they would see inside.

Three women scrambled to their feet, immediately imposing themselves between the newly appeared party and the form of a man lying on the ground.

Rowan had quietly stewed in all sorts of doubt while on their way there. Would Blake be different? Would he still be the friend he'd known for so long? Not once, however, had he suspected that he *wouldn't* find him alive.

"Blake!" Rowan stormed forward, completely ignoring the questions and warnings the women threw his way. Some kind of mana bolt slammed into Rowan, but Marcus's defenses held and he didn't even notice.

He pushed his way past them and collapsed on his knees as his eyes fell on the pale face of his best friend. There was blood smudged there, and cold sweat collected on his brow. Rowan's stomach flipped, then fell, before a dizzying sense of relief when he noticed the slow rise and fall of Blake's chest.

"He's alive." Rowan breathed out quietly, screwing his eyes shut. "He's alive."

"Who do you think you are, doing something like that?!" A surprisingly strong hand closed on Rowan's shoulder, then stiffened when Rowan didn't budge at the attempt to shove him.

He turned slowly, cold eyes falling on the auburn-haired woman, whose expression was starting to look a whole lot more worried when faced with his glare. "Better question is, who are *you* to stop me from checking on my best friend?"

The answer was as smug as it was instant. "I'm his fiancée."

Rowan blinked. *Oh. Well, all right, then.*

CHAPTER TWENTY-TWO

To Face a Legend

Fiancée?" Rowan repeated, startled enough to momentarily forget the urgency of their situation.

He wasn't the only one who had something to say on the subject.

"Since when?!" another woman snapped.

"Can the two of you stop fighting *for a second*?" the last member of the party demanded, falling to her knees next to Blake just like Rowan and quickly grabbing his hand. A soft glow rose from her skin, slowly seeping into the hero's body. His eyelids fluttered, but he gave no further signs of life.

Rowan refocused. "What's wrong with him?"

"We were doing fine, making solid progress into the wastes, when we got attacked. I—I think that thing was at the Legendary tier. It just stabbed Blake through the stomach and then disappeared. That's when the other monsters showed up . . ."

The third woman trailed off, but Rowan could guess what had happened from there. Judging by all the bodies they'd encountered on the way, the soldiers had been slaughtered.

"And you can't heal him still?" Rowan asked.

"No. I'm not actually a healer," the woman said, taking a second to brush her brown hair out of her eyes and glare at the huffy blonde who had taken exception to the other woman's claims of Blake's marital status. "She is. I am just boosting his natural regeneration."

"It's not my fault the wound is cursed or something!" the other woman snapped, clearly still paying attention. "I tried everything—healing, purification, and cleansing rituals. All my cards, too! It's like the wound is a permanent part of him."

Her voice hitched at the end and she turned away. Whatever their issues with each other were, Rowan strongly suspected that they still cared about Blake. Mostly because he wasn't sure anyone could truly hate the man if they gave him a chance.

That wasn't enough to stem Rowan's frustration, though. *Are you telling me he's dying and they're still stuck playing out a stereotypical anime harem scene?*

Before he had to contemplate that further, Blake's eyes shot open.

The hero coughed, then broke into wheezes, rolling over on his side as a foul, tar-like liquid came streaming out of his mouth, eyes, ears, and nose.

Rowan recoiled so quickly he was almost on the other side of the barrier by the time he caught himself. His reaction was instinctual, a deep-seated revulsion that threw him for a loop.

"Blake?" Rowan asked quietly when the man gagged one last time and collapsed onto his back again.

Blake's eyelids fluttered, and a moment later he was on his elbows, squinting in Rowan's direction. "Rowan?"

Rowan really didn't want to, but he made his way right back to his friend, doing his best to ignore the foul liquid. "I'm going to kill you for worrying me like that," the Stalwart Hero hissed, drawing the other man into an awkward hug.

Blake returned a weak laugh, leaving Rowan alarmed at his lack of strength.

"What's happening to you?" Rowan asked quietly. There was a tear in Blake's shirt, he finally realized, and all Rowan could see through it was blackened skin, obsidian-like in its quality.

"You shouldn't try to stand, Blakey." The auburn-haired woman intervened immediately, going to kneel behind the hero and drawing his head back onto her lap. The glares the other two sent her were glacial. "He's been like this ever since. He passes out, wakes up, throws up, and then passes out again."

Her confession didn't make Rowan feel better.

"Can we risk moving him? We need to get out of here, quickly. If you really saw a Legendary demon lurking around here, then we're all as good as dead at the moment. One and a half heroes and a single army isn't going to cut it," Rowan said.

"It's fine, Rowan. I'm fine. I'm not going to fall here. Lady Sarina wouldn't allow it." Blake spoke with such strength, such conviction, that Rowan looked at him with disbelief.

"What's happening, Blake?"

Even Rowan wasn't sure what he was asking. Was he asking about his injury? Or about why he said the name of a frustrating, no-good goddess with such devotion?

"I think the demon is trying to possess me. Or corrupt me. I'm not sure. It's using the wound as a link of sorts. When I pass out, I encounter it in my dreams. It's . . . gotten close, a few times. There's no need to worry, though. My goddess had protected me each time."

Rowan looked the man in the eyes and, for the first time, realized he could see a light in them. Not a metaphorical light or even a reflection. It was honest-to-goodness, inner-glow nonsense.

With what he had encountered very recently, Rowan suddenly had a very bad premonition. "You picked the blue class, didn't you?"

Blake's eyes widened in surprise for a second, and even though he said nothing, Rowan had his answer.

"Shit. Okay. Shit. Never mind." Rowan shook his head, trying to refocus. "Listen, we need to move. How sure are you that the demon isn't going to reappear?"

"Very. As long as it's focused on corrupting me, it's not going to be able to move around or even do much. I know it's somewhere relatively close by, which would typically be a great opportunity to strike, but . . ."

"But you're half-dead and there are Epic-tier monsters out there. Listen, I need to know what the lot of you can do if we're all going to make it out of here alive."

Rowan addressed that last sentence to Blake's party, to the immediate displeasure of them all.

The blonde didn't hesitate to protest. "You can't just demand to know such—"

"Amanda Rhys, [Light-Winged Saintess]." Blake cut her off, pointing at her and giving Rowan a mini heart attack when he recognized the surname. "Jacqueline de Vort, [Bulwark of the End]." Blake's hand pointed right at the auburn-haired woman, who scoffed. "Mirabella Treagon, [Blessed Fortifier]."

Rowan heard Olivia's sharp intake of breath and a hiss of recognition at the last name, but there was little he could do about it at the moment.

"Thanks, Blake. So, healer, defender, and buffer," Rowan concluded.

"Barrier master—there's a difference," Jacqueline grumbled, crossing her arms. "I'm the whole reason we can chat here like this and why our hero is even still alive."

"And my buffs are just, what? Entirely unnecessary for you? Because if you can keep going without me, I'll happily focus on amplifying Blake's healing," the Treagon grumbled, her words ignored by everyone except for Blake, who sent her a winning smile.

Rowan wanted to pull his hair out.

"Okay, okay. Blake, you're going on my back and I don't want to hear any complaints." Rowan addressed his friend first before refocusing. "Can you empower us the way you can him? Because if what he said about the demon is right, we can probably kill most of the powerful enemies here and then flee."

The trio grimaced and exchanged looks, but the desire to see Blake safe clearly won out against whatever issue they had using their abilities on anyone else.

"Fine. We can use our buffs on you, I guess. We swore to act in service to our hero, and this is close enough."

Please, princess, don't sound so thrilled, Rowan complained in the safe confines of his mind, but didn't voice anything.

"But if I stop, will you be okay?" It was the Treagon that protested, looking genuinely terrified to stop using her amplification on Blake.

"I'll be just fine, my lady. Have faith in our goddess and she shall provide." Once again, Blake sounded so sure that Rowan's stomach turned.

"Yes, well, let's see about securing you and get a move on. Just please try not to puke on me?" Rowan asked hopefully, even as Olivia pulled a length of rope from her ridiculously and unnaturally large bag with a sadistic grin.

When the barrier suddenly fell, Rowan realized just how much it had been doing. The sights, the sounds, the *smell* of battle all became briefly overwhelming.

The Mercenary King was pulling off a small miracle, fighting three Epic beasts with only his lieutenants by his side. Tamara had another two distracted, raining what Rowan could only describe as ordnance down upon them while her apprentices worked to distract, defend, and corral.

The normal soldiers were doing quite well, too, though Rowan didn't miss the bodies, torn apart and squashed under the feet of the advancing horde.

Their chat and preparations had cost precious lives in the army, and Rowan was ready for payback.

That's when the buffs hit him. The Treagon girl erupted into a cascade of light far brighter than what she'd put on earlier, and the corona of light broke up into four strands that sank into Rowan and his party members.

Instantly, he could feel every last source of his strength surge in power, his body, mana, and spirit magnified in a way that felt glorious and left him feeling like he could topple mountains.

A moment later, the princess took action. Her power was equally impressive as a massive sun erupted out of nowhere overhead then collapsed into a million shooting stars.

Most of these landed on the bodies of the soldiers or the hero party, but quite a few sank into the bodies of monsters, too, with the largest number congregating in the five Epics.

The effect was immediate as a gentle warmth spread throughout Rowan's body. Meanwhile, each and every affected monster broke into pained howls, yips, hisses, and a myriad of other sounds.

Emboldened, Rowan rushed forward, heedless of the strangled gasp Blake made when they suddenly accelerated.

His first victim was a monster fighting against the Mercenary King's group, a humanoid with spindly arms, a twiggy body, and absolutely no facial features.

As he channeled power through his body and into his spear, Rowan marveled at how easy it was. The amplifier's abilities gave him so much more to work with, and the saintess's blessing made *handling* it all so much smoother.

Rowan experienced a brief surge of jealousy.

The power of the buffs meant that the second his spear so much as touched the odd monster, a whole section of its body disappeared in a shower of gore. A good third of its torso was gone. All Rowan had to do was hop back and watch as his card synergy drained the creature of all its blood due to the excessive damage he'd dealt.

His spear rejoiced at this, all the flecks of blood and flesh disappearing into its shaft, and Rowan relished how *easy* that was. If he had had buffs like that from the start, what would he have been capable of?

Of course, that's when explosions erupted around the other two Epic monsters, frighteningly contained and literally blue. The bolstered flames made possible by Olivia's new class drew cries of agony from the monsters, and his jealousy evaporated.

Sure, Blake had a whole party designed solely around buffing the power of a hero to the absolute utmost.

However, did he have a kick-ass alchemist girlfriend?

Milena, too, seemed reluctant to be upstaged. She raised her hands and a storm of black bolts erupted out of them. She was obviously relishing the moment, and as the bolts made contact, Rowan could tell why.

Every single enemy touched by the bolts showed immediate signs of one of her curses.

Some were suddenly weakened, ghostly faces pushing against their skin from the inside of their bodies in a way that made Rowan want to puke. Some collapsed, writhing in agony as their bodies cooked from the inside. Many more still were suddenly rendered blind, deaf, and incapable of feeling anything, stumbling around like newborns.

Rowan swallowed thickly, recognizing that the Epic tier was treating the wolfkin well.

He turned toward Marcus, half expecting to see the man suplex one of the monsters into submission or cow them all using his aura or something. The shield bearer just gave an awkward smile back.

"I mean, they're not going to be able to touch a single one of our people from now on until I go down?" Marcus offered weakly. Rowan laughed.

Then Rowan was moving again. He trusted his party to have the original trio of beasts handled, especially since one was down and the other two were almost cooked to death. He decided to make the most of the occasion and go for the other Epic-tier monster.

The monsters harassing Tamara and her mages were the oddest of the bunch.

One of them was a squid-like thing with far too many legs that were stretching to impossible lengths. Tamara was successfully burning the legs that came close, but the creature kept regenerating and trying harder.

The other resembled a statue, and it seemed to just be standing there, staring at the different mages. The only sign of anything being wrong was that a few mages would suddenly stumble at times and then send a volley of attacks against the creature that it just tanked through, not even moving.

Rowan chose to deal with the statue first.

"You won't be able to hurt it," Blake rasped in his ear, almost making Rowan stumble. "Here, let me help."

Before Rowan could stop him, Blake reached out and gently touched the shaft of his spear. The weapon lit up, and through their bond, Rowan could feel that it was suddenly *more*. Tougher, heavier, sharper, pressing against the very world around it.

Gritting his teeth at the way Blake was pushing himself, Rowan nonetheless committed to the strike. His body grew visibly gaunt in a matter of seconds while he positioned the spear like a lance, pointing it straight at the monster's rocky head.

The monster actually turned to face him, even if it didn't bother to dodge, and its eerie red eyes met Rowan's. The hero felt like someone had taken a sledgehammer to his head, but the impact was blunted, robbed of most of its strength.

The saintess's blessing wavered in strength, but it didn't matter.

Rowan's spear didn't falter.

It met the creature's face, taking it right in the eye.

Rowan had to admit that without Blake's help, he likely would have failed. It felt like he was trying to drive his spear straight into a diamond wall. But when his spear pulsed with the bright golden light, the wall gave way.

Ironically, the creature wasn't made out of rock throughout. Once its stony exterior cracked, brain matter and blood were sent soaring into the sky. A couple of the mages cried out, and Rowan laughed at their expressions of disgust. Blake whooped right with him.

"Goddess, I dislike mages. That was great," Blake chuckled, his arms briefly tightening around Rowan's chest. "By the way, whatever card you're using, it's freaky. Why are you almost reducing yourself to a skeleton?"

"Blake, if you keep distracting me, I'll feed you to the thing," Rowan threatened jokingly, making his friend laugh again.

"You wouldn't dare, you loooooove me too much," Blake teased.

"Why, Hero Blake, are you coming on to me? Is there something you'd like to tell your girlfriends about why you haven't picked one of them?"

Rowan marveled at the way he could *afford* to joke with his friends as he dodged the whiplike appendages of the squid monster. Just a couple of days ago, a single Epic-tier monster would have pushed him to his utmost.

Now? Now he was having fun.

Blake laughed louder, but before he could make an inappropriate comment about how Rowan was the one tying the two of them together, the sky turned into flames.

Tamara was clearly not amused by the hero intervening and stealing her experience. The entire light show turned into a single, thin column of fire. It barely covered the main body of the monster, but then the flames went from red to white to blue and the thing *evaporated*. For just a moment, Rowan was thoroughly impressed by the woman's strength and control.

Then her apprentices started falling down while she just looked smug, and Rowan realized that her attack wasn't without its costs.

Blake shared Rowan's insight. "Did she train up a whole lot of apprentices *just* so they could manage the fallout of her spells?"

Rowan strongly suspected that the answer to Blake's question was yes, but they didn't really have more time to waste. A glance back told him that the other two Epic monsters were dead, too, and that it was time to run before the Legendary showed up again and ruined everyone's day.

"Lucius! Lead a retreat!" Rowan bellowed across the battlefield. A card effect swept over the army, and then they were moving, fighting against what monsters they had to while struggling to get away.

At least Marcus was as good as his word. Rowan saw plenty of monsters take advantage and strike against unprotected backs, but all that led to were a few grunts from the shield bearer.

Not that they could afford to let them take potshots forever.

"We'll cover the retreat!" Rowan really shouldn't have bothered with that particular order, because his party members were already on it.

Olivia was chucking her conjured potions left and right, this time focusing on explosion range instead of on focused strikes. While Milena and Rowan demolished the monsters and Marcus focused on protecting everyone, she was building a barrier of fire none of them dared try to pass.

That did leave them on the wrong side of the conflagration, but Rowan met Marcus's eyes, nodded, and decided to trust the man. He plunged right into the flames, and while Blake let out a strangled grunt and started glowing of his own accord, neither of them felt the sting of heat or the choking of the smoke.

They were through in a couple of seconds.

Any monsters that tried to copy them bitterly regretted it and were burned down in seconds.

"Keep retreating. Lucius, if you can push them faster somehow?" Rowan yelled. "We need to put as much distance between us and the Legendary as possible."

That earned Rowan a wild-eyed look, but to his credit, the Mercenary King didn't even bother to ask. He just intensified his card effect far past what they'd experienced in the past and the entire army practically flew down the path they'd followed previously.

Rowan felt a grin sneaking its way onto his face and exchanged a victorious look with Olivia, who was suddenly by his side. His fingers twitched toward hers, but even he felt a little awkward trying to hold hands while fleeing a monster horde and carrying his best friend on his back.

Nonetheless, they'd done it. The Legendary hadn't shown up, their losses weren't catastrophic, and they'd gotten Blake and his party out. The three women with Blake were sort of struggling to follow along because they were, for some reason, unaffected by the Mercenary King's buffs, but that didn't matter much.

They were alive.

"Don't mean to alarm you, Rowan, but I might be taking another nap soon." Blake's voice was thoroughly drained of energy, so much so that Rowan almost stopped in his tracks to check on him.

"What's happening? Talk to me here," Rowan said.

"I can feel it coming on. Every time. The thing in my chest *squirms* and then tries to extend up into my head. Either I manage on my own, or Lady Sarina protects me, and I end up puking it all out. It's just unpleasant."

Rowan's heart started beating faster as his mind replayed the moment when the knight demon grabbed him back at Felton's Mill.

"Jeesh, mate, you really got yourself into a mess this time." Rowan tried for a joking tone but just ended up sounding miserable.

"Tell me about it. My goddess didn't even want me coming here. Wanted me to finish getting rid of all the *heretics* back in the capital, but I didn't want to keep waiting and let people get hurt."

The way he said *heretics* was so vicious and full of vitriol that Rowan shuddered. He wasn't sure what to think or feel on the subject.

This was Blake. His best friend. He kept catching glimpses of the man he knew and cared about. However, this new Blake the zealot was a grim reality, too.

I already no longer trust Kayla. Now, something weird's happening with Blake, too. How do I even know I can trust him? Unless . . .

It suddenly hit him, and quite hard, at that.

Running at the back of his own army, surrounded by party members he was willing to trust with his life, Rowan realized how much he'd changed.

He was more than willing to put his life into the hands of Olivia, Marcus, and Milena, no questions asked. He was so afraid of messing up those friendships, he didn't even want to bring up his new class feature with them.

And yet, the second Rowan was reunited with Blake, he was tempted to offer him a spot as one of his [Knights]. Somehow, a space had grown between the two of them. But Rowan also had a practical reason for the thought. His regeneration card might help the situation.

After all, it was supposed to "restore a body to its *natural* condition." This wasn't like with Bron, where giving him the card would have been useless since the card was too low-tiered. The card was at Epic now, and its effect was far more powerful and pervasive.

And making Blake a [Knight] would let him pick one card out of Rowan's deck to copy.

"Hey, Blake. Might have a solution." Rowan wet his lips, hesitating just for a second before pushing on. "I just got to Epic, and my class is called [Spear of Unity]. I can select eight people to link my class with. If I do, they get access to a copy of one of my cards, of their own choosing. It doesn't count against their deck, either. And I have an extremely powerful regeneration card . . ."

Rowan trailed off, ignoring the startled looks of his party members and the way he was pushing his guilt down.

"Really think it would help?" Blake asked.

"Didn't have time to switch cards around with us in combat and rushing about right now, but yeah, I think it would. The card says it returns your body to its 'natural state.' I doubt that means corrupted as hell."

It didn't take Blake even a second to decide. He didn't even ask about potential drawbacks to doing it, or what Rowan would get out of the whole thing. "Let's go for it."

So, for the very first time, Rowan reached out for his new card, triggering its effect.

"Huh, yeah, got a window asking me if I want to accept and an offer of cards to select," Blake said. "You've got some pretty nice ones. Good. See the card, too. Well, here goes."

Blake finalized his choice and hit the final yes. A stream of power opened up between the two heroes, linking them, letting them tap into a part of each other's strength.

A smile touched Rowan's lips as he felt the blazing ball of trust, friendship, and care emanating from Blake toward him. All doubts were squashed. All suspicions washed away. This was still his best friend, even if things had changed a bit.

And then a flash of something cold and dark sneaked through the bond, too, and Rowan barely had the time to gasp before he was falling.

Rowan jerked and blinked awake, only to hiss in pain and confusion. All around him, a blighted land stretched, dead and barren. In spite of the cloudless sky, the only source of light was the weak, reddish glow of a flickering sun. Even with it at its zenith, the sky was practically black as pitch.

"Rowan? What are you doing here?" Blake's voice was hurried, panicked.

Rowan blinked and looked around again, this time immediately spotting his best friend. He wasn't sure how he'd missed him the first time, with the land as open as it was and the link between them still blazing bright.

Except, not everything was as it should be. Rather than a man of flesh and blood, Rowan realized that Blake was cast out of pure, golden light. Every detail was there. Everything was moving and working as it should. He just didn't look like a human being. And right there, in his chest, a ball of miasma and foulness coiled, trying to stretch its tendrils higher. They were already up to the hero's neck and grasping ever onward.

A startled glance down revealed that Rowan wasn't exactly in his own body, either. His form was made out of reddish energy with a black tint, but at least he didn't have a parasite squirming in him.

"I—Wait, where am I?" Rowan demanded, quickly clambering to his feet. His spear materialized in his hand, almost like magic. But looking at it was a challenge. The entire weapon was darkness, blood, and some strange matter wrought together in a beautiful whole.

"This is what happens every time I pass out," Blake said. "Though I don't know why you're here, or why you can summon that." He pointed at Rowan's spear, almost pouting. "I'm stuck with only my class and cards. You know what? It doesn't matter. He's coming. I can feel it."

Rowan didn't have time to wonder at the fact that Blake didn't have a bound weapon, especially when his friend was sponsored by the king instead of a backwater baron. Rowan was a bit preoccupied by the storm cloud tearing its way across the horizon, making an even bigger mess of the blighted lands.

There really wasn't much the two heroes could do. They fell in together, Rowan clutching his spear, Blake summoning a sword and shield made of light.

Finally, just before swallowing them whole, the storm cloud stopped.

"My lord will be so proud of me. Two heroes, for the price of one!" The voice was ripe with madness, malice, and a twisted kind of worshipful devotion that made Rowan feel sick.

When Rowan finally felt the thing's aura sweep over them, almost driving them to their knees, there was little doubt left.

They were face-to-face with a Legendary demon.

CHAPTER TWENTY-THREE

Broken Light

Rowan made the first move.

His spear became a blur as it shot straight for the demon's face. Unfortunately, it was flicked away before it could ever get close.

Rowan tried again, undeterred. His sweep was kicked away, his stab was simply blocked by an impenetrable hand, and his furious kick was absorbed with no trouble while leaving a dull ache in Rowan's shin.

Blake wasn't faring much better. The other hero was glowing in a corona of light, hacking and slashing, but each and every one of his attacks was outright absorbed by curtains of darkness that would flicker into existence a fraction of a second before the attacks would impact.

"Just. Die!" Rowan hissed, struggling to empower his spear for some reason. His mana was flowing into it, but it was sluggish and difficult to control. But he managed a decent strike with the renewed effort. The tip of the spear exploded against the hand the demon was blocking with, and a couple of its digits were lost in the process. A large cut marred its palm, too, bleeding black ichor that repulsed Rowan.

The demon grunted and took a quick step forward. Before Rowan could react, the demon used the very same appendage to backhand Rowan across the face.

The world turned into nothing but dizziness and pain. Rowan was vaguely aware that his body was tumbling over the ground, but awareness was an impossibility when faced by the sheer agony of having his face entirely caved in.

And yet, with a gasp and a whimper, he came to. He was on his back, staring at the depressing sky, with actual, functioning eyes.

I don't want to think about it, but . . . Hadn't one of his eyes popped out of its socket, and wasn't the other reduced to a mess running down his face?

He lifted a trembling, *functioning* hand up to his face and gingerly touched it. Everything was still there, all the bones and skin and other pieces in the right places. The only trouble was, when he pulled his hand back, it was covered in a red-black residue.

"Rowan, don't just stay still!" Blake's shout jerked Rowan back to awareness, even if he sort of wanted to continue ignoring reality when he laid eyes on what was happening.

Blake was getting savaged.

The hero was bleeding gold all over, and the mass of darkness was already inching its way up his jaw. Rowan suspected that the only reason Blake was still in the fight was the glowing silhouette embracing him from behind.

The figure was barely there and the most visible features were the arms crossed around Blake's neck. Even then, when the silhouette turned and looked in his direction, Rowan instantly knew who it was.

The goddess of light herself, protecting her champion.

With gritted teeth, Rowan managed to force his protesting body upright, focusing on shoving more power into his spear tip. It was even harder this time around, both because his mana was fighting him more ferociously and because there was less of it.

Rowan could tell that his regeneration was working, but like everything else, it seemed muted, barely there.

They were losing.

At least the demon was focused on Blake at the moment, a cruel smirk on its lips as it methodically worked to dissect the hero. The demon seemed to benefit from the oddness of the place. Like Rowan's face, its hand was back to normal.

Shuffling slowly to the creature's back, Rowan tried to find anything resembling a weak point. The closest he came to one was the creature's tail, which Rowan spotted for the first time, long and sinuous and deadly looking, adorned with a myriad of spikes.

If I cut that off, I don't think anything's going to change . . . Then again, I'm not too sure if anything changes with how everything seems to heal in this place.

Rowan grimaced and decided to just commit. Steps lighter than they'd ever been, Rowan drew closer, counting on Blake and the sounds of the ongoing battle to mask his approach.

"Honestly, the two of you." The demon giggled and then his head turned to the sound of a snapping spine a full circle to stare right at Rowan. "What are you hoping to accomplish?"

Its tail moved faster than Rowan could react, blood filling the hero's lungs as the spiky appendage speared right through his chest.

Rowan would have collapsed on the spot as a pain worse than anything he'd experienced before filled him. The only problem was that he was literally dangling on the demon's tail.

Blake screamed a wordless cry of frustration and fear, erupting into an ever-growing ball of light that managed to make even the demon frown. The monster whipped around, launching Rowan straight into Blake's chest and making both of the heroes crumple to the ground in a heap.

Blake's light continued to build.

"Don't worry, I've got you," Rowan's best friend whispered, and then the world was consumed by light.

Rowan blinked his eyes open to the same depressing scenery, struggling to make sense of what was happening. They were obviously still in whatever hellscape the demon favored for its shenanigans, but the creature was nowhere to be seen. Which was definitely a good thing, considering the way Rowan's body ached and protested even the slightest bit of motion.

"You okay there?" Blake grunted, and Rowan startled upon realizing he was still lying on top of the other hero.

"Sorry, sorry," Rowan mumbled, managing to stagger upright and offer his friend a hand. Blake took it, and then they were both standing. "What in all the hells is going on?"

Blake just sighed. "The same thing that happens every time I pass out. I have no clue what this place actually is. A mental realm? The demon's mind? Whatever it is, I always fight it here. And I always lose."

The other hero absentmindedly rubbed at his throat, and Rowan realized there were runes, sigils, and more engraved there. Like the thickest choker in existence, they encircled Blake's throat, glowing brighter every time the tiny smidgen of darkness tried to worm its way higher. Even though the darkness's progress had been reset, Rowan just wasn't willing to bet on the effectiveness of Blake's new defensive measures for very long.

"How do you always get out?" The question was a little desperate, but who could blame Rowan for trying?

His friend, unfortunately, shook his head. "I don't, Rowan. So far, Lady Sarina was able to pull me out every time I'm on the verge of . . . not dying, exactly. Just . . . it feels like I'm getting slowly unmade while fighting the thing."

Rowan was forced to reexamine them both and he didn't like what he saw. The color of their "bodies," which had once been so rich, was slowly leeching away. Blake was more an off-white than golden now, and Rowan's own red and black were diluted.

Granted, he had no clue what that meant, but it couldn't be good.

"You're clearly doing something right, though. You managed to drive him off, for now," Rowan said. And it was true. Whatever the light Blake wielded against it was, the demon was nowhere to be found.

So, Rowan didn't like the odd look Blake gave him. "I didn't drive him off. I shifted our location. I can't win, but I've been learning how to run and buy time to recover a little. Problem is, every time I do, he ends up finding me."

"Oh."

Rowan really couldn't find a single difference about the plains they were currently in compared to their previous location. Everything was still dead and barren and the sky was just as gloomy as before. Blake pulled him from his contemplation by tugging on his hand. Rowan didn't know where exactly the other hero wanted them to go, but he wasn't about to doubt his expertise on what they should do. "Where we headed?" Rowan asked.

"Nowhere. Just can't stay still. He shows up faster when I do that. Listen, Rowan . . ." Blake trailed off, refusing to look at him.

"Whatever you want to say, just do it. We've known each other for long enough that I can tolerate a stupid question or two," Rowan said, desperate to lift the mood a little. He didn't like the gravity Blake had injected his voice with.

His friend sighed. "Please . . . I want you to break whatever bond we formed before we both ended up here."

"What? No! I know I'm not much help, and my healing card isn't working the best here, but it's still helping, and I won't leave you here!"

Rowan was pretty sure he was right on every count, too. While his regeneration card wasn't its usual reliable self, he could *feel* it working when he focused, struggling to pull color back into his ethereal frame.

"You wouldn't be here without the bond. And I . . . I don't think we can win, even if we're fighting together. That thing's a Legend. We need all our armies and Kayla by our side if we want to actually kill it," Blake said. There was a deep bitterness there, especially when he mentioned Kayla's name.

Desperate both for some answers and to change the subject, Rowan latched on to that. "Speaking of, I met Kayla briefly. She wasn't really, how to say it, herself? What happened in the capital after I left?"

Blake hunched in on himself, and Rowan was briefly worried his friend would just shut him away and refuse to talk any more. The emotions he was feeling through their bond were a mess. It was a churning storm of doubt, fear, disgust, anger, regret, and so much more.

"When we ended up here, Kayla started . . . changing. I don't know what she went through, exactly. We only had brief chances to meet up with each other," Blake said, his voice growing low as he forgot about moving and stood in place. "Still, she grew colder and colder, and then she stopped visiting altogether. The last time we met . . ."

After the moment of silence stretched into two, Rowan asked, "Yeah?"

"She said a bunch of stuff about how I shouldn't trust Harold. The king, I mean. How he's been plotting since before we arrived in the world. She insulted my goddess and said that Lady Sarina was just using me, too. The fight got bad and she left. She hasn't spoken to me since."

Rowan wasn't sure what to say. More to the point, he wasn't about to disagree with any of the stuff Kayla had apparently told Blake. The king was suspicious at best, and the less said about the goddess of light, the better. Frankly, a part of Rowan was upset that Blake was so mindlessly following a goddess who was at least half the reason they were here in this mess. Rowan took a deep breath and picked a different approach.

"Why do you think she said all that?"

"I don't know!" Blake exploded, teeth audibly clenching as his hand tightened on Rowan's arm. Rowan thought he looked desperate for reassurance. "I don't know . . ."

It wasn't the best approach, but Rowan wasn't about to just drop the subject entirely. Especially not if he wanted to keep his friendship with Blake. "Well, did the king say or do something to her? Surely you didn't just dismiss her without asking?"

"He didn't. I'm sure of it. Why would he? He's been nothing but nice to me, and Amanda says . . . never mind what she says, Harold has our best interests at heart, okay? And my goddess has protected me time and again! I wouldn't be here if she didn't pull me out every time things got really bad," Blake protested.

Rowan sucked in a frustrated breath through his teeth, taking the time for fear of saying something indelicate. He observed Blake's current state. A gold color was definitely leeching back into his frame, and the more of it that accumulated, the faster the process got.

"You're healing up pretty nicely," Rowan tried.

"Yeah." Blake allowed himself a smile. "I still think you should break our bond and leave, but the card *is* helping. This is the first time I'm actually healing while stuck in here."

Rowan hummed in contemplation, then decided to go for the throat. "Do you actually trust the king and his daughter?"

To his credit, this time, Blake didn't rush to answer. "I think so. They helped me. Got me good equipment. Trained me. Helped me level up. Wouldn't have even met my current party without all their help."

"The party that can do nothing but buff you up? You saw what my party could do, back at the fight."

"Please don't remind me—that wolfkin mage was scary." Blake actually shuddered, making Rowan smirk.

"Shaman. But point still stands."

"I know, I know. But . . . trust me, they're not . . . bad. They like to argue, but they work great as a team when they're supposed to. Besides, you caught them at their lowest. They've burned through a bunch of their mana protecting us and trying to keep me alive," Blake said.

"Blake, just because someone does the bare minimum after stealing you away from your own life doesn't mean you should trust them."

Blake slumped even farther down.

"We can't just keep second-guessing everyone's motivations, Rowan," Blake said. "They want their world to be safe. Sure, they summoned us without consent, but would you really just go back right now if you could?"

Rowan tried to say yes. But stopped just short of the words forming in his throat. The second he thought about Olivia, his party, and even the baron and his wife, he couldn't say the words anymore.

"Thought so. You're way too nice to walk out on all the people who need you." Blake offered Rowan a smile, but it was a small, fragile thing. "Kayla would leave. She just wants to be done with it, I bet. You know she always had trouble caring about anyone or anything."

Kayla had some issues. That was true. However, that sounded more like self-justification to Rowan, but again he said nothing. If he defended Kayla, he would also feel compelled to admit that until very recently, he was fully on board with leaving the second he could.

Eyes fixed on the ground, Rowan struggled to come up with an argument, any argument, to make Blake understand how horrible an idea it was to trust the king. Instead, he got thoroughly distracted by the soft, green shoots under their feet.

"Blake, does this ground look different to you?" Rowan muttered, looking around.

While there were a ton of differences he was only starting to understand between his real body and the one he was currently stuck in, it seemed that stats carried over well enough. The extra perception helped Rowan spot all the emerging greenery all around them.

The problem was, he was pretty sure that hadn't been there before, since they hadn't made much progress walking and he would have noticed if they suddenly popped up.

"There are plants? Why are there plants here? This is the first time I'm seeing anything like this," Blake said in wonder, stopping and kneeling to gently inspect one of the fragile shoots struggling to grow.

"You really shouldn't make it a habit to run like this, you know. It's horribly rude to give your host the slip like that." The oily voice of the demon had both heroes spinning around, only to find the creature examining them with more than a little amusement.

"We're in your world then, are we?" Rowan asked, mind racing for ways to distract the creature for as long as he could. Anything was preferable to getting outright curb stomped.

The demon just shrugged, offering them an open-mouthed smile with far too many teeth. "Shall we continue where we left off?"

Blake seemed to have an objection to that, however, seeing as the hero grabbed Rowan closer and once more erupted into a storm of light.

The scream of frustration from the demon would have been amusing, if the two heroes didn't just blink into existence in yet another stretch of lifeless wasteland. Well, not entirely lifeless. With a frown, Rowan realized that the same shoots were present all around them once again.

"I managed to do it again," Blake said, wonder in his voice. "I typically don't manage to do the disappearing trick twice." He looked down at his hands, clenching and unclenching them with wonder. "I feel so much better than I did before."

"My card is working, then," Rowan concluded, and a simple visual inspection proved him right, too.

Blake was back to where he was upon their appearance in the infernal realm, golden and glowing. In fact, a closer look even told Rowan that the darkness swirling in the hero's body was shrinking. It was sluggish now, its grasping tentacles barely rising from the hero's chest.

"It is. It really is. If we can just stay ahead of the demon, we might win." Blake gave Rowan a dazzling smile, making it difficult to continue being upset.

"We should get moving again, then. We're safe for now?" Rowan asked and got a nod in return. "Then it's time to talk about something else."

"I don't like that look in your eye, Rowan," Blake said.

"Then you shouldn't have gone and accepted a party with three women in it, Blake. Now, before that freak catches up again, spill the beans. What's up with the whole harem-protagonist thing you've got going on?"

Blake groaned and blushed, but Rowan wasn't about to just drop the subject.

"It's nothing, really. I honestly think most of them don't even like me," Blake groused, making Rowan quirk an eyebrow his way. "I'm serious! Getting a hero into the family is a big deal. Pretty sure they were ordered to pursue me, so I don't want to force them into an awkward position."

Rowan had to agree with part of that, making him wince a little. "Still, you can't tell me they're constantly fighting over you like that without at least some personal feelings involved."

Blake blushed again, making Rowan laugh. "Oh, shut it. Okay, so maybe they care a little. Honestly . . . I think Mirabella actually does like me. If any of the three do, it would be her. And, I mean, I *might* like her, too."

This time, Rowan couldn't help himself. He groaned in frustration. "The Treagon. Out of all of them, you like the Treagon?"

"What's wrong with that?" Blake asked defensively, giving him side-eye.

"Oh, nothing much. They just stole all the land, power, and even the card collection of my girlfriend's family." Rowan scowled, giving his best friend the stink eye back.

At least Blake seemed suitably shocked. "What? That can't be right. I didn't hear anything about that."

"Well, I bet they don't go around discussing how the only reason they're dukes is because they stole everything they own from the

Suttons. Honestly, you saw how slimy and disgusting the nobles were during that whole mess they called a welcoming feast," Rowan said.

"I mean, he's not pleasant, sure, but his daughter's not like that. Honestly, you'd probably like her if you gave her a chance. I can see the two of you talking about some random book together," Blake teased, even if there was a slight edge of discomfort to his voice.

"We'll see. I'll have to make sure she's good enough for my best friend. Still, you actually care about her? It's not just infatuation, or whatever? You're in love?"

Faced with the earnest question, Blake blushed and nodded. This time, Rowan managed to restrain the groan he wanted to let out. After all, there *was* a chance that Blake was right and the woman was a sweetheart. It didn't change Rowan's feelings on the matter of her family, though.

"Well, as long as she makes you happy, I guess. I can at least promise I won't be mean on purpose. And I'll stop Olivia from poisoning her. Or I'll try to," Rowan said.

"Your girlfriend's the alchemist then, I take it?"

"Yeah, she's amazing, right?"

"Well, if you fancy dating someone who can literally blow you up," Blake teased, and the two friends exchanged glances.

Even stuck in a nightmarish reality, hunted by a too-powerful demon, the two broke down into laughter as they allowed themselves to finally relax a little.

Sure, things were horrible. But at least they now knew their friendship wasn't over, as Rowan had privately worried it might be. Blake was probably in the same camp.

"I've missed talking to you, man," Blake admitted quietly, a smile on his lips.

Rowan was about to agree when he ran face-first into a tree. "What the heck?" he sputtered, trying to get what he was fairly certain were pine needles out of his mouth. His mouth had been open when he ran into the branch and the earthy taste was altogether not pleasant for him. "There are trees?"

"First time I've seen any," Blake admitted, glancing around in worry at the veritable wall of trees that had formed up in front of them out of the blue.

A quick glance back revealed the same plains as before, with the exception of the plant shoots now standing even higher.

And then the angry roar of an approaching storm also announced the unwelcome return of their stalker. As he looked in the approaching demon's direction, however, Rowan was more confused than anything. He could spot the monster's head forming up out of the cloud, and its expression was livid. It was also wreaking complete destruction as it went, leaving the ground barren in its wake.

Things were changing, and Rowan had no idea if that was good or not.

"Can you get us out again?" Rowan asked.

Blake looked worried, hesitation obvious in his posture and features, but still nodded. "I'll try."

"No!" the demon screamed. "Don't you—"

The light flashed again, cutting off the angry demon's bellows.

When Rowan looked around, he was surprised to find they were standing, once again, at the edge of the tree line. Somewhere far off in the distance, he could even spot the lightning flashes of a storm.

"We should keep moving," Blake insisted, plunging into the forest without a single look back. A contemplative look on his face, Rowan followed.

The trees were thick, and growing thicker as they went, but that wasn't what worried Rowan. The demon was finding them faster and faster. At first, they'd walk for half an hour or more before the monster reappeared and Blake was forced to pull off his disappearing trick.

Now, however, they were barely lasting ten minutes before the demon showed up, roaring in fury and demolishing the trees around him.

Another thing that worried Rowan was the darkness in Blake's chest.

Natural Renewal was clearly doing work, because Blake's golden complexion was shinier than ever. Even the darkness had curled into a tight ball, but that's where the progress on that front had stalled out. The obsidian ball of shifting shadows stood lodged right above Blake's heart, and it was stubbornly resisting any further attempts at diminishing it. That, along with the rapidly improving color of the trees and the quality of the soil under their feet, got Rowan thinking.

Clearly, they were moving closer to the center of *something*, seeing as they could physically spot the places where they'd fled the demon behind them, darkness howling above the treetops. But was that a good thing?

Would they manage to get away from the demon entirely, or would the infernal simply corner them at the center and devour them on the spot?

More importantly . . .

Rowan took a deep breath. "Blake, I don't think we're in the demon's world at all. I think this is *your* world. Or mind. Or soul. Or whatever. Why it's a prairie followed by a forest, I don't have a clue."

Blake stopped, looking back at Rowan with wild eyes. "You think? I mean, I feel something calling for me, from up ahead. I feel like I *have* to get to it. Think we'll be able to leave if I do?"

"I don't know, but I guess we'll have to find out?"

Blake didn't need more encouragement, and the two heroes broke into a run. They'd been hesitant to do so before, since the ground was oddly treacherous and full of roots, but the enraged roars of the demon in the distance were good motivation.

As they drew closer to whatever was calling to Blake, a smile slowly grew on his face, and his steps became surer and more hurried. "I can feel it. We just need to get there, Rowan, and—"

Blake cried out in pain as he ran headfirst into an invisible barrier. A barrier that, a second later, turned pitch-black and rose into the sky, shouting their location for all to see.

"There you are, you fools." The demon's voice echoed from everywhere, and its storm corrected its course, coming right for them. "Think you can run from me? This is *my* playground. Mine." The trees around them were violently ripped out of the ground as the demon once more coalesced into physical form. "Foolish. So foolish. Misery was lost to us, but I was hoping at least Ennui and Malice would come along more easily. Now, I see I was mistaken to be as kind as I was to you two. One [Holy Paladin] and one [Spear of Unity]. Your precious gods and classes won't protect you."

Rowan's mind raced, looking for any possible solution. He wasn't going to let the demon's ominous words come to fruition. Failing to come to an obvious way to fix what ailed them, though, he desperately fell back on the only thing he had. Words. "Why do you know what class I was offered when reaching Epic?"

The demon cackled, shaking its head. "Oh Ennui, *dear* Ennui. Did you think you can travel between the planes unnoticed? That your soul can slip into the world we've been monitoring for generations unaltered? We know you. We know all of you. You would do so much *better* on our side."

"How? Why would we even want to join you?"

Rowan was barely aware of what he was saying or hearing; his eyes were staring at the squirming ball of darkness in Blake's chest.

"Why wouldn't you? You would have to give up the local spark of divinity, true. But what we offer is so much better. Why not ascend early and take your place by our side as we bring this world to heel?"

Rowan didn't dignify that with a response. Instead, his gaze met Blake's, and he asked a question of his own as his energy slowly seeped into the tip of his spear. "Do you trust me?"

Rowan received a nod without any hesitation, and with a sad smile, Rowan drove the spear right into his friend's chest.

CHAPTER TWENTY-FOUR

Peace at Last

Several things happened all at once when Rowan's spear sank without resistance into Blake's translucent chest.

First, the demon screamed as the ball of darkness evaporated at the spear's attack. Second, Blake let out the startled gasp of a man who had just touched a red-hot stovetop but somehow expected it to be cool. And third, the glowing outline of the goddess Sarina formed behind the partially corrupted hero.

Rowan's power exploded the very next instant, opening a sizable hole in Blake's back and eradicating every last trace of the corrupting influence within him. As Rowan took stock of the damage, his eyes met the glowing orbs of the goddess, and he could see the distaste there plain as day.

"This once. *Once.* I help you in return for this favor," Sarina sneered, her voice echoing within Rowan's mind as she thrust her hand in his direction. A beam of light erupted from it, striking the Stalwart Hero right in the middle of his chest, and then his senses vanished in favor of absolute darkness.

Words unfurled before Rowan.

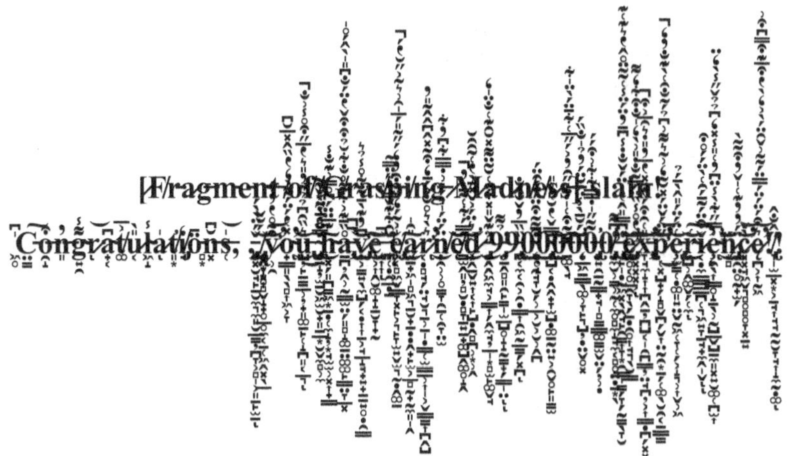

Seeing the obvious corruption of the status window didn't startle Rowan nearly as much as seeing the garbled font in *blue*. Still, he didn't have all that much time to reflect on things, since the very next instant, he was gasping back into awareness.

"Rowan! Rowan?"

Rowan cracked open his eyes and saw Olivia's tear-streaked face. A goofy smile rose on his face. "Oh, hello there."

And then he passed out.

When Rowan woke up again, he did so slowly. He first became aware of the softness under his skin, enveloping most of him in its embrace. The next thing he noticed was the sound of humming and tinkling glass. His heart skipped a beat when he recognized Olivia's voice. He relaxed into the bed. Olivia wouldn't be humming a tune if they were still in immense danger.

Rowan finally blinked his eyes open and dispelled his last vestiges of terror and anxiety. A smile found its way to his face as he watched his favorite alchemist whirl between the working stations around her.

For some reason, he was laid out on a bed that had been brought into her potioneering lab. Despite the potions being brewed, it was a pretty good place for a nap. All the windows were heavily curtained. Rowan could even remember a rather tense conversation where the baroness forbade her daughter from fully boarding up those same windows.

He wasn't sure how long he just lay there and watched her work, but Olivia eventually put down the various vials, stretched, and took a glance in his direction. The second she spotted him, she was by his side like she'd learned to teleport.

"You're awake. *How long* have you been awake? No, wait, don't answer that. I feel like you're just going to upset me." Before Rowan could answer, Olivia was kissing him, and Rowan *definitely* didn't want to interrupt that.

Some fifteen or so minutes later, once Olivia had worked through most of her frustration by assaulting his lips, she was curled up on his chest and Rowan could no longer continue ignoring reality, no matter how tempting.

"How *are* we here? What happened?" Rowan asked.

"You passed out and traumatized the lot of us, is what happened," Olivia grumbled, but there was no real heat in her voice.

"A bit more detail, dear?"

"Well, after you used the secret new ability you refused to share with us, you and the other hero both passed out. His party freaked out, and we weren't far behind. The corruption on his chest briefly flared up, but then it actually got better. We all calmed down a bit, at least until you both woke up again. You were fine, but seeing him throw up blood all over the place and pass out was . . ."

"Traumatizing?" Rowan offered hesitantly, earning a glare for his efforts.

"Sure. *Traumatizing* is a serious enough word. Anyway, after *that*, he was finally corruption-free, so we figured you were both well enough to move. There was a thoroughly terrifying roar somewhere in the distance, felt like it flattened us all for a second, but nothing all that significant happened."

It was Rowan's turn to pause as he caught the implication she'd tried to gloss over. "Nothing *all that* significant? Meaning something happened?"

Olivia huffed, but clarified. "There was a bit of a disagreement," she hedged. "You know, with the other hero party. Well, and your fellow hero Kayla, when she finally showed up."

Rowan tried to sit up, but with Olivia intent on keeping him down, the attempt promptly failed. He settled on using his words. "Kayla showed up? When?"

"Just about when we were arguing with those infuriating women about how we *weren't* about to escort them all the way to their frontier town, and that they'd have to either shut up and come back to Rest's Remorse with us or be left behind," Olivia grumbled, and while that was very interesting, it also wasn't what Rowan was in a hurry to learn about.

"Focus, please, dear. Kayla?"

She sighed, sinking into his chest again. "Not much to tell, I'm afraid. She showed up with her mage army and then demanded we hand both you and Blake over to her. We refused, obviously, which she wasn't entirely happy with."

"Did she try to push the subject?" Rowan asked.

"Might have, if we didn't have so many Epic tiers with us. I don't think she ever expected to see so many gathered in one place. Did you know she only has her mentor at the same tier as her? She doesn't even have a proper party, apparently," Olivia said.

That was definitely a surprise for Rowan. He'd been under a strong impression that Kayla would have way more Epic tiers following her than either him or Blake. If that was true, then he had to wonder why she was in such a disadvantageous position.

"That honestly doesn't sound like the Kayla I know. She's many things, but she wouldn't just cripple her own power base like that," Rowan said.

Olivia simply shrugged, prodding him in the side when Rowan spent a little too much time fidgeting and too little time acting as a proper pillow.

"Anyways, we scared her off. Then the brainless trio finally realized they didn't have an army or particularly useful classes, so they stuck with us. Much to my regret. More to the point, much to my mother's regret. The princess is becoming an issue," Olivia said.

"An issue I need to go out there and do something about?" Rowan ventured, feeling quite reluctant to follow through on that particular course of action so soon after waking up.

Olivia considered that for a moment, then thankfully shook her head. "No. Not that urgent. She's just trying to boss everyone around and take the place over. Surprisingly, those other two aren't as bad. Anyway, my mother just stonewalled her, citing that you're currently in a coma and therefore incapable of turning over control of your army to a passing royal."

"She wants my army?" Rowan's voice dropped an octave, betraying his feelings on the matter. "On an unrelated note, how hard would it be to cover up the death of a princess?"

"Let's not go committing regicide. *Yet.* If she pushes too far, I'll let you know when it's okay. And yes, she wants it, but can't rightly have it. Legally speaking, the nobility isn't obligated to give up private armies to the crown. *Technically*, as a hero of the kingdom, you count as a high noble."

Rowan let out a relieved breath, then decided that the princess and the rest of Blake's party were a future problem. For the time being, he was going to spend some time with his favorite alchemist and then work on his problems from there.

Gods dammit, past me, Rowan complained, staring blankly ahead while the blonde woman in front of him prattled on and on for what seemed like an eternity.

The moment word got out that Rowan was once again up and on his feet, the princess had started demanding meetings. If it weren't for the Rare-tier guards that were posted outside his room, she would have simply barged in. Point of fact, she had tried to do just that *in spite of* the guards. Ironically, she simply didn't have the strength to force the issue in the way she wanted to.

As it turned out, being a saintess left a person with very few offensive measures against anything that wasn't a corrupted, demonic, or undead creature. Rowan was just happy that the blast of light did nothing more than temporarily blind his guards and make them feel oddly warm, like they were in someone's embrace. Otherwise, he would have been forced to hunt down a princess, and neither of them would enjoy the fallout of that.

Rowan couldn't rightly avoid meeting his nominal ruler's daughter forever, though. Which was why he was stuck in a meeting featuring the baroness, the Mercenary King, the full hero party, and the saintess-size menace.

The Rhys princess was trying her best to clobber everyone over the head with bogus justifications on why they should all bow, kiss her feet, and then pledge themselves to her service forevermore in a glorious show of devotion to king and country. Everyone was refusing to do so, much to her frustration.

When she started up a fourth round of circular arguments on the same subject, Rowan finally had enough. "No, I will not hand over authority over my army. No, the Mercenary King will not be leaving with you. And no, my party and I will not subordinate ourselves to Hero Blake so we can attempt a 'thorough and righteous cleansing of the wastes.' We barely survived. I'm not throwing everything away to charge at a Legendary demon." By the end of his words, Rowan's voice had grown to a complete shout. Noticing that, he collapsed back into his seat. "Princess Rhys, I understand where you're coming from. Blake is my friend. I won't let anything happen to him. But there's more at stake than just him. Plus, he's *still comatose.* I believe he could benefit from your healing."

The princess sputtered, spouted some nonsense, and finally left. Rowan wanted to groan in relief, but reined himself in to look relatively dignified.

The Mercenary King, on the other hand, didn't care about looking regal. He chuckled then broke out into full-on laughter. "Well, look at you, lad. Right as day. If you can shout that loudly, you're recovered. Still, had a question on my mind, you see. Why didn't she ask for Tamara to be present, too?"

Camilla scoffed, crossing her arms and bringing her elbows down on the huge table they were sitting around. "She's the princess. Probably doesn't want to associate herself with a disgraced, banished member of nobility, Epic tier or not."

That made perfect sense, though Rowan felt like it wasn't quite enough to explain everything. Nonetheless, they had other things to worry about. "What is Blake's condition like? Tried to visit him, but his party members weren't letting anyone into his room."

"I saw him, briefly, when the soldiers brought him in," Camilla said. "He looked fine. A little pale, sure, but fine. I'm guessing he was just more badly hurt due to whatever happened while you were passed out. Speaking of, I'm told it was due to a card effect?"

Rowan flinched a little. Curiosity was plain on all of his party members' faces, and even the Mercenary King leaned forward a little. Frankly, he trusted all of them, but he still hesitated to speak.

"Of course, you don't have to tell us if it's a secret." Olivia came to Rowan's defense.

"It's okay. But what we talk about here doesn't go beyond that door," Rowan demanded, motioning toward the double doors that the princess just used.

"Aye, lad, we're fine with that," the Mercenary King rushed to agree, ignoring the glare Camilla sent him for trying to work his way into the group.

"Right. So, I picked up a class called [Spear of Unity], which gave me slots for eight [Knights] that I can designate at will. When I do, and they accept, which is a requirement, they get to use a duplicate of one of my cards. It doesn't count against their deck, either."

The Mercenary King whistled, leaning back in his chair, and Rowan could tell that everyone else was obviously interested, too.

"And the cost the [Knights] have to pay for that privilege?" Camilla asked.

"That's honestly why I didn't bring it up before," Rowan admitted, worrying at his lower lip. "I'm linked to all my [Knights]. I can feel most of their emotions, and though I didn't really push at the link yet, I *might* be able to catch snippets of thoughts, too."

That definitely did the job of quashing further interest, since everyone looked understandably reluctant to place themselves in such a position. All but Olivia, who was looking at him contemplatively.

"I also get ten percent of the stats each of my [Knights] have, as well as thirty percent of all experience they earn. The stat sharing is sort of like yours." Rowan nodded at the twins. "I don't steal those, just share them."

"And the experience?" the Mercenary King asked, frowning.

"I don't know. Haven't had much chance to test it out. Though . . . I'll note that there's no tier restrictions on choosing knights. If I can just pick a Common-tier soldier, and then help them level up quickly to the peak of Rare? That's a very nice chunk of experience instead of having to exclusively hunt Epic-tier monsters."

"You could go all the way to the peak of Epic, all without getting stuck because of a lack of monsters," Camilla said, catching on to the implications of what the class brought. "And you're *already* linked to the other hero."

"Unless he asks me to break the bond." Rowan tried to temper her expectations, though he didn't deny the usefulness of having Blake be one of his [Knights].

"We need to test this. I'll find you a promising Common tier," Camilla said. "We can't waste that slot on someone you won't fully benefit from in terms of stats, especially if class quality somehow affects things. Hero Blake might ask you to break the bond? That means you can cancel your link to your knights? Are there drawbacks to doing so?"

Rowan grimaced, a part of him instinctively unhappy with the mere suggestion of doing such a thing. A second later he realized it was his new class card influencing him and pushed the feelings down as far as they would go. He used his deck. He couldn't afford to let his deck use him.

"Yeah, I can cancel the link," Rowan said. "Unfortunately, it takes a year for the slot to refresh."

The baroness hummed thoughtfully, fingers drumming on the table. "It makes sense. Otherwise, you could just continue training people from Common to Epic and then dropping the link, never even having to risk your life for progression."

Rowan shrugged in resignation. He wasn't entirely sure he'd go for such a thing regardless. Somehow, he wasn't entirely sure it was healthy to be power-leveled that way, even if it could theoretically let him improve his tier. Case in point, he was thoroughly unimpressed by Blake's party, even if they did have fancy class names.

"We can look for [Knights] and experiment with my class later. For now, I'd honestly prefer we figure out what to do. Can we help Blake awaken sooner? What do we do with him and his party once he is awake?"

"That depends. How much do you know about the man? I know you mentioned you were friends, but is he likely to cause problems if he stays here?" Camilla responded.

Thankfully, Rowan didn't even need to lie or try to twist the truth.

"Blake won't be any trouble, trust me. We talked a little already, and he hasn't changed much from when I knew him. He seems pretty big on Sarina nowadays, but otherwise he's the same good guy I know."

"You talked? I heard everything that happened, and from what I've heard, that didn't seem like enough time to reconnect," Camilla said.

"The two of us didn't *just* pass out," Rowan admitted, then launched into the explanation of what they'd gone through together, leaving out a couple of details about what the demon said in the end but otherwise relating his entire adventure. "I still don't know what that was all about. Were we stuck in Blake's head? His soul?"

"It's a mental-realm battle," the Mercenary King said. "There are records of high-tier demons doing so, but most such battles are lost."

"Lucius's right. There's simply not enough knowledge about such things. Sarina would know, obviously, and she might share her knowledge with Hero Blake," Camilla said.

The baroness's suggestion was sound, but Rowan winced at that, knowing there was little to no chance of him ever getting that kind of explanation from the goddess's champion.

"Do you think Blake will wake up soon? He has my card, but I honestly don't know what my attack might have done to him, or how quickly any such wounds would heal," Rowan asked.

Camilla glanced at the others before responding. "I don't know. Hero Blake is alive because of divine intervention. Typically, people corrupted to that extent would either perish or turn. Without seeing him, I can't tell you what might happen."

"Right." Rowan didn't like it, but the baroness was right. "What about our army? What are our losses like? It didn't seem like we'd lost too many before I passed out, but . . ." Rowan trailed off, hating the fact that he was thinking in terms of numbers instead of human lives. Those people had trusted him, put their lives into his hands, followed him into danger.

To Rowan's surprise, it was the Mercenary King who answered. "It wasn't too bad altogether, lad. Twenty-seven of mine and six of yours. Tamara lost none of hers, of course. Frankly, I'd call it a miracle, but I know we have mostly your shield bearer to thank."

"I was just doing my job," Marcus mumbled when all the eyes focused on him, blushing even harder.

"Well, it's a good thing that you're so great at it." Rowan stretched to pat the man on the shoulder. Then he turned his attention to his sister. "And Milena, I saw you unleashing hell in the fight. What in the world did your Epic class do to you?"

Milena hadn't stopped grinning since the conclusion of the battle, and it didn't seem like her good mood would run out any time soon. "I can finally fight properly, that's what it did to me! No more waiting forever or casting lengthy rituals for the most basic spells and curses."

"Yeah, you were eradicating those monsters almost as fast as I was. But still a bit slower than me," Olivia said, and when the two women's eyes met, Rowan could practically see the sparks flying. Frankly, he was feeling sorry for whatever enemies they would encounter in the future of their newborn rivalry.

The baroness's face lit up at the reminder of her daughter's Epic class. "Olivia, don't be rude to your party member. Especially now that you're an Epic class. You have to have some dignity."

"Because Father was refusing to let me fight on my own! I told you I could do it," Olivia grumbled and crossed her arms, a picture-perfect copy of her mother.

"Gotta say I'm a little jealous, kids," the Mercenary King admitted, leaning back in his chair. "Can't tell you how long it took me to claw my way up to Epic. It really does pay off, teaming up with a hero."

"Well, you're welcome to join us more officially, if you'd like," Rowan offered, knowing it was unlikely that anything would come of it. After all, the Mercenary King had all but outright stated that the reason he was stuck in Rest's Remorse and so unwilling to ally with the new mayor was pressure from the kingdom. If he was seen as making moves in direct opposition to the official king's interests, he could get into a ton of trouble.

Much to Rowan's shock, though, the man didn't immediately turn down his offer. If anything, he was holding the gaze in a way Rowan wasn't sure he liked.

"We'll see, lad. We'll see. For now, I'd like to excuse myself. Gotta make up for the losses we took, if I still have your permission for recruitment?"

"Just keep in mind that we need a couple of good candidates to test out Rowan's new class," Camilla said. "If you find someone promising, send them our way. I bet they wouldn't say no to having access to an Epic card at Common."

The Mercenary King huffed in amusement but nodded. "Sure. Rob me of my best potential recruits. I'm leaving before you shake me down for more."

The fact that the man actually jogged out of the meeting room sent the hero party, and even the baroness, into soft chuckles.

"We really should think about doing another recruitment drive, too. If we can afford it?" Rowan aimed the question at the baroness, who looked thoughtful for a moment before nodding.

"It's not impossible. We'll need to plan around our expenses a bit more carefully, but we should be able to pull it off. As long as you don't outright double your army. We should be able to support another two hundred or so recruits."

"I don't think we could find enough people to double our numbers to begin with," Rowan said with a grimace, and by lack of disagreement, he was probably spot-on.

Rest's Remorse wasn't the biggest of frontier towns, even before it was attacked twice. Now? They would likely be scraping the very bottom of the barrel when looking for recruits, and they might fall short regardless.

"We'll think of something," Olivia reassured Rowan. "We can put out a recruitment notice through messengers and send those to the nearest settlements. Likewise, we can even petition the king for more troops."

Rowan didn't think it would be that easy. Stealing people from under the noses of other nobles wouldn't be easy, frontier or not. Similarly, he legitimately doubted that the king would be willing to do anything to help. And even if the king did, that help would likely have strings.

Still, Olivia was right. They'd think of something, together.

CHAPTER TWENTY-FIVE

To Do One's Duty Still

Rowan's worry came to pass over the next few days. There was very little progress on finding good recruits, let alone one who could help him test out his new class feature. But he was frustrated by an entirely different problem. One that stemmed from his best friend and the trio of women who were part of his party.

"Three days," Rowan hissed, stomping around his room as Olivia watched in amusement. "They've been stopping me from visiting him for three days!"

"Rowan, you're going to fall through the floor at this rate," Olivia quipped, and even though he felt the urge to glare, Rowan took the moment to assess her claim.

His angry stomps weren't exactly raising dust clouds, seeing as the room was meticulously clean. He did, however, have to admit he was causing actual damage to the carpet. And, now that he was looking a little closer, maybe to the floor, too?

"How . . ."

"We're at Epic now, you dummy. And one of your *main* stats is strength. I wasn't exactly kidding. If you put in enough effort, you're going straight through that floor," Olivia said.

Rowan scoffed, but there was no denying the blush that graced his cheeks. Typically, his increased stats and newfound abilities didn't get in the way of his daily life. Although each increase in strength meant he was significantly stronger, he had to make an effort to use the added power. Ever since his ascension to the Epic tier, everything felt more instinctual. His cards, especially the Epic-tier ones, felt more like extra limbs than something he needed to tap into.

He could wield his stats with much higher proficiency and power. It wasn't that Rowan couldn't use them before. But he now had better instincts on how to handle all his rapidly accumulated power, whereas a part of him felt that his past self was like a toddler stuck in the body of a superhuman athlete. Could he walk, talk, and function normally? Sure. Could he do it at peak efficiency? Hardly.

"Sorry," Rowan grumbled. He strode over to collapse on the bed, his head falling onto her lap. "You know, your mom is scary."

"Scary is the least of it," Olivia replied.

Rowan had been briefly carried away with his new Epic-tier class and its stats. So much so that he'd asked the baroness for a spar. It didn't end well.

Apparently, **Natural Renewal** could do much more than patch up simple wounds. That was both a good and bad thing. Camilla began cutting away deeper and deeper chunks of Rowan during their fight until Rowan had to stop because of the pain. It was true that he learned more in that spar than he had in weeks, but it was also the case that parts of him were still suffering phantom pain even now.

"If those three were as scary as Camilla, I would have given up. But they're not. I just want them gone, you know? I guess the other two aren't that bad overall but the princess is making me want to lead a rebellion. Is she next in line to the throne?"

"It's still up in the air, actually. Her older brother, the king's eldest, is the crown prince right now. However, she is part of the hero party, and aiming to marry the hero, too. She might end up inheriting the throne if she pulls that off and proves her power," Olivia said.

Rowan grimaced, shuddering at the mere idea of having that woman on the throne. "I really hope not. If she does end up taking over, we're rebelling against the kingdom—please promise me that?"

Olivia froze for a moment, her hand pausing where she was running her fingers through his hair. And then the spell was broken with a giggle. "I promise. You and me against the kingdom. Well, my parents would probably join in, too."

"That's all we'd need, no?" Rowan teased in turn, grabbing her hand and pressing a soft kiss against her wrist. "I bet your mother could take out most of the capital all on her own."

Olivia sent him a smug smile full of confidence before her eyes caught on his lips. She leaned down and Rowan closed his eyes. And then a knock jerked her away from him and Rowan himself shot upright, eyeing the door.

"Who is it?"

"Excuse me, sir, but there's a commotion at the training grounds. I thought it best to inform you personally." Henry's voice floated through the heavy wooden doors.

"I'm coming," Rowan groaned as he stood and rearranged his clothing a little. It would not do for the mayor himself to show up to resolve a problem looking all disheveled. "You've got more information for me than that, right?"

"I'm afraid it has to do with the princess."

Rowan groaned again, much louder this time.

The training ground of Rowan's army had undergone a rather positive transformation as of late. For starters, the baroness's work meant that the town had many more resources to spruce the place up. Higher-quality training equipment, like dummies that could slowly regenerate from damage, were merely the tip of the iceberg. The ridiculously heavy weights meant for people with high stats were a particularly nice benefit and one Rowan was starting to take advantage of himself, too.

The most significant change, of course, was to the soldiers themselves. There was a morale to them that hadn't existed before. Whereas they used to carry themselves listlessly and like they were afraid someone would beat them senseless for stepping out of line, they now stood proud and confident.

They had reason to feel that way.

They'd reached heights they previously thought impossible with regard to personal strength. They were paid much better, letting them take good care of themselves and their families. And, perhaps most importantly, they knew they had the support of their mayor.

The dead soldiers from their last mission had been few, but seeing the families of the fallen receive their pensions, along with all personal possessions of their fallen and even several high-quality cards, was enough to bolster the army's loyalty to Rowan. It was, after all, something Rowan had promised to do. He knew that the hallmark of a great general was following through on promises and building trust.

It was for this reason that the army had taken such exception to the princess barging in on their training and demanding they swear their loyalty to her.

When Rowan arrived, things were on the verge of violence. The princess was shouting about loyalty, royal rights, the stupidity of peasants, and quite a few insults aimed at Rowan himself. The soldiers were silent and gripping their weapons tightly.

Rayne, on the other hand, was nodding along with a smile. "With all due respect, Your Highness, please fuck off."

Rowan blinked. The princess blinked. Both of them stood frozen for a long moment, before the princess cocked her arm back, her hand whistling through the air in what was looking to be a devastating slap.

Rayne didn't flinch, just smiled at the other woman and let the blow come closer and closer to her face.

In a flash, Rowan appeared right next to the two, his hand clamping down on the princess's wrist. He stopped the attack before realizing that the woman's main attributes were wisdom and intelligence. There was little chance of her getting free, but even less of a chance for damage even if she could strike an unencumbered blow.

"Release me this instant! You have no idea what you're doing!" the princess hissed, spinning around to face her newest adversary before freezing in place once again.

Apparently, she hadn't expected Rowan himself to show up, because she looked at him like a deer caught in the headlights.

"Can you explain to me, Your Highness, why you are here and harassing my troops?" Rowan asked as calmly as he could manage, which wasn't all that calmly at all. "Especially when I've told you, time and again, that you don't have the authority to claim them?"

The princess flinched, then her own glare redoubled as she gave her arm a sharp yank. Rowan let her free herself before he folded his arms behind his back.

"You will regret treating me this way, *Mayor*." She hissed his title like it was an insult. "Hero Blake, chosen of goddess Sarina, will awaken soon! Then we'll see whether you can afford to be so rude."

With those parting words and another venomous look, she stomped away. Rowan let out a long sigh, trying to cleanse himself of all the frustration and anger the woman's sheer presence had caused to bubble up in him. It wasn't enough that they were blocking his perfectly normal and justified request to see his friend in his own home, but she was also set on pissing him off every time they crossed paths.

Like Blake is going to take your side, Rowan thought bitterly, before facing his troops again.

"Thank you for not stabbing her," Rowan said sincerely, to the chuckles of his troops. "If she shows up again, which I will try to prevent, simply ignore her. In fact, it's about time we got back to our excursions into the wastes. That will help you stay far away from her and earn some loot and levels besides."

That, at least, was met with approval. No one would say no to more levels and cards.

It was two birds with one stone. Now that the soldiers were strong enough, they could push back the demons and keep Rest's Remorse safe. And they'd gain valuable combat experience for the future.

If Rowan was being entirely honest, though, that wasn't the main reason he wanted to get away from the town.

The bond he'd established with Blake was once an indelible link straight to his emotions. Near or far, he was supposed to have a solid grasp of whether his [Knight] was in good condition or not, and a rough idea of what he was feeling.

Now, the bond was all but dead.

Only flickers of *something* passed through it, and Rowan was terrified that it might entirely wink out at any second. What exactly that meant for Blake and his current state, Rowan wasn't sure. He did know it was unlikely to be anything good.

At least that same vague sense of his understanding implied that Blake did still have access to his card's effects and that his friend was alive. That, more than anything, was helping Rowan cling to the dregs of hope.

Regardless, a sense of foreboding had taken root in him, and it refused to let go.

Nothing major happened for the next few days. And in spite of his worry, Rowan was deeply enjoying the new routine.

He and Olivia were spending more time together, even if most of that was spent in her laboratory as she guided him through her latest experiments and brewing efforts. Now that she was more or less officially the main alchemist of Rest's Remorse, she couldn't dedicate all her time to new recipes. Most of the time she was making potions that had a clear need. She didn't really complain, though. If anything, she seemed to take an inordinate amount of pride in the fact that she was supplying the town with a frighteningly large number of potions.

The other addition to Rowan's itinerary was the resumption of his classes with the baroness. The never-ending stream of laws, leadership know-how, and so much more was mind-numbing. At least Olivia was being forced to endure it all right alongside him.

It was, however, at the start of one of these classes that the baroness greeted them with an unusually bright smile.

"Something good happen, Mom?" Olivia asked as she seated herself, a smile rising to her own face in response to her mother's good mood.

"For once, yes. Your father is going to visit us in about two weeks. He wants to see the town himself, and he's found a couple of promising candidates for Rowan's [Knight] slots."

That caught the hero's attention completely, both due to the fact that his class would finally have a chance to grow and because Olivia's father would be arriving soon.

He exchanged an excited, if slightly worried, look with his favorite alchemist.

They would have a lot to discuss with her parents when they arrived. For the time being, however, all they could do was prepare.

*   *   *

Almost a week and a half after coming back to Rest's Remorse, a message found Rowan while he was engaged in some light sparring with Marcus in the training yard, if "light sparring" was the fitting description for a clash that left literal craters in the ground.

Blake was finally awake.

It should have calmed Rowan down and finally let him breathe a little easier. Instead, he found his heart racing ever faster as he drew closer to his friend's room. His bad feeling was reaching a crescendo, and in spite of the assurances from his class, he was convinced he'd open the door and find Blake dead in his bed.

When Rowan finally reached his door, he couldn't even bring himself to open it for long, painful minutes. It was the brief sound of laughter that finally compelled him to act, even if the sound was definitely off.

The three women immediately bristled at the mere act of the door opening, but he caught tears glistening in their angry eyes.

However, his full attention was squarely on Blake. The room had a large set of glass windows on the wall opposite the door. Those windows were wide open, letting the gentle afternoon sun filter into the room and paint everything in shades of yellow and orange.

Even under those hues, Blake was deathly pale.

His skin glistened with sweat that reflected the light, making apparent the fact that his every movement and exertion was a torment. He looked, well, like someone who had spent a week and change in a coma.

"You are not supposed to be here," one of the women said.

"Amanda, please. Can I have a bit of time alone to talk to Hero Rowan?" Blake's voice was scratchy and as weak as the rest of him. In spite of that, there was an undercurrent of authority and steel there that had the frustrating princess clamping her mouth shut. Rowan was genuinely surprised to see her defer to him so readily. With how many times he'd had to stop her from ordering his staff and soldiers around, not to mention thwarting her many poaching attempts, Rowan was fairly certain she would be more than happy to get rid of him if she could.

"You know, I genuinely admire you," Rowan opened the conversation as he sat on one of the chairs conveniently positioned next to

Blake's bed. "How have you survived having them in your party? Without killing one or more of them, I mean. All they do is argue and cause trouble."

Blake sighed, sinking back down onto the bed now that the women were out of earshot. Instantly, an even deeper sense of weariness settled about Blake, and Rowan hated the fact that he apparently thought it was important to push himself that much just to put on a front.

"They're not that bad," Blake said.

"Once you get to know them, I assume?" Rowan asked.

"No." Blake smirked, even if the expression quickly shifted into a grimace. "They actually get worse once you do that, for a little while. It all evens out when they figure out they *don't* have to be awful and prickly around you."

"You have the patience of a saint, Blake. I really don't. So if you don't tell your princess to stop trying to poach all my soldiers and a good chunk of my staff, I'm going to chain her up and throw her into the dungeon. I haven't seen it, but I'm sure I have one somewhere around here."

Blake laughed. "Please don't. Can you imagine how annoying she'd be if you did? She'd drive all your jailers insane, and then what would you do?"

"I'm only part joking, Blake. Olivia's mother is on the verge of stabbing her, and she's had decades of experience holding back her real feelings as a duchess."

"I'll do something about it, promise," Blake said, his smile once more growing brittle as a surge of pain flashed through his body.

Rowan instantly felt worse about taking up so much time talking about someone who, on the whole, wasn't that important. Now that Blake was awake, the connection between the two of them was stronger. Rowan could tell, vaguely, just how much pain his friend was in. How hollow and tired he felt. To say Blake wasn't feeling the best would be an understatement.

"Do you want me to post up a guard next to your bed?" Rowan asked. "Might not be able to manage it easily, but I can probably get the Mercenary King and Marcus to take up the shifts. I don't want those three getting ideas about forcing you to marry them on your sickbed."

Maybe it was a bit crude, but Rowan tried for the joke anyways. Apparently it worked, since Blake first sputtered, then laughed.

"I can handle them just fine, thank you very much. What about you, though? That alchemist of yours pushing for a wedding already?"

Rowan did blush, but it was just a light reddening of his cheeks. The last few days had definitely been good for him and Olivia—their relationship didn't feel like something vague and barely defined anymore.

"She doesn't have to push me. As soon as all this mess is sorted out, I'm planning to ask her to marry me," Rowan said, his heart jumping to his throat. The admission was more meaningful than anything else he could say. He'd finally sorted his feelings out, fully and truly. There was no more escaping the truth. He cared about the people around him now far more than he'd ever cared about anyone back on Earth.

Blake fell silent, eyeing his friend carefully for several drawn-out moments. To Rowan's surprise, he broke into a soft smile right after.

"So, you're staying." That wasn't a question. It wasn't judgmental, either, which Rowan was rather thankful for.

"I am," Rowan said.

"Good. This place is good for you, Rowan. You've always been withdrawn. Hesitant to engage with anyone. I . . . I'm proud of you, you know? Hell, you came to save me. And now you're planning a future with a beautiful woman!" Blake exclaimed.

Blake's voice was slightly teasing, true. But the sincerity that shone through was almost enough to make Rowan choke up. A couple of tears escaped from him.

"You really think so? It's not . . . wrong, to just stay? I mean, I know we haven't even won against the Legendary demons, let alone the big boss, so it's a bit early to be thinking about stuff like this."

"I know you love to ramble and second-guess everything, but don't. We'll be fine. You'll be fine. Then you'll have your happily ever after and everything is going to be okay." Blake said the words forcefully.

Somehow, Rowan didn't feel like Blake was entirely talking to him. It felt like a mantra the man had been repeating since waking up, and the deepening pallor of Blake's complexion worried him.

"So, what about you? Planning to stay as well?"

Blake blinked a couple of times, breaking himself out of the stupor that had claimed him. The smile he offered Rowan was blinding.

"Yep. I can do so much more here than I ever could have back home. There are people in actual danger here. People who need me. My goddess still needs me to go back to the capital and eradicate all the malicious heathens there!" As Blake spoke, his cheerful voice rose, and the end of his sentence might as well have been a shout of pain. Rowan watched, stunned, as Blake's lips quivered and tears started to slip down his cheeks. He quickly covered them with the back of his arm. There was little Blake could do about the way sobs jerked his body around, however, even if the way he was biting down on his lower lip silenced them.

"Blake? What's wrong?" Rowan hovered half out of his chair. He had no clue what to do or say. Making people feel better was typically Blake's job when they were together, and to see him so vulnerable was entirely enough to knock even the alarms going off at the mention of heathens out of Rowan's head.

"I'm useless now, Rowan." A sob escaped the other hero as he spoke. "Useless. I can't help you. My party's probably going to abandon me, too, when they find out. I can't help anybody anymore."

Rowan's mind spun, his eyes immediately flashing over Blake's body. His first thought was a crippling injury, but the fact that all of Blake's limbs were moving normally definitely precluded that one.

Blake was still weak from his coma. However, Rowan was fairly certain that he would recover rapidly between the potions Olivia could make and Rowan's own regeneration card.

"Blake? Why do you say that?" Rowan asked slowly. "I don't know what's wrong, but we can fix it. I promise you, we'll fix it."

Rowan's best friend removed the arm covering his red eyes and peered into Rowan's face. "I was lost, Rowan. My goddess told me as much. She was trying to delay the inevitable, but I was . . . I was going to get corrupted, sooner or later."

"But you're not, right? You're *not* corrupted. We got rid of what the demon was doing. I got the system notification and everything."

"You did." Blake chuckled, the smile he offered Rowan profoundly sad. "I don't have a clue how, but between what you did and your class effect, you did. Corruption isn't so easy to deal with, though. It has consequences."

Rowan's worry and stress and days of waiting were starting to make him irritable. A ball of emotions swirling in his chest pushed him to demand an answer. Instead, he closed his eyes, took a deep breath, and spoke gently.

"What kind of consequences, Blake?"

In lieu of an answer, the other hero shared a system screen with him.

Blake Trevlin
Level 56 [Fragment of Light]
EXP: 843/6,000,000
Deck:
ERROR!
Your deck is currently locked!
Card detected:
[Heart] Light Scion (Epic)

"I'm broken, Rowan," Blake whispered quietly, averting his eyes. "I'm not even at Epic anymore, and my class and deck . . ."

Rowan could see it in his expression. Blake was convinced that it was over and that there was little he could do to recover from this new kind of injury.

Rowan wasn't as convinced.

"You still have your Heart Card," Rowan said, sticking to the facts. "And you still have the ability to earn experience. We're going to fix this, Blake. I don't know how, but we're going to fix this."

His best friend gave a sad little smile, shifting just enough to give Rowan an awkward hug. The Stalwart Hero didn't mind.

He wasn't lying.

They'd find a way to give Blake back the power that was stolen from him, and then they'd take the fight to the demons, the kings, and even the gods. Whatever it took to help his best friend.

About the Author

A. T. Valentine is the author of the Legend of the Spear Saint series, originally released on Royal Road. He strives to write the best possible books across a variety of genres. Valentine resides in Potomac, Maryland.

RESPAWN YOUR CURIOSITY

follow us on our socials

podiumentertainment.com

@podiumentertainment

/podiumentertainment

@podium_ent

@podiumentertainment